BROOKE STAYROOK

Tell Me a Tale of Rebirth

Book 1 of "Tell Me a Tale" Series

First edition

Editing by Doreen Martens
Cover art by Teresa Jenellen

This book was professionally typeset on Reedsy.
Find out more at reedsy.com

For Mom,
who told me bedtime stories that fostered my imagination to create continuously.

Contents

Acknowledgement

As all stories do, this book started out with an idea - or rather a philosophical conversation among coffee lovers neglecting their studies to delve into a fascinating idea that we as humans have a tendency to fill the unknown void with mythology.

The friend studying psychology, who is a therapist today, surmised that stories of lore and myth are coping mechanisms to give tangible explanations to a convoluted world. Her example: the bubonic plague was blamed on witchcraft because people needed to feel control of this devastating disease else they fall deeply into fear and anxiety.

The theologist in the group, now a journalist, countered that religious institutions perpetuate these myths to bring people closer to the church. Hence, if you carry a crucifix on you, then the vampires can't harm you.

That was when the philosophist, now a doctor, spoke up about myths giving us meaning and fulfillment. Why else do we still cling to Norse and Greek mythology? These stories motivate us forward and bring us together in tight knit communities. Stories as grandiose as Thor or Hercules also were an uplifting distraction from the drudgery of life.

However that didn't sit well with the writer in the group, who is a Literary English teacher today. Her argument settled well with all of us. Myths and Lore were used as lessons for children and to remind adults of behaviors expected of them. The Grimm Brothers collected stories from all around Europe that had ghastly endings with a purpose to teach children serious lessons about listening to adults. Even religious texts used stories to guide adults towards expected societal behaviors. Do not steal, covet, murder, etc.

In that silent moment of contemplation, it was my video gamer friend who really drove home a single idea that would spark on an adventurous trilogy. What if these myths were actually true? If vampires, witches, werewolves, changelings and other mythological beings existed, then how would that shape our economy? Would that change racism?

It is because of this ragtag team of dreamers and deep thinkers that such a novel was created. This book is dedicated to the group of friends, and those out there like them, who didn't let school get in the way of their imaginations.

Reward

As the author of this work, I offer you, the reader, the opportunity to redeem a cash award for introducing this work to any literary agent, publisher or film producer that offers an acceptable contract [to the author] for this work. The reward offered is 10% of any initial book advance or option contract for film up to a maximum of $10,000.00.

Why am I offering a cash reward to readers?

- **Odds**: 98%+ of all works published today initially found their way to a publisher by introduction as opposed to arriving "over the transom" so the odds are better doing it this way.
- **Volume:** Writing is an inherently solitary endeavor. Offering readers a reward to do it multiplies the effort as each volume in the hands of reader starts diverse chains of discussion and introduction, one of which will lead to success.
- **Collaboration:** Reading is unique among all entertainment vehicles in that it requires effort from the reader: the author and reader collaborate to tell the story. Hearing what readers enjoy is exciting to any author and the collaboration of this reward program offers the reader a chance to help jump start the career of an author he/she enjoys. Besides, publishers are much more interested in readers' opinions vs authors' offerings.

Suggestions:

Via this reward, our mutual goal is to introduce this work to literary/publishing professionals or TV series producers. Many are likely familiar with the term "six degrees of separation," the theory that anyone on the planet can be connected to any other person on the planet through a chain of acquaintances that has no more than five intermediaries. This is what I aim to accomplish here with your help.

- Think about who you know in publishing (literary agents, editors, readers, executives, etc.) or film producers (agents, directors, editors, etc.) and pass this volume on to them.
- Think about who you know and who they might know in publishing or film.
- Think about who you know that reads and would enjoy this book.

Send any leads, or opportunities, or introductions via the email link below.

Thank you in advance for your help.

Brooke Stayrook
@brookestayrook
https://brookestayrook.wixsite.com/home

*Inspired by D. Erick Mairkranz's REINCARNATIONIST PAPERS Reward

THE SOUNDTRACK

Follow the QR code below to listen to the music that inspired the tale, from the joyful highs to the tragic lows.

THE PROPHECY

The prophecy calls a child born into sin
With a mark that will magnify the demons within
Beset to an existence of prodigious suffering
Innocence lost in a malevolent plundering
Immortal decay will shape its existence
As it gains power in suffering's persistence
In its final supreme rendition
Humanity's fate will be left to paradise or perdition

1

A TRAGIC BEGINNING

NEW YORK CITY, NEW YORK

FEBRUARY 4TH, 2001

Valda Enterprise is a well-known medical equipment company. Fifty floors to the top isn't such a huge feat in New York City. Yet, amid the hustle and bustle of the Big Apple, this building stands out in a special way. Instead of standing straight and tall, it curves similar to a DNA strand—an idea that originated with Ronald Valda, CEO, who executed the architectural plans. Today will begin a chain of events that will rock the fabric of reality, and it all starts with an interview.

A heavy knock rattled against a large wooden door, on which was a silver plaque: *Ronald Valda, CEO Valda Enterprise.* The knock startled the CEO, even though he was expecting someone—and at ten minutes early, no less. His back to the windows revealing a beautiful city landscape, Ron stood up from his cushioned chair and straightened his suit jacket. The CEO walked to the door with his chest puffed out with obvious pride.

"Ah! You must be Connor Roberts," he said in a jolly tone as he exchanged a firm handshake with the young man.

"It is a pleasure to meet you, Mr. Valda. I have read so much about you and your successful company," the young man said with professional formality and a polite smile. Connor stood straight, making him just a hair taller than the CEO. He wore a plain black suit and red tie. Clean-shaven, with well-groomed, short black hair, he projected an overall professional appearance for the interview.

"Please have a seat," the CEO said, indicating an upholstered chair facing the large oak desk.

"Thank you," Connor said, sitting down carefully so as not to wrinkle his suit.

"I understand you are interviewing for the tutor and caregiver position."

"That is correct, sir."

Ron chuckled. "You can call me Ron. *Sir* makes me feel old. Thank you for completing the personality test and the lengthy three interviews," Ron began. "I reviewed your resume and see that you might be overqualified for this position. Tell me how you got a master's in psychology and a teaching license in only one year, when that would normally take six."

Connor smiled. "Well, you see, *Ron*, I happen to be brilliant and motivated. I tested out of all the required classes with flying colors. The only reason I had to spend a year in school is because of the field work I had to do for certain classes."

"Mmhmm," Ron said as he looked over the resume. "Looks like the only experience you have is research. Tell me why you would be a good fit with my little princess if you don't have any experience with children."

Connor's smile deepened as he realized he now had the upper hand. "My research was underneath a highly qualified team over at Yale. I worked with children of all ages for a couple months. The research was on the developing child and their educational capacity. Your daughter's preschool was one group I interviewed. Samantha really stood out to me. She was very smart and had plenty of potential for growth. Unfortunate that such a bright young girl with so much potential would be hindered by peers who held the class back, as prestigious as the school was. When I saw that you

2

posted a job listing for a full-time tutor and caregiver, I jumped on it. This would be the perfect job to give me some more experience in enabling the development of a shining genius while fostering psychological safety throughout her childhood. If given the position, I would like to conduct a case study on the relationship between education and mental health."

"That's great," Ron said enthusiastically. "Wow! You are brilliant and motivated, aren't ya? Now I don't mean to be sexist, but a lot more women applied for this job. It's not a typical job for men. Plus, my child is a female. So ..."

"Ron," Connor interrupted, "you are welcome to check with my references ..."

"They all had amazing feedback about you—"

"You are also welcome to do a background check."

"Obviously I did, or we wouldn't be speaking right now. Once again, flawless."

"I can promise you that your daughter Samantha shall receive the best education and care possible. I also promise that if anything were to happen to her, then you could throw me into prison and I will go without a fight." Connor smiled at his own joke.

"Well, you definitely are the best candidate for this position. So, do you have any questions for me?"

"Will the mother be around much?" Connor asked, as if expecting a certain response.

Ron's face fell. "Unfortunately, my wife died in labor. It has been Sammy and me for quite some time now. Which is why I need more help raising her as the demands of the company increase. Originally, I thought a feminine presence in her life would be useful, but you seem to provide much more for her health and well being than any of the other candidates."

"I am so sorry to hear that, Ron," Connor said sympathetically, "but I would be honored to accept this role and provide some additional support to Samantha and yourself."

Ron's face lit up a little more. "Any more questions?"

"Will I be living in the house?"

"Yes, I need someone 24/7 to watch Sammy. That being said, I have full security surveillance and constant recordings should anything happen." Ron replied with a warning, "Anything else?"

"If I have any more questions, then I'll be sure to ask you," Connor said with a smile.

"Great! I do have an odd question to ask you."

"Go right ahead."

"Are your eyes really purple, or are those contacts?" Ron asked curiously as he stared deep into Connor's almost hypnotic eyes.

Connor chuckled, his purple eyes calmly swirling. "Purple is my natural eye color. It's a unique genetic mutation. Nothing to be worried about." Ron was right to wonder: the swirling purple mist in those eyes spoke of ominous prophecies, the ancient secrets of a people lost long ago, secrets a mortal such as Ron could never fathom.

Ron was caught in Connor's cryptic eyes for a moment and couldn't seem to look away. Connor blinked and broke the gaze, which prompted Ron to snap back to himself again. "Oh, okay. Well, I see no reason to not hire you. Congratulations, Connor Roberts. You're hired!"

"Thank you, Ron. I won't disappoint you."

"Would you like to meet Samantha? She's in the playroom, since there's no one else to watch her."

"Yes! I would love to meet Samantha and introduce myself as her tutor and caregiver," Connor said, smiling softly but maintaining the composure that came with his analytical mind.

"Right this way." Ron led Connor out and into a large, open area, elegantly decorated. The receptionist sitting at a beautifully carved oak desk inlaid with gold winked playfully at Connor, who ignored her and continued on. They approached a large door that was similar to the rest, except that taped to it were three crayon drawings of animals that appeared more advanced than a 5-year-old could typically produce.

Ron passed his badge in front of a small black rectangle with a red light. The light turned green and the door was unlocked. "Standard protocol for most doors. Sammy can get out, but only those with access can get in. I'll get you a badge soon enough."

Connor appreciated the attention to safety and followed Ron in. The room was filled with educational toys and stuffed animals. There was a small bookshelf filled with books, each about three to five years above the average five-year-old's reading level. A 500-piece puzzle was lying nearly completed on a round table surrounded by butterfly-backed chairs. There was a bathroom to the side with a small toilet and aquatic décor. A large beanbag chair with a princess canopy and rolled-up blanket sat in the corner. At the side of the room was a small sink and a fruit basket filled with juice boxes and water bottles.

In the middle of the room, coloring with crayons, was Samantha Valda. Auburn hair flowed over her shoulders and down to the middle of her back. Her small green eyes sparkled with delight. It was obvious she had been visited by the tooth fairy recently, because she was missing two front teeth. Sam wore jeans and a pink shirt with an image of Cinderella on the front, which matched the pink socks.

"Papa!" she squealed as she grabbed the paper she was working on and ran to him.

"Bonjour, mon aimé!" Ron greeted his daughter as he wrapped her in a hug.

"Nein!" the daughter said sternly, "Ich spreche heute Deutsche!"

"Ah, es tut mir leid," Ron responded in German, "Wie geht's?"

"Es geht mir gut!" she replied happily, then raised her picture up that looked convincingly like a golden retriever. "Machst du meinen Hund?"

"Ah! Dieser Hund ist super!" Ron commented and kissed her on the cheek.

"Who is that?" Samantha pointed at Connor. "Does he speak German?"

Before Ron could reply, Connor answered her question, "Guten tag, Samantha. Ich heisse Connor." Connor knelt down and shook her hand.

"Connor?" she asked curiously, then added excitedly: "I know you from preschool!"

"Yes," Ron said. "He is going to be your new caretaker."

Connor gave a deep bow. "The pleasure is all mine, princess. I'm more than happy to help you with anything you need." He realized he was behaving subserviently—old habits and all. He was used to finding her when she was around her mid-twenties. This was by far the youngest he had ever found her. It felt awkward, this dynamic. Luckily, she didn't retain any memory of those times.

Samantha didn't like his formality and instead jumped up to Connor and wrapped her arms around his neck. "Let's be friends!" she said with a large, gap-toothed smile.

Connor smiled. "Yes, let's be friends."

Ron gave Connor two big thumbs up.

* * *

NEW YORK CITY, NEW YORK

SEPTEMBER 11, 2001

The next three months proved busy for Connor. Within a couple of days of being hired, he moved in with the Valda family. Their Manhattan high-rise condo was grandiose. There were four rooms and three bathrooms. Ron's master bedroom was a simple yet functional room without much decoration, other than a few framed pictures of his departed wife. Samantha's bedroom was filled with toys, stuffed animals, books and puzzles. Another room was dedicated to Ron's home office, where he spent the majority of his at-home time these days. The last was Connor's: a simple room with no decorations or flourishes, which was fine with him.

The condo had a large living room with a state-of-the-art sound system and flat-screen TV that was rarely used. The kitchen had state-of-the-art equipment and appliances, used mostly to reheat takeout leftovers. Connor did note security cameras in each room, as Ron had mentioned in the interview. It was hard to say whether they had always been there or had been added recently. One thing Samantha loved about the condo was the large terrace that overlooked the city. Her favorite time of the day was when she could sit in her dad's lap while he drank his scotch and watch the New York cityscape. It was the one bit of quality time they spent together every day, and Ron always made sure to be home to give her this little slice of his valuable time.

Other than that, he wasn't home much, which left plenty of time for Samantha and Connor to attend to their own busy schedule. Every morning, Connor prepared a healthy breakfast, except for the weekends, when she was spoiled with waffles, cinnamon rolls or crepes. After breakfast, he would get Samantha ready for the day, prompting her independent hygiene habits. Then there were morning stretches and warm up exercises, followed by academics: English arts/reading comprehension, arithmetic assignments, science, history and current events, arts and crafts, piano lessons, practice in French and German, and puzzles or other thinking games.

Weekends were different, though. On Saturdays, Connor made an effort to take her to zoos, parks, museums, or other places she could learn from. Sundays were "Fun-days" dedicated to doing kid stuff, such as going to the movies, amusement parks, shopping malls, or plays. Connor enjoyed giving Samantha these opportunities to be a kid and do what kids do best: play. Samantha was disappointed that her father never joined in, but was mature in her acceptance of it.

This morning, as Samantha was in the shower getting ready for the day, Connor stood in front of the floor-to-ceiling windows. Uncharacteristically, he had the TV on this morning, which was filling the quiet apartment with frantic news reports as, down on the streets below, people ran and screamed in horror. He stood there frozen, not knowing what to say or do. Deep down, he knew that Samantha was about to face the first great hardship in her life: the death of her father.

This morning, Ron was scheduled to be at the World Trade Center, building working relations with a foreign company. Samantha's father was one of the poor souls trapped in the burning building, and now it had fallen, killing innocents by the thousands. A hopeful person would start calling authorities, asking them to search for Mr. Valda. A hopeful person would wait for a phone call to hear that he was all right. Connor was too practical for that. There was no way Samantha's father had survived. The first plane hit dead center on the floor where his meeting was to take place.

Connor felt no sympathy for the people dying in that tower or in the plane that crashed into it. But glancing back at Samantha's bedroom door, his heart grew heavy. He had hoped that she would live as good a life as he could give her. Yet now, she was facing tragedy at such a young age.

"Connor!" Samantha yelled in her five-year-old high pitch. Normally, this was how she told him she was ready to have her hair done for the day. Normally, he would go in and start a fancy braid or up-do so that she could feel like a princess. Today, Connor stood there staring at the debris that was now clouding the air so badly he couldn't see the next building over. He was at a loss for words.

"Connor!" Samantha called again, with a little more whine in her pitch.

It had only been few months since he was hired, not long enough to be considered family. He didn't even know how he was going to talk her through this. He had read every book out there on child development and how to raise a child in a healthy environment. He even perused new research on a daily basis to see how he could improve general psychological well being. Anything to relieve the inevitable turmoil of emotions that would be coming her way. Out of all that Connor had read, he couldn't remember anything now about how to help a child grieve for a lost loved one. His mind was pulling a blank at the worst possible time.

Samantha came out of her bedroom with her long, auburn hair dripping wet. Her pink Barbie shirt and blue skirt were already dampened. "Cooooonnnnnnooooorrrrrr," she whined.

Before she made it to the living room, Connor quickly turned off the TV and stood to face her. "Es tut mir leid," Connor apologized in German.

"Wo sind Sie?" Sammy asked with folded arms, scowling at Connor.

He took a deep breath, then sat down on the couch and motioned for Samantha to join him. "Come have a seat next to me," he said in a very serious tone.

As she walked over, Samantha peeked outside and asked, "Why is it cloudy?"

Connor could feel his heart growing heavier as he replied, "That is what I want to talk to you about."

Samantha's face fell. She crawled up on the couch and stared at Connor with curious green eyes.

"I'm afraid I have some very bad news for you, Sammy," Connor said.

Samantha looked outside, then back at Connor. "Okay," she replied calmly.

Connor took a big breath, then slowly explained to Samantha. "You know that your daddy was at a very important building called the World Trade Center, right?"

Samantha nodded.

"Well, there was an accident at the World Trade Center. A very big accident." Connor paused to take a deep breath. Samantha's green eyes were glued to him, watching closely. "Your father was killed in the accident. I am so sorry, Sammy."

Samantha stared blankly at Connor as if she didn't understand or didn't want to understand.

"What?" —She looked outside at the debris floating in the air then back at Connor— "Does that mean he won't come home anymore?"

Connor's heart dropped. "Yes, Sammy. Sadly, you will never see him again."

Samantha's eyes welled up with tears. "But … but … I never said goodbye. We are supposed to sit on the balcony tonight!" —Tears streamed down her face— "Bring him back, Connor. I want my daddy!"

"It is okay to be upset, Sammy. Unfortunately, I can't bring him back. No one can." Connor's heart hit his stomach and twisted viciously.

Samantha cried louder and her tears flowed. "Bring him back, Connor, bring him back!"

"I can't, I'm sorry," Connor replied.

Balling up her little hands into fists, Samantha beat on Connor's arm and chest as hard as she could while crying hysterically, "Bring him back, bring him back, bring him back!"

Connor wasn't sure what had come over him, but he pulled Samantha into his embrace and held her tight. Although she stopped beating him, she didn't stop crying. Nestling her face into his muscular chest, she continued to scream and cry as Connor held her in a warm embrace that seemed to ease the terrible sinking feeling he was experiencing in his heart. Connor could feel his black button-down shirt growing wetter by the second as her tears flooded from her eyes. In a way, Connor understood all too well what it felt like to lose a loved one. Without thinking, he held Samantha closer and rubbed her back to help her calm down. Even with the obscure reality of offering another human being compassion, this small gesture helped him as well, in a way he could never have expected.

Connor turned his gaze to the window. The debris in the air was so thick he couldn't even see the balcony anymore, but he could hear sirens below. He could imagine the faces of humans wailing in agony as they searched blindly in the debris. There were probably thousands of bodies lying dead, burning, and dismembered inside and outside the World Trade Center. He knew the entire nation had to be watching in terror as this terrible tragedy. When both towers collapsed, thousands of souls were released into the afterlife. Yet here and now, one little girl, seven miles away from the scene, was mourning the loss of her father. Connor had no sympathy for the many who had died, but his heart was breaking over this little girl hysterically crying in his arms. It was almost too much to bear.

After two hours of constant crying, Sammy finally fell asleep in his arms. The condo was quiet. Connor peered down at Sammy, asleep, with her hair now a dry, tangled mess and her face streaked with tears. Yet she slept, too exhausted to do anything else. To make her more comfortable, Connor picked her up and started walking to her room.

"Connor?" she asked weakly, her voice cracking.

He had hoped not to wake her. "Yes Sammy?" He laid her down in bed and handed her the half-empty glass of water on her nightstand from last night.

Greedily, she took the cup and drank it in two large gulps. Then she looked up at Connor, who was grabbing blankets to tuck her in. "Please don't leave me," she said, her voice made rough by the hours of hysterical crying.

Connor sat down on the bed next to Samantha, who instantly hugged him tight. "I can stay here with you. I'm going to help you through all of this, Sammy," he said.

"Don't ever leave me," she said, as she clung tightly onto his shirt. "Don't leave me like Daddy."

Connor smiled warmly as he accepted her first command to him. "I will never leave you like your dad left you."

Samantha's green eyes glistened as she asked, "You promise?"

Connor replied, "Samantha Valda, I promise you that I will never die and leave you all alone. I promise to always be here for you as long as I am able."

"Pinkie swear!" she demanded, holding out her pinkie.

Connor chuckled and hooked his finger with hers. "My pinkie also swears to always be here for you." Satisfied, Samantha snuggled up with Connor. "You have had a rough morning. How about you take a nap and when you wake up I will make you something super special for lunch."

Samantha sat back up, "I can't sleep right now. Tell me a story."

"A story?" Connor asked, clearly surprised by the request. Samantha nodded eagerly, with big, puppy-dog eyes he found.

"How could I say no to a face like that? Let's see..." he said, searching through his memories. Connor finally remembered a story that a five-year-old would enjoy. "All right. Let me tell you a tale of a princess ..."

* * *

LONDON, ENGLAND

MAY 22, 1536

Deep in the heart of London, at the height of the tallest tower, sat a princess curled tightly in a ball. The full moon cast a soft light on the princess, but it did nothing to relieve her sorrows. She showed no care for the fine purple dress that she freely stained with tears. She had disdain for the braided auburn hair pinned to her head that she now tore at with shaking fingers. Preoccupied by her own misery, this young princess of sixteen remained unaware of the dark shadow perched outside her window.

Suddenly she heard a light knock on her window. Confused, she sat up slightly and looked toward the four large windows, currently covered by curtains. Another knock sounded. Curiosity getting the better of her, the princess went over to the window. Standing very still, she listened closely for another knock. Silence.

"It was probably a bird," she told herself. The second she took a step away from the window, she heard three more knocks. The once tearful green eyes now widened. Swallowing the lump in her throat, she drew open the large curtains. Since the candlelight cast reflections on the window, it was difficult to see out into the dark night. Prompted by her curiosity, she opened the window and leaned out. The cool night air dried the tears on her cheekbones. Sweet aromas drifted up to her from the garden below. The stars twinkled up in the sky similar to fireflies. She couldn't see the source of the knocking. As she began to close the window, a large mass jumped through the window and landed directly on top of her. The princess closed her eyes as she hit the floor but then opened them wide when her mouth was covered.

Straddling her was a young man dressed all in black, from his short, black, wavy hair to his shiny black boots and his scandalous black shirt, which showed a portion of his chest. The young man appeared to be in his early twenties. What was most stunning about this young man were his intensely dark and mysterious eyes.

While he firmly held his hand over her mouth, the young man bent in close and whispered in her ear, "I'm not here to hurt you. If I remove my hand, do you promise not to scream?" His voice was silky, with a hint of desire, as if he were a lover whispering into her ear.

The princess nodded her head.

Cautiously, he removed his hand and sat up for a moment, as if waiting for her to scream for help. Instead, she lay there silently while admiring the attractive young man on top of her. Finally, the princess awkwardly asked, in a hushed tone, "Can … can you please remove yourself from my person?"

The young man chuckled, his smile charming enough to make even the most determined woman melt. He responded, quietly so as not to be overheard, "I knew you weren't the real Princess Mary of House Howard. The real princess would have yelled for help." The young man hopped off and then helped her up.

She kept her distance from this man who had unexpectedly popped through her window on her first night in the castle. Ready to flee at a moment's notice, she maintained a coiled tension. Quite opposite of the proper posture with which a princess would hold herself. "Who are you?"

"Ah, pardon my rude manners." —The young man in black made a low bow— "I couldn't help but notice your arrival today. By the number of ogres surrounding your carriage, I take it that you didn't come willingly, either. Hence, I am the thief in the night, here to steal you away from what appears to be a cruel fate." He gave her a deep bow.

The fake princess looked out the window into the dark night. Her bedroom was easily four stories up. "How did you climb up here? And what is your name?"

Once again, he gave her his charming smile, his eyes glistening purple. "I climbed the wall, of course. As for my name, I will answer to whatever name you give me."

A little taken aback, she smiled, a blush blossoming on her perfect cheeks. "Do you not have a name, castle climber?"

Observing the room, amazed at its ornamentation, he answered, "I have gone by many names. What would you prefer to call me, other than your

13

thief?" He winked at her playfully.

She blushed brighter, then tried to hide it. "Fine, then. You shall be called Cleon, since you enjoy climbing walls."

The young man clicked his heels together and announced, "Well, my lady, my name is Cleon the fortress climber, and your own personal thief. It is an honor to be in your presence. And what name blesses a beauty such as yourself?"

She answered rigidly, "My name is Mary of ..."

"Please don't even try," Cleon interrupted, "I know you are not Princess Mary. Tell me your real name and I promise to keep it our little secret."

Relaxing, she finally revealed, "Serena. My name is Serena. I was Princess Mary's chamber maid."

"How fascinating!" —Cleon spun around on his heels, elegantly snatching up a chair and plopping himself down on it— "Tell me how a chamber maid was elevated to be a princess in one day."

The tears returned to Serena's glistening green eyes as she lost all her composure. "It was horrible! Princess Mary was a cruel, spiteful girl who delighted in the suffering of others. If anyone dared to disobey her, then she would order them whipped. But she didn't deserve such a fate!"

"What happened?" Cleon honestly inquired.

Serena inhaled deeply, her jaw quivering intensely. It was the exhale that appeared to calm her enough to explain, "This evil king sent ogres, wolves and knights to slaughter the noble family because they had land he wished to seize. I waited with her in her bedchamber for death to come. There was no escaping.

"Death, dressed as knights in shiny, bloody armor and ogres adorned in human flesh, were coming to kill everyone in the castle. Feeling useless, with nowhere to run, I did what I was raised to do. I asked, 'Is there anything I could do to help you, my lady?'

"For a moment, Princess Mary directed her fear and anger at me. She picked up a doll and raised her arm to throw it at me, when she suddenly froze. The princess's face lit up. Holding my shoulders, she bounced as if she were a little kid and exclaimed, 'We can switch places. The knights are coming to murder a princess. They aren't looking for a servant. If you dress as me, then I can sneak away in your clothes. The worst that could happen to me is that I get a little dirty during my escape. But that can be fixed with a hot bath. I'm sure another noble family will take me in. Isn't it a brilliant idea?'

"I honestly didn't know what to say. I didn't believe her plan would work, but I knew I was going to die either way. So I agreed, 'If that is what my princess commands, then I shall do my best.'

"I went fast to work at stripping the princess down while getting myself undressed. The princess stood surprisingly still, even though she was overwhelmed with excitement that she would survive. As I put my servant clothes on the princess, she complained about how scratchy the material was. I rolled my eyes and put on the princess's beautiful blue dress. The fabric was so soft on my skin, as if I were being kissed all over. I had only ever dreamed of wearing such fine clothes. I felt blessed that I was able to wear one fine dress before my end.

"A loud banging hit the door so hard that it splintered the wood. It made both of us jump. With one more earth-shattering crack, the door flung open. We stood side by side, frozen in place, as we watched three giant ogres barge inside. Blood dripped off their swords. They wore sharp-edged helmets that hid their grotesque green faces, and their evil, piercing eyes zeroed in on us.

"It was so horrible! Immediately the princess begged for her life. One of the ogres took his battle ax and swung it through her body, cutting her down to the core. There was blood everywhere— all over the walls, the furniture, and even on me. I can still hear that wet sucking sound as the ogre pulled his ax free from her body." Serena covered her face in her hands and wept.

Cleon stood up, wanting to comfort her. Remembering that he was a stranger in a princess' bed chamber, decided against it and resumed his seat. "That sounds traumatic for someone who has never seen death."

"That's not all," Serena said, "A knight with golden armor entered. He inspected me, and said, 'This is her.'

15

"The other two ogres grabbed my wrists and dragged me out of the room. I was terrified that they might kill me at any moment if I resisted, so I let them take me. We passed through the castle, stepping over countless bodies until we were outside. It was even worse out there. I saw the most incredible display of dead carcasses rotting in the heat of the night. The King's head was pierced on the gate like a grape on a knife. The Queen's was on the other side of the gate. Then there was the young prince and princess, both hung near the stables. Men had died by the thousands trying to protect the castle from the ogre horde that King Henry VIII had sent their way. Now, all was lost.

"Seems King Henry needed an heir. Hence my capture and delivery to London." Serena's lip quivered and she clasped her arms together tightly, trying to calm herself.

"You are so young to be exposed to such tragedy. My heart bleeds for you," he said. It was a lie, but convincingly told.

"Shall we be off, then?" he said, popping up from his chair.

Serena's nose crinkled as though she'd caught a whiff of something pungent. "What did you say? I can't leave! They'll hunt me down with those wolves! Plus, why would I run away with you?"

Cleon pointed a finger to the ceiling and opened his mouth to make an intelligible argument. At that moment, the door slammed open, startling Serena. The hardened eyes of the knight in the doorway scanned the room, then came to rest on the fake princess. "Who were you talking to?"

Serena whipped her head around to the window, to see where her mysterious castle climber had gone. There was no sign of him, just an open window where the draft pulled the curtains outside into the brisk night air. Correcting her posture, Serena answered the knight, "No one. I was practicing what I might say tomorrow when I see the King."

It was clear the knight wasn't entirely convinced. He stormed into the room and ripped the curtains away from the window. Cleon dropped from the windowsill. Keeping to the shadows, he disappeared around the corner of the castle. Rescuing the princess from her tower would have to wait.

At the expected time the next night came a familiar knock on the window. Serena jumped out of bed and ran to open it, throwing the curtains open as if making a grand entrance on stage and then unlatching the window. As it slowly swayed open, Cleon climbed through calmly, as if this were the normal way to enter a room. Seeing Serena blushing, Cleon felt a fluttering butterflies in his stomach, but was careful not to show it.

Standing straight and tall, he announced, "Serena, I shall now save you from your awful fate and whisk you away into the night." From behind his back, he brought out a unique flower that was foreign to these lands. It was a brilliant shade of purple, with wild petals that stretched and curled. In the center were brilliant pink stripes. Serena admired the flower with delight, and upon receiving it, held it close to her chest.

At first, Serena was stunned to silence by the wonderment of the flower. Recollecting his question, she continued her game of cat-and-mouse. "Not tonight, castle-climbing Cleon."

Cleon admired Serena's breathtaking face, complemented by wavy auburn locks. Her brilliant green eyes drew him in, as if he were trapped in a whirlpool. Yet he couldn't allow her to sway his mind so easily. "Stop this silliness and hop on my back, I'll carry you down the wall," he stated.

"I said, NO," she replied stubbornly.

Cleon's smile twitched to the side for a moment. He was growing impatient with this argument. Cleon reminded her, "You realize you will die in this castle."

Smiling, Serena mocked him by saying, "Why would it be safer for me to travel with you than to stay here? I have no experience beyond castle walls. I dare I would last a day trying to rely on my scant survival skills. I believe I am more likely to die outside the castle should I choose to escape with you."

Cleon growled in frustration and argued, "I can protect you!"

"I'll take my chances here behind the security of stone walls," Serena said, folding her arms defiantly.

Disgruntled, Cleon turned around and walked to the window. "I shall return tomorrow, when you will hopefully see the error of your refusal."

Then he was gone, leaving Serena to stew in her decision.

When he returned the following night, something had changed in Serena's demeanor. Her abnormally downcast appearance was a drastic change from her normally upbeat attitude. Taking hope in that, he prodded, "Is this a change of heart I see? Will you now depart with me far from this castle?"

Serena sighed, then picked up the flower from the previous night to admire its beauty. "Did you hear news of the castoff queen Anne Boleyn?"

"Yes, she was beheaded a few weeks ago," he replied, as casually as one would talk about the weather.

Serena recoiled at this. It wasn't normal for someone to be so nonchalant about death. "It might mind *you* little, but I had to suffer through listening to every detail the ladies were compelled to tell me. They warned me that I might meet the same fate."

"That makes your decision easier. Come with me to spare you such a fate," Cleon offered.

"I can't. Not after what happened today," Serena withdrew as if saving herself from temptation.

Cleon settled in and listened intently.

"As I entered the dining hall, the rows of nobles whispered and gossiped as if they were snakes slithering through tall grass, foretelling my own demise. The closer I got to the king, the more I feared for my own life. The king sat laughing over a shared chalice of wine. To the king's left was another woman I had never seen before. By her mannerisms, I could tell that this woman was high-born, most likely a princess or duchess. The woman hung upon the king's arm and laughed alongside him. The perfect accessory for the king! I walked up to the king and curtsied, as was proper. For a moment, the king didn't even notice me. It was the woman—with deathly cold eyes—who redirected his attention.

"The king turned around in his drunken stupor. For a moment he appeared lost, as though he had never seen me before in his life, then his face brightened up. 'Ah! Princess Mary! Glad you could join us.

Unfortunately, child, I have some bad news.'

"My heart raced. I felt as though my fate now hung in the balance, upon the edge of the ax that had so swiftly spelled out the fate of so many others.

"'I found a more suitable wife, Lady Jane Seymour! So it would seem'—he eyed me up and down with a touch of regret, as if he believed he was missing out—'I shan't be needing your services anymore.' My heart sank into my stomach as the king waved me off. Before I could react, two men grabbed my arms and led me away. I screamed, but no one said a word as they watched me being dragged away. I lost all hope and regretted not running away with you.

"Then my hero stepped from the crowd and told the knights, 'Stop right now!'

"The knights promptly stopped, as the king put up his hand to order them to cease. This young man, whom I'd been introduced to at court as Henry Fitzroy, is rather unusual. He has oddly feminine features, wavy blond locks, a soft face, and baby blue eyes. The way he holds himself suggests that he was not high born. There's a slight slouch in his shoulders, and he doesn't hold his chin in that aristocratic way. He seemed to me the sort of man who had always sought to blend in, not wanting attention on himself … until today. I was shocked by what happened next.

"He walked boldly up to the king and requested my hand in marriage! The whole hall instantly burst into an uproar of whispers.

"'Why would you want to marry this princess, Henry, m'boy? She has nothing more to offer you. Her land belongs to me, along with that heap of a castle her family built,' the king grumbled.

"The young man held his chin high, 'Father … your majesty… please grant me permission to marry this princess so I may be entitled as a duke. instead of merely your bastard.'

"I was shocked again. I'd always thought that the king had no heir, hence his dire need for a fertile bride.

"The king seemed to be mulling this request over in his head, a moment that lasted an eternity. The tension built so high that it even silenced the whispers. I felt my heartbeat pounding through my entire body, especially where the knights were still holding me, bruising my upper arms. After what felt like an eternity, the king replied, 'Because you have always been so loyal and because I am a just and fair king, I shall grant you the title of duke in the course of marrying this lowly princess, who shall henceforth be your duchess. May you father many children.' All of the dinner guests burst into applause and praised the king for being so fair.

"My resentment for the king burned deep within my heart. When the knights released me, I almost fell to the floor. Luckily, I managed to stay on my feet and shakily walked over to the bastard son of the king. Fighting the ache in my arms, I gave the most gracious curtsy I could and spoke the words that betrayed my own heart: 'I thank thee both for your generosity. I shall never forget this moment, your majesty.'

"The king took a long swallow of his wine, then gruffly commanded, 'Be a dutiful wife for Henry, because of his sacrifice to marry you. And marry, you shall.' —Then the king turned to the crowd, which was still cheering— 'For tomorrow they shall be wed,' the king said, pulling his new bride closer to him. 'Then our marriage shall be as soon as the grand festivities can be planned!' The crowd cheered and applauded. The drunken king moved toward the face of his betrothed to give her a sloppy kiss, which appeared to repulse her.

"I was grateful that this bastard had saved my life, but I knew he regretted it as much as I did by the reluctant way he looked at me." Serena breathed heavily after her lively reenactment of this tumultuous day.

Cleon eagerly ran to the window and stretched his right hand out to Serena, "Run away with me! We can flee far from this evil place and all that haunts your dreams."

Instead of taking his hand, Serena sat back down on her bed and shook her head. "I can't. I'm betrothed now."

Cleon's heart plummeted. This rejection stung worse than the others. "I see …"

Then he was gone.

Panicked, Serena ran to the window, but no matter how much she called out for him, he did not return to her that night.

The next day was the rushed ceremony to unite the bastard, Henry Fitzroy, and the alienated Mary of House Howard in holy matrimony. Despite his heartbreak, Cleon couldn't stop himself from going to the ceremony. Unlike the dark garb of his nightly escapades, Cleon wore to aristocratic clothing befitting his class. The front of his black overcoat was intricately embroidered with a gold and black dragon. Golden chains and ruby clasps accented his princely undercoat. His thick black locks were swept back, allowing his face to be seen fully from every angle. Adorning himself in princely attire, Cleon blended in with the rest of the nobility, and he tucked himself away at the very back of the high-vaulted church.

When Serena stepped out, he was overcome with a mix of jealousy and awe at her beauty. Ahead of her at the altar stood a large congregation of priests and altar boys. Angelic music resonated throughout the cavernous church. Serena's beauty was illuminated by sunlight cascading from the stained-glass windows. Her beautiful locks of auburn hair were twisted up into braids woven into a bun. So much wax had been added to her hair to keep it in place that its naturally fiery color was muted to a dull brown, decorated with tiny flowers. A long yellow veil embroidered with flowers hid her face and drifted down her back. The green dress was an extraordinary layering of lace, gold trims and tightly stitched flowers. Upon her chest was the gold crest of House Howard, so no one would forget she was a princess.

Taking as deep a breath as her corset would allow, Serena took her first step towards the altar. As she walked, six ladies held her veil and the hem of her long dress as they proceeded along the church's stone floor. Serena buried her face in the bouquet of roses. Finally, the long walk was over, and Serena stood facing Henry Fitzroy. He puffed his small chest out proudly. In unison, the audience sat down as the priest began to speak in Latin. .

Finally, the priest asked the most important question of the whole ceremony, "Princess Mary of House Howard, do you take Henry Fitzroy to be your husband?"

"I do." Her words were as hollow as if echoing in a canyon.

"Then I now pronounce you husband and wife. Duke Henry Fitzroy, you may now kiss the bride!" the priest said in a celebratory tone. The crowd roared in excitement, with the exception of Cleon, who stared silently at his boots. Serena stared at her new husband as he slowly lifted her veil. The new duke was gentle, perhaps timid, as he placed the veil behind her head. Then he gingerly leaned in and gave Serena a quick peck on the lips. The crowd applauded as he turned toward the pews with a triumphant expression, as though he had slain a dragon.

Hand in hand, they walked down the aisle. Serena glanced back at the ladies charged with holding her train, who were scrambling to pick it up quickly enough. As she looked ahead at her new husband pulling her forward, her eyes locked instead onto Cleon, whose princely attire outshone that of her new duke. In this fleeting moment, Cleon's dark purple eyes replicated the despair in Serena's green eyes. Then he averted his gaze and turned to leave through a side door.

Impelled to torture himself further, Cleon numbly walked into the great dining hall later that night, where the new duke had arrived early to bask in the glory of finally being accepted as one of the nobility. Cleon declined to pay respects to the duke, instead preoccupying himself by running his fingertip around the rim of his wine glass. When Duchess Mary Fitzroy was announced, however, he snapped to attention.

Serena made her way past the dancing courtiers and drunken lords, over to the table where the king was sitting with his betrothed. She curtsied low in her flowing green dress to pay her obeisance. Not even noticing his new daughter-in-law, the king accidentally spilled food on his irritated bride-to-be and then ordered a steward to bring more wine. Serena quietly took her place next to her new husband and started picking at the plate of food placed before her.

After a long hour of being ignored, she took one more bite and asked her husband, "Shall we dance?"

Henry appeared confused for a moment, as if dancing with his new wife was a foreign custom. Then he looked over at the king, who, for once, seemed to actually be acknowledging him. "No, Lady Mary, you may dance without me this time."

Serena recoiled as though he'd just told her to sleep with the pigs. "Well, if you change your mind, just let me know," she said, rising to join the crowd twirling about on the dance floor.

It seemed everyone was now prancing about in intricate steps. Hand in hand, the lords and ladies were lost in their partners and being swept away by the rhythm of the music. Serena awkwardly stood alone near the edge of the dance floor. She wrung her hands and watched the happy, nameless faces, dancing flawlessly. The song ended with polite applause, to which Serena joined in. The orchestra players whispered amongst one another before beginning the next tune.

This was Cleon's chance. He cut through the crowd and extended his hand to Serena, asking, "May I have this dance?"

Startled, Serena quickly said, "Yes!" before turning to see who was speaking. Cleon had swallowed his ego and his pain to save her from this awkward social situation. Those mysterious eyes of his were so dark that a color could no longer be registered. Leaving no time for Serena to comment on the change, he instantly guided her onto the floor. As the music picked up, he put his hand on her lower back and held her other hand.

"I don't know this dance," she whispered in a panic.

"Do not fret, my duchess, allow me take over," Cleon said with a smile, as he pulled her in closer. Serena did as she was told and allowed her feet to follow. With Cleon expertly leading her in a dance she knew none of the steps to, they floated as though they were dancing on air, their footsteps soundlessly flitting across the marble floor.

"Where did you get those clothes?" she whispered into his ear.

"They are mine," he responded distantly.

Serena's eyes widened as she said, "That means you are a ..."

"Focus on my lead," he instructed.

She winced as she stepped on his foot. Gentle and yet firm, Cleon guided Serena so precisely that they flowed as if they were one. Even though the music had stopped, they were still dancing, causing everyone else to stare at the two. After a few moments of silence, the audience abruptly applauded the magnificent performance of the new duchess and the stranger in black.

The music started up again, this time with a livelier beat. As the dancing began again, Cleon leaned in and whispered to her, "I must pass you off now."

Panic erupted on her face and she gripped his hand tighter. Cleon was calm and sympathetic as he kissed her hand and said, "It was a privilege to dance with you, my Lady Mary. I hope to dance with you again." Then he turned Serena around by her outstretched hand.

Henry bowed low and said, with fake sympathy, "I feel terrible for interrupting your elegant dance, but I would appreciate to dance with my wife now."

"Well, of course," Cleon said happily, as he gracefully transferred Serena's hand to Henry. "'Tis only proper for you to dance with you wife on your wedding night."

Henry took Serena's hand and held it gingerly while excusing Cleon, "Thank you for making my wife look beautiful upon the dance floor."

Cleon bowed low and glanced at Serena, saying, "Until next time, my lady."

"Until next time," she whispered.

It was agonizing to disappear into the crowd when all he wanted was to escape with her into the night. Unfortunately, social pressure held her fast in her place next to her new husband. This time, the dancers parted to give Serena and Henry plenty of space. It wasn't the most graceful dance— Henry would try to lead, but his forceful manner made her stumble. The dance was almost more awkward than their short-winded conversations. Compared to the dance with Cleon, they danced if they were as two fish flopping around on dry land. Both were visibly relieved when it was finally over.

"Enough dancing!" the king hollered out, prompting the room to quiet instantly. "For now we must pardon the newlyweds so they may produce an heir of their own!" The king raised his chalice, as did a couple of hundred others, in unison. They all drank to the newlyweds' fertility and shouted in joy. Henry looked awkwardly at Serena, whose frightened eyes peered back into his empty ones. Hand in hand, they walked out of the room, everyone cheering them on as if they were off to challenge some large feat.

Cleon grimaced, thinking about what must occur next. It should have been him happily married to Serena, not this feminine duke. He knew he should leave, but the masochistic side of him was prompted to stand guard outside the honeymoon cottage nestled next to the gardens. The only comfort he could find was in contemplating the vastness of the stars above. For no matter what happened down below, the stars remained unchanged in their cycle through the heavens.

Keeping watch, Cleon was stunned to notice something unexpected: the new Duke Henry Fitzroy was sneaking out of his honeymoon cottage. Curiosity getting the better of him, Cleon crept inside.

Lying prone on a clean, white—and undisturbed—bed was the new duchess, her eyes closed. Cleon silently approached her and tenderly brushed her cheek with the back of a finger, finding it moistened by a tear. "Do you often cry while you sleep?" he whispered.

Serena shakily sat up and opened her wet green eyes. Blinking away the tears, she saw a princely Cleon standing next to her. "Cleon," —she sobbed, jumping up and burying her face into his shoulder as she breathed in his aroma— "I thought I would never see you again."

Cleon pushed her away gently and smiled warmly.

Serena lowered her head in shame. "I'll run away with you. Please, take me far away from here!"

Remorse shrouded Cleon's face as he replied, "I can't anymore, Serena. You are now a duchess, married to a duke."

Serena clung tighter to his cloak, fearing he would leave again. "Henry ran off and wouldn't tell me where he was going. The marriage has not yet been consummated, which means it isn't official. Please take me away from here."

Cleon rested his hand on hers and whispered in her ear, "Then perhaps now is our chance. Grab everything you need. We leave immediately."

She shocked him by jumping into his arms and placing her lips upon his. At first, he resisted her but then quickly melted into her embrace. The whole world seemed to spin around them and then melt away, as if nothing else mattered beyond this moment. This perfect embrace felt as if it could last for a lifetime, but all too soon it was interrupted by the sound of barking dogs.

Cleon broke away, urgency in his pitch-black eyes. "Hurry and grab anything of value!" he commanded. He turned to see where the dogs were and prepared to protect Serena from them, instantly regretting that he had worn easily traceable cologne.

Serena quickly stuffed things into a sack and made for the garden door, only to be pushed forcefully back into the bedroom by Cleon, repelled by the gnashing of canine teeth just outside. As he flung her back, a flailing limb caught the canopy over the bed and tore it down, tangling both of them in a mess of translucent fabric as several arrows flew in through the open window, hitting the floor.

To add to the chaos, the front door opened and a maid blindly hollered, "Quickly, rest your eyes upon the adulterer! He's been sneaking into the princess' bedchamber every night!" Shortly after, the clanking of metal armor announced the four knights entering the room.

Serena screamed, "Wait!" But the knights ignored her and raised their weapons. Cleon, freeing himself, fought back with fury, but one of the knights managed to thrust his sword into his belly. Blood spurted from Cleon's mouth as the knight withdrew the sword, and he fell down, lying curled up and motionless on the floor. Serena screamed in horror as she watched Cleon's blood pool around him. The knights, deaf to her screams, grabbed her arms and dragged her away to the dungeon, where the king would decide her fate.

* * *

Connor paused in telling the story and noticed that Sammy had fallen into a deep sleep. This was probably for the best. He realized that his stories never had happy endings. Not wanting to disturb her much-needed rest,

Connor replayed the ancient memory in his mind as if it were yesterday.

* * *

Cleon groggily awoke. It took a moment for his eyes to adjust to the dim light, which revealed an orange glow in which several people were gathered—one of them the king.

"What do you mean he can't die? Blasphemy!" the king said, a hint of fear in his voice.

"I'm telling the truth, your majesty, this *thing* was run through with a long sword and completely bled out, yet he healed within a matter of minutes. We shot an arrow through his heart and threw him in this hanging cage," said a gruff, yet deformed voice. It sounded to Cleon as if the speaker was missing teeth or half his tongue, neither of which would be surprising.

"What arrow?" the king asked in disbelief.

"It fell out about ten minutes ago, your majesty," said another deep voice.

"Fell out? Fell out! Arrows simply don't *fall* out!" the king raged.

"Pardon me," Cleon interrupted, his voice weak. The collection of executioners, knights, a bishop and a king around him all yelped in shock as one and jumped back a step. The bishop crossed himself and began muttering prayers. The hands of the knights went to their weapons, and the king stepped quickly behind the burliest of them. Cleon was covered in his own blood, with more pooling beneath the hanging cage that confined him. His overcoat and black shirt were ripped in places where he had been run through with swords and arrows.

"It is fun to watch you all scatter similar to field mice," Cleon said, with a humorless chuckle. "I was wondering if you wouldn't mind giving my friend over there a proper room. A cell isn't comfortable enough for a princess."

Serena gasped from a faraway cell.

"Demon, be gone!" yelled the priest, as he showered Cleon with holy water.

Once again Cleon merely laughed, licking of the drops that beaded around his lips. "Thank you for the water. I was a bit thirsty. You missed my mouth, though."

The priest made the sign of the cross and took several steps backward, to place himself alongside the king.

"Now, are you gentlemen going to get the lady a proper room, or am I going to make you do it?" Cleon said.

The men remained frozen, dumbfounded. Nonchalantly, Cleon shrugged. "I guess I'll help the young lady myself." As he grabbed the bars of his hanging cage firmly, Cleon's eyes burned red, and the bars of the cage grew red hot.

"Do something!" demanded the king as the bars started to melt.

Snapped out of his stupor, one of the knights stepped forward and plunged his blade through Cleon's abdomen. As he pulled his sword out, part of Cleon's entrails also spilled out. Cleon coughed up blood and struggled to remain conscious.

Frightened by what he was seeing, the king commanded, "Every time the creature stirs, kill him again! There has to be a limit to how many times the devil will resurrect this monster."

The king then turned a hateful eye on Serena. Tears were running down her face. "As for this wench, who was clearly consorting with the devil, kill her before she also gains demonic powers!"

Overwhelmed, Serena could muster no more than a whimper. Pulling her legs close to her body for comfort, Serena wept into her knees as the men left. Cleon lost consciousness with the executioner at his side, ready to stab Cleon with a spear should he wake again.

The first sensation he had upon awakening was the smell of blood. A smell that normally energized him now shamed him. Feigning sleep to appease the guard, who stank of sweat, Cleon focused on what he could hear. Somewhere in the distance, a crowd had gathered outside, hollering for the beheading of the new duchess. Chains scraped along wooden boards.

The bishop's voice trembled as he loudly pronounced her sentence,

"Mary of House Howard, you are guilty of the crime of adultery and consorting with a demon. You shall be beheaded for your crimes. Do you have any last words?"

Cleon heard her proudly proclaiming to the crowd: "My name is Serena. Not Mary."

He thought he heard fear shaking the king's voice as he shouted the command: "Off with her head!"

Time seemed to stand still as there was a pause and he imagined the executioner raising his large ax. The crowd was now cheering for her death. The king shouting. The bishop trembling. Then a sudden hush, in which Cleon heard a quiet drip of his own blood coming off his foot. Then the soft whisper from Serena's lips: "Caspian!"

The ax fell upon her neck with an ominous THUD.

The crowd gasped in astonishment when no head rolled away from the condemned woman. Instead of the ax slicing clean through her neck, it fell heavily to the ground. Her dismembered body burst into millions of tiny purple wisps that floated off into the air. The rabble erupted in a frenzy, screaming of witchcraft as every one of them ran for the exits. Mass chaos took over, with no head to put on a spike and no body to throw over the castle wall. *Witchcraft* was the word that would be whispered for years to come.

Deep within the dungeon below the castle, intense rage consumed Cleon until the cage melted around him. The terrified executioner stabbed between the melting bars with the spear. In one fluid motion, Cleon grabbed the spear, broke off its lethal head and thrust it into the executioner's forehead. The man fell limply upon the hard stone floor, his dead eyes filled with terror.

As if he were stretching after getting out of bed, Cleon pushed out his arms and legs and broke free of the red-hot cage. Blood dripped on the floor from his stomach wound as he walked through the dungeon. The wound soon closed up, healing at a miraculous rate.

Cleon's eyes pulsed red as a vengeful energy burned deep inside of him. His gait was slow and heavy, with the destructive power of an infuriated

Minotaur. His goal was painted clearly in his mind as he slowly made his way to the grand throne room, where the king sat surrounded by his court officials speaking in panicked voices, trying to make sense of the evil that had come upon them. Some unfortunate souls caught in the tornado of Cleon's path were turned into heaps of torn flesh as he ripped through them.

When he reached the grand throne room, a mighty blast from Cleon's fist turned the twenty-foot-high doors into a million shards of iron and wood. Some died instantly from the impact of the shattering door. The remaining two hundred or so would not be so lucky. The entire room was still for a moment as its occupants gazed upon this monstrosity with glowing red eyes. The king yelled for his guards as if they could protect him from this evil. Cleon gave them a devilish grin, knowing he would savor these next moments.

Hundred of short-lived screams echoed that day from the castle that would be remembered in history as the castle of blood. The few survivors would recount the tale of the mysterious stranger who unleashed his fury upon the Tower of London after his love was sentenced to death—a tale so strange it has sometimes been dismissed as a tall tale. What the history books don't record was this:

Cleon made sure to paint the throne room as red as his eyes— as red as his fury.

The king he saved for the very last. Similar to a lion playing with a field mouse, Cleon kept him alive in agonizing pain over the course of twelve hours until the king's body finally gave out. Even after his death, it wasn't enough for Cleon. That rage of not being able to save Serena ate him away inside. Cleon's heart wrenching screams echoed back to him within the cold castle walls, now dripping with blood. Exhausted at last, Cleon fell into the pool of blood he had created and looked up at the vaulted ceiling of the castle, his eyes turning as black and empty as his soul.

* * *

Sammy yawned and stretched, her bright green eyes fluttering open. After a moment, she recollected the last bit of the story. "Did they both die? Cleon and Serena?"

Connor suddenly felt guilty about telling such a horrific story to a girl who had lost her father. "Serena died ... as did many others ... I'm sorry, Sammy. My stories don't have happy endings. I should have read from one of your story books."

"Why did so many people die?" Sammy inquired innocently.

"An early death was common back then. People died of all sorts of things. Just like House Howard, rival families killed each other. They didn't have laws to protect them back then, so people died because someone with a pointy crown said so," Connor explained.

"But why must people die, Connor?" Sammy asked again.

This question was harder to answer, especially from a five-year-old. What was he to say? People die because they are blessed with mortality. The gift of an end makes the journey of life that much sweeter. A five-year-old wouldn't understand that. Finally, he came up with another answer. "You know how in *The Lion King*, Mufasa teaches Simba about the circle of life?"

Sammy nodded.

"So, it goes with humans, too," Connor smiled.

Sammy wrapped her arms around Connor and snuggled in close. "I don't want you to die, Connor. Please don't die."

"I can't die," Connor jested. When Sammy looked up at him in confusion, he continued, "I promised you that I wouldn't leave you, didn't I?"

Sammy nodded and hopped out of bed. "Can I have chocolate-chip pancakes?"

"Of course. Anything for you," Connor replied sweetly.

2

A FRESH START

NEW YORK CITY, NEW YORK

OCTOBER 2, 2002

The blue sky showered down happiness on the city of New York, whose citizens were beginning to resume normal life, though reminders of the terror of 9/11 still hung in the air and in every corner of the city where the debris had yet to be cleaned up. Still, life moved on as it always has: with hope.

It was hope that now hovered about a shy little girl with auburn hair who was sitting among men in suits at the top of the Valda Enterprise building. She peered out the door of her daddy's private office at the ongoing bustle. A little girl sitting still in a chair stood out in this environment.

She watched Connor, who was speaking with a woman of African heritage who was handing him a pen. As Connor signed, Sammy was distracted by an argument two men in the outer office were having about the future of Valda Enterprise.

"There has to be a simpler way to adopt Samantha," Connor said as he grudgingly signed the papers.

"As I mentioned, we first must investigate her only living relative before

32

giving you full custody. The courts always prefer blood relatives in these situations," the woman said, pulling on her blazer with an air of authority.

The paper Connor had signed gave him temporary guardianship over Samantha. "Samantha Valda's only blood relative is an uncle convicted on three charges of grand larceny, one count of breaking and entering, and multiple counts of drug possession. Additionally, he has been in and out of drug rehabilitation programs with no signs of long-term recovery. I, on the other hand, have a spotless record, incredible resources and the financial means to take care of Samantha without touching her inheritance. Why wouldn't you grant me custody at this moment?"

The worker from the Department of Child and Family Services grabbed the papers from him and straightened them out. "While I will admit that you appear to be a fit guardian, you can't wave a magic wand and get what you want. There are rules and procedures that must be followed, like her being evaluated by a therapist."

"I'm glad you brought that up." Connor motioned to a woman standing in the corner of the room who, at his signal, walked forward, trailed by several men in sharp suits. "This is Dr. Kleinschmidt, the top child psychiatrist in the nation. Following her is Dr. Stanley, a professor of social work, and Dr. Azadea, a renowned expert in behavioral sciences. Then of course you've met my lawyers."

The DCFS worker stiffened. "Yes, I have conversed at length with your lawyers."

"Lynne, was it?" Dr. Kleinschmidt asked, while extending her hand.

"Yes." The DCFS worker shook the psychiatrist's hand.

"I've spent the last two weeks processing and playing games with Samantha Valda. Would you have a moment to come with us and discuss options with Samantha? I'm sure she would love a say in where she goes," Dr. Kleinschmidt asked, so soothingly that it instantly released the tension in the DCFS worker's shoulders.

"Uh, yes." Lynne nodded again.

"Let's go to the playroom." Dr. Azadea offered a hand to Samantha, which she instantly took, and they walked hand in hand back to the playroom.

Now alone in the room, Connor rubbed his temples. It was nauseating to have to do these things right.

A woman dressed in a tight gray skirt and blazer poked her head into the office. "The boardroom is ready for you, sir."

Connor threw on his suit jacket. "Thank you, Morgan." As he stepped into the boardroom, he had the look of the wealthiest man on Earth, with the authority to buy out every single man in the room, in one way or another. As they recognized the alpha in the room, the chaotic chatter ceased.

"Thank you, gentlemen, for coming here today. I hope you are enjoying your food and beverages." Connor seated himself at the head of the table, noting the lack of diversity in the room.

"Well, you are the one with the agenda," the interim CEO responded, politely but with a hint of cynicism in his voice.

"And I'm sure you all have your own hidden agendas, too," Connor responded nonchalantly. Morgan began passing out thick folders to each director sitting at the table, each of them carefully compiled for the person she was handing them to.

Connor pressed his fingers together and began his presentation. "Valda Enterprise has redeeming values: Collaboration, respect, ownership, charity, community and research. All are backed by the mission of the organization: 'To support the life of our neighbors so they too can achieve great things.'

"I know that since your founder has tragically left us that there has been some instability in this publicly traded company. Which is why I am giving you all a generous offer. As your biggest shareholder, I'm offering an additional investment to allow all medical equipment we sell will go to non-profit hospitals at half price ..."

"Do you really think this measly annual sum will cover our charitable contributions?" the operational director scoffed, looking at the document in front of him.

"That is monthly, not yearly, gentlemen. Please read the fine print." Connor continued, "as your biggest stakeholder, I also request charitable donations be increased by five percent annually. Research funds shall increase twenty-five percent. I get a say in who you hire on as the new CEO, and I am given a full report on all strategic initiatives each month. This will all be handed over to Samantha Valda when she comes of age."

"While your investments are quite generous, do you really think we can operate with such margins?" the financial director asked.

"You must," —Connor leaned toward the man, casting a shadow over his face— "If you do not follow my instructions to the T, then I will sink this company into the ground."

"What makes you think you have the ability to do that?" scoffed the interim CEO.

Connor leaned back in his chair, "Because I have purchased eighty-nine percent of Valda Enterprise stocks at two percent below the asking price. Now, do we have a deal?"

When Connor walked out of that room, he had less faith in humanity than when he entered, though that kind of disappointment was something he was accustomed to. Once back in Ronald's old office, he felt a familiar presence, one he had hoped would have arrived a couple of days earlier.

A gentleman was sitting in the late executive's high-back leather chair and swiveled around as Connor entered. His dress reminded Connor of the crisp anonymity of a secret service agent, but with a coy smile and an expression that said "up to no good"—the kind that often brings women to their knees. In his hand was the sweet portrait of Samantha playing in the fall leaves with her departed father. "How intriguing! When you told me she was young, I didn't expect her to be a child," he teased. "You are robbing the cradle these days, aren't you Ca—"

"You may call me Mr. Roberts," Connor quickly corrected. "Do you have what I requested, Dorian?"

A sigh of boredom escaped the man as he continued to swivel in the chair. On his next circuit, he placed a packet of papers on the desk and then propped his Gucci's on its corner.

Connor opened the packet and reviewed the housing information enclosed. "I am to assume that the security system is up and running?"

"And Morgan has done her own round of protection on it," Dorian added.

"Hmm," —Connor continued to flip through the loose papers— "It's in the middle of a cul-de-sac."

"Well, the best-kept secrets are always hidden in the mundane, are they not, Mr. Roberts?" Dorian's sarcasm bled through his truthful observations.

"Very well," —Connor sealed up the packet again— "Any word on the terrorist attack?"

"You know as much as I do," Dorian shrugged.

Connor shot him a reprimanding glance.

Dorian rolled his amber eyes in response. "The United States is still under the assumption that the Werewolf Clan was behind it. Causing quite a lot of press around the issue, pressuring the already unstable relationship between France and the U.S."

"Yes, I know our French prime minister has her hands full. Have we found evidence of foul play?" Connor asked.

Dorian's obvious annoyance created a slight tension in the air. "I'm your entrepreneur, not your errand boy."

"How is that going, by the way? Keeping you occupied for once?" Connor grabbed the photograph back from Dorian and gently set it back on the desk.

"It was exciting at first but grew dull after sustaining Fortune 100 status for five years and garnering more profit than I can invest. No, I think I might sell here soon enough."

"Do one last thing for me first."

Another eye roll.

"Wipe Samantha Valda from the map. I don't want anyone to track down her location after we move."

"Aye aye, sir." Dorian mockingly saluted Connor upon his departure.

From the other side of the playroom door, Connor could hear Samantha practicing her French with one of the doctors while hushed conversation continued at the other end of the room. He pressed his badge to the sensor, triggering the door to unlock.

"Connor!" Sammy cried out. Dropping her book, Sammy ran over and jumped into his arms.

Although Connor normally didn't condone that much affection, he allowed her this small comfort. "Did you have fun playing with the doctors, Sammy?"

"Mmhmm," she nodded vigorously. "But they said we are leaving."

"We are! Remember, you get a new house with a large bedroom and an even larger back yard!" Connor talked it up.

"But what about our home right now?" she asked sadly.

"It will stay right here, waiting for you! How about we come back from time to time to celebrate your daddy."

Sammy nodded.

"Are we all set?" Connor asked Dr. Kleinschmidt and Lynne.

"Your colleagues have really proven your ability to be an adoptive father. I see no further reason why I can't recommend that you be granted full custody," Lynne answered.

"Does that mean you get to stay with me?" Sammy asked excitedly.

"It means I'm stuck with you until you're sick of me,"—Connor playfully booped her on the nose— "probably at about age eighteen."

The doctors laughed.

"I have a few more papers for you to sign and then you are on your way," Lynne said, pulling more documents from her briefcase.

An hour later, Connor was helping Sammy into the back of a long limousine.

"Get comfy, because we are in for a long drive," Connor warned.

"Why don't we fly there?" Sammy asked naively.

"Funny enough, I'm not quite in the mood for flying these days," Connor jested as he opened the door to the limo.

Her eyes widened in joy as she saw the back of the limousine crowded with her toys and stuffed animals, along with her favorite treats and snacks stored where wine was normally held. "Wow! Thank you, Connor!" she squealed as she jumped in.

Connor slid in behind her and closed the door. A few moments later, they were on their way. "I thought that bringing along some of your favorite toys and activities would help make the move more tolerable."

Sammy opened a package of Kinder Chocolate and took a big bite. Her face lit up and then melted, similar to the chocolate in her mouth. After politely swallowing it, she asked, "Where are we moving to?"

Connor settled into a content smile. Seeing her happy made him feel warm inside. "A quiet little town in New Hampshire. The crime rate is incredibly low. There is lots of forest for you to play in. The house is quite large, so we can customize it any way we want ..."

"Like a swimming pool?" she asked excitedly.

"Sure, why not?" he said, chuckling.

Sammy giggled and took another greedy bite of chocolate. But her face fell as she remembered. "What about Daddy's business? What about his suits?"

"All of his belongings are in New York, right where you left them. We can go back and see them, as long as it won't make you too sad. Okay?" He paused expectantly until she nodded. "As for your daddy's business, it now belongs to you. Until you are old enough, it shall be run by your father's board of trustees and esteemed executives. When you feel you are ready, you can either take ownership of the company ... or you can sell it and live the rest of your life a wealthy woman."

"I'm scared, Connor," Sammy said, as she nestled her face into Connor's chest, the car now leaving the city behind.

For a moment, he didn't quite know what to do. After an eternity of isolating, it was strange to comfort her. Her warm little fingers clung to his shirt, which was slowly growing damp from her tears. Instantly, he melted and embraced her back, wanting to wipe away all her fear and sorrow. "I know it is scary, Sammy, but I am right here. I am not going anywhere."

She lifted her head, her green eyes glistening as tears ran down her soft, round cheeks. "You promise?"

Once again, Connor felt like putty in her hands. "I promise I will never leave you, Sammy. I will always be close by to keep you safe and happy."

Sammy started playing with her hair—a gesture Connor had seen many times when she was hesitant or unsure.

Doing his absolute best to help Sammy through this transition, Connor suggested, "How about we talk about what you want your new bedroom to look like."

"Okay!" Sammy bounced on the limousine seat excitedly.

It was dark by the time they finally reached the new house in New Hampshire. Sammy lay curled up, fast asleep. She clung tightly to her favorite teddy bear, which was wearing one of her father's old t-shirts. At times Connor would catch himself watching her chest rise and fall as she slept. He couldn't help but think how innocent and vulnerable she was. He hoped he was able to keep her safe through the coming years.

At last the limousine came to a stop. The chauffeur hopped out and opened the door for his passengers.

Connor took great care not to wake Sammy as he got out of the car. He closed the door quietly and told the chauffeur he was grateful to be out of that stuffy limo.

"I know! About damn time! With the bazillion bathroom breaks she needed, I didn't think we would ever get here," the man complained.

"Peter, what are you wearing?" Connor scolded, just now taking in his appearance.

The chauffeur had made a half-hearted attempt to appear professional. On the plus side, he had spotless black shoes, pressed black slacks, and a fitting cummerbund. Adversely, there was an ugly, heavily worn, brown messenger bag slung across his shoulder. Plus his dirty blonde hair stuck out at every angle and smelt as if it needed a good wash.

"If I added a black bow tie, then I'd look like a Chippendale. What do you think?" Peter teased.

"I think you'd better not let Sammy see you. You look ridiculous," Connor coldy criticized.

"Don't get your panties in a bunch, Master. I was able to gather the information you requested on the limo's phone," Peter expertly flicked off the annoyance.

"Were the Werewolves behind the attack?" Connor asked. A note of seriousness was added into the conversation.

As though a switch had been flipped, Peter went from jester to militant informant. "No. It was a set up by a handful of changelings. The CIA is staying pretty hush-hush about it all. They see some benefit in confronting the French Prime Minister and her WolfGuard Army— something about strengthening their position about keeping Werewolves illegal in America. Politics are a bitch, huh?"

"Damn." Connor had meant to whisper, but it came out a little loud. He double-checked on Sammy to confirm she was still sleeping before continuing, "Just when I think I've exterminated all those lowly shape-shifters, they pop out of the shadows. Such a pain in the ass! The WolfGuard are definitely being set up. I find it confounding, because changelings have never been organized enough to coordinate a terrorist attack on this scale. Can you make sure that the Vampire Federation is not involved?"

"You know our Miss President of the Vampire Federation won't like me poking around in her business," Peter warned, mischievously.

"I'll give Veronica a call later tonight. She'll play nice, but don't go pissing her off like you normally do. If her hands are clean of this, we need her to support the fact that Wolves were not involved," Connor sighed, "Which means I'll need Dorian to pull political strings between America and France as well."

Peter mockingly pulled out an invisible set of pen and paper. "So, I'm spying on the Feds, infiltrating the vampire layer, and exposing the changeling's involvement with the 9/11 attack. Would you like fries with that?"

Connor ignored the tomfoolery and gave him a stern glare.

"Roger, roger," Peter saluted.

"Now get back in the driver's seat before she sees you," Connor scolded.

The reprimand bounced off Peter, evident in the bubbly way he slid into the driver's seat. It was always amusing to be around Peter and his happy-go-lucky attitude— sometimes irritating, but mostly amusing. Connor ducked into the limo, where Sammy was still fast asleep on the back seat.

"Sammy"—Connor nudged her awake— "we're here."

She grumbled and clutched tighter onto her teddy bear.

"Come on, Sammy, don't you want to see your new home?" Connor nudged her again.

This time she peeked up at Connor. "Mmhmm," she nodded, and then rubbed the sleep from her eyes.

A warm smile spread over Connor's face. Helping her along, Connor picked her up in his arms and held her tightly as he walked up to the entrance of the new house. Arriving at the door, he shifted Sammy over to one hip so he could pull a small envelope from his pocket. Inside it was a key and several folded-up papers. The key made a grinding sound as it slid into the lock, making it apparent that this house hadn't been opened in a while. The door creaked loudly as he pushed it open. Connor flipped open a control panel and entered in the key combination, disarming the state-of-the-art security system.

Sammy lifted her head off his shoulder to look around. She uttered a sharp little gasp, then hid her face.

"What is it, Sammy?" Connor asked, then he saw it, too. The walls of the living room and hallway were entirely covered in pictures. Most were paintings: landscapes and portraits. Others were photographs of random people. The elegantly framed pictures filled the walls so tightly that hardly an inch of white space peeked through. It was easy to see why a child would be frightened of a hundred paintings of people staring back at her in the dark.

Connor comforted Sammy by putting his hand on the back of her head. "Don't worry, Sammy, I'll make sure they are all burned by morning." A small, maniacal glint sparked in his swirling purple eyes at the thought of burning the pictures.

Sammy buried her head deeper into his shoulder.

Connor reassured her, "It's okay, Sammy. You don't have to look. I'll just take you upstairs to your bedroom."

Padding softly through the house, Connor turned a corner and walked up a staircase lined with even more paintings. He couldn't help but roll his eyes at the excess.

Luckily, Sammy's bedroom was bare of everything but a bed with a plastic sheet cover. Connor took a deep breath and closed the door so she wouldn't have to see the paintings in the hallway.

"I'm going to put you down now, okay?" Connor said soothingly, as he gently set her down on her feet. In the distance, he could hear Peter bringing their bags into the main living area. It wouldn't be much longer before he departed to carry out his new errands.

Sammy looked around at the plain white walls and boring gray carpet. She walked into the bathroom, which was similarly boring and gray.

"Don't worry, Sammy. Tomorrow we will go shopping and design your bedroom precisely how you want it. In fact, you can help me design the rest of the house as well," Connor said. While she was taking in her surroundings, he pulled the plastic cover off the bed and tucked it away in the corner. Then he went straight to the closet and pulled bedding from large, airtight packages.

"This doesn't feel like home," Sammy finally said, mournfully, "I want to go back to New York." Tears started to roll down her face.

Connor stopped making the bed and kneeled down in front of her. "Hey, there's no need to cry," he said, wiping her tears away— "First nights can be scary, but trust me when I say that I will make this house feel like home. Whatever you want this house to have, I will put in it. Tonight, I will be cleaning out the cobwebs, in case you need me at any point. Because your happiness is the most important thing."

A small smile inched across her face. Sammy jumped up and hugged Connor around the neck. "Thank you Connor."

Connor hugged her back, the same alarm going off in his head: it wasn't natural for him to be so affectionate. Oddly, it was his impulsive need to stop her tears that kept him in that warm embrace.

"Now, time for bed." Connor pulled the blankets up and helped Sammy get under the covers.

She snuggled in, clutching her teddy close to her chest, and said, "Goodnight, Connor."

"Sweet dreams, Princess Samantha," Connor responded, as he flipped off the light switch.

3

FRIEND OR FOE

MAY 16, 2003

The large house, hidden by trees, stood quietly in a wealthy neighborhood in New Hampshire. A six-year-old girl with waist-length auburn hair was hunched over her desk, a couple of sheets of math homework sitting unsolved. Instead of focusing on her school work, her mind drifted to what was outside the window. She couldn't see much, just the leaves on a couple of trees. She yearned for some noise. So used to the cacophony of New York City, she felt strange in a world that was so quiet and serene. Her green eyes stared out at the leaves on the trees, and she wanted to be outside.

"Studying hard, are we?" Connor asked from behind.

Startled by his noiseless approach, Sammy turned around in her chair to see Connor holding a tray of sliced apples and peanut butter. "I'm sorry, Connor. When can we go outside and play?"

Connor calmly set down the tray and leaned over to see how much homework she had completed. He picked up the sheets disapprovingly.

"You haven't even started your math yet, Sammy."

Not listening, Sammy turned again to the view outside her window. "Do you think Daddy would have liked it here ... in this house?"

Connor's heart sank. It was perfectly normal for a child to continue to ask questions about someone they'd lost, but it hit Connor hard every time. Everything he had tried to keep her mind off things had worked only a little to prevent her from crying every so often. It was understandable, though. Samantha's father had been the only person in her life. When he died, she had lost everything.

"I have an idea!" Connor perked up. Sammy turned around, her attention now fixed on Connor, who always had great ideas. "Let's go to the zoo! York's Wild Kingdom isn't as large as the zoo in Central Park, but it has amusement rides and carnival games."

"Okay!" she exclaimed, "I'll get my jacket!"

Connor smiled as she ran off to her bedroom. As he put down the paper, he thought, *there will be other days to finish homework.*

* * *

Sammy bounced up and down while holding Connor's hand. They were greeted by a large, blue-brick entryway with a snake on one side and a lion on the other. As they passed underneath, Sammy grew even more ecstatic about the zoo. Bouncing up and down uncontrollably, she was enthralled by the flashing lights, mechanical rides and animals. It was as if she might explode from excitement. Connor's heart grew warm as he saw her childish awe and wonder and listened to her chatter at a million miles an hour as she quickly rhymed off all the wonderful new things she would like to try.

Despite the chaos of kids running amok and his niggling concerns about the possible dangers of ride malfunctions, Connor felt more at peace. Watching Sammy grow in fascination and wonder, or perhaps simply connecting to the happiness that emanated from her, Connor finally felt as if he were doing something right. Whatever the reason, he didn't want this peace to dissipate, and so he gave in to her every whim. If she wanted to ride the spinning cups a hundred times, he would tag along. If she wanted to eat cotton candy, it was hers. If she wanted the big teddy bear offered as a prize at the ring toss, he would win it for her. The world was hers, and he would be damned if he couldn't give it to her.

As Sammy calmed down, her interests turned less to the amusement park and more towards the animals.

Sammy stared at a tiger lounging on top of his wooden hut. So lazy and motionless was the tiger, tired of the hordes of gawking kids.

"Why don't we go look at another animal that is more active?" he suggested.

"Mr. Tiger," she called into the metal netted cage, "Won't you come say hello?"

The tiger flicked its tail a couple of times.

"Sammy, I think he is trying to get some sleep," Connor responded, "Let's leave him alone."

"Mr. Tiger," she called again, ignoring him.

Raising his enormous head and flicking his ears back and forth, the tiger sat up to look directly at Sammy. A long, low noise came from its throat as the tiger yawned, displaying its massive canines.

Sammy giggled and said, "Wake up sleepyhead, and come over!"

Connor watched in fascination as the tiger obeyed. Sluggishly, it rose and stretched, its sharp claws scratching the wood on the roof of the hut as the powerful muscles stretched beneath the striped coat. Then the magnificent creature hopped down and slowly made its way over. The tiger stopped and sat down right in front of the metal net.

"Wow, you sure are beautiful, Mr. Tiger," Sammy praised. "Thank you for coming over to say hello."

By now, a crowd was starting to form around Sammy and Connor. Everyone wanted to see the big cat active, since it mostly slept during zoo hours. Connor tightened his grip on Sammy's jacket, more for his own mental security; he was wary of losing her in the crowd.

The tiger made a deep rumbling in its throat, similar to a purr, and rubbed up against the fence. Cameras started clicking.

Sammy giggled and commented, "I like you, Mr. Tiger. I wish we could play together like Calvin and Hobbes."

Connor bent over and whispered, "Come on, Sammy, let's go see something else and allow everyone else to have their own encounter with this majestic animal." Connor was leery of drawing too much attention. Most people didn't know what had happened to the daughter of the CEO of Valda Enterprise. It was better this way, safer this way.

"Okay," Sammy said, disappointed, "I can't wait to see you again, Mr. Tiger!"

Connor successfully steered her away from the mob that had formed around the tiger, each desperate for selfies with it. Not long after, Connor was buying a large ice cream cone for Sammy to make up for tearing her away.

"That will be $3.29," said the acne-faced teenager at the food stand.

Letting go of Sammy's hand, Connor fished in his pocket for the change. After a moment, he handed the money to the teenager, who passed the cone over and said "Enjoy!" before his eyes suddenly widened as he saw something happening behind Connor.

Connor whipped around to see a crowd running chaotically in his direction, parents carrying or dragging their children while racing from danger, eyes wide with panic.

That was when he saw it: a flash of pink weaving between the legs of the fleeing families. It took only a moment to register that Sammy was no longer by his side—and was headed in the direction everyone else was fleeing from.

Connor's heart hit the bottom of his stomach as he sprang toward Sammy. His mind cleared, focusing his senses precisely to gather the most information possible from the environment. He could hear every heartbeat of the people rushing by and feel every fiber of their clothes as they brushed him. The mass momentum of the crowd was like climbing up a waterfall, delaying his pursuit of Sammy. Small and agile, she had no problem weaving between the adults' legs. Connor tried to call out, but his voice was lost in the screams of the crowd. How Connor wished he could cut down everyone who stood in his path. In the past, he would have had no hesitation about decimating every man, woman and child that stood between him and her. Now there were cameras everywhere, and anything he did out of the ordinary would be publicly displayed all over the media. He couldn't risk drawing attention to himself, for it would risk Sammy's safety. Going into hiding would be almost impossible with the technological advances the military would have to track them down. He had no choice but to push against the crowd.

Sammy could be headed straight for danger, and she'd found ways to get herself into trouble in all her past lives. If something were to happen to her, Connor worried about the destruction he would leave in his wake. The suffering it caused him to watch her die time after time always led to cataclysmic endings. All his human anchors in morality would vanish, turning him once again into a monster. As the crying children and panicked mothers rushed past him, Connor hoped their fates wouldn't be connected to Sammy's. Not today.

Finally, the crowd cleared, and Connor sprinted ahead at human speed. Though Sammy wasn't within his sights, he could feel her nearby. He rounded the corner of an interactive animal information station and saw her little pink jacket. Relief washed over him. She was safe and unharmed. But he suddenly understood why she had run towards the danger everyone else had run away from: she wanted to see the tiger.

Sammy stood innocently before the tiger, which was easily four times her size, fearlessly talking to it as if it were another child on the playground.

"Mr. Tiger!" she chided, "you are not supposed to be out of your cage."

The tiger appeared calm, standing only ten feet away from her— easy striking distance for the tiger. Its eyes glowed as it stared intently at the little girl. Luckily, Connor was downwind as he crept closer, at a slow, steady pace. Any quick movements would be sure to set the tiger off.

"I know you wanted to play with me, but you caused everyone to worry. So hurry and go back to your cage, before they hurt you for getting out," Sammy continued, pointing a little finger at the tiger.

The tiger by now had noticed Connor and turned its attention his way, growling in a low tone. Sammy turned and smiled at Connor, then faced the tiger again. "Oh, don't mind Connor. He is my friend. He is your friend too!" The tiger ceased growling and continued looking intently at the young girl.

Connor was finally able to reach Sammy and, with relief, pulled her behind him. Silently, Sammy obeyed, but peeked around him to see the magnificent predator. The tiger looked up at Connor and got caught in his gaze. Connor's purple eyes started to swirl with darker shades of purple, which drew the tiger's interest. The big cat's eyes locked with his in a stare that Connor refused to let go of. The longer they both stared, the redder Connor's eyes became. After what seemed like an eternity to Sammy, the intense staring finally eased.

"Sit," Connor commanded. The tiger promptly obeyed.

Suddenly they were startled by the sound of a gunshot. The tiger was hit right between the shoulder blades and roared in pain. That broke the connection. Vengeance in his eyes, the tiger glared at Connor, wanting blood. As it crouched low, ready to pounce, two more echoing shots rang out. Sammy screamed, terrified for the tiger. Both shots appeared to have found their mark, in the middle of its back and in the rump. The tiger lunged clumsily at Connor with intent to kill, but another shot echoed as the tiger was in mid-leap, fangs bared. Sammy screamed, closed her eyes and covered her ears.

What the security cameras caught next was later deemed to be a hoax—a tampered piece of video that would sweep through the media for three days before disappearing. The tiger lunged at its victims, who seemingly stood still. Then, at the moment of the glitch in the video, the tiger was suddenly flying sideways at a ninety-degree angle from its original projection, and the two victims were miraculously twenty feet away, in the opposite direction of the tiger's leap.

Sammy opened her eyes slowly and found herself cradled in Connor's strong arms. For a moment, she seemed dazed, as if the two events didn't add up. What made sense was for the tiger to be on top of them. But, looking around, she spotted the tiger lying limply on its side, far from where they were standing. "No!" Sammy screamed as she wriggled free from Connor and ran over to the cat. Connor followed closely behind. Breaking into tears, she knelt by the tiger and ran her fingers through its deep fur. "Why did they kill him? He wouldn't have hurt anyone if they would have left him alone!"

"Sammy," Connor said, rubbing her back. "He's not dead, merely asleep. Look at his breathing." True enough, there was a steady rise and fall to its chest.

"But he got shot!" Sammy sniffed, as she rubbed her running nose.

Connor pulled out a long tranquilizer dart with red fuzzy feathers at the end. "They put him to sleep to save us. He will be just fine, Sammy."

"What's going to happen to him?" she sobbed, slowly calming down.

"We are going to put him in isolation for a month or so until we figure out why he acted so out of character. If he is still deemed dangerous by his veterinarian, then we will have to put him down," said a female voice from behind.

Sammy turned around to see a woman coming toward them. She was wearing a zookeeper's uniform, though hers was a bit tighter than most, cut to accentuate her voluptuous curves. She had long, brown hair flowing down her back. Sunglasses hid her eyes, but there was a smile on her ruby red lips, evidence of her pride in her marksmanship. Over her shoulder was a large hunting rifle.

Connor smiled, recognizing the voice. Turning around to smile at the approaching femme fatale, Connor greeted her in a flat business tone. "Your response time has some recent need of improvement, Morgan."

She took off her sunglasses, revealing her hazel eyes, and sarcastically replied, "It's good to see you too, Cas—"

"Connor," he interrupted.

"Connor," she corrected.

"Who are you?" Sammy interjected.

Immediately, Connor's matter-of-fact attitude warmed up in response to Sammy. "Morgan here is an old friend of mine."

"A very old friend ..." Morgan added, one eyebrow arched.

A vivid memory of their first meeting whipped through Connor's mind:

He was walking past a row of cages, one of the inhabitants stood out. A 19-year-old Morgan was grasping the iron bars tightly. He could see the iron shackles on her ankles had rubbed through the skin. Similar to the other women here, doomed to burn for witchcraft, she was imprisoned in a dank cage that smelled of feces. Unlike the other witches, Morgan had tucked herself in her own little circle of protection. How curious this circle was to him, but it didn't matter at the moment. A plethora of other witches had already met their fiery fate. It was inevitable that she was going to die in her beloved homeland of Trier, Germany, and nothing could save her. Soon it would be her screams echoing into the dusty sky, just like the rest of this cursed village.

He marched forward, leaving the young witch with fierce hazel eyes behind. The air grew hotter, almost to the point where it was difficult to breathe. The sound of the crowd waiting for the execution changed from celebration to screams for help, as great wisps of purple flames began to encompass the villagers. The purple flames grew and grew, reaching up toward the sky. He stood in the center of those flames, manipulating them as if conducting an orchestra. His fluid movements were as smooth as water, but his heart was controlled by unspeakable rage. For how can humans possibly call their murder justice when they are more monster than the witches they burned at the stake?

The human mob screamed as the flames consumed their bodies faster than those of the witches they'd set ablaze. Soon, the spreading conflagration was headed towards Morgan and the other women locked in the cages.

Afterwards, he found one witch still alive and unharmed: the one with a protection circle. This witch could prove useful to him. Unsympathetically, he kicked the bottom of her foot hard enough to jostle her awake. Blurry-eyed, she awoke. Her hair was frizzled with the heat, but she had suffered only mild burns. After a few blinks against the bright light, she was able to bring the man towering over her into focus.

"How interesting," he said, with as much fascination as that of a cat bored with the mouse it has already trapped in its paws.

51

Morgan, confused, observed that the iron bars imprisoning her had literally melted to stubs. The village had been reduced to ash and rubble.

"Where did you learn how to protect yourself?" he asked curiously.

"Um, I learned from my mother and her sister. They taught me healing and protection spells." Morgan's dress was smoldering to almost nothing, which left her attempting to cover her nakedness in front of this dangerous stranger.

He observed her with eyes deeper and blacker than the deepest pits of Hell. His face held no emotions, not even a hint of remorse. He found it curious that even though he had slaughtered an entire village, this witch didn't fear him. No. It was almost ... a look of admiration.

"Will you join me? I could use someone of your talents," he asked flatly.

Morgan again appeared confused. "Join you?"

"Yes," he responded, his voice remaining monotone, "you will teach me what you know of protection spells. I will give you enough power to never get locked in a cage, doomed to die by the hands of crazed villagers."

"Why would you do this? Why don't you kill me like you killed everyone else?" she asked hesitantly.

"I can kill you if you would prefer," he responded, emotionless.

"No! I'll teach you," she responded hastily.

"Then it is decided," he said, as he lifted her up. "Allow me to make you my official follower." His hand morphed into demonic claws that dug under her rib cage and branded her heart with his bonding curse. She screamed in pain and reflexively withdrew from his grasp, falling to the ground. Morgan tore at her dress, expecting to see a gaping hole under her rib cage where his claws had penetrated, and was surprised to find her skin intact and an intricate purple mark there. Similar to ivy scaling a castle wall, the mark twisted around her left rib cage and up over her shoulder. First brilliant purple, it dulled to a darker shade as if it were a hot iron cooling down.

"What ... what is that? What did you do to me?" she asked, terrified.

Once again in that flat tone, he responded: "You are immortal until I no longer have use of you. Tied to my soul, you shall serve me well and I shall reward you with your greatest dreams. Turn on me, and I will make you wish you were never born."

Speechless, Morgan gazed up at the man who had altered her entire existence. Finally showing some softness in his face, he knelt down so that he could see his black eyes reflected in her hazel ones. Already they were beginning to lighten up a little, with very slight shades of purple. The burden lifting from his shoulders, he caressed her chin and held it in his hand. "Now, you shall be known as Morgan le Faye, named after the most powerful witch that ever walked this earth. Learn as much as you can and grow strong. I anticipate you living up to the title, evolving into the most powerful witch this world has ever known." With that, he turned and walked away, intending her to follow. Quick to learn she kept two paces behind and followed him from that day forward.

"Thank you for responding when you did," Connor acknowledged. "What has been occupying your time?"

"I've found some prestige rubbing shoulders with historians and philosophers. Turns out they'll pay quite a price to know the secrets of the past, including some mysterious catastrophes that remain unsolved."

The casual way she brought this up jolted a spike of suspicion in Connor's gut. "Some secrets are better left untold," he warned.

The unspoken message was delivered. Turning attention off the subject, she motioned towards Sammy. "Appears like you both are living a quiet life."

"And that's the way I'd prefer it to stay," Connor commented, directing his attention back down to Sammy who was still petting tiger's soft fur as it snored peacefully. Connor picked up Sammy and threw her on top of his shoulders. "Let us go home so they can take care of the tiger."

Sammy nestled onto his shoulders and ran her fingers through Connor's loose, short black hair. "Okay, Connor. Bye, Morgan!"

"Bye, Sammy!" Morgan waved back and then turned her attention to the crew who had come to haul away the tiger.

"She was nice. Will we see her again?" Sammy asked.

"You'll definitely see her again," Connor said with a smile, as he calmly headed towards a back entrance meant for employees only. If it weren't for the police, news crews would be storming into the zoo for their scoop.

That sort of attention was not something Connor wanted to deal with at the moment.

"What about you?" Sammy asked. "Do you want her to be your girlfriend?"

Connor laughed. "Oh, you occupy my time well enough. I have zero capacity for another woman in my life. Women can be such a handful."

"Not me!" Sammy said proudly. "I am not going to be a handful."

"Oh really? I think you'll be more drama than I can handle," he replied playfully, while reaching an arm up and giving Sammy a light tickle in her rib cage.

Sammy giggled and shied away. As they walked to the car, Sammy kept looking back to see if the tiger was safe, although it was long out of view.

When they finally reached home, Connor parked the car gently to avoid waking Sammy. It had been a long day. All the adrenaline and candy had worn off, leaving the girl sleepy enough to allow Connor to unbuckle her and carry her into the house without waking. Entering the house, he heard the beeping alarm telling him to disarm. Grumbling, Connor switched her over to one arm so he could disarm and re-arm the perimeter. As he pushed in the code, Sammy stirred awake.

"Connor ..." she grumbled as she rubbed her eyes.

Quickly, he punched in the last few numbers and closed the key pad. "Go back to sleep, Sammy. I'll take you up to bed."

"I had a bad dream," she mumbled.

"About what?" Connor was concerned. He had hoped the nightmares wouldn't start until much later in life.

"That they were going to kill the tiger," Sammy said.

Connor chuckled and reassured her, "Silly Sammy, you know they are not going to kill the tiger. It didn't harm anyone. It just went for a walk to see you."

"Why did it like me more than the other kids?" Sammy asked curiously.

"Maybe you have a special way with animals," Connor said, with a sparkle in his eye. He headed upstairs to her bedroom.

"Will you tell me a story?" Sammy asked, waking herself up with excitement.

"The princess story again?" Connor said in disbelief. "I have told you that one many times."

"No," Sammy said with newfound enthusiasm, "A new story about animals."

Connor thought for a moment, then held up an expectant finger. "How about this: you get ready for bed and I will tell you a story. It won't have a lot of animals in it, but it is a story about a special girl who could communicate with the creatures in a forest. It was her job to keep the harmony between man and beast."

"Yeah, yeah, yeah!" Sammy yelled with fists pumping up and down. "I'll go brush my teeth and get my jammies on!" She ran off to the bathroom while Connor took to setting things out for the morning. Sammy soon came rushing back into her bedroom and enthusiastically jumped into bed, happily anticipating a new story.

Connor chuckled at her eagerness. "I need to remind you that my stories don't have happy endings," Connor warned.

"That's okay!" Sammy said jubilantly. "I like your stories much better than the ones on TV."

"All right," Connor said as he sat down in a small chair opposite her bed. "Let me tell you a tale about a girl who spoke to forest creatures!"

* * *

PRUSSIA

JULY 2, 1070 A.D.

A soft breeze whistled through the old trees as though whispering secrets from far-off lands. Though the sun warmed the dense coniferous trees as they reached into the sky, minimal light reached the forest floor, making it appear dark and fraught with danger. The speckles of light that penetrated through appeared deceivingly similar to countless pairs of eyes. Branches creaked and leaves crunched as little creatures scurried through the underbrush. Otherwise, it was deathly quiet, but none of this appeared to concern a young man cloaked in black. He tramped over broken tree branches and dead leaves without bothering to hide his tracks.

A young woman with flowing auburn hair was running as fast as humanly possible through the ancient forest, not daring to look back lest it slow her down. It would appear that today she was having a stroke of bad luck.

The man simply watched her run, without fear of what she might be running from. Still, his pitch-black eyes searched for the reason of her flight. Trees fell and wood cracked as a predator hunted the maiden. Nonreactive, the young man stood his ground and watched the woman approach. As curiosity got the better of her, she whipped her head around to see if she had gained any distance—and so ran blindly into the young man at full speed. Her bright green eyes locked with his black ones as they fell together so that she ended up straddling the stranger in the most intimate way. Her hair cascaded around his face and shielded his view as if it were a curtain. The frozen moment made time stop for a moment until the loud cracking of trees grabbed their attention.

"RUN!" she yelled into his face, frantically scrambling to get up and grabbing his hand. Without a word, he leapt up and started running at her side. They weaved through the trees, trying to lose the unseen pursuer. The maiden appeared afraid for her life, but the young man remained as calm and composed as if he were on a light run through the woods.

The couple parted around a boulder, but the pursuer stayed on the girl's track until she desperately climbed up a large, dying tree in hopes of disappearing from view. As she reached the top branches, she stopped to regain her breath. Out of the darkness a black beast bigger than a bear and faster than a wolf ran at full-speed to the tree, slamming into it with such force that the maiden was almost shaken from her perch. Then the beast, with gnashing yellow teeth and long, dagger-sharp claws, ripped away at the tree trunk, determined to obtain his prey at any cost. The tree shook as she hung on desperately.

The man leaped up into the tree and grabbed her from behind, pinning her arms tightly to her sides. Before she could react, the two were being launched off the tree, falling backwards, as if in slow motion. The beast disappeared behind the tree and the sky came into view.

Her captor whispered in her ear, "Breathe."

Complying before thinking, she inhaled as much air as her lungs could hold. Immediately after, ice-cold water swallowed them both. Only moments after they fell harmlessly into the murky water, the tree fell next to them under the beast's onslaught, its branches twisting around them.

Shocked into stillness, her heart beating fast, she held her breath. Above the surface, a distorted image of the great beast stepped atop the broken trunk. The man switched his grip, so one arm held her tight while the other covered her mouth to keep her from exhaling and sending out bubbles. The branches crunched around them as the beast walked hesitantly farther up the trunk, as though there was something about the water that the beast feared. After what felt like a lifetime, the beast left with a disgruntled growl.

The maiden struggled to break free but was held underwater by his iron-clad grip. Losing strength, she released the air from her lungs, which found its way through his fingers and up to the surface of the water. There was no reaction from the beast. As her limbs eerily relaxed, the man released his grip, and they instantly burst out of the water. Clutching onto a tree branch, she coughed and greedily gulped the air.

Once she caught her breath, the young woman began analyzing this man. She eyed him as he calmly got out of the water, as though he could have stayed under for longer. He was dressed entirely in black, with a thick black cloak fastened at the neck by a golden emblem of fire. His shaggy black hair, which he needed to brush out of his eyes, was dripping wet, like the rest of him. It was his pitch-black eyes that gave him an ominous presence.

The young man caught the young woman's stare. She wore mostly animal pelts that were roughly sewn together and seemed warm despite being soaked. She had a couple of small blades strapped safely to her hips, along with a slingshot and bag of sharp rocks. This equipment confirmed she was from a small village on the outskirts of the forest, a place known for its hunters. What was most striking about her were her magnetic green eyes, so warm and familiar to the young man. Relief washed over him, and once again he was entranced by her beauty, only to be snapped back to reality by her loud mouth.

"Who in the gods' names do you think you are!" she yelled.

Taken aback, he responded, "I'm the one who saved your life."

"Ugh, I'm not some damsel in distress!" she said as she trudged through the water, pushing him as she got out of the pond.

"You could at least show a little gratitude," he replied while flicking the water off his hands.

She took off her patchwork shirt and wrung the water out, now wearing only a small strip of cloth used to flatten her breasts against her body. The young man tried to not stare at her unabashed indecency. She ignored him as he copied her by wringing the water out of his cloak. Filling the awkward silence, he asked, "What name do you go by?"

For a second, he thought she wouldn't tell him. As she put her shirt back on, she groaned and replied, "My name is Sibilia. What is yours?"

"Sibilia. Such a beautiful name. Do you have a surname?" he ignored her question.

"It's just Sibilia. My mother died during labor, and my father died shortly after that. I was raised by the village. And your name was?" she asked again, irritation in her voice.

"What village do you live in? Is it nearby?" he asked, avoiding her question yet again.

Sibilia stopped and snapped, "I'll tell you where my village is if you tell me your name."

With a sly smirk, he replied, "I'll go by any name that you give me."

Sibilia rolled her eyes and huffed: "Fine, your name is Caeronvar. My village is not far off. I'll take you there if you are looking for a place to sleep. It's not much, but I call it home."

"Thank you, Sibilia. I greatly appreciate it," he said as they started on their way. "So why was a hellhound after you? What did you do to deserve such a cursed animal's wrath?"

She continued through the forest and replied, "Was that a hellhound? Huh. I tried to stop it from killing another woman and it turned on me … after killing her. I guess I bit off more than I could chew."

"Hmm. Let's hope he doesn't come back for seconds," Caeronvar replied. "Do you normally go out into the woods alone? These are not the normal woods where people hunt for roots."

"I have ventured in these woods every day since I was young. They don't scare me, and I'm aware of the creatures that inhabit this forest. I respect their space and they leave me alone. Why were *you* in the woods?" Sibilia asked, her attention still focused ahead of her.

"I was searching for you," Caeronvar said bluntly.

This made Sibilia stop in her tracks. She whipped around and glared at him, studying him hard to reevaluate whether he was an enemy or an ally. "Why were you looking for me? I didn't kill whatever you think I killed, and I didn't steal whatever you think I stole. I haven't done any wrong by any of the neighboring towns."

Caeronvar chuckled. "I'm not a bounty hunter. I have come to protect you." Caeronvar puffed his chest out proudly, expecting praise.

For a moment, Sibilia appeared confused. Then she laughed heartily. "I don't need your protection! I've been protecting myself from the horrors of the world my entire life. I don't need you." She started walking away again, this time at a faster pace.

"Let me stay with you for a short while. If you absolutely detest me, then I will leave. After all, I protected you earlier from the hellhound. That should at least give you a little faith that I mean what I say," Caeronvar continued.

"Uuuggghhhh!" Sibilia moaned. She abruptly turned around to face Caeronvar, who ran into her, bumping her to the ground. At first she had fire in her eyes, then she softened when he gave her his charming smile.

"That was my blunder," he apologized, as he reached down to help her up. As he took her hand, Sibilia peered curiously into his black eyes, which gazed longingly, into her green ones.

"All right," she agreed. "You can *protect me* for a few days. If I grow weary of you, then you must disappear."

"Deal," Caeronvar agreed enthusiastically.

"Ooooooh, what did you find in the forest today?" a voice from afar called out.

A middle-aged man was walking towards them.

"Hello, Garrett," she greeted as she met the man at the edge of the forest.

"Welcome back, Sibilia," he responded. "I have seen you carry some weird critters from the forest, but this is the first time you've brought back a man."

"I found him scurrying through the woods. Thought he could help out with some heavy lifting," she jested.

As Caeronvar approached, Garrett gave him a once over and remarked, "He's not more than a dainty noble. Won't fit in around here."

Sibilia started to respond, but was interrupted by Caeronvar, who chose to speak for himself. "Good day to you, sir. I believe I overheard your name is Garrett?" Caeronvar stretched out his hand.

Garrett cautiously gave the hand a firm shake. "Yes, sir. Do you think you can handle some manual labor? If you pull your weight, then we will feed you."

Caeronvar smiled mischievously. "I'm stronger than I appear. I can easily pull my weight around here, and you won't need to worry about feeding me."

"Hmmm ..." Garrett, not convinced, eyed Caeronvar up and down once more. "You're a cocky one. Well, I guess we shall see what you are worth. Come along."

Sibilia and Caeronvar silently followed Garrett to the village. Caeronvar curiously observed the layout of the village, which was completely open to attack. There were no walls nor guard posts to warn the villagers of intruders or a lurking predator. It was almost as if the villagers' naivety protected them from the beasts that would eat them in their sleep.

The village appeared small and insignificant from the outskirts. From the inside, it was a maze of wooden homes with more people than expected. Multiple gardens grew fruits, vegetables and herbs next to a pen full of livestock. The streets were busy with children playing together and the occasional dog romping after them. Most of the adults were too busy to notice Caeronvar walking through, while others silently sized him up. Contrary to how they treated the stranger, the villagers warmly welcomed Sibilia with a small handout of food.

Finally, they came upon a small hut. Garrett and Sibilia walked in, and Caeronvar followed. The interior was as simple as the village, furnished with a single bed and thick animal furs for blankets. There was a wash basin with a comb that was made from bone. A small chest sat in the corner, most likely holding Sibilia's clothes and personal effects. The hut was barely big enough to comfortably hold the three of them.

"So, did you find anything of interest in the forest today, Sibilia? I mean, other than the fellow in black?" Garrett laughed.

"Nothing in particular," Sibilia shrugged as she collapsed on her bed.

"What do you mean?" Caeronvar interrupted. "I had to save you from a hellhound that wanted to rip you to shreds."

"What?" Garrett asked, surprised and angry.

"Ugh, Caeronvar! I was going to save that story for tonight at the tavern!" she groaned. "Why did you have to go and ruin it?"

Caeronvar was dumbfounded. That beast was a real threat, yet she had tried to brush it off as if it were nothing more than a tale to tell her friends.

Garrett stared at Sibilia, expecting more. Annoyed, she gave him the answer he wanted. "There's unrest in the forest. Something is upsetting the balance, stirring the creatures. While I was investigating further, I was targeted by a hellhound. I would prefer to save the rest of the story for later at the tavern."

Garrett seemed suspicious and eyed Caeronvar again. "And this fellow saved you from the beast?"

Caeronvar proudly answered, "Yes," while Sibilia simultaneously said,

"Not exactly."

Garret's brow wrinkled as if trying to piece it together.

Sibilia added, "I had it under control."

"Says the girl who was treed by a hellhound," Caeronvar interrupted.

"I wasn't treed like some helpless cat!"

"That's what I saw."

"I had a plan. I was going to jump!"

"Was your plan to get eaten? Any other place you jumped to would have made you dog food." Caeronvar was certain he was right and that he deserved praise for saving her life.

Sibilia quickly accused, "You almost drowned me!" This made Garrett look menacingly at Caeronvar.

Shocked she was making such an accusation, Caeronvar responded, "I pulled you into that pond so the hellhound would lose your scent. We stayed under the water together until I knew the hellhound was gone. If I didn't intervene, you would have been killed. Now, will you stop arguing and thank me for saving your life?"

Sibilia had fire in her eyes.

"All right, children," Garrett interrupted. "Why don't we stop this bickering? Yes? Caeronvar, come help chop firewood. Sibilia, why don't you relax and unwind. I don't need you riled up and starting another fight tonight."

"Oh, please! I only broke a table last time," she said, with sass.

"Yes, but the time before that, you sent a young man through a door. Cool your temper." Garrett gave her a fatherly glare that seemed to quiet her down. He then turned to Caeronvar. "Come on, son."

Caeronvar quietly followed Garrett out the door. As soon as they were far enough away, Caeronvar asked Garrett, "Has she always been that fiery?"

Garrett chuckled. "Well, she has been on her own for quite a while. She had to get tough to survive." Caeronvar noticed how peaceful and calm the village was. If anything, this appeared safer than other places he had traveled to. Caeronvar didn't respond, though, and remained quiet for the rest of their walk.

Soon they came upon a large stack of logs that two burly men we chopping. Both stopped for a minute to examine the approaching stranger.

"Hello, boys," Garrett called out. "I brought someone to help with the load."

They laughed.

"You expect him to help us?" one asked.

Nearby, a few women were laundering clothes at a well. Their ears perked up, and they all gaped at the stranger.

Garrett chuckled with them, "Well, we shall see now, won't we? Caeronvar, why don't you work on that tree." Garrett pointed to a slightly smaller tree than the other two had felled.

"Do you need firewood size?" Caeronvar asked.

Garrett nodded and pointed at an ax next to the tree. "Show us what you got, boy."

Wordlessly, Caeronvar strode over to the tree and studied it. He sighed deeply, took off his cloak and hung it on a nearby tree. Then he took off his shirt and hung it on the tree as well.

The onlookers were surprised by his muscular physique. True, he didn't have bulk, but he had muscle density that exceeded that of the large brutes. Additionally, Caeronvar had a glistening scar running up his back that shimmered in the sunlight; close up, it shined almost like scales against his white skin.

Caeronvar picked up the ax effortlessly. Each swing of the ax made a whistling sound as it cut the air. The first time the ax hit the tree, it cut clean through with one chop— unimaginable to the two burly men, who needed at least three chops. Caeronvar worked quickly as he chopped the trunk and limbs up as easily as a cook would cut carrots. It took only ten minutes for the tree to be chopped up into firewood-sized pieces. Caeronvar turned around and let the head of the ax fall to the ground while leaning on the handle. Not even a shimmer of sweat showed.

Proudly, Caeronvar asked, "What's next?"

The two burly men puffed up their chests.

"Beginners' luck," one sniffed.

"It was a small tree," the other said.

"Bet you can't do that all day," the first egged him on.

"To a larger tree, too," the other added.

"I bet we can even go faster than you," the first added to the bet.

Caeronvar smiled. "All right, let's do this."

Garrett chuckled and walked away to do other tasks.

After three hours of chopping wood with the two competing brutes, Caeronvar was finally starting to tire. He was lightly glistening from sweat and felt hot from the sun beating down on his back. The other two were dripping and doubled over from exhaustion, irritated at Caeronvar's amazing endurance and strength. They were surrounded by enough firewood to supply a 500-man army.

The female onlookers were rosy-cheeked as they watched the men compete. Most had their lustful sight set on the new stranger. One approached Caeronvar with a leather pouch of water. "Thought you might be thirsty," she offered. Using her youth to her advantage, she attempted to seduce Caeronvar by pulling her sleeves down to reveal her bare shoulders and cleavage.

Caeronvar wiped his brow with the back of his hand and smiled at the young maiden. "That is very kind of you. Although I do believe these men are in more need of water than I."

The two glared at Caeronvar. The young woman appeared disappointed that her wiles had failed.

Seeing this, Caeronvar added, "If you could show me where the tavern is, though, I would be most appreciative."

The young woman lightened up— "Of course!" — and led him there. Caeronvar grabbed his cloak and shirt, putting them on as he followed. The two burly men brooded in their defeat.

It wasn't far to the tavern and, truthfully, easy to find. It was by far the biggest and loudest building in the village. Before entering, he turned to face the young maiden. "Thank you for your assistance."

She smiled seductively. "If you need anything else"—she paused to peer down— "please don't hesitate to ask."

Caeronvar politely smiled and took a step towards the door. "I will keep that in mind."

He turned inside to find Sibilia, now sitting on the bar counter regaling the townsfolk with her story. Caeronvar was sad to have missed her version of the event.

"... And so, here I was. A strapping young man, clad in black, holding me down under the water. All the while the great hellhound was sniffing for me from above. I could feel the ripples from the drool of the hellhound hitting the water. He was hungry for me and wanted to devour me whole. Still, I patiently waited under the water for the beast to disappear. Because boys, as mighty as I am, I can't take on a beast like that bare-handed ..."—Sibilia paused while the crowd laughed— "... So I waited patiently in the water until I knew the beast was gone. Then, when the coast was clear, I burst out of the water, instantly on guard to see if the beast was going to take me again. Nothing! So, since the coast was clear, I pulled the strapping young man up from under the water and smacked his princely face until he breathed ..." Once again, laughter. "So proud, so humbled was he"—she winked at her audience— "that, after fighting to overcome his ego, he was able to thank me for saving his life. He bent down on one knee and proclaimed himself my protector until his dying day. So I say back to him—"

Sibilia paused, seeing that Caeronvar was actually there. She blushed, her bravado gone, and continued, "I say to him, 'Thank you, my humble prince. You have served me well today. I shall allow you to stay by my side. If you are unfit to serve me, then I shall relieve you of my service.' Well, gents, can you believe it, he agreed and then tried to kiss my hand as if I were some sort of lady. I would not let him, though, because you all know that I am not a lady. I am a fearless warrior who traverses the forest every day without so much as a scratch on me." The crowd applauded her bravery.

"Were you scared?" asked one woman.

"For a moment I was, but in order to survive I had to ignore the fear and focus on the danger at hand," Sibilia replied.

"Where is this young fella now?" asked one of the gruffer men.

"Why, he stands by the door," another said.

The crowd turned towards Caeronvar. He could feel their burning eyes judging him and didn't much appreciate the attention. As Sibilia was getting down from the counter, the crowd surrounded him and hammered him with questions.

"Where did you come from?"

"Are you a real prince?"

"Why do you wear all black?"

"What were you doing in the forest?"

"Were you scared of the beast?"

Overwhelmed, Caeronvar excused himself from their demanding attention and went outside where the sun was setting behind the trees. Some followed, so he rounded the corner to find some quiet.

"I didn't mean to corner you," Sibilia spoke up.

The setting sun cast a warming glow upon her, making her appear even more lovely. Caeronvar couldn't help but smile. "Being surrounded by unfamiliar faces puts me on edge."

Sibilia laughed as she stood closer to him. "I would have figured that you were used to public attention, what with you being royalty and all."

"I'm not royalty," Caeronvar corrected her.

Sibilia laughed. "Yeah, you can't convince me of that with a face such as yours. You must have some sort of pure breeding. Come back in. I'll make sure that they don't crowd you."

The sun had barely set, fading the glow on her beautiful face. "You go in, princess. I'll be in shortly."

Sibilia was astonished. "I'm not a princess!"

Caeronvar gave her a clever smile and retorted using her words. "Yeah, you can't convince me of that with a face such as yours. You must have some sort of pure breeding."

Sibilia gave him a playful smile and a light punch on the upper arm, then returned to the tavern. Caeronvar stopped to watch the sky for a moment.

There was always something magnificent about how the sky could change every night and the stars would pop out. There were so many nights where Caeronvar wished he was up in the stars. It was probably simpler up there than it was down here in this dirt.

Finally ready, he went back into the tavern where everyone had dispersed. Some were gambling. Others were sharing grand stories over a few mugs of ale. A couple turned to get a better look at the stranger. Sibilia was sitting at the bar. Standing next to her were the two burly men that Caeronvar was chopping wood with earlier. Caeronvar stayed back for a few moments to listen in.

"What makes you think you can just bring in a stranger?" one asked her.

"I didn't see a reason not to," she replied, calmly sipping her ale.

"Did you bring him here to have your way with him?" the other asked.

"Obviously not, or I would already be *having my way with him!*" Sibilia replied rudely.

"You know, we could offer that to you any time, sweetie," the first said, with lust in his eyes.

"Yeah, you don't even need to bother asking us, we can just give it to you," the second said as he reached to grab her butt.

Suddenly Caeronvar was at her side. Before they could lay a hand on her, he slammed both of their faces hard into the bar counter, and they fell to the floor as if they were big lumps of meat. Taken off-guard, Sibilia was aghast at Caeronvar, who was once again expecting praise.

"I can fight my own battles!" she yelled at him.

Confused, Caeronvar defended, "I protected your honor."

When the would-be groper started standing up, Sibilia punched him in the face. As he toppled, Caeronvar kicked him in the stomach, sending him in the opposite direction. Sibilia glared at Caeronvar.

He shrugged and explained himself, "Garrett told you to not break any more furniture. He would have broken a chair if I didn't kick him away from it."

This made Sibilia laugh. She shot down the rest of her ale and exited the tavern, with Caeronvar on her heels. "I think we both have had enough fun for one day," she observed.

They reached her little hut, Sibilia paused, chewing on the words that were difficult to say. "Well, I guess you can sleep on the floor."

Caeronvar put up a finger and said, "Don't bother. I'm going to explore the layout of the village."

Sibilia raised an eyebrow and asked, "You aren't going to sleep?"

"Not yet." Caeronvar had a purple glint in his eye. Before she could say another word, he had disappeared into the night.

* * *

In the morning, Sibilia ran out the door—and nearly ran into Caeronvar standing nearby.

"What's on the agenda for today?" he asked.

Sibilia stared into his eyes that he knew were a darker shade of black, then responded, "Breakfast, and then we go into the forest."

"What are you looking for?" Caeronvar asked as they winded through the village. One of the elderly women handed Caeronvar and Sibilia meat wrapped in bread. Sibilia instantly tore into it. Caeronvar held onto his as they walked further.

"Aren't you going to eat anything?" she asked, eyeing him suspiciously.

Reluctantly, he ate the sandwich, which absolved him of suspicions for now.

"I am the peacekeeper. I go into the forest every day to ensure that balance is kept," Sibilia said, answering his earlier question.

"Why you?" Caeronvar asked protectively.

"I'm better at handling these situations. Apparently they used to put up effigies of their gods at the border, which only angered the creatures." Sibilia laughed as she fearlessly headed into the dark forest.

Caeronvar observed her work throughout the day. There was something magical about the way the forest seemed to bend around her, as if giving way to her. She traveled respectfully, never breaking a leaf nor tree branch. When she thirsted, there was clean water available on a leaf. When she hungered, she would instantly find some edible vegetation. When a little critter ran across her path, she ensured it was healthy. If it appeared weak, she would give it a remedy from her satchel. There was a magical connection that bonded Sibilia to nature in a way that Caeronvar had never even known existed.

At the end of the day, Caeronvar observed how she resumed her tough exterior around the villagers. There was two sides to her: the maternal side that cared for all living things and the abrasive side to keep everyone else at bay. She'd joke and brawl with the men while the women turned up their noses at her rough ways. Caeronvar found something perfect about her in this way. More than that, he was lucky to be given the opportunity to see both sides of her. Every now and then she would give him a shy glance, as if scared he would reveal her feminine side.

After she would tire of the tavern, she would retire to her hut.

"Are most days like this?" Caeronvar asked.

"For the most part, this is my life. Every now and then, I need to settle a dispute between my village and the forest," Sibilia explained, entering her hut.

Caeronvar remained outside the door.

Sibilia turned around and motioned him to come in.

"I'm not quite tired yet," Caeronvar explained.

"Well then, I'll see you when you finally get tired," Sibilia bid goodnight, then paused and leaned closer. She brought a hand up to touch his cheek. Realizing that his eyes were a lighter purple than when she last saw them, Caeronvar shied away and took a step back. Embarrassed by her own actions, Sibilia blushed and closed the door. This left Caeronvar to once again disappeared into the night.

When morning came around, Caeronvar was waiting outside, his eyes returned to pitch black. Sibilia opened the door and pulled him into the hut.

"Why are you going into the forest? Do you want to be killed?" she yelled at him.

"It is hard for me to sleep—" Caeronvar started.

"No, when someone has trouble sleeping they drink more ale or take a tonic. They don't go off into the woods at night. That is suicidal! What are you thinking?"

"I'm not harming any of your creatures," Caeronvar excused.

"Then why are you going into the forest? And why are your eyes always purple at the end of the day, yet black by the next morning?" Sibilia shouted, frightened and concerned. Caeronvar couldn't answer, so she asked, "What are you?"

"I'm human, just like you," he lied.

"Humans don't have black eyes. Humans need food and sleep. What are you?" she demanded.

"I'm human!" he yelled, almost as if he were convincing himself, along with her.

Sibilia seemed unsure. "Then why do you go into the forest at night?"

"I search for the hellhound," he revealed. "Once a hellhound has your scent, it never stops. There are a couple of ways to kill a hellhound, but first I need to find it."

Sibilia's expression fell into helplessness, unable to find the words, "Why?" was the only word she could utter.

Caeronvar took a step closer and held both of Sibilia's shoulders. He gazed deep into her green eyes and softly said, "Because I love you."

Sibilia took a step back as a tear ran down her face. A loud knock interrupted the moment.

Garrett's voice called out, "Get decent, you two, I'm coming in."

"Like I would ever do that, old man," Sibilia said crossly as she quickly wiped the tear from her face. Garrett barged in, appearing distressed.

"What's wrong?" Caeronvar asked, his voice betraying his annoyance at the interruption.

"A child was stolen in the night and replaced with a changeling," Garrett said, panic in his voice.

"This doesn't make sense," Sibilia contemplated with a furrowed brow. "The changelings agreed to never target our children. Someone must have upset them." She glared at Caeronvar.

"What will we do? It was my grandchild, Sibilia!" Garret asked, pulling his trembling hands into fists.

Sibilia thought for a second, then walked closer to Garrett and slapped him in the face. For a moment he was in shock. It put Caeronvar on edge, thinking that Garrett was going to yell at her or hit back. Neither happened.

"Get a hold of yourself. Garrett, the rest of the town looks up to you for guidance. You can't show weakness, because of a mere changeling. Bring me the changeling child. I will replace it with your grandchild." Sibilia laid her hand gently on the spot where she smacked him. "It's going to be okay. I will get her back. I promise!"

Garrett raced off to grab the changeling child.

Sibilia turned to Caeronvar and pointed a harsh finger in his direction. "I don't know if it was your stupidity that caused this to happen, but it stops now! No more gallivanting through the woods at night!" She took a deep breath and, with a little sorrow in her eyes, added, "We can talk later tonight about whether you should stay. I hardly know you and am not ready for commitment."

"Do you at least feel something for me as well?" he asked desperately.

Her eyes welled up and replied, "Whether I do or not doesn't matter. Right now, we need to get that child back before it's too late." She rummaged through her chest and pulled out a small silver coin. "If you have any weapons on you, then I suggest to take them off, unless you want to be torn apart by the changelings."

Sibilia was trying desperately to hide her emotions from Caeronvar, though he could tell by her somewhat choked voice that she did indeed feel something for him. She had far too much pride to admit it.

Caeronvar lifted his hands and said, "I don't have any—"

"Good," she interrupted and pocketed the coin in one of the folds of her shirt.

"What is the coin for?" Caeronvar asked.

"Changelings like shiny objects. They should be happy with this trade. It's worked in the past," Sibilia said, her voice growing serious.

Garrett appeared in the doorway and handed Sibilia something moving in a tweed sack. "Here you go. It's sleeping right now."

Sibilia took the sack.

"Good luck," Garrett told her, then nodded at Caeronvar, who nodded back.

Carrying the sack close to her bosom, Sibilia raced out the door with Caeronvar hot on her heels. They dashed into the forest, which welcomed Sibilia with a joyful birdsong. Together they jumped over and ducked beneath tree branches. It wasn't so different from the first time he met Sibilia, but this time they were venturing further into the forest.

The forest grew darker the deeper they went into it. Soon, nearly all light disappeared and they were at the mercy of the beasts that lurked in the shadows, making Caeronvar worried the hellhound could burst forth at any moment.

Sibilia stopped short of a compacted mesh of trees. She whispered, "Let me do the talking."

Ducking down, she crawled through a hole in the mesh of tangled branches, with Caeronvar following. The hole formed an entrance to a tunnel that continually sloped downwards into a vast room with walls made of thick foliage. On the floor was a mess of dead and decaying animals. In the dim light, eyes popped from holes in the trees. Sibilia took some flint and steel from her pocket and lit a small blaze on a dead tree branch, which immediately illuminated the room. Caeronvar was startled by the mass of creatures crawling and slithering along the walls. He was outnumbered a hundred to one. Sibilia showed no fear, instead walking forward with the torch outstretched in one hand and the changeling child cradled in her other arm.

As they passed into a larger area, Caeronvar watched as hideous creatures growled and slinked away from the light. Sibilia's attention was focused only toward her destination: a large throne made of broken tree branches. It was clumsily decorated with miscellaneous shiny objects, all man made: swords, shields, spoons, rakes, combs and jewelry. Atop the throne was a rotund creature composed of slime and grotesque boils. Mold grew on its skin where hair normally would have been. Its eyes were two black pits with shining yellow irises. Its fingers resembled that of a tree branch, angular and sharp at the end. On top of its head was a rusted crown, worn by a princess once upon a time.

"This creature," Sibilia whispered to Caeronvar, "is king of the mystic forest."

She handed the torch to Caeronvar, then turned her attention to the creature king. "I have come to bargain with you," Sibilia shouted, loud enough so all could hear.

The creature king growled and hissed at her.

Appearing to understand him, she replied, "This is my friend. He is here to keep me safe. He holds no ill will against you or your kind."

The creature king growled and made other strange guttural sounds.

"I have come to get back what is mine and give back what is yours." Sibilia opened up the sack and pulled the grotesque changeling child out for the whole room to see. It wailed from being taken out of the warm bag.

The creature king growled at her some more.

"I also offer you a sign of peace," Sibilia held up the silver coin so it glistened in the light of her torch.

The creature king made softer growls and then roared loud enough to echo throughout his lair. Other creatures added to the call with their own roars, sending up a cacophony of noise. All the while, Sibilia showed no fear and stood strong in her resolve.

A strange creature that resembled the changeling child appeared from the darkness, delicately holding a human baby in its arms, swaddled in cloth. It approached Sibilia carefully, terrified she might lash out. Sibilia held out the changeling child, which the creature took back reluctantly, sadly giving up the human baby in return.

Sibilia held the baby close and softly kissed its forehead to show the creatures how much the baby meant to her. Then she carefully set it on a tree branch and walked up towards the creature king, extending the silver coin to him. "Whatever we may have done to upset you, I hope you may forgive us."

The creature king made soft guttural noises and stretched out his hand to take the coin.

As she was handing the coin over, a long arrow pierced through the creature king's heart. Green blood splattered Sibilia as the creature king died on his throne.

Sibilia screamed in horror, "No!"

The creatures were suddenly in an uproar. They screamed for revenge on Sibilia and Caeronvar. Before Caeronvar could react, the changeling lunged towards the helpless child and kidnapped it into the darkness. This child was now claimed by the changeling and would never be given back to its rightful parents. This was a cry of war. What was worse was that her village was the closest and would be the first targeted.

Caeronvar and Sibilia looked up to see a hole created in the roof, which was now raining down sunlight. In the hole they spied a human with a bow and arrow, who promptly disappeared.

Sibilia called out to Caeronvar, "If you wish to assist me, then kill anything that is a threat to the village. I'll find the shooter." Sibilia quickly climbed the mass of tree branches and disappeared out the hole the shooter had made.

A long sinister smile grew on Caeronvar's face, revealing such bone-chilling, malicious intent that the attacking creatures hesitated their counterattack. Caeronvar couldn't imagine a more perfect task being handed to him than exterminating the whole lot of 'em. Regathering courage, the creatures sprinted at him, screaming battle cries. They easily outnumbered him five hundred to one.

* * *

After the slaughter, there were so many dead bodies that the dirt floor was no longer visible. In the middle of the hundreds of dead creatures stood Caeronvar, basking in his own bloody accomplishment.

Caeronvar was caked with their green blood from head to toe. His fine black clothes were nearly torn to shreds, but his skin remained flawless and untouched. The setting sun, now glinting through the hole in the forest canopy, shone orange upon the smoking and disintegrating remains of the last mythical creatures.

Sundown triggered an alarm in his head. Sibilia could be in danger! Caeronvar raced to the village as the last rays were leaving the sky. He was horrified to see the entire village ablaze. Men clad in metal armor were rampaging through the once peaceful town. Caeronvar knew these men. Swords for hire paid for by the Viking Earl he had defeated over three years ago. It would seem they had finally found him. This wasn't the first time that these Viking sell-swords had taken advantage of other creatures' desires to distract him from what mattered most. The last time he had slaughtered half their number. Judging by the screams echoing in the night, they were getting revenge. As Caeronvar approached the clearing, his resolve grew and his black eyes transformed into a dangerous, burning red.

Upon the ground he spied the archer who had shot the creature king. This dung-stirring scum squinted up at Caeronvar, blood flowing from his nose. Caeronvar stomped on his groin, crushing the tender flesh. The archer screamed in agony but was quickly silenced when Caeronvar kicked his head hard enough to break it open as if it were a melon.

Caeronvar picked up the bloody bow and the quiver full of arrows. In quick succession, he shot each man in the clearing with spot-on accuracy. He continued through the village, slaughtering any sell-sword that crossed his path. Rage consumed his heart at the mere thought of what they might be doing to Sibilia. If there were any gods out there, he would pray to all of them just to have her safe and unharmed. Finally, he reached the clearing where he had chopped wood days earlier. At the well stood a crowd of the same sell-swords who barely escaped with their lives the last time they had angered him. The two wood choppers he had beat up were also proudly wearing Viking armor. *Spies! I should have recognized those smug faces from the heathen Viking army that I obliterated during their raid on France.* In their midst, Sibilia was tied up tightly, beaten and bruised. Her only crime was getting too close to the warrior Caeronvar.

When she saw Caeronvar, she screamed, "Help!"

The other sell-swords turned to Caeronvar and immediately advanced on him, while one pointed a dagger at Sibilia's back. Blind with rage, Caeronvar picked up an ax and hacked away at the approaching men, who dropped like flies. He had easily cut down five men before he felt something hit him in the back. Disoriented, he dropped the ax and touched his back where blood was flowing.

One of his burly wood-chopping rivals punched the ax deeper into Caeronvar's back and laughed. "Look who's the better man now!"

Losing feeling in his legs, Caeronvar hit the ground.

Sibilia screamed, "Caeronvar! Caeronvar!" Then everything faded to black.

* * *

As if waking from a deep sleep, Caeronvar awoke with a massive headache. Opening his eyes was a challenge. His chest throbbed. The world was spinning and he couldn't make it stop. Struggling to open his eyes, he saw nothing but a red blur. At first, he tried to wipe the stickiness from his face, but his arm wouldn't obey him. The other arm worked only slightly better. Realizing the obstruction in his back, he reached around as best he could and grabbed hold of the ax. It took all the contortion his muscles could handle, but finally he was able to free himself from the blade lodged there. Instantly, his muscles healed freely.

There was no choice but to be patient. Caeronvar lay there for a moment, to give his body time to heal. His lungs at last were able to fill with oxygen, allowing him to breathe deeper and heal faster. The pain in his skull that kept him cemented to the ground was dissipating. A distant ringing increased to an unbearable, ear-shattering siren. Caeronvar's stomach shrank and his heart grew cold when he clearly heard Sibilia whimpering and begging for it all to stop. The strength returned to his arms, allowing him to wipe the blood from his eyes. What he saw would be burned into the back of his skull for the rest of his abnormally long life. Sibilia was still tied tightly up to two posts, with her arms and legs spread apart as far as they could go. A stream of blood trickled from her multiple wounds, staining the dirt beneath her. The men around her admired their work as they joked. No one noticed Caeronvar and his quick regeneration.

One of the men whistled and explained to her, "It cost me only one pretty gold coin to bribe a witch to set that hellhound on his trail. Who'd have thought the beast would take a liking to you? And what luck, because I can't think of a better sound for him to hear as he enters the gates of Valhalla than your agonizing screams as the hellhound rips you to shreds. Nothing personal against you."

From behind Sibilia, a dark creature appeared from the smoke. Steam wafted from its nostrils. Blood dripped from its enormous, protruding fangs. The hellhound's black eyes burned with desire for its next feast. His body was not quite ready, but Caeronvar pushed past the pain and groggily stood up. His spasming muscles didn't want to obey his commands, but he fought through their resistance and picked up the ax. The men were too distracted enjoying Sibilia's terror to notice the threat advancing from their rear. Caeronvar held the ax up in the air like a crazed murderer, his blood-red eyes set on his prize: the master of the hellhound.

It all happened within the blink of an eye. Some of the men noticed Sibilia's gaze and turned around to see the dead man rising from the ground. A couple of them stepped forward to attack, but the rest only watched in horror as Caeronvar rushed forward and chopped the attackers down with one swing of the ax. As he rushed to kill the next three standing dumbly in his way, the hellhound bit down on Sibilia's abdomen, wrapping its teeth completely around her stomach and back. In a frenzy, Caeronvar beheaded three men and jumped into the air to land his final strike upon the hellhound's master. The dumb human in his glistening armor and fine furs held up his arms defensively, as if that would help. Meanwhile the hellhound was shaking and ripping Sibilia off the posts as she wailed in agony. Just as the hellhound pulled her loose from her restraints and sent her bloodied body flying, Caeronvar was slicing clean through the master from skull to groin. The two halves of the master fell apart and twitched on the ground while his entrails spilled loosely, as if he were filled with snakes. The hellhound disappeared into black mist. It was over.

Caeronvar dropped the ax, his strength waning. He ran over to Sibilia with the last of his energy and knelt down beside her. The dirt and grass were drenched in her blood. Her body spasmed as her eyes stared up in shock. After all his promises that he would protect her, he had failed in the end. Tears coursed down his face as he helplessly watched her die.

Looking up at him, she managed to speak only a couple of words— "Caspian, I ... love..." —then her eyes dulled and her last breath exited her soft lips. He picked her up from the ground, held her bloody body tightly to his chest, and screamed into the night. As his screams echoed through the trees and shook the forest, her body disintegrated into purple wisps that flew up into the sky.

The next moment, Caeronvar's arms were as empty as he felt inside. Tears flowed down his face in silence. Lost in his own despair, Caeronvar looked back down at the spot where her body had lain and saw the blood still soaking the ground.

Suddenly, his eyes turned an intense red as he screamed out in anger. Purple flames erupted from his body with such speed and ferocity that they soon consumed not only the village but also the surrounding forest for miles around. That fire burnt down one of the most ancient forests of the time. It decimated nearby towns and villages, along with the thousands of people, animals and mythical creatures that were caught in its path. Purple fire burnt all night and well into the next day before it died down. All that remained was a single man asleep in the ashes, with a tear-streaked face.

4

THE TRUTH ABOUT PIRATES

LONDONDERRY, NEW HAMPSHIRE

JULY 12, 2004

The soundtrack of *Pirates of the Caribbean* echoed deafeningly through the pine trees surrounding a large, elegant house in a wealthy neighborhood in New Hampshire. The archway leading into the house was decorated with balloons, streamers and cartoony pirate symbols. Inside, a battalion of neighborhood children wearing plastic pirate hats and eye patches were chasing each other with plastic swords.

Their parents watched the children, bemused, doing little to keep their offspring under control. In the two-acre backyard, a sleepy teenager who was supposed to be monitoring the number of kids entering a large, inflatable bounce house was busy texting. Kids who weren't playing pirate were watching in fascination as an actor-for-hire, dressed as Captain Jack, inflated balloon pirate hats and swords.

Sammy stood atop her two-story tree house as if commanding a pirate ship. The other children played along, indulging the birthday girl as she commanded her scurvy crew as Captain Valda the Brave. When her crew failed to follow her commands, she would make them walk the plank, falling four feet into an inflatable pillow that cushioned their fall. Some kids enjoyed the jump so much, they would refuse to "swab the poop deck" so they could earn another leap to the pillow.

Despite a house full of chaos, Connor remained as calm as a monk strolling through an abbey. Connor weaved through the galloping children holding foam swords. He grabbed empty cocktail glasses accumulating around the adults. The bartender in the front room appeared pleased about her overflowing tip jar. Alcohol was the best way to keep adults busy for an hour— a commodity he was happy to provide.

Though the house was as chaotic as an amusement park, it was all worth it to see Sammy happy. There had been so much suffering in her past. He was determined that this story would not be filled with such woe, but instead with happiness and fond memories— she deserved that much. Currently, Sammy was lost in make-believe— a whole world she could create with her imagination. It was a world where there were happily-ever-afters and naïve bliss.

Disappearing into the kitchen for a moment, Connor pulled out three bulk-sized bags of chips and proceeded to empty them into large bowls. Snacks completed. The chef rushed in to start preparing the ice cream sundaes with pirate sprinkles and chocolate ganache swords, just as Sammy had ordered.

Connor calmly left the kitchen with the snack bowls and distributed them around the main level. All the while three of the childrens' mothers gave him suggestive glances. People of this level of wealth didn't normally dote on their children unless they have done something outstanding — or horrible. Undoubtedly, the husbands were making better use of their time playing golf or smoking Cubans at the country club lounge. The thought of this made Connor smile. *Some things never change, class behavior being one of them.* The prowling women, so hungry for attention, had seen his smile and flattered themselves by assuming he was smiling at them.

Ignoring the lustful housewives, Connor tracked down the birthday girl. Following directly behind, the chef wheeled out a magnificent cake intricately detailed to match the Black Pearl pirate ship, with a sugary Captain Jack Sparrow at the tiller. The cake even had caramelized blue sugar resembling waves lapping up against the side of the ship. The flags and sails were made of edible rice paper.

Up in her tree house, surrounded by kids wearing eye patches, Sammy stood on the tip of the "plank" with her back to the large inflatable pillow underneath. Judging by all the kids with foam swords pointed at her, they had finally decided it was time for mutiny.

"You'll be sleeping with the fishies tonight! Arrgghhh!" said one of the kids.

"This is mutiny! My own crew!" Sammy yelled dramatically with a joyful smile.

The kids thrust their foam swords forward. The audience of parents was watching with amusement while the audience of kids watched in terror as the captain met her doom. Sammy fell backwards. Her bandana flew off her head, releasing her waist-length, auburn hair so that it briefly floated upward, covering her face. She outstretched her arms as if someone might grab her and save her from the fall—a sight that brought back a sore memory to Connor. He tore his gaze away as she landed on the inflatable pillow, but peeked back in time to watch her bounce a couple of times, giggling. With a warm, playful smile, he leaned over her.

"Connor!" she screamed in excitement and latched onto his neck.

Connor tickled her until she let go. Her laughter was akin to silver bells on a sunny morning, and her smile was contagious. It was so good to see her happy. The past couple of years had been tough on her. Connor moved her to a new place where she had no friends. The one person in her life she was close to was gone. All she had brought with her to remember her dearly departed father was a jacket that had long ago lost his musty scent. It had been a long transition to reach this blissful place she now called home. Now she had friends in the neighborhood and was back into the routine of her studies. Best of all, she considered Connor her best friend in the world. It had been a lot of work, but he was pleased to have finally reached the point where she could be a normal kid, living a happy life.

81

"Come on, pirate queen, it's time for you to eat your cake," Connor said excitedly.

"Yay!" she yelled as she scrambled off the side of the pillow. The other kids heard the word *cake* and promptly followed, some jumping off the plank and others scrambling down a rope ladder. They wove their way through adult legs to arrive, mouths ajar, at the monstrous pirate ship cake.

Sammy had already seen the cake, but still stood in amazement at the size of it. Connor picked her up and sat her on a high stool next to the cake as the chef lit the last of the candles. Once the last one was lit, the crowd began to sing:

"Happy birthday to you ..."

Connor looked at Sammy's beaming face and couldn't help but smile himself.

"Happy birthday to you ..."

Her face, illuminated by the candles, glowed with euphoria, a childish naïvety Connor wished would never go away.

"Happy birthday dear Samantha ..."

But at the same moment, despair weighing on him. *She is so fair and innocent, why is she always crumpled by the cruel hand of fate?*

"Happy birthday to you!"

Connor watched as she closed her eyes to make a wish. He could only guess that her wish would be for a pony or some popular toy. Then she blew on those candles as if her wish might come true. Connor also made a wish that he could protect her from all harm... that he could finally end this cursed cycle that sent him spinning in torment, era after era.

The crowd cheered as the birthday candles were blown out, one huffing breath at a time. Everyone clapped as Sammy beamed proudly, as if she had won a gold medal. Connor applauded alongside everyone else, but behind the feigned smile was a host of worries and sorrows.

Connor hugged Sammy so tight that her adorable giggle tumbled out. "How does it feel to be eight?"

Sammy smiled up at Connor and said, "I feel as if I could take on King Henry myself!"

Caught by surprise at this inside joke, he laughed heartily. "You should probably learn how to wield a sword first," he said, laughing. Then he brought up a large butcher knife, "Would you like to cut the cake, Captain?"

"Argh!" she replied. Connor lowered the knife and allowed her to grab hold. Carefully, he wrapped his large hands over her small ones and guided her in cutting the first piece of the pirate ship. With focused determination, Sammy sliced down, willing herself not to mess it up, and then carefully placed the slice of cake onto a skull-and-crossbones paper plate. Overjoyed at her success, she called out to her crowd, "Who wants the first piece?"

A couple of kids raised their hands, while others threw out requests: "I want part of the sail … Can I have the poop deck? … Give me the mermaid on the front!"

Still holding Sammy's small hands wrapped around the knife, Connor stopped her from cutting another piece, drawing a puzzled scowl. Connor smiled warmly at her curious expression. "Don't you want the first piece, birthday girl?"

Shaking her head and grinning, Sammy replied with a sparkle in her eye, "Nope! I want to serve all my friends first. I like cutting the cake with you."

Connor's heart melted at her sincerity. At moments such as these he was putty in her hands. He would go to the ends of the Earth and would topple any mountain to see her smile. The warmth in his heart quickly spread through his body. "All right, let me know when you grow tired of serving cake and we'll cut your slice."

Sammy smiled and took requests from her friends. Connor was amused that she would call them friends after playing with them for an hour or so. Honestly, most of them were neighborhood kids that he'd invited to this party. Being home-schooled, she didn't have many opportunities to make friends, and the turnout was a bit of a surprise. He excused that as human curiosity, an odd behavior that prompted people to crawl out of their comfort zones to answer questions that lingered in their heads.

Human curiosity had baffled Connor for a long time, but what baffled him even more was the heart of a child. Here are these children who had never interacted with Sammy before. What started with playing a simple carnival game turned into an entire adventurous world of make-believe. Adults could never assimilate this quickly. It was children who could instantly become friends without judgment—a rare behavior Connor wished adults could learn from. In contrast, the adults at the party seemed locked into their familiar gossipy groups. Children simply lived in the moment. Connor hoped one or two lasting friendships would come out of this party for Sammy. Friendships were healthy at her age and taught her vital social skills.

Sammy continued to pass out slices of cake until everyone in the party had some, even the bartender, maid, and the chef. Connor was surprised to see that two-thirds of the cake was gone and people were coming up for seconds, just to be served by the adorable birthday girl. Connor finally had to stop her from serving. "How about you have a piece of your birthday cake, Sammy?"

"Okay, Connor. I want a piece with lots of frosting!" Sammy said, with hungry eyes.

Connor rolled up his fake sleeves in exaggeration and flipped his short hair back dramatically. Sammy giggled between her fingers at his silliness.

"One piece of chocolate cake coming right up!" With an air of confidence, Connor used his superhuman speed to cut and serve her piece within the blink of an eye.

Sammy, awed at his talent, had her jaw ajar as she took the plate. "Thank you, Connor!"

"Go enjoy it with your friends while they are still here. We can open presents later tonight!" Connor called back to her as she ran away with her cake.

With a warm heart that fluttered with happiness, Connor watched Sammy go eat cake with her new set of friends. It was sometimes difficult to watch her, he reflected. Every little movement she made was a shadow of previous memories of her. It was almost shocking to Connor that she maintained the same mannerisms, gestures and personality as in her previous lives. Yet there were some small things that would always change about her. Every trauma seemed to add to the legacy of her previous lives. The nightmares grew worse with every painful life full of trials. In her current youth, Sammy had been fortunate that the nightmares hadn't started yet. Connor dreaded the day they would wake her screaming and shivering in the night.

Innocence. That was one trait he longed to keep intact for as long as possible. The longer Sammy could hold onto her innocence, the longer she could maintain some small sliver of happiness.

Out of the many past lives in which he had found her, this time was the most precious. Never before had he felt so attached to her. He was always drawn to her and felt insurmountable torment when she suffered. This time was much different. Connor knew deep down that he had reached a tighter bond with her than he had ever had in her previous lives. If she were to die this time, he knew it would destroy him completely.

After a few hours, Connor was bidding farewell to their last guests. Sammy was shredding open her expensive presents as the women said goodbye, their children already in the cars. Connor closed the door, locked the two deadbolts and set the security alarm. Connor sighed, realizing that he still had to clean up the rest of the house before Sammy got up in the morning and back to the regular schedule. On second thought, he pondered letting her sleep in. It was the day after her birthday, after all.

"Connor! Connor! Connor!" Sammy yelled in excitement from the other room.

Pretending it's an emergency, Connor came running in with playful shock. "Oh no, Sammy, whatever could it be?"

Proudly, she held up a necklace with a rare Roman gold coin embossed with the profile of Caesar Augustus. "Argh! I got a cursed piece of gold!"

With his hands extended as though playing the "I'm-gonna-getcha" game, Connor tip-toed forward. "I sure hope a pirate ship doesn't come and ..." He paused as Sammy held her breath in anticipation. *"... get you!"*

Connor leapt forward and tickled Sammy, who laughed joyfully. After a couple minutes of tickling, Connor finally let up so she could catch her breath.

Sammy sat up and put the gold coin necklace around her neck, a piece of jewelry she would wear for every *Pirates of the Caribbean* premiere to follow. "Can you tell me a pirate story for my birthday present?"

Connor was momentarily surprised as he chuckled and reclined on the floor, crumpling the mess of gift wrap currently covering the carpet. "A story? I already got you a couple presents, though."

Sammy admired her stack of new puzzles and educational games, along with a couple of movies. "I know ... thank you for the presents, but I would much prefer another story. You have only told me two so far, and I want another one!"

Connor laughed at her enthusiasm.

"A pirate one!" she added.

His wide smile shrank a bit as he peered down at the gold medallion around her neck. "You know, Sammy, my stories don't have happy endings to them. They are nothing like the *Pirates of the Caribbean.*"

"I love your stories, though! They are so much better than the ones on TV! Will you please tell me a pirate story? PLEASE!" she begged, flopping her hands around dramatically.

Her childishness was so darn cute that Connor couldn't help but laugh as she continued to repeat "please please please please please ..." He grabbed her arms and held them by her side. "All right, all right. I'll tell you a story."

"Really? A pirate story?" Sammy perked up.

Connor's purple eyes sparkled as he started in, "Let me tell you a story about ... pirates!"

* * *

ATLANTIC OCEAN

MARCH 27, 1719

Thundering black boots stormed up the plank to the mighty Fiery Dragon. Hearing their captain fast approaching, the pirate crew stood at strict attention, lest they be at the receiving end of his bad temper. And there was much to fear. The terrifying Captain Condent walked with the air of a warrior and showed no mercy, not even to his own men. Matching his black-bellied ship, Captain Condent was clothed in black from head to toe, with an impressive tricorne hat shadowing his misty, swirling purple eyes.

Captain Condent held a rolled-up document towards the sky for his black-clad pirate crew to see. "Behold! Here be the contract from the crown. It would appear we have been hired to free these seas of Dutch merchants and pirate crews who are unlucky enough to sail in our path."

"Arrrghh!" the crew shouted triumphantly.

"We sail to Madagascar!" Captain Condent hollered, echoed by the crew. After that boost of morale, the captain threw the document back at his first mate, a mousy little man who scurried along at Captain Condent's heels as if he fearing a backhanded slap at any moment. His arms were filled with maps and documents, less the one Captain Condent had thrown at him. Fumbling clumsily, the first mate dropped a map to save the King of England's contract.

"Come along, Robertsy, prepare the ship for our voyage," Captain Condent commanded the first mate, the way one would instruct a dog at heel.

Robertsy straightened his small green tricorne hat and cleared his throat. "Ye heard ye Captain! Hoist the sails!"

The energetic crew leapt to their positions, motivated by the heaps of treasure they envisioned in their future. Long black sails extended, casting an ominous shadow on the sea. A black flag climbed the pole until it was flapping against the biting wind. On it were three skull-and-crossbones emblems, signifying the level of destruction that followed this black-clad crew.

Two weeks under the hot sun and barely anything to do. Captain Condent took up a position lying precariously perched on the port railing near the bow. Nothing else to do but flip a gold coin in the air, Caesar's face glistening in the bright sun with each rotation. Down below he could hear his crew gambling for gold they had yet to plunder, their conversation bouncing around superstitions that a storm would soon roll in over the horizon. Captain Condent spotted one thin cloud on the horizon ahead. It would be a miracle if their predictions proved true.

Tossing his gold coin in the air, Captain Condent wished for something to come his way. Finding a ship to plunder on the open sea was similar to feeding a string through a pinhole leagues away. He hoped their voyage to Madagascar would hold at least one lucrative encounter.

Breaking his train of thought was a low rumble far off in the distance. Could it be that a storm was coming? Popping up, he scanned the horizon and could only see bright blue sky against blue ocean. Another boom rumbled across the water.

Perhaps it's not thunder. Propelled by the anticipation of battle, Captain Condent raced down the deck and leapt upon the mast, climbing it with the ease of a monkey. The lethargic crew watched him but didn't move a muscle to follow. The loner in the crow's nest was startled that his Captain had come all the way up there. Ignoring the head-scratching lookout, Captain Condent perched himself on the ledge of the crow's nest and lightly tiptoed around the edge, gazing into his long brass nautical telescope. At last he saw it!

Three ships off in the distance. The first was the *Saint James*, an enormous ship captained by Thomas Cocklyn, famous on these seas. Cocklyn was known to sink merchant ships from every nationality; a pirate who prided himself on taking captives, then torturing them for weeks until he grew bored and fed them to the sharks. Preferring to stay in open water, Captain Cocklyn rarely made port except to barter his pillaged treasures. As the distance between them shrank, Condent thought he could see Cocklyn standing on the deck, mockingly dressed as an English gentleman. *A wolf in sheep's clothing*, Condent thought. Fine clothes couldn't mask the pirate's sea-legged gait. He wore a tall tricorne hat decorated with emblems of his triumphs, one of them a lady's garter belt. Now he was using a bullhorn to hail orders to another ship on his starboard side: the infamous *Le Victorieux*— a ship legendary for its speed and its captain's ruthlessness on the attack. The French Captain La Bouche's fearsome reputation was contradicted by his appearance. He was known to spend exorbitant amounts of time perfecting his appearance, including a wet powdered wig and heavy makeup, in the manner of a pampered French aristocrat, albeit tattered by life at sea.

A third ship, the *Rover*, sat off in the distance. Although it was not quite as infamous as the other two, Captain Condent knew of this pirate's trickery. Captain Howell Davis focused mostly on slave ships and would fool militarized naval ships into surrendering despite his lack of power. Davis was keeping his ship at a safe distance, his arms folded tightly against his barrel chest. This was a man who didn't try to disguise what he was, a pirate with a scarred face who knew battle all too well and had little mercy for others.

Though Captain Condent didn't understand the nature of the three captains' relationships, he was aware that these were some of the most feared pirates on the sea. There was sure to be rich booty hidden in the bowels of their ships. Captain Condent's jumped down from the crow's nest as the crew scrambled around him, eager to hear his news.

"Tell us, Captain, what has ye magical eyes seen?" asked the first mate.

Captain Condent collapsed his telescope and proudly observed his crew. "Rejoice with me, ye scurvy dogs! For just on the horizon sits not one, not two, but three pirate ships— their bellies full of gold. It is time to relieve them of this heavy burden."

The crew nodded and chuckled, unsheathing their swords and loading their pistols.

"What say ye? Shall we plunder the likes of these bloody pirates?" he shouted.

"Aye!" the pirates rejoiced.

"Then let us rip the bellies of those ships open and pour the gold into our pockets! For England! For glory! For our own greedy pockets!"

The crew hooted and hollered, celebrating the victory that would soon be theirs.

"Ye heard ye captain!" Robertsy spoke up. "Grab ye seaweed! Set the sails! Prepare the guns! May ye swords be drenched with pirate blood by sundown!"

Captain Condent bounded up to the helm and rested his hands on the wheel. Taking command, he steered the ship directly towards the battling trio of ships ahead. Once they were within visible distance, the first mate came to report: "Captain, the crew is ready for their victory."

Captain Condent glanced around and, sure enough, they had eager grins, sharpened swords and seaweed in their ears. The captain nodded at his first mate and handed the wheel off to him, making sure to give one more command that he himself wouldn't abide by: "Stuff the seaweed in ye ears now, Robertsy."

The first mate did as commanded and took the wheel. Immediately, Captain Condent jumped up on the stern's railing and whistled towards the water. He continued whistling until heads began to bob above the surface. It was the lovely mermaids that he called to, with their long, flowing hair that drifted similarly to ribbons blowing in the wind, and their lovely voices that cried out for lost souls. Mermaids would grant wishes and were good luck to sailors lost at sea. There were heroic tales of sailors, shipwrecked, who found their way back to land aided by these magnificent creatures.

But this was not entirely the truth, which the *Fiery Dragon* crew well knew.

"Good day, lovely ladies," Captain Condent called out to them.

The gorgeous women trailing the ship flitted about flirtatiously. The sunlight glistened from their colorful tails while their siren songs filled the air, heard only by Captain Condent— the sole man aboard who was immune to their charm.

"We were wondering when you would call," one mermaid with glowing green hair called out in a sultry voice.

"Aye, the seas have been quiet of late," Captain Condent agreed.

"That's what happens when you keep sinking ships," another mermaid giggled, echoed by her companions.

"Well, today I have a treat for ye lovely ladies," he said, drawing out the silence to build suspense. Then he held up three fingers. "I'll be delivering three pirate ships to ye today."

Joyously, the mermaids twirled and flipped their tails in harmonious unison. None of the crew was watching, fearful of being drawn into the water by their charms and drowned.

"Atlantis thanks you for your generosity," the green-haired mermaid graciously accepted. "We follow your lead, Captain." On cue, the school of mermaids disappeared under the water.

Captain Condent gazed toward the bow, at the trio of ships he was advancing on. *The Rover* had spotted the Dragon and was already fleeing. Frantic to not lose a third of his bounty, the captain climbed the net to the crow's nest again. This time, his lookout was prepared for him, standing by to hand the captain his bow and arrows. Captain Condent flipped a few long, scraggly locks of black hair out of his face and blew on the tips of the arrows. Magically, purple flames attached to their tips. Captain Condent nestled three flaming arrows to his bow and pulled it taut.

"I bet three silver pieces you miss," the lookout said snarkily, a reasonable wager considering the ships were well out of range for even the best archers. But the captain's limits exceeded all others.

Keeping his focus, the captain aimed high and loosed the flaming arrows, which whistled as they soared. When they struck two of the ships, fire immediately devoured the sails and flags.

Captain Condent arrogantly regarded his lookout, "Ye owe me three silver pieces fe doubtin' ye captain."

"Argh ..." the man sulked.

"Prepare to board! Leave no survivors!" the captain hollered to those below.

"Argh!" The crew saluted and readied themselves for glory.

Captain Condent's attention was drawn back to the other ships' pirate captains who were busy blaming each other for the pending catastrophe.

"Stop blowing holes in my ship, ye stinking pig!" yelled Le Bouche to Cocklyn, who was laughing maniacally as he stood on the rail clinging to a rope.

"This is what ye get for shooting my men!" Cocklyn retorted, before turning around and yelling, "Fire!"

The thunder of cannons was followed by the sound of wood splintering and men screaming as the cannonballs found their marks. This, Condent thought, would be easy pickings for the *Fiery Dragon*.

As his ship was nearing boarding distance of *Le Victorieux*, he saw a young woman frantically calling out: "Le Bouche! Le Bouche!" The young woman stood out as if she was a tulip in a swamp, with electrifying green eyes now wide at the sight of the incoming danger. Her messy auburn hair was tied up in a ribbon to keep it out of her face. The rags she wore didn't fit her fair complexion in the least. She wore short trousers that covered her upper thighs but left her calves exposed and had a hole in the upper thigh where it appeared an earlier owner might have been stabbed. Her black, buckled shoes appeared as if many men had walked in them before her. Her bosom peeked out from a shirt held closed by a string.

Captain Condent's eyes narrowed in on the one prize he desired. "The girl is mine!" he hollered down to his crew, who were busy screaming their own battle cries.

The French captain paid her no mind as he continued screaming to Cocklyn amid the chaos of men throwing buckets of water on what remained of the mainsail. Then the auburn-haired woman ran over to the wheel, turning the ship's course toward what Condent suddenly realized was a small island in the distance. He was dismayed by the abrupt change in direction; if they got closer to the island, chances were high that there would be survivors. He preferred to leave none.

Le Bouche, alarmed his ship was moving without his command, looked to the upper deck and spotted her. "Sarah! You little—!" He pulled out his gun, while Cocklyn laughed hysterically at Le Bouche for allowing a woman to steer his ship.

"But Captain!" she screamed, pointing out the incoming ship with black sails.

Le Bouche, finally grasping the danger both of them were in, hailed Cocklyn. "You filzy pig! Ahoy a ship!"

Startled into action, each captain actively commanded their crew to prepare the big guns for battle. But it was too late for both ships. The *Fiery Dragon* was within range. The *Saint James* and *Le Victorieux* had cannons set up only along their starboard and port sides. His oncoming ship had two cannons angled from the front. Le Bouche and Cocklyn noticed this a moment too late.

A soft, warm breeze blew back Sarah's auburn hair, a whisper of impending death. She dived for cover. Cannon fire echoed, followed a half-second later by splintering wood. The bows of *Saint James* and *Le Victorieux* tipped forward and then rocked back from the force of the barrage, their sails already reduced to ash. The men in the crow's nest, now aflame with purple fire, fell to the deck, dying instantly. The crews were frantically trying to put out the blazes that were spreading like wildfire. Clothes caught fire, and sailors flung themselves into the sea. The burning mast of *Le Victorieux* toppled, clipping the deck of the Saint James so that the two were connected in their final hour before being claimed by the sea.

The *Fiery Dragon* crew, clever to block out the siren call of the mermaids with their seaweed-plugged ears, jumped over the mermaid-infested waters onto the two burning ships to claim their prizes. The *Saint James* and *Le Victorieux* crews were less prepared. Survivors on board, popping up from below deck as if they were rats in a flood, were mesmerized by the mermaids' song. Their eyes glazed over as they walked in a stupor to the edge of the deck, climbed over the rail and then dropped blindly into the ocean. The second they struck the water, the mermaids' song became a glass shattering wail. Rows of shark teeth appeared behind their ruby lips and latched upon the men, tearing them apart. The lucky pirates stuffed their ears with seaweed before the mermaid song would transfix them to death. The mermaids did however claim a handful of men who were ill prepared. The woman upon whom Condent's eyes were set, Sarah, screamed in terror as she watched the water around the ship turn blood red.

"Abandon ship!" yelled Cocklyn, whose crew quickly obliged and fled in the available rowboats.

"No one takes my ship from me!" growled Le Bouche, drawing his sword and screaming "Attack!" as the Fiery Dragon drew up alongside. The sword was pointed towards Captain Condent, the first to board *Le Victorieux*.

Each step Condent took was heavy with purpose. His large hat hid his mystical swirling purple eyes. Directly behind him came his crew, hand selected from the best warriors in the recent war against the vampire hordes. Each was heavily armed and ready to shed blood.

As the crew lunged forward, the woman crawled underneath a stairway for cover. But it took only a moment for one pirate to spot her and grab her out by the ankle—only to find himself being whacked across the head by Captain La Bouche's short sword. That pirate fell to the deck with a cracked skull, blood seeping from his head. La Bouche fought on valiantly, the woman watching from her hiding place in amazement as he skillfully cut through four pirates' skulls. Given a moment of reprieve, she scurried out and made her way over to a row boat fastened near the bow as battle cries and the collision of steel upon steel resounded all around her. Neither La Bouche's nor Cocklyn's men stood a chance against Condent's bloodthirsty sailors.

Condent, who had cut down one of the French pirates, caught sight of the woman fearlessly darting into the battle zone. She ducked low to narrowly avoid a sword swing by a *Fiery Dragon* pirate who caught his sword in the wood railing. As he struggled to pull it out, one of *Le Victorieux's* pirates ran up and shot him with a musket, splattering blood on her back. As she headed towards the boat again, her eyes locked onto Captain Condent's now fierce, dark purple eyes. Taking long, heavy strides, he advanced towards her, and in a panic she climbed over a broken barrel of gunpowder and vaulted herself forward.

Hindered briefly by one of the French pirates, Condent grabbed the man's head and smashed it against the broken mast. She had almost reached the boat, where a French pirate with the same idea was pushing it off the side, only to have his throat slit by one of Condent's men. The boat toppled empty into the water below.

Condent could tell from the leer on his man's face that he had set his gaze on the captain's prize, and a second later his blade was pointed at her neck. The captain grabbed her arm from behind and reached over her shoulder to strike down his own pirate with his sword, his body slapping the deck like a wet fish. The woman turned around and came face to face with Captain Condent.

Snapping herself out of her fixed gaze with Captain Condent, she tried to yank her arm away, an impossibility as his vice-grip tightened around her arm. She winced in pain, crying "Let go!" with a pleading look into the captain's eyes.

Condent was furious, his eyes now swirling with black and red. How dare she treat him this way after he had just sacrificed one of his own crew for her. This woman was going to come with him, whether she liked it or not!

From somewhere behind him, a voice called out, "Captain Condent!" La Bouche threw a long knife straight for Condent. The knife went twirling through the air straight for the woman, but Condent put his body in front of the flying dagger as he shoved the woman over the railing and into the water below. As she fell, Condent winced and pulled the knife out of his back. Then he effortlessly flicked the blade back; it twirled elegantly toward Captain La Bouche.

* * *

Connor paused the story, struggling to continue.

"What happened next?" Sammy asked, sitting on her hands to keep them from flapping excitedly.

Connor was ashamed of himself for getting this far in the story. Sometimes he got so wrapped up in reliving the past that he completely forgot the gory context of the stories— mermaids tearing men apart and pirates slicing each other open. These stories were far too gruesome to tell a little girl, on her birthday of all days!

"Connor!" Sammy said playfully, "What happens next?"

Hanging his head in shame, Connor replied, "Sammy, I just realized that this isn't the best story to tell you."

"Yeah, yeah, it doesn't end happy. What happens to the girl Captain Condent found?"

Connor looked seriously at Sammy. "Are you sure this isn't going to give you nightmares?"

"It won't! Just tell me, tell me, tell!" she begged, bouncing up and down on the couch.

Connor chuckled. "All right, where was I?"

"The mysterious woman with a beautiful face was pushed overboard by Captain Condent!" Sammy recited dramatically.

"Oh yes," Connor smiled. "That's right—"

* * *

La Bouche evaded the knife, then taunted Captain Condent about his poor aim. Thinking he had the upper hand against a wounded opponent, he drew out his fencing sword to prepare a duel as Condent spun around.

Similar to a bull charging a red cape flapping in the wind, Captain Condent lunged for the French captain, whose arrogance was his own undoing. A split second before the fencing sword would have pierced his heart, Condent rolled into a fall and grabbed the blade. The next second, the sword was bent and had pierced through the French captain's shoulder.

La Bouche watched the warm trickle of blood run down his chest. He observed the fading chaos on his ship, now strewn with dead French pirates. Knowing he had lost, La Bouche turned back towards Captain Condent with fading eyes and then fell as stiff as a board face down on the deck.

"Are all you Frenchies this weak? I didn't stab your heart, just barely stabbed above it," Condent said confidently as he stood over La Bouche, who lifted his head enough to spit on Condent's shoes. Captain Condent responded with a light chuckle, then stomped on the French captain's knee so hard that he screamed in agony.

Then, over the side of the ship, he noticed the woman, who had somehow survived the fall into the mermaid-infested waters and made her way to the side of the rowboat that was still bobbing alongside the ship. Flipping her hair back, the woman hoisted herself into the boat and collapsed on the bottom.

Blinded by the high sides of the boat, she didn't see the danger coming for her. It was one of Captain Condent's men, known for his penchant for collecting women's hair from their scalp. A stubborn fixation so strong that he braved the mermaid-infested waters and jumped off the plank straight for her rowboat. He'd obviously set his gaze on the auburn-haired beauty, but Captain Condent had declared the woman his prize and wasn't about to let even his own crew get in his way. Looking around for a suitable weapon, he spotted a harpoon.

Before she had a chance to pick up the oars, the pirate jumped into the rowboat with a knife drawn. The woman screamed as the ugly pirate brandished his knife high in the air, relishing the moment before the kill. At that moment, Captain Condent hurled the harpoon at the rogue crewman with the grace of an Olympian throwing a javelin. The harpoon shot through his chest with enough force to come out the other side. In shock, the pirate looked down at the harpoon piercing his body as if he didn't believe it could exist. Blood sprayed from his mouth as he was yanked backwards into the water. Captain Condent handed off the harpoon rope to one of his men and ordered him to reel in the catch of the day. Nervously, the crew mate drew in the rope as if his life depended on it.

La Bouche, still on the deck at Condent's feet, was blubbering in pain. "Tell me about the girl," Condent said, contemptuously.

"Go to hell, you pig!" La Bouche spat back.

Captain Condent straddled the French captain while crushing his shoulder until it cracked and popped. The Frenchman screamed in agony.

"Maybe you didn't hear me ... Tell me about the girl!" Condent shouted.

The French captain wept, "All right, I'll tell you ... just don't kill me!" He spilled the words like vomit. "Her name is Sarah ... Sarah Hughes. Her father was a merchant sailing to Africa. We captured the *Bird Galley*, her father's ship. Naturally I would have let her sink with the ship, but Captain Cocklyn had an eye for her and kept her on his ship for nearly a week."

"What did Cocklyn do to her?" Condent growled, showing an odd protectiveness for the woman he was hunting.

For a moment, La Bouche had a glazed look in his eyes. Then he answered, "Nothing. She wouldn't let him. Scratched his face up pretty good, too. She was too strong fo—"

"Then how did she end up on your ship?" Condent demanded, growing impatient.

"Cocklyn threw her to his crew. I would not put up with that, so I took her," La Bouche answered.

"And did you ..."

"Never!" La Bouche responded, aghast. "I do not care for women. If you didn't blow up my ship, then you would be more my type."

Condent had had enough. In one fluid motion, he threw La Bouche over the side of the ship, where razor-sharp teeth spelled his doom. Condent gazed out toward the island. Sarah was already more than halfway there, her oars splashing awkwardly.

"Robertsy!" Captain Condent yelled out.

The first mate was instantly at his heels, "Aye Captain!"

Lifting his spyglass to his steel-cold purple eyes, he fixed his gaze venomously on Cocklyn's men scrambling over the beach to the protection of the jungle.

"It would appear that our dear Captain Cocklyn and Captain Davis have hidden themselves upon the island," he shouted to the crew, who had put down the last of the French pirates. "What is our code?"

The crew shouted back in unison, "Leave no survivors!"

A grin so maniacal that even Satan would shudder slithered across Captain Condent's face. "Yo ho, yo ho, a-sailing we shall go ..."

Sarah made it ashore without difficulty. Ditching the rowboat, she jumped into the water and waded onto the land. Meanwhile, Captain Condent was quickly advancing on the island, perched at the bow of the first rowboat making its way to shore.

Desperate for a weapon, Sarah searched the two rowboats Cocklyn's crew had come ashore with. Both boats were bare of any objects, let alone weapons.

"Oh shit!" she screamed out in frustration, "Oh shit! Oh shit! Oh shit!" Sarah kicked the water, sending chunks of wet sand flying, before desperately scrambling for the shelter of the jungle.

The first boat gently ran aground. Condent quickly jumped out and immediately marched towards the jungle.

"Captain Condent?" the first mate called out, running after him. The captain stopped for a moment, irritation clearly written on his face. Two other boats came ashore next, spilling his black pirate crew onto dry land.

"What is it, Robertsy?" he asked angrily.

The first mate appeared as if he had been whipped. "I'm sorry Captain ... but aren't you going after the escaped crew with us?"

Captain Condent admired at his crew for a moment. Even fresh from battle, all of them were ready to shed more blood. "Find the cowardly crew!" he shouted to his men. "We take no captives!" The crew celebrated with hoots and hollers and brandished their weapons.

The first mate moved closer to Captain Condent and softly asked, "What about the girl? Your prize?"

Captain Condent patted his first mate on the shoulder, "That is the girl I have been searching my whole life for. If I don't return to the ship by sundown, then you are to take my name and my ship. Sail to the tip of Africa. There is much treasure to be found there. Do you understand, Robertsy?"

"Aye aye, Captain Condent!" he saluted.

Without further distraction, Captain Condent followed Sarah's footprints into the tropical jungle. He tracked them deep into the jungle, occasionally finding broken branches and scraps of cloth torn from her clothes, evidence of her haste.

After what felt like forever in the hot jungle, Captain Condent finally caught up to Sarah, who was sitting on a rock, exhausted and trying to catch her breath. Startled by a rustling in the bushes opposite the spot where Condent was silently watching, she sprang up with her back to him, obviously preparing to run again—or fight, an admirable quality in a woman, he thought. Condent was surprised to see Cocklyn pop out of the bushes, smiling gleefully to see his prey had jumped right in front of him, like a fleeing deer running straight into your arrow. Sarah screamed as Cocklyn lunged toward her and, to Condent's amusement, punched him in the face.

"You little bitch!" Cocklyn spat while struggling to hold down her arms, "This is all your fault ..." He finally got her arms pinned above her head. "I'm going to make you pay for all of this!"

Sarah struggled against his grip, fruitlessly. Sighing out of boredom, Captain Christopher Condent decided it was time to make his presence known and stepped out of the foliage. Cocklyn saw the dark Captain Condent reflected in Sarah's horrified green eyes and reflexively rolled, putting Sarah on top. She kneed Cocklyn in the testicles, forcing him to let go immediately and hold his crotch tenderly. Sarah scrambled over him, pushing his face into the mud with her boot as she went. Without looking back, she bolted up a hill.

"It would seem I have discovered a man with no honor," Captain Condent smirked. "I know just the thing to fix that."

Cocklyn's eyes widened in horror as Condent struck at the perverted man's groin, severing his member. Cocklyn's blood-curdling screams echoed through the forest as he bled to death. Although Captain Condent was enjoying watching the perverted pirate suffer, he had a more important goal. He set off to track Sarah down, determined to carry her back to his ship, whether she liked it or not.

Sarah slid to a stop as she reached a sharp ledge, gasping as immense, sulfurous heat billowed up into her face, blowing back her auburn hair. Carefully, she leaned over and peered down the edge; about a hundred feet below was a crater of boiling red liquid, at the edges of which a layer of black crust floated similarly to sea foam. Glancing over her shoulder, she saw Captain Condent standing a short distance behind.

Condent's heart stopped when he saw her leaning over the ledge of the volcano. His voice involuntarily projected, "STOP!"

Sarah turned her head again, her hair whipping around her face as she looked at the monstrous Captain Condent standing there, with his open hands reaching out to her. Then she looked down again into the pit of red boiling liquid.

"Don't jump!" he begged, "Please ..."

The wheels turning in her head, Sarah continued to weigh one evil over another. When she noticed he had taken another couple of steps forward, she screamed, "Stay back! Don't come near me. I know what you are: a monster!"

This cut Captain Condent deeper than a sword through the gut. A deep sadness shadowed his black eyes. "I know... just step away from the ledge and I will take you safely back to England."

Sarah shook her head slowly back and forth, refusing to believe him. A tear ran down her face as she decided which way she was to die. Sarah turned around so her back faced the crater, her heels hanging off the edge and her arms outstretched.

Captain Condent, suddenly understanding her intentions, bolted forward to snatch her away from the edge.

The billowing heat blew her long auburn hair in her face. Tilting back, Sarah let gravity take her. A simple and easy submission to death.

Captain Condent pursued her, his reach was a hair short of catching her. Instead of stopping at the edge to save himself, he dived off the cliff after her. His arms reached out in vain to grab hold of her, as though he could still save her from the fiery pit below. The sulfur-laden wind hit him in the face, obscuring his vision. Her auburn hair whipped his outstretched fingertips. The peaceful sky was changing to shades of orange and purple through the setting sun.

In that frozen moment, Sarah looked up into the captain's eyes. Those unfeeling black pits she had peered into earlier were rapidly changing to a vibrant purple, and from those eyes came all the caring and love in the world. Captain Condent could see his own swirling purple eyes reflected back in the green eyes of a woman who had mysteriously crossed his path in a moment of fate so perfect he would never understand it. In that final moment, Sarah reached out for his hand, which he instantly took in his.

The second they touched, her all-knowing green eyes flashed in recognition. "My love," she whispered as a single tear flew onto his cheek and evaporated from the intense heat.

He watched her face wince as her body hit the surface of the lava. Before her bones cracked on the dense lava ... before her body could settle into it ... before he could land atop her ... her body burst into a million tiny purple wisps, which soared into the sky, rising on waves of heat.

* * *

Sammy's brilliant green eyes glistened with tears, her young mind trying its hardest to understand. "Why'd she jump?"

Connor opened his mouth to answer, then closed it to think a moment. He resolved to answer her question with a question, "Why do you think she chose to jump?"

"She thought she was going to die either way. But she didn't know that Captain Condent would have saved her. They would have sailed the sea together ... right?" Sammy sounded unsure, but her pure naivety, the light of her angelic soul lightened Connor's heart.

A sigh escaped his lips. "The older you get, the more you'll understand that everyone has a choice to make. Our choices help define us. Sarah could have chosen to go with Captain Condent, but she might have suffered on that ship. Captain Condent could have chosen to go back down the mountain so he didn't scare her into jumping into the volcano. There are many choices we can make. As you get older, you'll have even more difficult choices to make than deciding what type of birthday party you want."

Sammy rubbed the authentic golden Roman coin, bearing the image of Caesar, that Connor had given her for a birthday present. It glistened, as though it held a truth she couldn't quite grasp yet. "But you'll still be there to help me make those choices, won't you Connor?"

"Even if I am with you, there will still be choices you have to make on your own. Don't worry about that right now, though. Right now, it's time for bed." Connor stood up, straightened his shirt and motioned for Sammy's hand.

Sammy obediently took his hand and walked with him upstairs to her bedroom, "So what happened to Captain Condent? Did he die, too?"

Connor didn't want to think about that, let alone relate the aftermath to Sammy. No, he would keep that piece of his memory to himself. Still, the memory plagued him similar to a howling cat that can't be silenced.

Caspian floated atop the liquid lava. His clothes quickly caught on fire and were turned to ash, but his pale skin remained intact. Alone and full of regret, Caspian inspected the empty hands that had held her mere seconds ago. He trembled with self-hatred. The lava swirled around him as if it were a tornado of fire, its edges climbing the sides of the crater, swelling upwards. Looking towards the heavens, Caspian screamed as loud as his lungs could allow. A purple fire erupted from his body and burst towards the sky, as if to burn down God himself. Standing up, Caspian screamed louder as the lava erupted out of the volcano, reaching high into the sky. Tears evaporated on his cheeks as he continued to curse heaven and hell and every living thing. Caspian screamed as the lava spilled down the sides of the volcano, melting everything in its path. The lava flowed all the way to the sea, where a ship with black sails was hastening to make its escape.

The new captain looked back at the island, hearing the cries of his former master. Caspian's rage did not end until the entire island and all living things on it were covered in lava.

Caspian returned to the top of the volcano where he had watched Sarah jump. More than anything, he hated himself for putting her in so desperate a position that she would take her own life. Caspian stepped away and made his way down the mountain, the molten lava quickly hardening into black rock behind his footsteps. He felt emptier than he had in a long time, walking naked as the day he was born, with a long mark glistening on his back, as if made of scales. At the bottom of the mountain, Caspian sat down on the hard black rock, still steaming as it cooled, and gazed out over the vastness of the ocean in the light of the setting sun. No longer having a direction, but no longer caring.

5

LOYALTY TO A FAULT

LONDONDERRY, NEW HAMPSHIRE

OCTOBER 23, 2005

Visions of the past flashed through Connor's eyes. The memories were coming in as if they were oncoming lights of a freight train, too terrifying and fast to move his numb body out of the way in time. Screams echoed in his ears of all the times she had died— the death rattles of all the people he had slain, both warriors and the innocent. The faces of the slain vivid in his mind. He remembered how he had shown no mercy to not just men, but women and children, too. To think of them at such a time as this was insane!

"Are you even listening to me?" chided the blonde beauty to his side.

Connor came back to the present and reacquainted himself with the peaceful environment. The autumn leaves were a breathtaking array of gold, orange and green, slowly drifting to the ground. The wise, ancient trees surrounded a small park fully equipped with three slides, a jungle gym, monkey bars and a swing set. This was Sammy's favorite park, which is why Connor enjoyed bringing her here to socialize. He could see her now, crawling on top of the monkey bars as her friend hung from below. Always the center of attention, Sammy turned around and waved at Connor. It was difficult to believe she was already nine years old. Even her auburn hair had grown long enough to be braided and wrapped around her head as if she was a princess.

Time passed so quickly for Connor, perhaps because of his insufferable immortality. Yet now that he was always with her, it was as if time had slowed, if for no other reason than to enjoy each precious moment with her. Time was now a blessing, no longer a curse. Sammy turned her attention back to the game she was playing with a boy on the monkey bars.

"Hello?" snapped the blonde, mother of the boy.

"I'm sorry. I spaced out for a moment. What were you saying? Something about Becky getting fat again?" he asked though honestly he had zero interest.

"Well," she stopped for a moment to think, while playing with her hair. "She is putting it on. Maybe she'll go get more liposuction done. But I was talking about that dreamy guy jogging by that you apparently missed. I thought all gay guys were aware of the hotties around them."

She had gone on believing that Connor was gay. In her mind, it was the only explanation for why he didn't want to pile-drive her over the park bench right this minute. Connor never did correct her. He put up with this mother enough to ensure Sammy had a friend to play with for a couple of hours a week. Normally it was at the park, but every now and then they would go play on their family yacht.

"I didn't see the guy jogging, but I would assume that he was attractive," Connor replied in monotone.

"Mmm, he would be a man I would actually enjoy sharing with you at the same time," she suggested with a raised eyebrow.

"Not interested," Connor replied bluntly.

"Are you really that repulsed by women?" she asked, taking personal offense to his statement.

Connor paused for a moment and redirected his attention to the two children, who were now at the top of the slide. Another boy, bulkier than

106

the other two, was currently climbing up the slide. Connor turned his attention back to the mother. "Maybe you should try a woman and see if you like it," he said sarcastically, with a smile.

Normally quick on her feet, she pointed a sharply manicured finger in the air to object, before pausing a moment. "Might be fun," she finally decided.

A scream cut through the serene day, jolting Connor out of his seat similar to a shell-shocked war veteran. He honed in at the children. The little boy was wailing as he ran towards his mother with scraped knees and elbows. Sand from the playground had dirtied his pants and part of his shirt. More screaming could be heard up on top of the slide, where, for a brief moment, Connor saw Sammy swipe her hand at the fat boy. Wanting to dominate the annoying little girl, he jumped on her and pinned her against the railing of the slide, her upper body hanging over the side in such a way that she was in danger of falling off. Connor ran over as the bully pushed harder and Sammy, screaming for Connor, fell head-first.

Reaching her just in time, Connor caught her in his arms. "Are you okay, Samantha? What happened?" he asked, inspecting her for injuries.

Vengeful, she pointed toward the bottom of the slide, where the bully had gone down. "He kicked Tommy in the back to get him to go down the slide!"

The fat boy flipped off Sammy, adding salt to the wound. Darkness was falling on the park as Connor's eyes turned a dark purple. Sparks of red ignited deep in his corneas. "How dare you!" he growled at the bully.

The kid stood there, terrified of the dangerous man approaching. Fear planted him in his spot as Connor set his sights upon the little shit that had hurt Sammy and her friend.

Recognizing the hell she had unleashed, Sammy panicked and held onto Connor's arm to stop him. His eyes grew bloodthirsty at the thought that Sammy could have died by being thrown off the slide. He took two heavy steps toward the little boy, who was now peeing his pants in fear.

"Stop Connor! Stop!" Sammy screamed, and threw herself in front of Connor, hugging him tightly around the waist. Shocked by her sudden embrace, Connor looked down at Sammy, her tiny grip tightening for dear life, begging, "Don't hurt him, Connor."

Connor melted, completely vulnerable to her will. Those big green eyes were almost hypnotizing him into compliance. How shocking it was that she had recognized his quick-to-kill complex, even though she had never seen him hurt a fly, let alone a human. Something deep in her subconscious had triggered her intuition, in a way she probably couldn't comprehend. Connor had a flicker of hope that her ancient memories of past lives could come back. And that hope completely disarmed him. "Okay, Sammy. If that is what you wish."

"It is. Don't hurt him," Sammy said softly.

The air lightened and Connor's eyes resumed his normal bright purple hue. He looked over at Tommy's mother, who was clinging to her child and looking fearfully at Connor with wide eyes. It was plausible that this was the last time Sammy would be allowed to play with her friend. Turning back to Sammy, who had finally let go of his legs, Connor said softly, "Let's go home."

"Okay," she said happily. Holding hands, they walked the three blocks to their house. "Did you see me hit him?" Sammy added. "Wasn't I brave?"

Connor chuckled, "Yes, you have a lot of fight in you, huh? That fighting spirit could get you in trouble, though."

"I live for trouble," she replied in a superhero tone.

"I sure hope not," Connor said. "If you were in trouble all the time, that would mean more work for me."

"I can protect myself," she said stubbornly.

"Hmm, let me double-check here," Connor said sarcastically while putting a contemplative finger up to his lips. "Who got pushed off the top of the slide? Who needed to be caught before she broke her neck on the ground?"

"Well. I. Uh. He. He was bigger than me!" she finally reasoned.

"You know, I used to know a heroine ..." he said with a sly smile.

Sammy's eyes lit up. "Another story?!"

Connor looked up, gathering his memories for the next story session.

This time he was determined to help teach Sammy a lesson about putting herself in danger. They walked into the house, Connor making sure to re-alarm the security system while she took off her boots. Grabbing a pillow and hugging it, she snuggled into the couch, ready for another adventurous story.

Connor sat down opposite Sammy, his purple eyes swirling with excitement and mystery. "Let me tell you a tale about a heroine facing incredible odds during the French Revolution..."

* * *

PARIS, FRANCE

JULY, 1789

The morning air felt crisp as a soft glow shone through cracks between the wooden boards of the rough shelter. Birds were chirping merrily outside, proclaiming to the world that it was now time to enjoy the day. A young man lay upon a straw bed surrounded by an odd variety of dogs. Some were favored by the higher nobility, no larger than a loaf of bread. Others were fantastic hunting dogs with rippling muscles easily seen beneath their layers of fur. Some of the dogs were more heavily coated than others, but all nine were closely gathered in this small hut. One of the great hound's ears perked up. The morning breakfast bell at the manor was gently ringing from across the courtyard. The first hound howled to the sound of the ringing bell, which woke the rest of the pack up. A cacophony of barks filled the quiet morning air.

"I guess it is that time again, isn't it," the young man said to himself as he swept his shoulder-length black hair into a loose ponytail. The rest of his outfit was fairly plain: a loose black shirt and tight black pants. Black shoes kept buffed to a high shine, part of the protocol when waiting upon aristocrats.

Well, *waiting upon them* wasn't exactly right. He was the kennel master, and his duties were to wait upon the dogs of Mademoiselle Stephanie Le Blanc. Although she was not permitted to keep the dogs inside the wealthy estate she had been adopted into, she made an effort to collect dogs she found unique. Some were retired hunting dogs the original owners had no use for anymore. Others were miniature dogs that required much grooming to keep their coats soft and untangled. Then there were the misfit dogs she would find on the streets, poor unfortunate souls born at the wrong time and trying to survive in the wrong place. Generously, she took them in and gave them a good life. Although she was bourgeois enough not to actually care for the dogs. She went out of her way to hire a kennel master to care for them— a young man she had stumbled upon who shared her generous attitude toward canines. He was loyal to her and dutiful in the care of her dogs. It was an odd arrangement, given the political turmoil that had befallen France. Dogs were the least of the nobility's concerns.

The young man rose and got to work feeding the dogs the best meat the chef had to throw out. Even eating the scraps from last night's supper, those dogs ate better than most of the townsfolk below the hill of the chateau. After feeding the dogs, it was the kennel master's job to keep them adequately trained, which he had grown quite skilled at, with the help of a couple of friends.

Then it was off with a bucket to the well, where they received regular baths and perfuming before a visit with Mademoiselle Stephanie. For the most part, the dogs were well-behaved while being groomed, but for some reason the hound he was bathing today kept acting up. It wasn't long before the kennel master was soaked and smelled as bad as his wet dog.

"Having some trouble there, Claude?" asked a voice from behind.

Claude smiled and glanced over his shoulder. "Well, I should have known you were around, Jean. Your presence always riles up the canines."

Jean smiled broadly, revealing his set of fine white teeth. Huskier than Claude, he had rippling muscles that revealed themselves under his shirt, with great tufts of brown chest hair that poked from the top of it. His hair was combed back smoothly for presentation, but his great big, bushy beard remained unkempt and wild. The same kind of wild was reflected in his eyes.

Jean walked with attitude—more than confidence, but not quite to the point of being arrogant. He knew no one would dare face him in a brawl. Yet he was humble enough to know that he wasn't the alpha in this city, and he respected that fact.

"You need to show them who the alpha is," he said with a cocky smile. In setting an example, he whistled and called all the dogs to sit promptly to attention.

Claude gave a small smile as he continued rinsing off the large hound, which was now sitting still. "Well, I have learned in my experience that authority builds followers, but it is compassion that keeps them loyal. Don't be too rough on your pack, Jean."

Jean's laugh was deep and hearty— a full belly laugh. "That is quite amusing, coming from you. Here, let me help you." Jean started to take off his shirt, revealing a rippling muscular torso along with the tips of a purple pattern on his right shoulder. The pattern swirled around his shoulder in an arc, similar to the hypnotizing pull of the moon. In the center of the design was a lone wolf crying out to the moon, the only one listening to its baying.

Claude's purple eyes glowed. "Don't go showing off too much skin. You might draw attention from the gossiping ladies of the court."

Blushing, he pulled his shirt back down. "Sorry, Claude, I forget about the mark." Getting down on his knees, Jean and picked up a delicate King Cavalier to clean and perfume next. Jean rinsed off the dog and working on untangling mud clots from its fur. "I could never forget how you saved my life, Claude. If you hadn't come along, my inner beast would have swallowed what remained of my humanity," he whispered the secret. There was a long silence before he spoke up again. "Why do you care for these dogs so deeply?"

"Because it pays well and gives me something to do in these long days filled with uncertainty." Claude finished with the hound and made sure to perfume it.

"There is another meeting tonight. Selina will be waiting for you," Jean hinted.

Claude didn't respond and gave no hint of his thoughts.

"I think she has a preference for you," Jean added.

A slight smile finally broke from Claude's lips. "She is a very admirable woman. I am glad that she invited me to these meetings."

"I think she wants your rod," Jean commented with a playful smile.

Claude nearly slipped on the wet stone in response to the straightforward remark. Jean always did speak his mind with no filter at all, but the fact that Selina's attraction to Claude was becoming common knowledge was bothersome.

"Then all the more reason I should attend the meeting tonight," Claude said. There was a brief silence before both men laughed. "Now, we must hurry if I am to bring Mademoiselle her dogs on time."

"Yeah, yeah. I have mixed feelings on that woman," Jean said with contempt.

Claude shot Jean a look. "Don't be harsh on her. She does what she can, given the constraints of her own status. It isn't all that easy being part of the elite, you know. Mademoiselle Stephanie tries to help out in the best ways she can."

"I still think she is two-faced. If she really supported the poor and the canines, then she would have given up all her possessions long ago and marched with us," Jean spat.

Claude refused to discuss this any longer. In times such as these, it was impossible to argue with the revolutionaries. Some were far too obsessed with their own beliefs to be open to other ideas. The two men finished washing the dogs and parted ways. Claude went to the gardens, where Mademoiselle Stephanie waited for her clean and pampered canine companions, while Jean went inside the mansion to wait upon other bourgeois needs and desires.

The dogs barked and yipped with glee at seeing their doting mistress.

Claude trailed behind the excited dogs toward Mademoiselle Stephanie, whose back was to him as she gossiped with friends. She was wearing a dress of embroidered silk, with a high collar and decorated with fine lace. Her powdered white wig rose had layers upon layers of white hair finely ornamented with silk flowers and leaves. As she turned to face him, her billowing dress flowed about her, revealing the intricate flower patterns stitched into it by a skilled artisan. Extending her white-gloved hands, she beckoned her beloved canines forward, their tails wagging madly.

"My beautiful dogs! It is so good to see you again," she squealed, her white, plastered face and exaggerated rosy cheeks glistening in the sun. Her rosy red lips were stretched into a thin smile as she picked up a small poodle. Instantly the poodle leaned in to lick her face. She chuckled and pushed the wet tongue away to avoid smearing her makeup.

"You all smell so good!" she commented, without the slightest attention to Claude, who had worked tirelessly to keep them groomed. Knowing his place, Claude stood by diligently, awaiting her next orders.

Mademoiselle Stephanie turned to her tea companion, similarly dressed in fine silks and jewels. "If you will excuse me, duchess, I must give these adorable dogs some attention before lunch."

"Go on and enjoy the sunshine, my dear," said the seasoned, older woman at the table, whom Stephanie was probably entertaining more out of duty than friendship. The young woman was not quite like the other bourgeois. Her father, a war hero, had sent her to Paris from somewhere in the east as a token of his loyalty. No one knew much about her, only that she knew the ins and outs of the French courts and could be counted upon for juicy gossip. Though assured that her bloodline was pure, everyone in the courts saw themselves above her. Stephanie might dress, speak, act, and be as conniving as the rest of the court, but she was looked down upon for not being a true Parisian. Still, her life was more comfortable than most Parisians, who had to scramble daily to find a scrap of food to eat.

Stephanie giggled and doted on the little poodle in her arms. "Let's go for a walk!" she said. The rest of the dogs bounced around behind her as Claude respectfully kept his place about ten paces behind.

As a good chauffeur would do, Claude assisted Mademoiselle Stephanie into her waiting carriage and then loaded all the dogs into a rack built for them in the back. Behind the carriage, he attached an additional, covered cart. Then, he snapped the whip and the horses pulled the carriage down the winding streets into the heart of Paris.

When the carriage finally stopped, Claude jumped off and opened the door for Mademoiselle Stephanie. She extended her hand, which he dutifully took to assist her exit from the carriage. Meanwhile, the dogs barked excitedly from the back.

Dutifully, Claude went to the back of the carriage and unloaded the dogs, who happily sprang out onto the street. Then he went to unhinge the cart from the carriage. A man approached nearby. Automatically, Claude put a large silver coin into his hand, and the man went to attend to the horses and find a more secluded place for the carriage— a silent agreement.

Mademoiselle Stephanie wore a large, red smile on her face. Not a normal reaction to the horrid smell that crinkled the noses of those unaccustomed to the stench of this neighborhood. What were once artisan shops and fine homes had become broken-down shacks in shambles that no one had even bothered to board up. Some structures had missing doors, while others were missing walls. If it weren't for the fresh piss and shit on the muddy cobblestones, it would be difficult to comprehend that people lived here.

Hungry little eyes of children and starving mothers gazed out from these dark abodes. Though Stephanie stood out similarly to a rose in a field of thorns, she seemed oblivious to the threat that lingered in the shadows. These days, it was dangerous to have any form of wealth. People of high social status had been dragged from their beds, butchered or shot while their homes were looted and burned. Some called Mademoiselle Stephanie naïve, while others called her stupid, but the poor called her an angel.

"Come here, little ones," she sang with her arms stretched wide. On cue, Claude uncovered the wagon, full of food: meats, breads, fruit and every scrap of food that hadn't been consumed during dinner last night. It might as well have been gold in the eyes of the hungry little children who darted

114

out first while the mothers waited warily in the shadows. Curious men craned their necks to get a better look. Keeping portions moderate to feed everyone, Claude handed out food to the children. They ravenously devoured the fine delicacies as their mothers came out to eat. The cart grew lighter as more and more hungry Parisians came out of hiding with empty stomachs.

Many had heard of a wealthy woman who came to feed the poor, but with her constant rotation through different neighborhoods of the city, only a few had ever encountered this generosity first-hand. Stephanie was gratified to be filling all the starving bellies with the finest food she could offer. Little did she know that most would suffer stomach aches afterwards, their bellies unaccustomed to such rich food.

"Stop!" gruffly shouted a dirty man on the street. "Stop it right now! Don't you realize that she could be poisoning us?" Angrily, he pointed a filthy, crooked finger at Mademoiselle Stephanie. "They want us dead so we will stop resisting them!" The women suddenly appeared concerned and stopped eating, regarding the food in their hands with suspicion.

"Monsieur, this is simply not true! I promise you, I only wish to help!"

The man spit on the ground in front of her, bringing tears to Stephanie's eyes.

"We should teach her a lesson! How dare she try to poison us?" he shouted to the crowd, which was getting riled up by his words.

A sharp, clear whistle cut through the air, prompting a sudden stillness after a sharp intake of breath. Before anyone could blink, three large hounds were pointing their sharp noses at the man, a low growl rumbling in their throats and rolling down the street as if it were a toxic gas. Frozen in fear, the man's eyes grew wide. No one made a sound.

Claude, in perfect command of the dogs, walked forward with the purposefulness of a predator, keeping his head low as he observed the fragility of the accuser. "No one ever said you had to eat the food presented. Why would such a man as yourself be threatened by a *petite femme* who only wishes to extend generosity to the needy?"

Claude's voice remained smooth and compassionate, yet his mannerisms suggested a deadlier secret. He walked closer to the man until their eyes were a mere six inches apart. The trembling brown eyes of the Parisian looked into Claude's cold, purple, calculating eyes. "I guarantee you that there is no poison in this food, because it was prepared by servants who walk these same streets at night. If you are too afraid to accept the gracious handout of a compassionate mademoiselle, then you can leave." One of the dogs barked as the other two growled ferociously.

"I'm so sorry, Monsieur, please have mercy." The man trembled.

"Don't apologize to me. Mademoiselle is the one you insulted," Claude stated coldly.

Peering over at Mademoiselle Stephanie, yet keeping an eye on the threat before him, the man mumbled, "I'm sorry, Mademoiselle. Please forgive me."

Astonishingly, she smiled back, grabbed a small loaf of bread, and ran over to offer it to the man. "Please, take some. If you have children, then feed them as well," she said graciously.

With a tremulous hand, the man took the loaf from her. "Merci. Merci beaucoup."

Before he could step away, Claude growled, "Take a bite of it, to show her that you are grateful for the food."

On command, he took a small bite and swallowed before he could savor the taste of the bread. "Merci." Then he bolted.

Loyalty chained the dogs by Mademoiselle Stephanie's side until the man had disappeared between the dilapidated buildings.

Turning towards the townsfolk, Stephanie announced, "Please take as much as you want. I promise you, it will help you feel better." To prove her point, she took a small cherry out of the cart and popped it in her mouth, savoring its flavor. Convinced now, the people scrambled towards the cart and cleaned it out, filling their stomachs and taking more to their neighbors. Stephanie happily watched the food being eaten. All the while, the dogs continued to roam between the legs of the Parisians, occasionally submitting to a pat. Claude remained a watchful statue, surveying the crowd for any signs of danger. Luckily, there was none.

Now that the wagon was empty, the crowd dispersed. Claude had retrieved the carriage and dutifully loaded the dogs in the back while Stephanie watched.

"Do you find my attempts silly?" she asked shyly.

He paused for a moment, surprised she had asked his opinion. Normally, she wouldn't lower herself to ordinary conversation with servants. He turned around with a light smile on his face, his purple eyes glowing. "Silly? *Non.* I don't think you are silly for wanting to share food with the poor. I find you incredibly stupid, though."

Shocked by his bluntness, Stephanie put a hand on her chest, offended. "Excuse me? Who said you were allowed to talk to me like that?"

"The one who prevented you from being torn apart by a mob. How many times has this happened in the last month? Oh, that's right … twelve! I find you incredibly stupid for thinking that you can walk through Paris, knowing that at this time the Parisians are tearing apart the bourgeois. Yet you foolishly think that if you give them food they will leave you alone. So, Mademoiselle Stephanie, I respectfully give my opinion, as the servant who has single-handedly saved your life a dozen times."

Stephanie desperately tried to think of some clever retort, but nothing came to mind. In her frustration, her eyes watered.

Claude felt abashed at his forwardness. He hated to see any woman cry. "I'm sorry, Mademoiselle Stephanie. It was not my place to state my opinion. If you wish to go gallivanting around the dangerous parts of town, then I shall dutifully trail behind you with your beloved canine companions."

Stephanie sniffled, "You only follow me because I pay you heavily."

Feeling bold, Claude did something he had never done before: he touched her shoulder to give her comfort. The warmth from his fingertips melted through her thick, decorous clothing and gave her some degree of comfort. "I have been dutiful to you and only you. Whether you pay me handsomely or not, I will be here to take care of the dogs and to make sure that you don't get murdered by a mob. … Now fix your makeup. Be sure you are always seen as high-born, lest you find yourself trampled under those bourgeois pointy-toed shoes."

Stephanie sniffled again, while dabbing her embroidered handkerchief at her cheeks, where the natural pinkness of her skin was starting to show under the pallid makeup. "Thank you Claude. Take me home."

"Of course, Mademoiselle," he said with a bow. Then he escorted her into her carriage and drove back to the safety of her chateau on top of the hill.

As he opened the door and stretched out his hand to escort her out, no hand appeared. A few moments passed. Thinking she might be napping, he peeked in and found her staring up at the chateau with an expression of dread.

"What's wrong, Mademoiselle?" he asked.

"At times, this feels like my prison—a place where I must be perfect or face the dire consequences," she said, her eyes brimming with tears that threatened to ruin her makeup again.

"Be strong, Mademoiselle, these fruitcakes dressed in drag are harmless," he encouraged with a wink.

A laugh erupted on her lips, which she quickly covered out of shame that it was not controlled. "You called them *fruitcakes*," she chuckled again.

"Well, what would you call them?" Claude joked.

Once again, her eyes gazed up at the chateau with resentment. "Cruel."

"Have no fear, Mademoiselle. You are safe in this chateau. It is heavily guarded and has thick walls." Once again, he stretched out his hand, which she finally took.

"All right, Claude. Thank you." Resuming her aristocratic posture, she climbed out of the carriage and proceeded inside, past the double set of guards. Claude politely waited for her to be closed within the safety of the walls before he set to his tasks of getting the dogs their evening meal.

A couple of hours later, Claude wove through a large crowd of slightly inebriated men all gossiping about politics. At the bar, the bartender greeted him with three large steins of ale, which Claude carefully carried through the crowd, being sure not to spill a drop on other patrons. He set the full steins down on a lopsided table where three others were already seated.

"Ah! The best way to end a day of kissing ass is to drown yourself in ale!" Jean announced triumphantly. Greedily, he took one of the steins and inhaled it so fast it dribbled down his beard.

"Don't drink too fast," joked a young man sitting next to Jean, "or you'll run out."

"Aw, Leo, that is when we buy more!" he shouted with rosy cheeks as he continued to drink.

Claude squeezed in on the other side of the table, next to a woman who winked and said, "*Merci, mon beau.*"

"Of course, *ma chérie*, anything for you," he said with a suggestive smile.

Her dark green eyes sparkled with hints of orange as her rosy cheeks reddened. Flirting her way closer to Claude, she fidgeted with the auburn hair that flowed down her back in a long braid.

"Oh Selina, stop the horseplay and have at him already!" Jean announced with a slight slur to his speech.

"You're getting drunk and rude," Claude chided him. "I'll cut you off early if you can't handle your liquor."

"Don't worry," Leo cut in, "he's jealous that a beautiful *femme* such as yourself would be interested in this odd guy."

"It's okay," Selina said with a smile, "I do find Claude strangely magnetic."

Claude exchanged a flirtatious glance with her, reducing his emotions to that of a juvenile. He could honestly say that he was attracted to her. Selina had introduced him to this bar, with its weekly justice rally. He supported their efforts in nominal ways to get closer to her. It was her resilience that drew him in, when normally he would not be so easily enamored. Known for drinking with the men, Selina could easily hold her own in conversation and feistiness. Men knew not to try to mess with her or touch her inappropriately, or they would find a dagger stuck through their hand.

Selina's readiness for the fight came from her upbringing as an orphan in the streets of Paris. She had learned to survive in ways that other women never found possible. There was never a man who slept with her whom she had not invited into her bed ... and never for money or favors. Most men could never meet her standards and would be thrown out of her room, buck-naked. No matter how much they begged to be allowed back in, her stubbornness always kept them naked in the cold. A strong and fierce woman, with dark green eyes and auburn hair. It was no wonder Claude himself had been curious and desired to get closer.

A man by the name of Rousseau stood upon a table and cleared his throat. The noise in the bar dulled to a whisper that snaked through the crowd. This was the man of the hour— the one man that everyone had come to hear. Rousseau spoke with the fiery certainty of a prophet, calling for the abolition of France's caste system and its wretched inequalities. To everyone in the room, he was their savior.

A charming smile that left dimples in Rousseau's cheeks only added to his magnetism. Clearing his throat again, he announced, "My brothers and sisters, I invite you all to think deeply on what I am about to say. We have accomplished much in the last months, yet we have so much longer to travel until we get what we deserve as citizens of France!"

The crowded bar roared in agreement.

Claude lost interest. His mind drifted to more mundane but enjoyable thoughts. To other Parisians, these midnight gatherings were history in the making. Yet Claude felt no interest; they seemed to be just another mob wanting their fair share of everything. He had seen it before, many times. It was all pointless, because he already knew the ending to the story. The villagers would either be cut down as the royal military infiltrated every street corner to enforce their justice, or the villagers would take over using their own cruel and bloody justice. Either way, it didn't matter to Claude. He had been in the middle of many coups, but this time he would stay out of it.

He peeked over at Selina, looking radiant, empowered by the words she felt were being spoken directly to her. She had so much drive and motivation, it was almost sexy. That fierce determination in her dark green eyes made Claude smile. He was happy to have come to the meeting, only to spend a little time with her. Selina was his picture of lady liberty, and he would fight for her to the death if given the chance. Claude hoped that she would stay alive long enough to see her efforts in this rebellion bear fruit.

To his surprise, she stood up and shouted over the crowd: "We shall get our justice, even if we must spill our own blood so that our children may live freely! We shall follow you, Rousseau!"

The rest of the crowd roared in excitement.

Claude was dismayed. Rousseau's speech went on for another hour, Claude paying more attention to the crowd than the speaker. It wasn't just burly men, but also women and the elderly. Children weaved between legs to deliver more drink to the already intoxicated. Claude drank another ale, knowing it wouldn't affect him in the slightest. After the speech finally ended, the crowd dwindled and it became possible to see the floor again.

"Wasn't he incredible?" Selina asked excitedly.

"He sure was!" Jean added.

"Anybody want another drink?" Claude proposed as he began to get up.

Selina grabbed his arm. "Please, Claude." She winked at him as she stood up. "Let me buy you a drink for once."

Claude sat back down with a smile on his face as he watched her walk away, her hips seductively swaying, accentuating her perfect curves.

"Do it!" Jean whispered as he leaned over the table.

"Do what?"

"Do her!" Jean said suggestively.

Claude laughed it off. Then a sly, cunning smile crossed his face. He wasn't about to kiss and tell.

"All right, boys!" she said triumphantly, holding a large stein. "Here you go, Claude." After setting down the stein in front of him, she kissed him on the cheek. Still not used to this sort of affection, Claude blushed slightly and then looked at his drink. He couldn't help but notice that something had been added to it, particles still swirling in the bubbling ale that soon dissolved. He first wondered if she was trying to poison him but quickly concluded that was ludicrous, seeing as how she was always flirting with him. Perhaps she hoped to get him to loosen up. He knew such efforts would have little effect on him, but he would let her believe it did. It would be more fun if she believed him to be intoxicated. Claude took a large swig and thanked her kindly. She seemed quite pleased with herself and grew more suggestive the more he drank.

After Jean and Leo were too drunk to hold a conversation, let alone hold themselves up without swaying, they stumbled out, singing their merry way home.

"How do you feel?" Selina asked seductively as she slid her hand on his upper thigh.

Claude quickly stopped her hand and checked to make sure no one saw. She chuckled, thinking him shy. The table was covered in empty beer glasses. He had consumed four giant steins himself and admittedly felt a buzz from the spike of the alcohol in his blood. Returning a seductively raised eyebrow, he replied, "I feel quite intoxicated, thanks to your efforts."

Selina wrinkled her nose and asked, "Oh really? Well, in that case, will you walk me home?"

"You might need to lead the way, as I have never been to your home," he teased.

"Mhm, sure you haven't. Come along," She pulled him up from his chair and led him by the hand outside. The air was getting cold, foretelling a winter soon to come. Selina bundled herself tighter into her thin clothes. Claude, always radiating heat, wrapped an arm around her to keep her warm. "Such a gentleman. I can't wait for you to show me how ungentlemanly you can be."

"Why, whatever do you mean? I wasn't planning on going into your house," he coyly smiled.

Playfully teasing back, she fluttered her eyelashes back at him, "Well I was."

Claude looked down at the temptress in his arms and was pleased that she was indeed more enamored with him than any other man. It surprised Claude is that he was so open to her. She was just a human, after all.

"How about this, I will do whatever you command of me," Claude started.

"Ooooh," she said rolling her shoulders back which made her cleavage temptingly available.

"In return, you stay with me and promise me you won't go to any more of those raids," he added in negotiation.

Selina shortened her step for a moment and gave him an incredulous look. "You almost sound sober."

On cue, Claude tripped and almost fell on his face.

Selina laughed it off. "Apparently not. Why does it matter if I go or not? I support a free France. *Liberté, égalité, fraternité!*"

Attempting to slur his words, Claude replied, "There are other ways you can help the revolution without picking up a musket."

Silence filled the small gap between them before Selina finally responded, "All right. I promise to not wield a weapon and go raiding. In return, I expect you to succumb to my every whim!"

"Deal," Claude agreed. Content that he was extending her life a few years longer.

They finally reached her house, a shack that was held together by scavenged boards and rusted nails. This didn't matter to either of them. Selina playfully handed Claude the key, which he took and started to open the door. The second the lock was released, she tackled him and pushed him in the house. The door was quickly slammed behind them.

* * *

"Uuuhh," Connor paused, a light blush growing on his pale cheeks.

"Why'd you stop? What did they end up doing?" Sammy asked.

Shyness descended on him. She was only nine years old, and though she'd had the talk about the birds and the bees, there was a way to go before she understood the intimacy between a man and a woman.

"They, uh,"—Connor cleared his throat— "They had sex."

It took a moment to register, but when it did, Sammy twisted her face in disgust and shook her head to rid herself of the thought.

A loud laugh burst from Connor, as he made the delicate decision to

123

skip pieces of story she wasn't old enough to understand.

Vividly aware of Sammy's eyes dissecting the intimate thoughts locked in his head, Connor cleared his throat and continued.

* * *

Two hours later, Selina woke. She looked over at Claude, lying on his stomach, breathing softly as he slept. Slowly, she sat up, careful not to wake him, and noticed a unique marking on his back. It looked as if someone long ago had ripped a large chunk of his skin off, in a strip that trailed from right shoulder to left hip. It had left a glistening scar resembling reptile scales in the moonlight. When she touched it, the mark felt smooth and warm to the touch. Not wanting to wake him, she resisted the urge to keep touching him and continued to slowly get out of bed, careful not to stir him. Soundlessly, she dressed, watching Claude to make sure he didn't stir. Then she grabbed her pistol off the table and headed out the door, glancing back for one last look at Claude.

The moment her foot left the front step, Claude opened his swirling purple eyes and sighed deeply. He had really hoped she stayed in bed.

Stephanie jolted awake and frantically searched her bedroom. Her breathing was rapid, her heart racing frantically, her pupils dilating in fear. Something had awoken her, but she couldn't discern what. Everything in the room was quiet and still. The tall white wigs still stood on the boudoir table as if they were lingering spirits. The separated layers that made up her daily outfits were awaiting the hours until they would once again constrict her breathing. The vast dimensions of her room were constant reminders of how alone she truly was. Then, over by the door, she saw a dark shadow, slouching. Stephanie gasped and pulled the covers tighter. The shadowy figure slunk forward as if it were a demon about to drag her down to hell. Fear overtook her as Stephanie inhaled deeply to let out a scream. Before a sound could leave her lips, the dark shadowy figure was suddenly on top of her. One hand held her mouth, while the other gently held her jugular, keeping her completely mute.

"Stephanie, please don't scream. I mean you no harm," whispered a familiar voice.

Immediately, she recognized that voice and the purple, swirling eyes.

"I'll let you go, but you can't scream. I'm here to help you, Stephanie. You are in great danger." The hands were slowly raised from her throat and mouth.

"Claude?" Stephanie asked in disbelief, "What are you doing here? How did you get into my room?"

"There's no time for that. I need to get you to safety," Claude said in a panicked voice as he pulled her off the bed.

"Let me get dressed first," she said, concerning her white silk nightgown.

Claude kept pulling her hand, forcing her to follow him to the window. "There's no time for that, we must go now!" he urged as he opened the curtains.

At that moment, Claude saw a mob of Parisians surrounding the chateau with guns and torches. A glass bottle tipped with fire came spinning through the air headed right for the window. Reflexively, Claude wrapped his body around Stephanie, protecting her. In the next second, the window shattered and shards of glass flew into the room. A fire erupted, rapidly consuming the curtains and moving to the wall. A shard had left a deep gash in Stephanie's arm. As Stephanie screamed in terror, Claude rose and made a sweeping motion with his arm, as if wiping mud off a flat surface. The fire obeyed and was immediately extinguished along their path to the door.

"Come on," Claude urged Stephanie, who was frozen in place, her green eyes glistening. Her long, auburn hair, normally hidden under a white wig, hung down around her face.

"We don't have time. I need to get you out of here now!" Forcefully, he pulled her towards the door. He kicked it right off its hinges, not caring about the intricately carved wood. The mob could be heard smashing and trampling far corridors of the vast house.

Claude kept his senses alert to danger. Soon, there would be no avoiding the mob. He had to get Stephanie out of there quickly if he wanted to save her life. Claude guided her to the servants' area in the kitchen and found himself confronted by two men with muskets. He pushed Stephanie down face-first to save her from being targeted, then jumped on the first man, twisting his neck at an angle that made a loud pop. Then he grabbed the musket from the stunned second man and used it to bash his skull in. As the second man fell to the ground, Stephanie watched Claude extending his hand. Bewildered, she took it and was sharply pulled up.

They bolted to the kitchen exit, only to be halted by a group of angry Parisians holding homemade weapons. Seeing Stephanie in her silk gown, the mob spilled into the room. Claude threw Stephanie over his shoulder and ran. A second later, he felt a sharp stab in the back of his upper thigh— a knife. He pulled the blade out of his leg with a grunt, blood pouring from the wound as he ran on, until he found an undisturbed smoking room. Carefully he put down Stephanie, her green eyes vacant, overwhelmed by the horrors she had seen. So many bodies Claude had jumped, so much death, so much rampant hatred.

"Stephanie," Claude spoke softly. Her vacant gaze gave no response. Claude grabbed her shoulders, "Stephanie, stay with me."

Tears once again poured down her face. "How did it all come to this? What did I ever do to deserve such hatred?" She cupped her face in her hands and burst into sobs.

"Stephanie, I need you to be strong right now ... just a little longer until we find a safe way out." Claude tried to get her attention again, to no avail.

He focused on the task at hand— to find a safe way out. Suddenly, he remembered a servants' passageway in the adjacent room. If they could get to it, they would be home free. "I think I know how we can escape," he said excitedly. Claude ran out of the room and across the hallway, where the entrance to the servants' secret door was still untampered. Relieved to have found a way out, Claude raced back to the smoking room.

Bursting in, Claude announced, "I found a way out!"

"Oh, did you now?" responded a cold, silky voice.

Claude's heart hit his stomach as his eyes fell upon Selina, standing to

126

Stephanie's side. In Selina's hand was a pistol, forcefully pressed against Stephanie's temple, tilting her head to the side. Claude looked at the two women who dominated his life. They were similar enough to be mistaken for sisters. Approximate ages with the similar facial features and body types. Both had green eyes and flowing auburn hair. Yet they were opposites in every other way.

Selina was a fiery woman, drooled over by men— a commanding woman who fought her way through life and demanded respect. Selina was courageous, tough, and a born leader.

Stephanie was delicate and had never gone without food for even a few hours. She had never been exposed to the harshness of the world, but knew about cruelty and loneliness. It had made her a kind and generous woman who tried her best to assist those in need, from poor child on the street to the forgotten mutt no one wanted. Her fearlessness fought the caste system in a different way. Stephanie had risked her entire livelihood to bring food to those in need.

"Selina," Claude whispered.

"I knew you would choose her over me." she spat, her face full of hatred.

"Please," Stephanie whimpered. "I can help you."

"Shut up!" Selina commanded.

Stephanie quieted down.

"Selina, put down the gun. It doesn't have to end like this," Claude said cautiously, taking a small step forward.

Selina pushed the gun harder into Stephanie's temple, prompting Claude to stop moving. "I knew you didn't fully understand why this revolution meant so much to us, yet I never thought you would stoop so low to save one of *them*."

"Stephanie is different; she supports your cause," Claude said, while venturing another small step towards Selina.

"I thought you loved me!" Selina screamed. "Why would you save a filthy wench?"

"I will do anything you tell me to do, Selina, just don't make this mistake. Do not stoop so low as to murder an innocent woman," Claude begged, while taking another step.

"Don't fucking move!" Selina screamed.

"I will do whatever you command of me, Selina. I will help you win this revolution. I can help you in ways that you could never imagine, but please don't kill her. You are not a murderer," Claude promised. One more step. Now he was within range to be able to reach them if he lunged, but it would still be a stretch he wasn't comfortable with … even with his superhuman speed.

A single tear ran down Selina's cheek. "I'm sorry, Claude." She closed her dark green eyes and turned her head away from the gun.

The deafening sound of the gunshot echoed in the smoking room. The smell of gunpowder permeated through the ancient smell of tobacco. Then came an unsettling silence that struck a chord of fear deep in the heart.

Claude stared at the ground. The silence of death rattled him deeply. He would have preferred a knife in his stomach to the twisted agony in his heart at this moment. In the profound silence, he heard a drop of blood hit the floor. He glanced at it, then at the dagger in his hand from which the blood came. It was the same dagger that had been embedded in his leg moments earlier— a wound that was already healed. Then a gurgling sound cut the silence sharper than the droplet of blood. Claude drew his gaze up into Selina's shocked eyes. A curtain of blood cascaded down her neck, drenching her front. Not a word was spoken, but her horrified dark green and orange marbled eyes said it all.

Claude watched her fall forward and bleed on the floor until her body lay still. He had grown fond of Selina and considered marking her. She was beautiful, brave, courageous, but uncontrollable. She would have been dangerous if given more power. Still, Claude couldn't help but feel saddened by her death. Perhaps she reminded him so much of *her*. Yet when the worlds aligned, Selina could never have been *her*. There were far too many signs that this was not the woman he was searching for.

As if finally connecting the dots, Claude looked over at the woman he had been searching for. Stephanie trembled fiercely from her unlikely escape from death. It had all been a blur to her. At one moment, the gun was pressed firmly against her skull. When she heard the click of the trigger, she closed her eyes, unwilling to see her own death reflected in Claude's gorgeous purple eyes. The gun resounded, and to her surprise, she was alive. The gun had been thrown to the other side of the room before it discharged, Selina's throat had been slit, and Claude was magically at her side. It had all happened so fast that Stephanie couldn't even begin to comprehend what had transpired. Staring down at Selina's body, lying in a pool of blood, Stephanie gasped and sobbed.

Instantly, Claude was in front of her, holding her tight. For a few minutes, she buried her face in his chest, moistening it with her tears. Claude held her close and rubbed her back. This was a comfort he secretly desired for a long time.

After a few minutes had passed, Stephanie looked up and asked, "Why did you save me and kill her?"

Claude's dark purple eyes remained soft and compassionate. "Stephanie, I saved you because I love you. I killed her before she could kill you. Is that not a simple enough explanation?"

Stephanie cried harder into his chest. Claude lifted her chin up gently to look him in the eyes. "Stephanie, we have to go now. There is a secret passage. Once we are out of this burning building and past the gate, you will no longer be in danger. Then we can leave this place and go wherever your heart desires, but we must leave now!"

Stephanie gave a slight nod. Grabbing her hand, Claude pulled her through the door into the room opposite, found the decorated panel that marked the entrance to the secret passageway, and gave the small upward tug needed to open it. It was small enough to crawl through to escape. Suddenly, he heard chaos in the hallway.

Claude grabbed Stephanie's arm, directing her towards the passageway. "You go first. I'm right behind you."

Obediently, Stephanie bent down and crawled in, as the door to the room burst open and men with muskets flooded in. Claude faced them head-on as they shouted: *"Vive la révolution!"*

As calm as a predator ready to strike, Claude steadied his stance and lifted his hand to his mouth. Extending his pinky, he inhaled deeply and exhaled through his fist, blowing out flames of brilliant purple that immediately consumed the entire room. All the men who stood before him were reduced to ashes. Content in his defensive measures, Claude turned back towards the hole and climbed in after Stephanie.

Stephanie kept crawling, but was hindered by her long gown catching under her knees.

"Move!" Claude commanded, "Go, go, go! Before they realize where we are headed!"

"I'm trying to move as fast as I can," Stephanie said, panicking, but pushed to move faster by Claude's commanding voice.

Finally, they felt a cool, fresh breeze that told them their salvation was near. The tunnel had felt miles long, though it was only about twenty meters. The end of the passageway was tilted at an angle, rusted and damaged.

"Keep moving! The second you get outside, run for the wall," Claude commanded from behind.

Stephanie pushed hard on the panel that enclosed the end of the tunnel. Luckily it gave way with ease and Stephanie tumbled out. As she rose, she stood still, her back blocking the entrance.

"What the hell are you doing? Run!" he yelled at her before nudging her away enough to jump out of the tunnel.

The second his feet hit the ground, a cacophony of gunshots rang out. Claude saw about a dozen men with muskets aimed right at him from various angles. He knew it was too late. The musket shot cut into their bodies before they'd even had time to raise their hands to protect their faces. Time seemed to slow as Claude watched Stephanie's body being struck, her face contorting, their blood being sprayed against the wall and each other. Stephanie's back arched delicately as she fell, similar to a graceful bird plummeting to earth from an interrupted flight. The world spun as Claude fell as well. The shot that entered his skull made the world fuzzy and full of shadows.

Stephanie looked over at Claude, her voice mute, yet he could make out one word on her lips: "Caspian." Before her body hit the ground, it burst into millions of tiny purple wisps that floated up into the air. Claude's body hit the ground as his world went completely black.

The sun peeked over a horizon filled with hundreds of columns of smoke escaping into the sky. Claude opened his eyes to see the sky painted red, a sign that much blood had been spilled that night. His body refused to respond. Already the flies were gathering around him. The more he stirred, the less bothersome they were. Inspecting his blood-spattered body, Claude knew he still had much healing left to do. If he pushed it too hard, it would shut down on him again. He could feel his organs rebelling at his attempts to sit up. No doubt there was shot remaining in his flesh. Pathetically, he fell back to the ground, his head lolling to the side.

So much blood had stained the ground that it was difficult to discern how much was his and how much Stephanie's. It's no wonder he had been left for dead. Anguish struck him hard in the chest, paralyzing him further. The emotional torture that constrained him was too much to bear.

"I almost saved her," he whimpered and put a hand over his eyes. When at last he removed his hand, his purple eyes had turned a red deeper than that of the bloody sky overhead.

"I almost saved her," he growled. A new surge of energy washed over him. Fighting against the stiffness, Claude pushed his body to sit up, which was no small task. He was panting but refused to stop.

"It's all their fault! They killed her," he growled deeper. He fought through the stiffness in his limbs and was able to get up to his knees.

"Humans are destructive, childish and cruel. They all deserve to die," Claude snarled. Using all the strength he could muster, he got to his feet. His body was resentful and weak, but Claude wanted to fill the streets with a river of blood.

For a moment, he staggered and swayed as his body rebelled against him and threatened another complete shutdown. Yet his anger and determination would no longer allow weakness to take over. Tilting his head back, Claude let out a long and powerful howl that rustled the leaves on the trees and produced ripples in the chateau's ponds and decorative fountains. His message sent, Claude stood stronger. His lips snarled in a constant low growl.

Barking could be heard in the distance, quickly replaced by the pounding of paws on the earth and stone. Within minutes, Claude was surrounded by the dogs he had trained, from the gigantic, ferocious hounds to the ankle-high toy dogs. They growled with him in unison. They would follow their master anywhere, he thought— perhaps even die for him.

A few minutes later, another, wilder pack appeared— four men and three women, led by Jean. All of them had a wildness in their eyes, ready for battle. Most were poorly clad, and one of the women appeared as if she had been living in the woods for some time.

Jean approached and asked, "What are your orders, Master?"

"Kill every last human who appears to be a threat. I don't care what side they are on," he growled. A couple of the others smiled, displaying a magnificent set of sharp, wolf-like teeth.

One of the pack, a female with bushy blonde hair and a curvy yet muscular body, gave her alpha a serious glance. They had a complete conversation with that look. Then Jean spoke for her, "Some are concerned that if they change when it is not a full moon, that they will never change back."

Claude looked at them all with piercing red eyes. In one quick motion, he ripped the shirt off Jean, displaying a large mark that resembled a tribal tattoo of a moon twisting around a howling wolf on his right shoulder. The thorns twisted and weaved on his skin, almost appearing to have a life of their own. Claude's own heightened emotions made the mark radiate purple.

"If you can show me your worth ... if you can deliver me one hundred dead bodies, then I will give you the ability to change at will and immortality," Claude stated and read the eager faces.

As the pack looked at one another in agreement, their eyes burnt yellow as their pupils turned to slits.

Claude barked orders, "Follow my command. Change only when you are ordered to. Bring me back one hundred dead humans, with your teeth marks verifying the killing blow. I do not care from which side you take them. Then I shall save you all from your permanent morph, just as I did for Jean."

The four men and three women celebrated their triumphs prematurely. Jean looked upon his pack with pride, but turned to Claude with some concern. "What if they die?"

"Do you believe them to be that weak?" Claude growled.

Jean didn't respond. He didn't have to. He had faith his pack would easily be able to accomplish the objective, yet he worried that Claude didn't care about them enough to even consider the possibility of their death.

"Today, I shall bathe in the blood of the cold-hearted and narrow-minded Parisians," Claude growled, as he surveyed the city with blood-red eyes.

* * *

Connor paused, realizing that once again he had gone too far. In the past, he had tried to save Sammy from gory endings that would haunt her nightmares. He didn't know what came over him, but he continued to replay the memory, hinting at the darkness in his own heart. Just as always, Sammy rocked on her hands anticipating the next part.

"Sammy, I ... you don't have to hear this next part." Connor hung his head in shame.

"This story is about the French Revolution, isn't it?" Sammy asked, "My history books said that many people died because they all turned on one another. Though it was the werewolves that ultimately led to a free France for all."

"You know about that?" Connor's purple eyes twinkled.

"Mmhmm." Sammy nodded her head. "I watched History Channel. They said they knew about werewolves ending the war but had a hard time finding out when werewolves were involved. Do you know the real story?"

In a change of heart, Connor gave a smug smile. "I do, actually."

"How do you know?" Sammy asked curiously.

"Because two of my closest friends are werewolves," Connor explained.

"How? Werewolves aren't allowed in America. They are illegal." Sammy had been well informed through her homework assignments on government.

"Whoever said I've always been in America? Did you know I was born in Europe?" Connor released a little information about himself, information that was rarer than his storytelling.

"I didn't know that!" Sammy gasped. "Tell me more!"

"About myself, or Claude?" Connor began to redirect.

Sammy thought for a moment. "Let's finish Claude's story first!"

Connor chuckled to himself. "All right, then, but this next part is particularly graphic."

* * *

The town was bursting with chaos and destruction. Blood stained the streets and mixed with the sewage. Triumphant yells of patriotic fervor, and the horrific screams of those being slain filled the air. The city was too full of hatred to notice a monster in its midst. Most of the townsfolk who were no longer pillaging and killing were gathered in the center of the city, where a line of the socially elite had been lined up for slaughter. The "fair" method of execution they had chosen: beheading by guillotine. They believed it to be quick and painless, though they had failed to notice the twitching bodies left after the guillotine severed the heads. The crowd, consumed by mob mentality, cried out for more bloodshed. Little did they know their wish would soon come true.

Cloaked in black from head to toe, Claude slunk through the crowd similar to a wolf unseen in a flock of sheep. His faithful canine companions were even more invisible to the flock. The canines dutifully paused at strategic distances from one another in their deadliest attack pattern. Once they were all in position, Claude started whistling a tune familiar to the crowd— their revolutionary anthem. After the first few notes, other members of the pack joined in and whistled the tune as well. Confused, the Parisians started to sing their anthem. Near the end, Claude whistled out a sharp, high-pitched note that most humans wouldn't be able to hear. The second his lungs were empty of air, the screaming began.

Blood sprayed the streets and filled the air with crimson, painting the town red with patriot blood. Terrified and bewildered, the crowd had no clue where the danger was coming from until it was too late. The dogs ripped through the crowd. Even the smaller dogs played their part, killing a person or two before they themselves were dispatched by a solid kick.

The werewolves, on the other hand, were magnificent. Each jumped out of their skin at the perfect moment, their human flesh buried in the accumulation of dead bodies they quickly procured. Massive and beautiful beasts, they mostly resembled wolves, but with larger mouths, sharper fangs, longer claws and faster reflexes. These extremely skilled and intelligent monsters ripped through the crowd as though they were nothing more than white sheets blowing in the wind. The more the werewolves ripped apart the humans, the more their humanity they lost. They all knew the risk, though. Changing when it wasn't a full moon was risky enough. But if they tasted blood, they would be doomed to live in werewolf skin forever. And yet, they trusted Claude... no, they trusted their alpha, Jean. They had heard his story many times over.

Jean had turned during a partial moon in order to save his soulmate's life. Claude saw this act of heroism and was able to save Jean by marking him. In so doing, not only could Jean turn whenever he wanted and still return to his human form, but he also had increased strength and agility. The others wanted this gift so badly that they were willing to kill for it— and kill they did. By the time they were done, thousands of carcasses would be strewn about the streets.

Claude walked through the chaos and bloodshed. He could smell the fear radiating from the sweat of every victim in the streets. Some fought and died trying to overcome the wolves. Most fled and still died. All hope vanished. The smell of fear invigorated Claude. The overwhelming smell of blood in the streets awakened a deep hunger that he hadn't satiated in a long time. Dying wails of horror were continuous enough to play off a beat that Claude could dance to, a raucous melody from hell rhythmic enough to click the heels and dance as if he were a dark lord in a puddle of blood.

Returning to his old self again, Claude indulged himself and released his beast. The consequences of his actions over the next two hours would go down in history. Books would recall this day as the Flood of Blood. According to historical records, two thousand four hundred people were killed in a single day. When most students learn of this tragedy, their minds can't comprehend the brutality. One or two people is easy for the average human to understand and sympathize with. Once the numbers enter double digits, it becomes data. Ordinary emotions can't grasp what it would have been like to be a victim caught in that trap. Historians have tried to piece together the events in Paris that day. The best guess they could come up with was that King Louis XVI had ordered a massive slaying by his own private army of werewolves.

What came after the Flood of Blood was an upheaval that involved all the citizens of France, so vicious and massive that it was censored in high school history books. Throwing away the guillotine, the French citizens had their revolution and made sure that every member of the upper class was tortured for their crimes. Some believe werewolves assisted the French revolutionaries in their quest for justice, yet little evidence of this has ever been found.

Claude calmly sat upon a broken-down wall as he enjoyed a juicy red apple he found in a market stand. Taking a bite out of it, he savored its flavor and wiped the juice off his lips, along with some lingering blood that stained his chin. As he enjoyed this simple pleasure, his pitch-black eyes surveyed the destroyed streets of Paris, piled high with bodies. He was proud of his handiwork and felt no regard for the poor souls who died by his hands.

"Claude!" Jean called out from behind.

Casually, Claude glanced behind him and saw a disheveled Jean. Although his wounds had healed, his clothes remained torn and dyed red by Parisian blood. Following closely behind him was his female lover, Renee, and one of the males in their wolf forms. Badly injured, the poor creatures could no longer carry on, but still followed their leader. Another wolf was being dragged over the piles of bodies by Jean. This one had been severely wounded by silver bayonets. The poor beast wouldn't survive much longer, yet Jean continued to drag it toward Claude, in hopes he had the magic to heal the dying werewolf.

Refreshed and quite pleased with himself, Claude bounced down to join what was left of the pack. "I must say, I am quite impressed with you all. This is a marvelous sight!"

Jean let go of the werewolf. He lunged at Claude, who didn't appear threatened, and grabbed a handful of his bloodstained shirt. "Save them right now!"

"Or what? You'll kill me?" Claude mocked. Jean loosened his grip and let go in defeat. "You can't break what's already broken, I'm afraid." Claude stepped past Jean and leaned over the dying wolf. The other two wolves growled at him. Claude shot them a sharp glance, which instantly shut the werewolves up.

"Master, will you please save them?" Jean rephrased.

"Of course!" Claude said jovially. "They have proven their worth to me!"

"Thank you." Jean sighed with relief.

"I don't know if this one will survive it, though," Claude said, shaking his head.

"What?" Jean growled, quickly followed by the growling of the other two.

"Jean, my friend," Claude said sympathetically, "I can easily help out these two, but in order to be marked, you must undergo excruciating pain, not only in your body but also in your soul. If you are already in a weakened state, you will die during the procedure... as you well remember. I will try my best, but there are no guarantees that this dying pup will survive. It all depends on his will to live and if his body can pull through the pain."

"Will you at least try?" Jean begged.

"Of course," Claude said, with a smile that was much too bright given the situation.

Claude circled the dying werewolf, who was whimpering in pain. After a few moments of judging where to begin, Claude made his choice. Kneeling, he gently petted the blood-soaked fur with one hand, in an attempt to calm the trembling beast. Meanwhile, the other hand grew massive black claws. Gently, Claude coaxed the werewolf to raise its head and bare its neck. In a quick motion, Claude shoved his hand through the flesh of the wolf's neck, digging his hand deeper and deeper as the beast's back legs kicked defensively. The werewolf whimpered as Claude finally found the heart. Claude's black eyes swirled with a red mist as he planted his mark in the werewolf's heart. Suddenly the beast stopped moving. Ending the procedure, Claude ripped his hand out of the wolf, spraying werewolf blood everywhere. The beast lay motionless on the ground as Claude wiped off his hand.

"Who's next?" he asked enthusiastically.

The other two growled. "Is he dead?" Jean asked uncertainly.

"Well," Claude replied, "We will certainly find out soon. Now, should we do ladies first?"

Both of the werewolves growled. Not appreciating their responses, Claude immediately appeared behind them and knocked them both unconscious.

"What the hell was that for?" Jean shouted in fury.

"I couldn't have them biting me during the process," Claude said matter-of-factly. Kneeling down next to Renee, he searched for her sweet spot, and when he found it, he drove his hand up her rib cage. The werewolf woke and howled in pain. Within moments, the act was done, and Claude was wiping off his hand on her white fur before turning to the male werewolf.

As he was looking for the right spot, Renee morphed back into her human form. As she did so, the wounds on her body began to heal. Soon, she was standing as a human, naked on the street and not a bit ashamed. Renee attained the same purple swirling pattern that Jean had on his skin, only hers was smaller and wrapped around the front of her shoulder, not the whole shoulder.

Flipping her blonde hair back, Renee looked at Jean. "I'm alive!" she said, rapturously. They passionately embraced as lovers do, and then turned to watch Claude perform his magic.

Claude furrowed his brow as if there was something wrong. Taking a deep breath, he plunged his long, clawed hand under the creature's armpit. The beast made a few whimpers and then remained silent. Claude ripped his hand out of the werewolf and then laid his hand on the thick fur. Claude looked up at Jean with sad eyes. "I'm sorry, my friend, but this one was not strong enough to survive the mark." True enough, its heartbeat had stopped, along with its breathing.

"So I was ze only one to survive?" asked Renee.

"I wouldn't say that," Claude said with a wink.

Jean and the female werewolf looked back at the first, the dying one, and saw that he had returned to his human form. His body was still recovering from the massive damage that had befallen him, yet he was conscious. A purple mark of a midnight moon twisting around a howling wolf glowed against the pool of blood in the streets, then dimmed. As Jean and his female companion shared words of encouragement and praise with their wounded brother, Claude walked away with a smile on his face. That day he walked away from Paris, content with the thought that it would be a long time before he ever returned to the city of blood.

* * *

"Wow!" Sammy said with wide eyes. "Did that really happen?"

"What do you think?" Connor teased.

Sammy thought about this a moment, kneading the teddy bear as she did. "I guess it could have happened. Why did Claude have to kill Selina, though?"

It was a tough question and an even tougher answer. Connor wrapped his arm around Sammy and drew her in close. "There's something to be said for loyalty. Claude was loyal to Stephanie, just as Jean was loyal to Claude. You see, Claude had promised to protect Stephanie, so in order to keep that promise, he had to eliminate the threat. It hurt him deeply, but that is what he had to do."

"But Stephanie still died," Sammy replied somberly.

"It appears you didn't quite catch her heroism in this story. Stephanie chose to stay in France so she could feed the poor. She felt she had a mission to save those whom she felt couldn't save themselves. Claude had an exit plan for Stephanie. Told her many times about a way out, but she never took it. Her heroism kept her in that chateau, despite hearing the stories of all the other wealthy houses that were getting pillaged daily. So in a way, it was her heroism that ended up killing her as well."

Sammy stared down at her teddy, the gears in her nine-year-old brain processing so hard that it might have created smoke. Finally, Sammy said, "I can see why you didn't want me to be a heroine today. Doing good still means that you can get hurt."

"That's my girl!" Connor congratulated her.

Sammy defiantly added, "But I still think what Stephanie and Selina did was right. I would rather be a heroine like them than a coward who doesn't stand up for what is right."

"Sounds as if my job got harder, didn't it?" Connor sighed, then turned on Sammy, his fingers wriggling under her armpits until she was laughing so hard she could barely breathe. Once she calmed down, Connor added, "I promise to protect you, if you will let me."

"Okay, Connor, but be better than Claude. Don't let me die," she responded.

"Haha! You won't die on my watch!" Connor said with a laugh. Sammy laughed with him, not knowing the painful truth in his statement.

6

MAN'S BEST FRIEND

LONDONDERRY, NEW HAMPSHIRE

DECEMBER 25, 2006

Sammy urgently raced downstairs with a smile on her face that reached from ear to ear. Her long, auburn hair hung down to her waist in two long braids that bounced against her back as she hopped down the stairs enthusiastically. The rush of adrenaline was making her sweat inside her brand-new Christmas pajamas. With both feet together, Samantha jumped down the last couple of steps and landed with her feet planted and arms raised as if she were a gymnast. Then she sped around the corner and ran into the living room, where her breath was instantly taken away. The whole room glowed with twinkling lights and tinsel. The space around the Christmas tree was filled with presents. Her stocking on the fake fireplace was so full that a second stocking had been added by Santa. A small train made little puffs of smoke as it circled the lit Christmas tree and the presents. On a small table in front of two beige leather couches was a plate with six partially eaten cookies, an empty glass of milk, and half-eaten carrots. Underneath the plate was a note written on red paper that glittered in the same manner as tinsel. Sammy ran over and picked up the note, which read:

Dear Sammy,

Thank you for the delicious homemade cookies and cold milk. They have helped give me the energy I need for my long night ahead. Have a joyous year, young Sammy.

Merry Christmas,
  Santa

Sammy read the note a couple of times, pausing to peek over at the Christmas tree with eyes full of wonder. Finally she dropped the note on the table and ran over to the tree. She was so excited at the abundance of gifts that she didn't know where to start.

"Merry Christmas!" Connor called out from behind her.

Sammy turned around. Connor was wearing a red, fluffy Christmas sweater with the image of a sparkling Christmas tree. This was odd attire compared with his normal head-to-toe black.

In one hand, he held a giant Santa cup filled with hot chocolate and marshmallows. In his other, a plate of coffee cake and breakfast egg-sausage casserole, all of which were Christmas traditions Sammy's father had set from the time she was born.

Over the years, Connor had always been sensitive to the little things, such as these Christmas traditions— setting shoes out for St. Nicholas Day, seeing the lights on Christmas Lane, going to pet and feed the reindeer at a nearby farm, baking Christmas goodies, attending a Christmas play, and reading a Christmas story on Christmas Eve. All the little things that mattered to Sammy had made a huge difference in giving her the Christmases she deserved. It also helped that Connor spoiled her beyond her wildest dreams. Still, it was all these little moments that Connor cherished the most, such as watching her tear through wrapping paper on

Christmas morning with a hot-chocolate mustache.

"Merry Christmas, Connor!" Sammy said. She ran over and gave him a tight hug. Connor cherished every embrace and sealed those memories away.

"What are you waiting for?" he asked with a jolly smile. "Let's see what Santa brought you!"

Sammy's eyes lit up. "Okay!" She took a long gulp of hot chocolate, then set it on the coffee table before running over to her presents.

Connor watched her open gifts for the next two hours. She started with her stocking first. Her greedy eyes surveyed all the chocolate it held, but it didn't occupy her for long before she dived into her mountain of presents. Among the many toys were games, both educational and fun. Ultimately, Sammy requested books … lots of books that were well above the normal reading level for her age. It amazed Connor that, although she was only ten, she was reading at a high school level.

As Connor watched her open up her presents with wide, glistening eyes, a warmth spread in his chest and a soft smile relaxed on his face. Sammy had this uncanny ability to bring a surge of a foreign feeling in Connor: happiness. He felt it genuinely whenever he witnessed all the perfections and imperfections that made her who she was … who she always was. Watching her as an innocent and happy child made Connor wish she would never grow up to face the horrors of the cruel world that awaited her. Part of him wished he could keep her boxed up in this happy little home full of presents, glistening lights, delicious smells of holiday food and Christmas music in the background. Sadly, he knew this was only a wish. Sammy would grow up and, as children do, would discover the world.

"I'm hungry!" Sammy complained.

Snapping out of his head, Connor readjusted his vision and smiled at Sammy. "Oh, really now?" He checked his watch. "I'll heat you up more breakfast casserole if you wish."

"Okay!" Sammy piped up, with a smile on her face.

As Connor was standing up, the doorbell rang. He expressed excitement towards Sammy and said, "I wonder who that could be!"

"I don't know," Sammy responded, puzzled. They never had visitors. Every now and again a missionary would show up and be escorted off the property. Occasionally, one of the administrators from Valda Enterprise would arrive to give Connor an official report. Then there was the rare "friend" that Connor would set up as a play date for Sammy.

"Let's go look!" Connor exclaimed, grinning from ear to ear.

"Okay!" Sammy jumped up and bolted to the door. Connor followed closely behind, put in the security code and unlocked the door. When he opened it, Sammy peered around the door and saw a large box wrapped in red velvet with a large green ribbon. On top of the box was a note. Curious, Sammy took the note and read its green letters.

Dear Sammy,

I am so sorry, but I appeared to have missed one present last night when I was making my delivery to your house. So I decided to make an extra stop so this very special present made it to you in time for Christmas morning.

Deepest apologies,
  Santa

While Sammy was reading the note, Connor picked up the large velvet box and brought it inside. After shutting the door, he balanced the large box on one hand while he put in the security code and locked the door. As he was doing so, the box nearly fell out of his arms, but he was able to catch it just in time. Sammy laughed at his blunder and then hopped behind him as he walked the box into the living room.

"What is it? What is it?" Sammy asked enthusiastically.

"I don't know," Connor replied playfully. "You'll have to open it and see."

The second he set the large velvet box down, Sammy unwrapped the cloth. As she did so, the box shifted. Sammy looked over at Connor with curious, excited eyes, then she tore the box open faster. The second the lid was open, a small golden retriever puppy leaped on her. Landing on her butt, Sammy giggled as she held onto the puppy licking her face. Connor pulled out a camera to take pictures as she rolled around on the ground with the puppy in pure glee. After a while, the puppy grew more curious about its surroundings and began sniffing around. Sammy ran over to Connor and hugged him tightly. "Thank you, Connor!"

"What are you thanking me for? Santa was the one who brought you the puppy."

"It's okay, Connor, I know that Santa isn't real. Thank you for the puppy! It's the best Christmas present I could have ever asked for." She dug her face into Connor's stomach and hugged him tight.

The warmth in Connor's heart spread throughout his entire body. He could remember only one time he had ever felt this happy.

"You're welcome," he said. "Anything for you. What are you going to name him?"

Sammy appeared perplexed in her response, "Connor, your eyes are green."

Connor was speechless.

"Sammy, are you going color-blind? My eyes are purple," he teased while pulling her off of him.

She stepped back in and palmed his cheeks to keep his head still. The puppy rustled the wrapping paper he was playing with as Sammy silently studied his eyes. "Nope, they're green," she said with certainty.

Still not believing her, Connor objected, "It's probably just the way the lights from the Christmas tree are reflecting in my eyes. That's all."

Noticing his bewilderment, Sammy suggested, "Go look in the mirror if you don't believe me."

"Fine, I'll go look in a mirror if it will make you happy," he said, shrugging. "In the meantime, why don't you go get your snow clothes on and take your new puppy out back to play in the snow."

"Okay!" Sammy rushed upstairs in a hurry, the floppy-eared puppy loping after her.

Connor went to the bathroom, hesitant to see his reflection. Exhaling deeply, he finally built up the courage and looked.

She was right.

Connor leaned in closer to inspect his eyes. No longer were they the swirling purple that he had seen for most of his life. They weren't even the bright red that glowed when he used his powers or even the pitch-black eyes that resonated with the horrors he had committed. No. His eyes were green— a green very similar to *hers* but not quite as vibrant. These were the same green eyes he'd been born with. It was so long ago since he last saw them that he had somehow managed to forget. It was with these green eyes that he first saw *her* ... it was with these green eyes that he first fell in love with *her*. After two thousand years, they were finally back.

Connor had never felt more vulnerable.

His first fear was that he had somehow lost his power. Double-checking, he snapped his fingers and created a small flame in the palm of his hand. In the mirror, he saw the red eyes ignite as they always had. Those red eyes were somehow more comforting than the green. From past experience, Connor knew that the second he was done using his power, his eyes should fade into a black, and then back to purple. To confirm this theory, Connor curled his fingers into a fist to extinguish the flame. Then he watched his eyes slowly fade from red and immediately return to green.

He was at a loss for words. Oddly, seeing those green eyes made him feel the happy nostalgia that green represented for him. Happy memories of *her* flooded his memory. They were memories of *her* laughing, rolling in fields of flowers with him, riding horses with him, and being alone together. All the memories of *her* that were so blissful and happy had historically caused him heartache. Now he felt something else ... Happy relief washed over him as if it were cleansing his soul. Watching those green eyes in the mirror, Connor saw a single happy tear form and then roll down his cheek. Connor touched the wet, foreign form of happiness and smiled.

"Are you crying?" Sammy asked incredulously.

Whipping around, Connor looked at Sammy layered in her snow clothes, with her new puppy patiently waiting by her feet. Connor knelt down and looked into the girl's vibrant green eyes with his own green eyes. That was when it all made sense. "Sammy, I haven't been this happy in a very long time. Making you happy and giving you a good life has been the best Christmas present I have ever received."

"Connor," Sammy asked, concerned. "Did you never get Christmas presents when you were a kid?"

Laughter erupted uncontrollably from Connor's mouth, and another tear of happiness rolled down his cheek. "Let's go out and play in the snow," he said with a larger smile.

"With Buddy?" Sammy asked, pointing at the golden retriever puppy.

"With Buddy," he confirmed.

Putting on not much more than gloves and a hat, Connor went into the large backyard with the girl and her puppy. It had been ages since he had been so carefree and blissful, throwing around snowballs and making a snow fort with Sammy.

In the midst of their play, Sammy surprised him with an authentic Christmas gift. "Smile!" she called out. As he turned to look at her, Sammy snapped a selfie of her big bright smile taking up half the screen, while Connor was half toppled by a snow-covered puppy.

Sammy turned the phone around and admired her photograph. "I like it! Can you print this one out for me? I want to put it on my dresser!"

Connor collapsed in the snow. He honestly didn't like pictures of himself, but there was no way he could deny her even this simple pleasure. "Sure!" he finally agreed, not knowing this picture would be the first of many she would collect over the years.

Sammy yipped with glee and jumped on top of him and Buddy, then proceeded to take more pictures of her first dog, Connor and herself.

For the rest of the night, Sammy drank hot chocolate with Connor while they played some of the new games she got for Christmas. Every now and then, Sammy would get distracted and play with her new companion, and Connor would simply watch, which was so profoundly satisfying he never wanted it to end. Connor couldn't help but think that this was the life she was supposed to live. All the lives she suffered through were never perfect. She had always experienced pain and fear at a young age. To Connor's best recollection, this was the first time she'd had a proper, naively happy childhood. Maybe, just maybe, this here was the answer—the thing that would break the curse that had plagued him for so long. Maybe the missing piece of the puzzle was happiness. If that was the case, maybe this happiness could even fulfill his own prophecy. Maybe … just maybe…

Sammy snuggled into bed after a long day. Buddy jumped on the bed with her and barked.

"No, no, no, down boy," Connor commanded.

Not understanding any commands yet, the puppy barked again.

"Can he please sleep with me?" Sammy begged, "just for tonight?"

"Now Sammy, you know that as soon as he sleeps on the bed once, he will always go on the bed. We should start training him now," Connor instructed.

Sammy pulled Buddy closer and wrapped her arms around his neck, "Please …" she said with puppy-dog eyes, "It is Christmas!"

He couldn't say no to those cute, glossy green eyes. It was embarrassing, letting Sammy have such sway over him. "Fine," he finally said, after raking his fingers through his hair, "but tomorrow he starts obedience training."

"Okay," Sammy agreed, as she snuggled in deeper.

"But if he pees on the bed, then you are cleaning it up. Not me," Connor lied.

"Okay," Sammy agreed nonchalantly as she petted Buddy.

"Was today as perfect a Christmas for you as it was for me?" he asked, sitting down in a chair next to her bed.

"Almost," Sammy said with a devilish smile.

"Almost?"

"Yep, I haven't gotten my story yet," she said, smiling from ear to ear.

Connor laughed. "Oh really now? But today has been so perfect, and my stories are so sad. I don't want to ruin today with another sad story."

There were those puppy-dog eyes again. "Then why don't you give an alternative ending this time … make this one a happily-ever-after," she suggested.

"I thought you said you didn't enjoy those ones? That they don't represent the real world?" Connor asked.

"I normally don't like happily-ever-afters, because they are fake. But … it is Christmas …" Sammy said.

"All right then. Let me think a moment …" Connor looked up and put his hand to his chin in an exaggerated fashion, then shot that same finger into the air, "Okay … I got one!"

Sammy excitedly hugged Buddy tighter and readied herself for another epic tale.

Connor's green eyes sparkled. "Let me tell you a tale of … the Samurai …"

* * *

EDO, JAPAN

DECEMBER 18, 1623

The carriage door burst open as a blur of green fabric and white lace jumped out. Her black boots hit the road, gathering dust around her feet. Standing up triumphantly, she took in her surroundings. The street was busy and full of foreign faces. There were women with white faces and red lips wearing floral kimonos with large red bows on their backs. The men wore plainer kimonos. Upon their hips were long katanas and short swords, tied in a ritualistic fashion. The locals had black hair that glistened under the hot sun. They all held their chins low and their backs straight. Some dared to peek at the bizarre pale-skinned girl with flowing, auburn hair that had abruptly jumped into the middle of their street.

For some, the English were welcomed as a way to bring prosperity to Japan. Yet most found the English very unsettling and did not like to acknowledge their presence in Japan. This social stigma flew right over the young girl's head as her green eyes surveyed the new town she would be living in for the next three months while her father conducted business. She was so excited for the new adventures that lay waiting for her in this bizarre town.

"Shelly! Get back in here this moment!" a gruff man yelled from inside the carriage.

Giggling mischievously, she disobeyed her father and ran into the crowd.

The man in the carriage rubbed the spot between his thick blonde eyebrows and wrinkled his forehead. He wore an English uniform befitting his high military rank. This was mostly for show, as he had never actually seen war. Mostly, he was a businessman who wished to establish trade with the Japanese. They wanted English firearms, and the English wanted Japanese teas, herbs and fineries. Ultimately, he would only give the Japanese outdated weapons, but these trades were going to open doors with these strangely foreign people.

Sir James Adams couldn't leave his eighteen-year-old daughter behind in England anymore because she caused far too much mischief while he was gone. Yet he now regretted bringing her along on this trip. In fact, he regretted following in his father's footsteps in trying to establish relations with the Japanese during such difficult times. The whole trip so far had been nothing but a throbbing headache.

Sir James picked up his ivory cane with a golden lion head and thumped it on the roof of the carriage. "Clark! Get down here at once!"

Some minor groaning sifted down from the roof. An empty jug of alcohol fell off the side and landed in the dirt. Then a person wearing all black clumsily fell off the top and barely caught his balance in the landing.

"Good heavens! Are you drunk again, Clark?" Sir James growled.

Dusting himself off, Clark picked up the jug and put it to his lips only to be disappointed by its empty contents. "I wish," he replied with a disgruntled sigh. He threw the jug on top of the carriage and leaned in the door. "How can I help you?" Clark asked with half-opened, pitch-black eyes and the smell of alcohol on his breath.

Sir James waved the air in front of his nose to help the stench go away. "Ugh, take a bath, why don't ya? Fetch my daughter again."

Clark turned around in a wobbly, drunken motion, peered into the thick crowd and then looked back at his employer. "Well, maybe you shouldn't have yelled at her again."

Sir James, infuriated by this insolence, pointed the cane into Clark's chest, pushing him away. "I did not hire you for your drunken wisdom, Clark! I hired you to guard my daughter. I will rip up your employment contract and leave you stranded in this godforsaken place if you give me lip again!"

Clark put his hands up and swayed backwards. "All right, all right, no need to threaten me. I'll go find her and bring her promptly back to the house, or whatever the hell they call it here," Clark responded, sweeping back the dirty, oily black hair hanging in his face.

"Then what are you waiting for?" Sir James asked.

"Aye aye, sir," Clark responded with a mocking gesture of an American salute.

Sir James merely glared at the young lad, standing there inebriated in the street. He tapped his cane against the front of the carriage, which the driver then put into motion.

Clark turned around in the crowd of curious Japanese that surrounded him and sighed deeply. "Why does she have to be so much trouble?"

Closing his eyes, he searched his intuition as to where she might have gone and then set off, weaving through the people. Curious and mischievous, Shelly would be drawn to the marketplace. He had made certain to walk the streets and map the area immediately after they arrived in port. He would need to know the ins and outs of the complex city of Edo and all the places an eighteen-year-old girl might hide from her father.

Clark didn't blame her for the impulse to run away from her hot-headed and sometimes violent father. It had been only three months since Clark had been hired as her bodyguard, yet he was already reaching his limit on standing idly by while she was disciplined for her curiosity. Whether it was being whipped for climbing trees in an orchard, being backhanded across the face for making inappropriate comments, or even being paddled for exploring London in the middle of the night, Shelly did not have it easy. Then again, it would be difficult for any child to have an overbearing father who demanded perfection from his only daughter. Sir James hoped to marry his daughter off to a wealthy nobleman and reap the benefits of the marriage … if only there was a lord foolish enough to marry such a wild woman.

That was where Clark came in. He was the glorified babysitter, tasked with retrieving the runaway daughter and keeping her safe from her own stupidities and her father's growing number of enemies. Not always an easy task, but Clark had ways of finding her.

He had a general feeling she was heading northwest, so he continued in that direction until he caught a whiff of her expensive perfume wafting in the air. He was getting close. As he passed by a public house full to the brim with men imbibing sake, Clark felt the addictive pull to drink some himself. Shaking his head, he realigned himself to the task at hand. There would be time for sake later.

Through a bustling crowd of topknots and plastered white faces, he saw her long, auburn hair drift into a building marked with a bizarre, segmented circle above the door frame. It took some effort to fight through the crowd, but he was finally able to cut his way over to the other side of the street. As he approached the building, the smell of sweet flowers and minerals overpowered Shelly's perfume. Taking a deep breath, Clark entered.

Immediately, he was greeted by a young Japanese woman who smiled and bowed as she said, in Japanese, "Welcome to Sakura Spa."

There was steam coming from cracks in the doors. Fresh, clean towels were neatly folded and stacked to about waist height.

"It will be 500 yen please," the woman continued.

Absentmindedly, Clark slipped some money into her hand without counting the amount. "Is this a bathhouse?" he asked back in Japanese.

"Yes, sir," she said with a sharp bow, slipping his money into her pocket. "This way, please." Silently and with small steps, she walked him to the men's bathhouse door.

Clark leaned in and saw about half a dozen naked men washing their bodies in preparation for entering the hot pools. Clark leaned in and asked her, "Where is the women's pool?"

"Sir, that is not allowed here. I'm sorry," she said with another short bow.

Irritated, Clark roughly pushed her aside and walked by. After catching her balance on the wet floor, she called after him, but Clark ignored her, poking his head into every entryway until he finally found the women's bathing area. Fully clothed and caring little for the naked women who shrieked around him, Clark hunted for Shelly.

He found her lounging in a green, outdoor pool filled with healing minerals. Closing her eyes, she dipped her head under the water, her long, auburn hair swirling around her. It was all so relaxing and calming she didn't care that the pool was filled with a dozen other naked women of all shapes, sizes and ages. As she was about to come up for air, a forceful hand grabbed her upper arm and yanked her out of the water. The pull was strong enough to lift her out completely and set her down on the stone path around the pool.

"What the bloody hell do you think you are doing, Clark?" she exploded at the bodyguard who was robbing her of her freedom.

A moment later he was wrapping a towel around her naked, dripping wet body. Clark noted the glowing purple mark hidden between her breasts, which trailed in a curving, symmetrical design down to her navel. "What am *I* doing? Shelly, what were *you* thinking? I told you not to draw attention to that mark! That was part of our agreement!"

"Stop yelli—"

"That mark is rare and can get you in a lot of trouble. I would have been less angry if you went shopping, not prancing around in your birthday suit where everyone could see you!"

"I'm sorry, Clark. I forgot," Shelly whispered ashamedly.

"It took you two days to heal from those wounds, even with my help. I thought you would be a little less reckless, knowing that you aren't invincible, just a little faster at healing," Clark grumbled.

"I said I'm sorry! What do you care? You get drunk all the time anyways!" Shelly shouted back with tears in her eyes. "In fact, you're drunk right now. Aren't you?"

"I am not drunk!" Clark yelled back, then felt the slight wooziness of the alcohol on his brain. "Possibly a touch inebriated— I wish I was drunk."

Shelly didn't respond to this comment. Clark could tell by the resentment in her face that she didn't exactly like him. Yet she felt obliged to follow his directions because he had saved her life and made it easier to heal.

"Come on." Clark motioned for Shelly to follow. "Let's go."

"I don't want to go back." Shelly pulled away from Clark, yet still held the towel up to cover her nakedness. "Father will punish me."

"Now, whose fault is that?" Clark spat back. "Besides, I was planning to find some way to persuade your father to spare the rod tonight. Now come on!"

"What do you mean?" Shelly asked curiously as she followed behind Clark.

"You got her a fucking dog?" Sir James screamed at Clark later that night.

Clark said nothing and took another swig of the sake he had bought earlier with his earned wages. After feeling the hot liquid coat his throat and warm his gullet, Clark finally answered. "Yes, I got her a fucking dog. She has been a nightmare for me as much as you. Now that she is responsible for something and preoccupied with training the mutt, she'll be less likely to create mischief." Or at least that was the agreement that Clark had made with her earlier that day. He hoped she could actually keep to this agreement.

"That girl deserves a belt, not a dog!" Sir James shouted.

Clark looked menacingly at Sir James for a moment, then averted his gaze to his sake bottle. "That girl got the beating of a lifetime a week ago. Why don't you try 'sparing the rod' for once like the good Christian you swear to be?"

"Fine!" Sir James agreed. "I'm too busy to deal with this, anyhow. If that dog ever becomes an inconvenience to me, then you have to be the one to kill it, Clark. Do you hear me?"

"Loud and clear," Clark responded nonchalantly, as he downed the rest of his sake.

"Not only do I have to do business with these stupid Japanese, but my daughter now has a yappy dog that *my* hired bodyguard bought for her. What a load of shit!" Sir James grumbled as he walked away.

Clark watched his employer disappear into his study. Once the coast was clear, he went into the enclosed garden, where Shelly was currently playing with her new best friend. The dog was cute, even for a mutt. Being only about knee height, the dog had yellow fur with brown blotches, including one that covered a floppy ear. It had a tightly curled tail that would wobble back and forth when happy. Ever since Shelly picked him out, the dog had been jumping and yipping in glee. Clark was happy to see Shelly happy. Knowing that she wasn't going to run away any time soon, and that she was safe in a heavily guarded house, Clark thought it best to reward himself with some more of that delicious sake.

Another month went by quickly. The days blurred into the same routine, which suited Clark and Sir James. Shelly was more studious than normal and took quickly to learning womanly arts of sewing and music. Occasionally she would beg Clark to join her, but he predictably chose the bottle over the violin. On the top of every hour, she would enjoy a fifteen-minute play session with her new dog, whom she named Inu, *dog* in Japanese. For her good behavior, her father allowed her to spend a couple of hours outside on the streets of Edo. Clark would, of course, have to accompany her along the way. Shelly enjoyed these outings the most, because she loved interacting with the Japanese, learning their language and customs. While Shelly enjoyed adventuring through Edo, Clark enjoyed new sakes he stumbled upon. Most people feared the pale foreigners and left them alone. So Clark didn't feel it all that necessary to be on high guard all the time.

One night, Clark was staring at the moon while drinking some cold sake, the taste of which reminded him of plums. The Japanese did have good taste in alcohol, and by this point Clark had tried every variety available in Edo. Suddenly there was a crash somewhere in the house, quickly followed by a shout from Shelly.

Ugghhh, Clark groaned to himself. *She's been good for so long. What now?*

Grumbling, he got up, staggering a bit before finding his footing. Sir James could now be heard yelling profanities at his daughter. Clark slowly sauntered into the house. The more the yelling increased, the slower he walked. He dreaded another confrontation that would give him a headache. The door slid open and Clark drunkenly entered the chaos.

Japanese businessmen were quietly excusing themselves from the room. Or rather, they were being escorted out by a couple of Sir James's bodyguards. Clark could tell by the sneer on their faces that these men were not happy with the business transaction that had blown up in smoke.

Sir James was red in the face from screaming, and a couple of veins in his neck were dangerously popping out. Seeing Clark, he pointed at the yipping dog behind Shelly and commanded, "Kill that mutt this instant!"

For a moment, Clark felt as if he'd been slapped in the face. It took him a moment to register what Sir James had commanded him to do. "You want me to do what?"

"Kill the mutt!" he screamed, his face growing as red as an apple.

"No! Inu was protecting me!" Shelly yelled back, defending her canine friend.

"Well, you shouldn't have spoken out of turn to my highly esteemed client!" Sir James said, pointing a shaky, accusatory finger at Shelly.

This time Shelly turned to Clark, knowing he was the only one who would understand, "Yamoto-san was going to hit me for speaking up. Inu defended me by biting his ankle. Please don't kill him for protecting me," she begged.

Clark saw the dog happily wagging his tail. The dog didn't understand that his fate hung in the balance, amid sharp words being thrown around as if they were knives. "Sir, if the dog was protecting her, then it shouldn't be killed."

Another vein popped out from Sir James's temple. "That dog"—Sir James's pointed towards Inu— "Cost me one of the most important business ventures in Japan so far. I told you the dog could stay so long as it stayed out of my way. You told me you would kill the dog if that happened, so kill it!"

"Sir, I don't think killing the dog is the right answer," Clark shook his head, trying to cut through the fog in his head.

"If you don't kill the dog, I will end your contract and send you back on the first ship to England!" threatened Sir James.

Mournfully, Clark pitied the dog hiding behind Shelly's legs. Tears were running down the girl's face. If he didn't kill the dog, he would be forced to leave. With how heavily guarded Sir James was, it would be impossible for Clark to stay close enough to Shelly to keep her safe. Not only that, if Clark wasn't there to keep her in check, she would most likely run away and get herself killed.

If he did kill the dog, then he would be allowed to stay and ensure Shelly was protected. She would hate him, but at least he would have the time to make it up to her. It was better to keep her safe than to have her like him.

Clark sighed regretfully, "Shelly, go to your room."

"Please don't kill him, Clark!" Shelly begged with tears running down her face in rivers.

Sir James reached over and grabbed her arm tightly. Shelly winced as he forcefully pulled her away from the dog. While Clark softly picked up Inu, Shelly melted to the floor in a puddle of her own misery. Clark could hear her crying harder as he carried the dog outside. The moonlight, so peaceful a moment ago, now cast an eerie light upon the dog who was doomed to die for his heroic deeds. Clark continued to pet the dog to calm it down.

From the house, Shelly yelled, "Don't kill Inu!" Sharply followed by a loud smacking sound, which was undoubtedly Sir James backhanding her across the face.

Inu looked up at Clark with his naïve black beady eyes, and Clark pitied the animal. The task of killing the dog left him feeling as though a knife was twisting in his stomach. He wished it was a knife, because that would be much easier to heal from than the memory of murdering Shelly's dearest companion.

"I am sorry, Inu," he spoke softly to the dog, as he wrapped his fingers around the back of the neck. "I will try to make this as painless as possible."

A sharp yelping echoed through the still night. A small gasp escaped Shelly's lips as she heard the yelp immediately cease.

* * *

"Did he really kill Inu?" Sammy whimpered as she pulled her own puppy closer to her chest.

Connor smiled, "No, he didn't, but Shelly didn't know that."

* * *

Clark hung the limp mutt in his arms, its head lolling over the side of his arm. The tiny heartbeat was still thumping strong in Inu's chest. Yet, he had the appearance of death, which was the next best thing.

Holding the dog by the scruff of the neck, Clark walked slowly back to the house. Shelly's cries grew louder as she saw the dog hanging limply from the scruff.

"Well done, Clark. You'll be sure to get a raise for getting your hands dirty," Sir James said.

"You murdered him!" Shelly screamed as she melted to her knees by her father's feet.

Sir James backhanded Shelly so hard across the face that she was sent sprawling across the floor. "Get out of my sight! Maybe now you will learn some respect!"

For a moment, Shelly continued to cry on the floor. Clark worried that if she didn't pick herself up, she might receive another whipping. As Sir James's opened his mouth to give the command, Shelly slowly scrambled up, her face streaked with tears and snot— a pitiful and guilt-inducing sight. Shelly gave one last, longing look at her only friend, hanging limply from Clark's hand. Then, bursting into tears again, she sprinted to her bedroom.

"Now that all that nonsense is over, I need you to come with me, Clark, and fix this mess," Sir James said as he poured two whiskeys and handed one to Clark.

Clark made no motion to take the drink. "With all due respect, sir, I would rather go drink alone than accompany you," Clark said darkly.

Sir James put the extra cup down and gave Clark a sharp look. "You have many flaws, Clark, but by God, you are the best hired man I have. My daughter made an enemy out of a powerful family. I need you to deliver the dog pelt to the family with me, in hopes that they will still do business with us."

"You can go grovel. I'm going to bury the dog. Then I'm going to drink alone," Clark said in a low voice. He could feel the mutt's heart rate increasing. He could wake up soon.

Sir James pointed a long finger directly at Clark, "I command you—"

"My shift is over. I did your dirty work. Now I'm going to drink. Get your other henchmen to grovel at your side. I'll have none of it." Without looking back, Clark walked out of the room. He could hear Sir James grumbling behind him, no doubt turning red in the face again. Clark didn't care. The only thing on his mind was the painful look of betrayal that Shelly had given him. Clark looked down at the dog, who was starting to kick his back foot as if running in a dream. Clark brought the mutt closer and cradled it in his arms to relieve the pressure from its scruff. As Clark walked away, he wondered how he would explain this to Shelly. Ultimately, he wanted to get those hurt green eyes out of his memory.

The closest place he could purchase more sake that was still open was a brothel about a fifteen-minute walk from the house. Clark made straight for it, ignoring the drunks passed out on the side of the road. As the mutt stirred in his arms, Clark cared only for the sweet plum sake that waited in the brothel.

As he entered, Clark walked straight past the beautiful Japanese women adorned in their intricate kimonos and hair jewels. He couldn't care less for the smell of hot food that wafted from the kitchen. Even the smell of opium and tobacco barely alerted him. Finding a table in a far corner, Clark placed the half-awake mutt down on a cushion and wrapped him in his own jacket. Then he sat and waited for the multiple bottles of sake that would soon be coming his way. He patted the mutt's head, encouraging it to go back to sleep. As the dog rested his sore head on his paws, a woman in a green kimono approached, her tiny feet shuffling toward him on her large platform sandals. The green silk of her kimono shimmered in the low glow of the paper lanterns hanging around the brothel. Her hair was tied up tightly into a bun, decorated with numerous jewels and small beads.

"How can I help you, sir?" she asked in Japanese, her red lips popped against her pale white face.

"Give me the strongest drink you have," Clark responded in Japanese.

"Is there anything else that you would like?" she asked, while motioning towards the other women, who were flirting from afar.

"Did I ask for anything else? Is my Japanese that poor?" Clark responded rudely.

"No sir. I apologize, sir." She gave a sharp bow and quickly disappeared into the kitchen.

After a few moments, she returned with a small tray holding a bottle of hot plum sake and a small cup on a serving dish. Wordlessly, she set down the tray without looking at the rude white man with bizarre purple eyes, and curtly shuffled away.

Before she could get far, Clark spoke up. "I'm going to need five more bottles." Then he threw down a crumpled wad of uncounted bills on the table.

The woman sharply turned around, walked to the table and picked up the stack of money. "May you have as much sake as you can pay for," she said in a condescending way.

Clark considered giving up on *her*. There seemed to be no point in following *her* around anymore. Clark had been at it for centuries, with no reprieve from the horrors he faced. He had been through so many wars and watched people tear each other apart over silly ideals. He watched *her* die more times than he would prefer to remember. Part of him felt cursed. The other part felt useless. The only reason he kept on pursuing this prophecy was to find one answer, an answer *she* somehow knew, though he doubted he could ever get *her* to remember that far back. Clark grabbed the sake bottle, ignoring the cup, and inhaled the sweet liquor.

Eight bottles later, Clark laid his head on the table, empty of thoughts and enjoying the blissful numbness he had envied of other drunkards. The world spun around him, making his stomach perform somersaults. Still, a masochistic side of him enjoyed the nauseating sensation, not wanting it to end. Time no longer had meaning, yet it was arguable that it ever had. The numbness was a relief; in these moments of intoxication, memories no longer plagued him.

"Where do you come from?" asked a gentleman in English with a thick Japanese accent.

Clark lifted his head and tried to make out the figure in front of him through blurry eyes. Squinting, he sat up a little straighter. The world was spinning and his head throbbed. He rubbed his eyes, which made the world appear a little clearer.

"Are you English?" asked the figure.

"No," Clark responded, in slurred English. The figure was a Japanese man with a black topknot, wearing a dark blue kimono and a white cloak with red trim. What appeared to be a large white rope was wrapped around his waist to hold up his black pants. It was clothing typical of samurai. This man was much larger than most Japanese men, but not from excess of food. No, his wide shoulders and muscular physique were barely noticeable under his loose kimono, as though his athletic form was a secret he didn't wish to fully reveal. This man could be a valued ally or a dangerous enemy.

"Are you Italian?" asked the man, careful to slowly enunciate his words so as not to cause confusion.

"No," Clark grumbled, rubbing his eyes again.

"Oh," said the Japanese man, nodding his head, "Are you Spaniard?"

"No, I'm not from anywhere. I don't belong anywhere!" Clark grumbled in Japanese as he grabbed the only sake bottle left.

"A man who is not from anywhere will belong nowhere," he responded poetically in English, then asked, "Where is your home?"

"I have no home," Clark said in Japanese as he took a long slug of his sake.

"A man who has no home will be cursed to wander forever," the man said eloquently in Japanese. "Your Japanese is much better than my English," he added.

"Well, who asked you?" Clark grumbled in English, slamming down the empty bottle, which cracked from the bottom to the top.

"A man who drinks this heavily is running from something," the Japanese man observed.

"Isn't it in your customs to introduce yourself before initiating a conversation?" Clark glared at the samurai, whose features were growing more distinct. He was perhaps five to ten years older than Clark appeared. His black hair, peppered with grays, had a blue shine to it that seemed abnormal. He had a sharp jawline and a tight mouth. His eyes were as dark as his hair.

"I did introduce myself. You were passed out on the table. It is you who was rude enough to not introduce yourself," the man said curtly.

"My name is Clark," he replied, leaning against the wall. The dog made a satisfied sound and shifted slightly in his sleep, so Clark patted him on the head.

"Are you the one who has been following around the English girl with red hair?" the Japanese man inquired.

"What has you so interested in a young girl?" Clark asked with an accusatory finger pointing at the man's chest.

"I find it irresponsible of you to leave your ward when you should be protecting her," the man said as he turned up his nose to Clark.

"What's that supposed to mean?" Clark shouted in English as he let his fist fall upon the table, cracking it under the pressure.

"It means I find you incompetent, Clark-san," the Japanese man responded in English. In a slow, ritualistic fashion he stood up, brushed himself off, and walked away.

Clark scowled at the man as he left. Everything was still fuzzy from the alcohol, yet Clark could sense something was wrong. It was as if there was a great pit in his stomach growing heavier with the awareness that he was forgetting something— something important. Clark tried to think what he was forgetting but was inhibited by the eight bottles of sake he had consumed. He looked down at the mutt as if it could give him some indication of what he was missing, but expecting answers from the dog was ridiculous. This was not reality. Reality was getting drunk to forget the horrors he had experienced over the centuries. Reality was watching humanity struggle and fight over petty things that mattered far less than the plagues that would wipe them out. Reality was the growing pointlessness of his never-ending search for the answer hidden in the depths of *her* memory.

That was when it hit him, as if it were a ram headbutting him in the gut. Shelly was alone. Although the house was surrounded by guards, Clark knew that an attack by a samurai family would cut through them as if they were butter. A sharp, burning sensation pierced Clark through his lower abdomen as if he had been impaled on a sword. Gasping for air, Clark leaned over the table, holding his stomach. Then the pain was gone.

Shelly, he whispered to himself. He shot out of his seat, only to fall back because of the heaviness of the alcohol on his brain. For the first time, he cursed the hindrance the alcohol gave him.

Similar to an infant learning to walk, Clark fought through the drunkenness that weighed him down. Grasping the wall for support, he moved as fast as he could towards the house. The short walk through the night seemed to last forever. His clumsy feet hit every pebble and groove in the road. Most of the time, he would drunkenly stumble and regain his footing, but sometimes he couldn't recapture his balance and would plummet to the earth, scraping his knees and elbows in the fall. Still, he fought hard to move as quickly as he could back to Shelly.

The night was hauntingly dark, with the moon hidden by clouds. The metallic smell of blood carried strongly on the wind. The road was empty of all life. Even the drunkards on the road had vanished to the safety of their homes. Clark was pathetically weak and alone as he stumbled to the house.

When he reached it, everything was so silent it disturbed him to the point of having slightly more clarity. The large doors that led to the inner courtyard were ajar. A trail of blood curved around to the opposite side of the door where Clark discovered a bodyguard cut from the collarbone to the sternum— a cut so forceful that it caused his entrails to spill over his belt. Another guard lay face down in dirt, stained with his own blood. The plants were sprinkled with red droplets from corner to corner of the once-peaceful garden. The sliding paper door was gashed open, as if a body had been thrown through it. Another of Sir James's bodyguards lay face-up, a curtain of red spilling from his neck. Still unsteady, Clark moved into Sir James's study to find it turned upside-down and his body in the center of the destruction.

Taking a moment to inspect the savagery inflicted on Sir James's body, Clark could tell he had deeply angered this high-ranking samurai family. Each hand had been severed clean from the arms. The Achilles' tendons were cut clean through, ensuring he could not have run away. The abdomen was stabbed seven times, each with exact precision. These assassins had made sure to keep Sir James alive through all of this, until the last stroke of the sword severed his head. The head was missing: a prize any samurai would take to his lord for compensation.

Clark believed Sir James got what was coming to him. He feared what had happened to Shelly.

Worry constricted his brain tighter than the alcohol had. Clark was more sure-footed as he ran down the hallway to Shelly's room. The screen door was pulled to the side, yet not damaged. The room was silent, and Clark feared the worst. He knew she wasn't dead, or else the mark he left on her would have told him so. He could feel intense pain, but no death. It was then that Clark noticed that the mattress had multiple stab marks in it. It was uncommon in Japan to have a bed raised above the floor; the Japanese slept on roll-up mattresses. Thinking this odd, he reasoned, they might have considered it a good hiding place and stabbed it several times to ensure there was no escape.

Clark inhaled deeply. He could smell her blood. Moving slowly to as not aggravate the pounding in his head, which was threatening to disable him, Clark peered beneath the bed. Nothing there but a small pool of blood that had soaked through the mattress. Hope seized his throat with an iron grip. Clark looked above the bed and didn't notice any blood.

"Shelly, are you in there?" he whispered.

The mattress shifted and a lump started to form. In a frenzy, Clark flexed his fingers, which elongated into claws. He ripped the top of the mattress off. Shelly lay in the middle of it, covered in cotton and blood. Her vibrant green eyes were wide with shock. She held tightly onto her stomach, staining her hands with her life blood.

Seeing her in distress brought clarity to his mind. The effects of alcohol were wiped clean, and his strength returned. Clark prepared to lift her from the hole she must have made in the mattress earlier, perhaps to hide from her father. Clark could only imagine what strength it must have taken to remain quiet as the samurai stabbed the mattress several times. Yet the samurai couldn't have known that he had stabbed her, because his sword was probably already drenched in blood. Clark knew he had to get her to a doctor, someplace far away, where they wouldn't be discovered by the enemy.

"I knew … you … wouldn't leave … me," she said through trembling lips.

Clark held her tightly in his arms. "I'm sorry I wasn't here to protect you. I promise I will make it better. Right now, I need to you to be strong."

"This … doesn't hurt … nearly as bad … as the mark … you … gave me," she said, smiling weakly.

"Save your strength, Shelly," Clark whispered, "and keep putting pressure on your stomach. The mark will help heal you, but not enough to save your life."

"What do we have here?" a gruff Japanese voice asked behind Clark.

Turning around, Clark faced a samurai wearing red armor, with an upward facing crescent moon on his black helmet. Gold and silver plates

165

of armor protected his core and limbs. On his belt were two sheathed katanas, and he held a spear in his hand. Clark smiled at how clumsy such a weapon would prove to be in close fighting quarters.

The samurai pointed his spear at Shelly. "Her head will be a fine prize for my lord."

"You should have left when you still had the chance," Clark said with an evil smile, setting her down gently and putting himself between them.

The samurai thrust his spear directly toward Clark's sternum. Clark deflected it with his elbow, but still got cut on the shoulder, thanks to his lingering intoxication. Angry about his own sloppiness, Clark grabbed the body of the spear with one hand and broke off the tip. Faster than the human eye could perceive, he drove that tip directly into the samurai's armor. Blood flowed freely as his heart ruptured from the blade. The samurai spit blood on Clark as he fell and died.

Clark growled and wiped the blood off his face. Normally he was better at not getting the enemy's blood on him. Once again, Clark turned to Shelly to pick her up. Shelly gasped with wide eyes as Clark heard the shuffling of armor behind him. Turning just in time to miss the blade thrust at his belly, Clark moved straight in and, in one clean movement, wrapped his arm around the samurai's helmeted head and ripped the head up. A horrendous sound came from the tendons, muscles and spine being torn.

Before Clark could respond, a knife flew at his head. Barely dodging it, he screamed in fury as he rushed toward the next onslaught of foot soldiers, backed up by two more samurai. Clark tore through the men, ripping them to shreds with his bare hands. Even though his sloppiness kept getting him cut and stabbed, Clark still fought on. Every trip and stumble increased his ferocity. Clark was angry at his own selfish stupidity for thinking he could be drunk and still take down an army— a mistake he would not make again. Finally having enough of battling samurai, Clark screamed and clawed the air, sending a flare of purple fire down the corridor, which soon filled the night with flames and the screams of mighty warriors.

Taking a deep breath, Clark turned back towards Shelly's bedroom, where the girl was hiding beneath the bed. "Come on out. We need to get you to a doctor quickly, before the house burns down," he said, kneeling and reaching out a hand. Shelly shrunk back deeper under the bed.

"Shelly, I'm here to protect you. I won't hurt you, I promise," Clark said, feeling the hurt more sharply than before. Hesitantly, weighing whether she could trust him, she finally crept out, leaving a smear of blood behind her.

Elsewhere in the house, beams were falling and acrid smoke filled the air. It was going up in flames faster than Clark anticipated. "We need to go quickly," he said, snatching her up in his arms. She winced in pain at his rough touch, but clung tight to him with one arm while continuing to put pressure on her stomach with the other. Clark raced out of the burning building, barely escaping a falling beam that would have crushed them both.

Clark cradled her in his arms, as he had done with the dog mere hours ago. Clark felt ridiculous for drinking the way he had been. Although his intoxication had worn off for the most part, without his full healing abilities it was taking his body longer than normal to recover from the alcohol poisoning. He was able to run only at twice the normal human speed, much slower than his normal pace— and at a moment when speed mattered most. Shelly felt heavier than ever, another testament to the fact that alcohol was making him sluggish.

Still, he pushed on until they found a place to hide in a bamboo forest. Clark felt he was at a great disadvantage, knowing only the layout of the city. He'd been too preoccupied with sake to care about surveying the landscape beyond the city—a huge mistake.

After running for thirty kilometers, Clark finally found a small village hidden up in the mountains, and in it was a house with the sign for a medicinal doctor. Not caring about custom, Clark burst in. A small, shriveled Japanese man with gray hair rushed from one of the rooms. From his disheveled clothes, it appeared he'd been roused from sleep.

Seeing the white man holding a barely conscious white woman, the elderly man started waving his arms in fear and shouting, "What are you doing here? Get out!"

"Please, she's hurt. Help her," Clark begged in Japanese, as he lowered her down for the doctor to see.

"You will bring trouble. I don't need trouble. Get out!" He pointed towards the door and started to walk closer to shoo them out.

"I can protect you from whatever may come. Please help her!" Clark begged again.

The old doctor folded his arms. "You will protect me? Like you protected her?"

It stung, but Clark took it. "I was wrong. I was incompetent and selfish. Please don't let her die from my mistake. Please help her, and I promise to give you whatever you want."

The doctor took a deep breath and looked at Shelly gravely. After a few moments, he finally sighed. "Bring her back here. I'll see what I can do."

"Thank you! Thank you!" Clark said, bowing several times in the local manner.

"But you will protect this house! You hear me?" The little old man pointed up towards Clark, who easily stood two heads higher.

"Yes, yes, thank you, sir." Clark bowed again.

The doctor gave him a small scowl before walking into his attached small clinic. Clark followed obediently to a small room with a futon rolled out on the floor. Its walls were lined with shelves full of medicinal herbs. Clark gently laid Shelly down on the mattress. She winced and moaned from being sprawled out. Noticing sweat on her brow, Clark laid his hand on her forehead, unknowingly smearing some of her own blood into her hair. Grumpily, the doctor shoved Clark away from her.

Shelly's hand was clamped tightly down upon her stomach, where the wound was. The doctor tried to remove the hand, but she refused to relieve the pressure. "Do you want to live or not? Remove your hand," the doctor barked.

"She doesn't understand very much Japanese," Clark informed the doctor.

He scowled at Clark. "We need to remove her clothes and I need her cooperation, or else she will die!"

168

Clark turned to Shelly and spoke to her in English, "Shelly, we need to remove your clothes so the doctor can sew you up."

"But … the mark …" she said through pants of pain.

"It's okay. The doctor is here to help."

Shelly nodded and removed her hand. Immediately, the doctor put clean towels on the wound and started applying pressure. Shelly groaned. The doctor commanded Clark in Japanese, "Tear off her shirt so I can get a better look at the wound. I'll hold pressure on her stomach."

Shelly remained still as Clark ripped the clothes from her torso, revealing the purple mark. Fortunately, the doctor didn't react to this mark and stayed focused on the wound. Clark discarded the bloodied fabric, leaving Shelly bare from the waist up.

The doctor grumbled, "Kimonos make it much easier to access a wound. These stupid foreigners with their constricting clothes." The doctor released the pressure. Clark had his first good look at the wound and was relieved to see that it was no more than an inch-deep cut; not a risk to any major organs. It was a wound most people could survive. But his hopefulness was not shared by the doctor, who ran a finger along the rim of the cut. Shelly gasped sharply from the pain. The doctor put the cloth back on the wound and ordered Clark: "Hold this down. She has an abnormal flow of energy that is quite concerning to me."

"How so?" Clark asked, as he put pressure on the wound.

The doctor laid his hand upon her sweating brow and then checked her pulse on three different spots on her wrist. "Her wound is normally not a mortal one. Tell her to to stick out her tongue."

"Shelly, stick out your tongue," Clark said softly.

It appeared to be a struggle to muster the energy to do it. The doctor inspected her tongue and grunted disappointingly. Then he hastily left the room. Clark could hear banging around outside of the room. The doctor's sense of pessimism was rubbing off on Clark. The man returned with a large pot of steaming water and what appeared to be a small hand-sized katana. The old doctor set these down right next to Shelly, then went to his shelves. Frantically, he searched his jars of herbs, retrieving the three he needed.

"What is wrong?" Clark asked uncertainly.

"Be quiet while I concentrate!" shouted the doctor as he put the herbs in a mortar and started grinding them with a pestle. For a few minutes, the only sounds were the grinding of the mortar and pestle and Shelly's sharp, heavy breathing. Finally, the doctor broke the silence. "Who did you anger?"

"I didn't anger anyone," Clark replied honestly.

"Who did she anger?" the doctor asked again irritably.

"I don't know. Some samurai family. She spoke out of turn while her father was doing business. The man didn't appreciate her speaking up, so he hit her and her dog bit him. Then later that night, they came back to kill the entire household," Clark recounted.

"Where were you during this attack?" the doctor asked with a hint of spite in his voice.

Clark looked down at Shelly. The truth hurt him more than anything else. "I was drunk."

"You really are incompetent," the doctor said as he rushed back over with a mortar full of orange-green paste that smelled of rotten dirt. "This family she angered is a well-known samurai family. Very powerful and not to be taken lightly. When they attack a family, they kill everyone. One way they ensure that everyone dies is by soaking their blades in poison. This poison normally kills people in minutes. Even a tiny little nick of their blade could prove fatal to an ox."

Clark's heart beat faster as he watched Shelly. Her pulse was racing, she felt cold to the touch, yet was breaking out in a sweat and her pupils were dilated. "Can you save her?"

"Hold down her arms and keep her still," barked the doctor.

Clark obeyed and moved around to her upper body, where he could hold down her arms.

"I will try to save her. It is a miracle that she has survived this long," the doctor said in Japanese. He removed the bandage. Clark peeked over and could see the dead tissue around the cut was growing. It was as if the flesh was slowly decaying around the wound. He worried what the poison was doing to the rest of her body. "Hold her down tight. She might want to buck."

"Do your best to hold still," Clark instructed her in English.

Shelly inhaled sharply and held her breath, preparing for more pain.

The doctor globbed on the medicine with his three middle fingers. Then he shoved his fingers as deep as he could into her wound. So deep that his fingers went completely inside her stomach. Shelly screamed in excruciating pain as Clark firmly held her down. The doctor removed his fingers and took another large glob of medicine. Shelly held her breath again as he plunged his fingers deep into her wound once more. She screamed again, wriggling and bucking. Clark had difficulty holding her down and wondered if it might be better to knock her unconscious.

"I need her awake for this," the doctor said, as if reading Clark's mind, "otherwise she won't have the willpower to stay alive."

Clark nodded and held her down tighter. The doctor continued until all the orange-green paste was gone. The last of it he put on the surface of her wound. Now she was no longer bleeding, but the area appeared worse with a grotesque mixture of colors seeping from the wound. Shelly's head wobbled back and forth as she fought sleep.

"Don't let her go to sleep yet," the doctor instructed, as he left the room with his hands covered in blood and medicinal herbs.

Clark turned to Shelly and softly smoothed her hair back. "Hey, don't go to sleep on me yet. I need you to stay awake for a little longer."

"Am I going to live?" Shelly asked shakily.

"Do you want to live?" Clark asked.

"Yes," she replied weakly.

"Then stay strong and you will survive this," Clark said, with a rueful smile.

The doctor returned with clean hands, holding a small cup of tea. Clark could smell the pungent aroma coming from the cup and wondered what nastiness the doctor had cooked up next. "Slowly sit her up," ordered the doctor.

Clark slowly propped Shelly up to a forty-five degree angle and instructed her in English, "This might not taste good, but you have to drink it."

"Okay," she replied weakly.

The doctor put the cup to her lips. The smell made Clark want to gag. Shelly wrinkled her nose at the horrid smell of the concoction.

"Drink," barked the doctor in Japanese.

Shelly obeyed and gulped down the hot liquid to the last drop. Then she grimaced and stuck out her tongue. "That was nasty. Do I have to drink any more of that?"

"She will need to drink the herbs four times a day for a week," the doctor instructed. "The medicine will need to be changed out on the wound daily until the puss stops running from it. If she can survive the next two days, then she will be in the clear." The doctor went over to his shelves calmly and started putting things away.

"What did he say?" she asked weakly.

"Get some rest," Clark encouraged. He didn't have the heart to tell her she would have to repeat this procedure multiple times. He could tell her when she awoke.

It only took a moment for Shelly to succumb to a deep sleep. As Shelly slept soundly, Clark refused to leave her. The doctor tried to coax him to eat or drink, but Clark refused everything. Now and again, he would have to wake her to drink more of the nasty medicine, which was slowly getting easier for her to consume. The doctor, who Clark later learned was named Takani, was much more pleasant than he had first presented. Turned out Takani did not care for early awakenings and generally resented the English influence on his country. But Clark found him to be a rather joyful man with a big heart, who deeply cared for his patients and tried his best to help them return to full health.

Clark would hear Takani talking to his other patients out in the front room. The only time he ever mentioned the foreigners occupying his back room was when a certain visitor would come by, which happened daily. Clark recalled him immediately: it was the man from that night in the brothel who called him incompetent. This man was even larger in comparison to the diminutive doctor and would come by to size Clark up. Irritated by these visits, Clark paid him no attention, and stayed loyally next to Shelly.

After a week, Shelly was finally awake and alert. Her wound was no longer flowing with puss.

"There, she is free of the poison!" Doctor Takani declared with open arms, then busied himself with tidying up his medicine jars. "She will have a nasty scar for the rest of her life. But at least it isn't as ugly as that purple tattoo on her stomach." The doctor laughed, throwing a keen glance in Clark's direction.

"I guess we'd best be on our way now," Clark said as he dusted off his blue and white kimono. Shelly had been dressed in a white kimono that was presentable enough, but the doctor kept telling Clark they were underclothes. Once she was more awake, the Doctor said he'd give her an old green kimono made of rough fabric that his late wife used to wear.

"You promised me you would protect this town," Doctor Takani said, pointing his finger at Clark. "Now you must pay for my services."

"Thank you for your services. I will be sure to repay you well. If you let us go back to her father's place, I'm sure we could find much more money than you could have earned in a lifetime," Clark responded respectfully, with a low bow.

"You insult me. Does it look like I need money?" the doctor growled. Clark looked around at the tattered old office and wanted to argue the point, but decided to keep his mouth shut. Doctor Takani continued, "I'm old and need help with heavy lifting and chores around the clinic. You can repay me for my time with your work."

"But we really must be going," Clark said, eyeballing the door.

The small, elderly doctor put his hands on his hips. "No, you promised me your services. Now I shall either have you protect me from the men who sought to kill her, or you can pay me through chores. It will take a while longer to fully heal from the injury as it is. No one comes through here anymore, so you won't draw attention to yourselves."

173

"What is he saying?" Shelly asked. "I can only understand a few words."

"Seems as if I need to help out around the clinic to pay for your medicine," Clark said with a smile.

"I'm glad we are staying," Shelly said with a bright smile.

Clark softly smiled back, happy that she was alive and healing.

* * *

"So she survived the poison?" Sammy asked happily.

"Yes, she did," Connor replied with a warm smile.

Sammy hugged her new canine companion. "What about Inu? Did he eventually find her again?"

Connor's smile faded slightly, then he forced the smile back on his face, "Yes, the dog did eventually find them in that little village."

Seeing the change in his face, Sammy asked hesitantly, "Do they die?"

"It's Christmas. We are not going to talk about such sad things on a day full of happiness and cheer." Connor's green eyes sparkled as he stood up and tucked her in.

"You didn't answer my question, Connor," Sammy said with a pouty face.

Connor looked seriously into Sammy's curious green eyes. "Everyone dies, Sammy. If you want to hear more about this story later, then I can tell you. But tonight," he perked up, "I want you to have sweet dreams."

Connor walked over to the door and turned out the lights. Right before he closed the door, he heard Sammy speak up. "Clark made a mistake, but I still think he was a hero."

How curious it was that such a naïve statement could render a monster helpless.

Sammy rolled over and snuggled in with her new puppy. "Goodnight, Connor. Merry Christmas."

"Merry Christmas, Sammy. Sweet dreams," he said over his shoulder as he softly closed the door. For now, the only sane thing to do would be to dismiss her comment and move on.

At times such as these, Connor was relieved by the simplicity of his mundane routine. From checking all the security systems to prepping meals for the next day, each task offered its own distraction. Yet Sammy's words buzzed around his head as irritatingly as a mosquito. Confounded by her statement, Clark sat on the couch and gazed at the Christmas tree. The lights on the otherwise jolly tree morphed into a memory of darkness. If only Sammy had known what happened next, she might not have labeled him a hero.

* * *

It had been a week of quiet country life in the mountains of Japan. Clark had been hard at work rebuilding and mending the clinic. Upon seeing his skills, other townsfolk had begun to ask his assistance. He was proud that his skills could be used to benefit the lives of others, but he continued to check frequently on Shelly's progress. The poison had taken its toll on her, but she was soon able to walk again and even learned from other women in the village.

That large visitor remained a mystery to Clark, his incessant need to check on them grew more irritating by the day— not irritating enough to overcome Clark's stubborn refusal to approach him directly. Clark's curiosity would get the better of him as he asked other villagers about this man, who apparently went by the name of Ni'itsu. Most said he was a quiet potter who lived upstream. Others said he was a grouchy hermit who hated the company of others. Yet no one could argue that this little town had remained untouched from violence thanks to Ni'itsu. Clark really didn't care so long as the man stayed far away from him and Shelly.

One day, a surprise came bounding into the small village. Inu yipped happily to announce his accomplishment at finally finding the girl he loved. Shelly squealed with joy at being reunited with her dog. Clark came into the clinic at the sound of the happy barks. It was an endearing sight to see her rolling around on the floor with her supposedly lost companion. Even though Clark had told her time and again he didn't kill the dog, she'd never quite believed him until this moment. Yet her smiles couldn't chase away the feeling deep down in Clark's gut that something was wrong. Peering out the window, Clark noticed that it would be dark soon.

"Won't you come inside?" Doctor Takani shouted out into pouring rain, hours after the dog had reappeared. "You will surely become ill."

"Don't worry about me, doctor," Clark hollered, "I'm protecting you from the dangers you can't see."

The rain poured hard enough to obscure the vision of a normal human, but Clark could see well beyond the trees and the bamboo that grew thicker with the heavy rain. Standing drenched from head to toe, he held his ground until he spotted someone coming.

A figure emerged from the woods, as Clark prepared himself for combat. He was taken off-guard by a small Japanese boy playing with a toy ball. He appeared to be no older than five— no threat at all. What he had imagined to be an army or at least a small league of assassins was merely a small boy. He couldn't understand it; Clark had an acute sense of danger, yet there was none. Relaxing his tensed muscles, Clark walked towards the young boy, who looked up and gave him a toothy grin.

"You should go back to your mother," Clark shouted through the rain.

The little boy paid him no mind and continued to play with his ball.

"Hurry, go home!" Clark shouted again. By now he was mere feet away. The boy looked up and smiled once more, then vanished right before Clark's eyes. At that moment, an arrow flew and pierced Clark in the chest .

All his fine-tuned senses returned as Clark realized the trouble he had put himself in. Crouching low, he scanned the trees while yanking the arrow out of his chest. Looking at the tip, he realized it had been smeared with poison. Already he could feel the poison impacting his muscles.

Clark looked up, knowing now that he'd been led into the middle of a noose. Dark figures moved through the trees, preparing their attack. The sound of armor and horses came from down the hill. Clark peered through the curtain of pouring rain to see about twenty armed samurai headed his way. Three more arrows fell, which he barely evaded. Kicking a tree with great force, he made it splinter, implode and fall, as a black figure—the archer—hidden behind it jumped for the cover of an adjacent tree.

Growing impatient, Clark put his hand to his mouth and blew hard as if sounding a trumpet. A long spray of purple fire came bursting out of his hand. The nearby forest immediately caught fire, the blaze rapidly incinerated the trees and their inhabitants until the rain extinguished it. Clark suddenly realized the huge disadvantage he had. The men coming up the hill were carrying spear, arrow and sword, which he knew they each had personal mastery in. These weren't typical soldiers on a battlefield; they were skilled assassins who had dedicated their lives to their art of killing.

Clark coiled tight and waited for an opportune moment to pounce on the onslaught of killers headed for him. The rain beat down upon his body with all the fury the heavens could muster. Before the samurai were within range, another rally of arrows cut through the rain in all directions. Clark narrowly avoided being struck by all but one, a delayed shot that struck him in the back as if it were strategically planned. Not paying mind to the poison arrow in his back, Clark leapt forward, towards the upward-facing spears of the small army. Rushing them as if he were a jaguar leaping on its prey, Clark evaded most of the spears while successfully crashing into two samurai, bringing them to the ground. A spear nicked his thigh, but this meant little to him. Using his massive claws, Clark tore through the armor of the samurai, who had their swords drawn. With every strike he delivered, three slashes found their way to his skin.

Clark felt weak and dizzy. At this point he couldn't even feel most of his body. So many poisoned arrows and blades had pierced him. It had taken pure willpower to kill off the last seven samurai, and now he could hardly see, even as more of them came at him. Multiple mortal strikes would slow down his healing process, and with the amount of poison coursing through his veins, Clark knew his body could not last much longer. His vision blurred and doubled, Clark swung his clawed hand out blindly while using his sword-wielding hand to swing in the opposite direction. His blade cut down something unseen before his body collapsed to the ground. The samurai closed in on him and began rapidly stabbing his chest. Clark no longer felt any pain. Instead, he looked up at the sky that sent the pouring rain onto his bleeding body. From the sky, a handful of purple wisps appeared and floated down to him. It would seem the assassins achieved their objective and killed Shelly. The superstitious samurai immediately screamed and chanted mantras to keep the evil spirits away. As the purple wisps landed on Clark's body, returning his healing ability to him, a single tear rolled down his face. Then the world went black.

When Clark awoke, the world was white as snow. His body was heavy and hard to move. Stiffly, he sat up and surveyed the white world. It was then that he noticed the snow didn't feel cold at all. Clark inspected his naked body and realized it wasn't snow he was covered in, but white ash. Sitting up more, Clark finally understood. The trees, the bamboo, the village and all the people had been destroyed by his purple fire. The snow-white ash hung in the air and settled down upon the blackened earth.

Though Clark had no recollection of setting the town ablaze, he knew he was the only one who could have incinerated an entire town full of innocent people with innocent lives. A town that had not only harbored Shelly and him, but welcomed them and treated them as if they were family. It was a town that did not deserve the fate that befell them by Clark's claws. Not being able to hold it in any longer, Clark screamed out all his anger towards the heavens. His reply was an empty echo of his own hatred. The despair was almost too much to bear.

Clark looked around the ash and noticed something glimmering beneath the white surface. His limbs stiff and sore, Clark laboriously pulled himself over to the object and pulled it free from the burnt earth. The katana was still mostly intact, with only the base of the blade burnt. Clark held the blade up and saw the ugliness of his soul reflected on its metal. Closing his black eyes, Clark took the sword and forced it through his stomach and then upwards towards his sternum. Already, he could feel his body healing and pushing the blade out. He withdrew the blade and stabbed, again and again, self-hatred motivating his relentless pursuit to end his own life.

Two days later, Clark lay on his back and looked up at the blue sky, feeling emptier inside than ever before. The ashy ground around him was a circle dyed red.

"Are you done wallowing in your self-pity? Or would you prefer to kill yourself some more?" queried a familiar voice from a distance.

Clark jolted up and looked across the field of burnt black soil, covered with a soft layer of white ash. At the edge of the burnt land was the mysterious man he had met back in the brothel, and who had monitored him while Shelly healed.

"Do you know why she died?" Ni'itsu asked as he came closer.

"Because I failed to save her … again …" Clark whispered to himself.

"No, that is not it at all," Ni'itsu replied, shaking his head.

Surprised that Ni'itsu had heard him, Clark sat up. Ni'itsu seemed surprisingly void of fear or hesitation. "Why did she die, then?"

"She died because you are a reckless fighter. The village died because you lack control. You failed because you lack discipline," he lectured, now a mere fifteen feet away.

"How dare you insult me, old man," Clark snarled. "I alone have won wars and slaughtered hundreds of men before tiring. I have conquered kingdoms and brought even the toughest opponents begging at my feet. I am the cruelest and fiercest warrior that ever—"

"She died when you were being impaled by four swords. Although you may be a great fighter, you don't know the first thing about self-defense," he growled.

Clark gave a smug smile. "If you haven't noticed, I don't need to defend myself. I heal quickly enough during battle."

"If you could have defended yourself from such attacks, then you would have been able to kill your enemies and save your ward," Ni'itsu said, with cold, black eyes.

Once again, Clark was speechless.

"Come with me. You may call me Sensei and shall be my apprentice, so your next ward doesn't face the same fate," Ni'itsu said as he walked away.

Clark sat for a moment, mulling over the possibility. Finally, he made his decision and ran after his new Sensei.

7

TO ERR IS HUMAN

LONDONDERRY, NEW HAMPSHIRE

AUGUST 2, 2007

"Aha!" Sammy shouted out as Buddy barked happily next to her, "I finally caught you sleeping!"

Connor startled awake and abruptly scanned the area with his vibrant green eyes. The living room was secured and there were no signs of immediate danger—just a proud Sammy, pointing her finger at Connor's nose. Her victory was proven true by the fact that he had indeed fallen asleep on the couch. At first, Connor was ashamed of this normal human behavior. The only time Connor slept was when his brain had to reset the body to preserve precious resources while healing egregiousness wounds. Yet here he was, awoken from a soft slumber that had stolen him away to a restful sleep.

It was odd how human tendencies had begun to direct his behavior, starting with the return of his natural forest-green eyes. These new green eyes had brought on a larger array of emotions for which he had always envied humans, such as true happiness, enthusiasm, hope and genuine laughter. Connor even found himself craving food he normally would have had no interest in. To top it off, he was succumbing to the natural rhythms of sleep.

It was all so strange and foreign that he didn't know how to respond. Centuries had passed without these basic human necessities, but now that he was spending more time with Sammy it was bringing the human out of the monster. Connor did his best to stifle the hope that this could be the long-awaited cure he had sought.

"It's true, you caught me at last," Connor said with a laugh.

Sammy giggled while Buddy barked happily. "I'm hungry!"

"Well then, what shall we have for breakfast? I think a vegetable omelet sounds delicious!" Connor suggested with a smile, his mouth salivating at the thought.

"How about some pancakes?" Sammy suggested.

"How about some *berry* pancakes?" Connor recommended with raised eyebrows.

"Okay, I guess I'll be a little healthy," Sammy joked.

"Come here, you!" Connor said playfully as he grabbed Sammy and tickled her. Her laughter brought a warmth to Connor's green eyes.

Moments later, Sammy was sitting on a bar stool at the marble counter top, lips smacking while enjoying the blueberry pancakes that were turning her lips blue. Buddy waited at her feet with a wildly wagging tail, in hopes that some scraps would happen to fall to the floor. Connor casually leaned against the kitchen counter top, enjoying a vegetable omelet. Buddy whimpered longingly, to which Connor responded with a sharp glance that immediately stopped the unwanted behavior.

"When can I go to school like a normal kid?" Sammy asked, with a disappointed face.

Connor felt queasy about this issue. He didn't want it to come up again, as it always ended in a heated argument. Derailing the dispute before it could start, he changed the subject. "You've surpassed kids your age, so it's really a mute point. Speaking of which, today we have a full day of English, History, German, French and then Chemistry. How about we end the day with music lessons?"

"Okay," Sammy said with a pout that indicated she was still unhappy about not being in a normal school. "Will you play with me this time?" Sammy asked hopefully.

"What would you like me to play?" Connor asked.

"Can you accompany my piano with the violin?" Sammy asked.

"I don't see a reason why not," Connor said with a smile.

"Then, after that can we take Buddy to the park?" Sammy asked with those puppy-dog eyes.

Connor laughed heartily, "Oh the pleading eyes! They make me so weak! I must succumb to your will!" Connor dramatically placed the back of his hand over his forehead.

Sammy giggled at his playfulness.

"Sure, we can do that. I'm sure Buddy would enjoy it as well," Connor smiled.

"Yay!" Sammy screamed with her hands in the air. Then she jumped off the stool and bolted to her bedroom, with Buddy hot on her heels.

A beaming smile refused to leave Connor's face. He couldn't even remember a time when he'd been this happy. Everything in the world appeared brighter, with more color. It was almost as if he had lived for centuries in a black-and-white world. It was only when she was around that the world regained its color. These days, it felt as though every day was a masterpiece to behold. Every second he spent with her was so fleeting that he wished it to last forever. Connor could only hope this happiness would last forever ... that it would be the cure to his unending suffering. It was a hope still too dangerous and fragile to depend upon, but growing nonetheless.

Once Sammy was all cleaned up, with brushed hair and teeth, she came out to the designated school room. Connor looked up as Sammy entered, ready for another day of study. He was amazed at how fast she had grown. A couple of years ago, she was wearing Dora the Explorer shirts and Barbie tennis shoes. Back then, this room was filled with puzzles and learning toys. Now, the study room was filled with books, activities and crafts. Now, at eleven years old, she had grown much taller, almost awkwardly so. Even with her long arms and legs, she still had that beautiful auburn hair that flowed elegantly down her back to her waist. It was that time of life; she was experiencing her growth spurt into a more womanly body. Connor dreaded the day he would have to talk about her changing hormones and how that would affect her. Luckily, that day didn't have to be today.

"Okay! I'm ready to learn!" Sammy exclaimed enthusiastically.

"All right, come on over here!" Connor motioned as he sat down in front of a pile of books and blank papers. "Why don't we get English out of the way?"

"Aw, okay," Sammy said. There was that pout again.

Connor ignored the attitude and focused more on the assignment. "First, I want you to complete these three pages of homework to show me you understand how to use certain grammatical structures. Then, write me a persuasive essay on whatever topic you want. Then we will move on to French & German, take lunch, then cover chemistry & history. Does that sound fair?"

"I guess, but I'm writing my essay on why I should be learning Mandarin instead of English grammar," Sammy complained.

"I can't wait to read it!" Connor said with a sparkle in his eye.

Five hours later, Connor was pointing towards a large map of Europe that he had pinned up on the wall. "And that was why the Germans decided to elect Adolf Hitler as their leader. After being thrown into the trenches as vampire and werewolf bait for the last two decades, the humans had reached their breaking point with these other species, turning the tides into the Great War. It was a multi-species war so devastating, reaching the far corners of the globe, that we will never see a world war such as that again."

"Didn't they know he wanted to kill *all* non-humans? Vampires? Imps? Satyrs? Werewolves?" Sammy asked in an condescending way.

"No one really knew what Hitler was capable of back then. And in the next couple of days, you will learn more about how that progressed. The execution camps didn't happen overnight. At first, Hitler did a lot of good for the Europeans and made them profitable," Connor taught as he looked back and forth between the map and Sammy.

"Do you have any stories about the Great War?" Sammy asked.

"Hmmm," Connor put his hand up to his chin to imitate deep thought. "I have one story about Pearl Harbor during the Great War."

"Can you tell me a story about Pearl Harbor?" Sammy asked, excited. She always loved the stories he told her and would ask him to repeat them several times over before they went on to a new one. Connor wondered if she had noticed any similarity between herself and the women in his stories yet, or if she was still too young to have memories from past lives return to her.

"I would be happy to tell you about Pearl Harbor, but not today. If you want to go to the park, then we need to practice the piano for at least twenty minutes first," Connor said as he put away the history book and a couple of diagrams.

"Will you still accompany me? You said you would," Sammy asked.

Connor chuckled. "I will accompany your piano with a violin piece. First, I want you to run down and play one classical piece of your choosing and one contemporary piece. Then I will pick up the violin."

"Come on, Buddy," she called as she patted the side of her leg. Obediently, Buddy got up and energetically bounced after her.

Connor continued to clean and tidy up the study room. It wasn't long until he heard Chopin floating on the air as delicately as a leaf in the wind. For a moment, Connor sat there and allowed the flow of the music give him a deep sense of peace. Then there was a sudden halt as Sammy messed up on one of the keys. A brief silence followed before she resumed playing.

Following the melodious sounds, Connor went downstairs to the music room. He paused at the doorway to watch her play. The light from the two-story-high windows cascaded upon Sammy and the piano, almost as if the room was caught in a dream. Only eleven years old and yet she showed the maturity of a thirty-year-old. She was an old soul, which was apparent at times like these. There was an expression on her face as if she were remembering something significant that wouldn't fully materialize for her— a memory that was out of her reach. Yet it wasn't out of Connor's reach. He had seen her play before. She'd always had an affinity for Chopin but could never quite tell him why. Maybe someday she could figure that out. Until then, Connor would simply enjoy watching her gentle fingers caressing the keys.

Sammy finished the piece and looked over at Connor, "I messed up," she said sadly.

Connor came closer and suggested, "You need to loosen the tension in your wrists a bit more. Sammy, you need to give yourself credit. Very few eleven-year-olds can play such a complicated piece of music as well as you can. Now play me something contemporary, and I'll get the violin ready."

Pretending to be a professional pianist, Sammy flipped her hair over her shoulder, straightened her posture, elevated her wrists and delicately rested her fingertips on the keys. After the first few notes, Connor chuckled, "The theme music to Harry Potter, huh?"

"I love that movie!" Sammy said enthusiastically as she continued to play. Connor opened up a large double-doored closet. Inside were multiple instruments carefully stored as if they were precious trophies. Among the many instruments were a violin, a cello, four guitars, a saxophone and a clarinet. From the collection, Connor pulled out the violin and started to prepare it.

Sammy ended her song and turned around, waiting for praise.

"That was excellent, Sammy! I am so proud of you and how brilliantly you play. Now, would you like to play something already written or do you want to continue composing your own piece of music?" Connor asked, as he stood next to the piano with the violin at the ready.

"I'm not as good at making up songs as you are," Sammy stated sadly. "Plus, you are perfect at every instrument, while I only know the piano."

Connor leaned over and placed a reassuring hand on her shoulder. "Hey kiddo, stop being so down on yourself. You're only eleven. I bet in eleven more years you can have all these instruments mastered. Don't compare yourself to me, because I have had much more practice over the years."

"Can you help me compose? I'm not that good at writing music yet,"

Sammy asked with a low affect.

"Only if you turn this negative attitude into a positive one," Connor said. "Why don't we start with a contemporary piece first? I know *Pirates of the Caribbean* theme music is your favorite."

Sammy giggled, "Okay, Connor!"

Both musicians readied their stance; then, with a single glance, they started on cue. The adventurous theme music drifted down the halls and filled the house with their synced melodies.

A while later, Sammy was throwing a Frisbee for Buddy in the park. She giggled and laughed as the red disc soared, with Buddy running underneath it. Connor sat on a park bench close enough to keep her in his sights. Connor sipped on a caramel macchiato, a drink he had grown fond of over the past several months. There were so many pleasures in life that he had neglected for so long.

Far to his left, Connor spotted a young couple. From their body language Connor guessed they were on their second or third date. The boy wanted to hold her hand, yet he was so shy. Feeling brave, he brushed her hand with his to give her a hint. She responded by grabbing the hand, then turned away to hide her blush. It was so innocent and romantic, almost as if watching a chick flick.

This glimpse at another couple reminded Connor that someday Sammy would be dating boys, with their own agendas. The thought disgruntled him. It was still a ways off, yet seemed far too close for comfort.

Connor shifted his attention back to Sammy, who was talking to someone hiding behind a large tree. His protective side kicking in, Connor went over to investigate. As he approached, he could hear a raspy man's voice.

"I have a puppy, too. Maybe your dog could come and play with my puppy. I bet they would have a lot of fun in my backyard," the stranger's voice said.

"Um, I don't think Connor would like that," Sammy said hesitantly, taking a step back. Buddy could sense Sammy's fear and defensively jumped in front of her with his hackles raised, ready to fight.

Connor could also sense Sammy's fear rise with her heart rate, which made his blood run hot. Within an instant, Connor was behind Sammy, gently resting his hands on her shoulders and pulling her in closer.

The creepy stranger was wearing old, holey jeans. What had been fine leather shoes were dirty and beaten. A stained, weathered sports jacket covered two unflattering layered shirts. Although the man appeared older, with weathered hands, a discolored complexion and disheveled, graying hair, Connor knew his age was somewhere in the forties. What stood out most about this man was the hunger in his eyes. Many times he had seen men do unethical acts with those types of eyes.

"Excuse me, sir, but we don't have any loose change on us today. So sorry, but the homeless shelter is about five miles south of here. If you leave now, you can make it for dinner," Connor informed.

The man replied with squinty eyes. "You are the bastard who kidnapped Samantha."

Connor was baffled by the accusation. "I beg your pardon, sir. There was no kidnapping involved with me adopting Samantha."

Sammy remained quiet, but Buddy's growling grew louder.

"I am her next of kin!" —the man pointed a long, crooked finger at himself— "I should be the one taking care of her. Not you!"

"Torin Schute? How did you find us?" Connor asked, confused. A million thoughts swam through his head. He was positive he had made sure no one knew where she was living now.

"Who is Torin Schute?" Sammy asked Connor.

Connor spoke in a gentler tone. "He is technically your step-uncle from your mom's side. When your maternal grandmother remarried, she adopted Torin, who became the step-brother to your mother."

"I am her family!" Torin said, still pointing a finger at his own chest. "I should be her guardian."

"You might be family on paper, but not by blood. Your documented history of drug use and felony charges has made you an unfit guardian for Samantha," Connor stated coldly. "Once again, I'll ask you: how did you find us?"

Torin looked down at Sammy with sad eyes. "I heard about your father, Samantha. I knew you would be all alone in the world and would need family to support you. I called many people at the courthouse. Your social worker, the one who checks up on you every year, she gave me your address so I can finally meet you."

"Excellent, the county social worker told you," Connor said, sarcasm dripping off of every syllable.

"You're my uncle?" Sammy asked gingerly. Judging by the disgust in her voice, Sammy was not thrilled to meet a long-lost uncle.

"I sure am, Samantha! I'm going to take better care of you than this con artist that is only using you for your money!" Torin spat at Connor.

Connor barely avoided the flying spit by tilting his head. "If money is what you are after, then I will write you a personal check from my own bank account if you will leave us alone." Sammy sank into Connor for protection.

Torin grew red in the face, his veins becoming more pronounced. "No, I don't want your dirty money. I want to be the rightful guardian of Samantha. You were the one who didn't disclose her status to me. For that I am going to sue you for everything you own. You did something illegal, I just know it!"

Buddy was barking aggressively as Sammy clung onto his collar to keep him from lunging on the screaming man. Connor wanted nothing more than to end this man's pathetic life right here and now. The idea of breaking his neck and burning Torin in his purple flame was quite tempting. Unfortunately, there would be far too many witnesses. The young couple Connor spied earlier were now pulling out their phones to dial 911, in case the situation escalated. Connor couldn't risk Sammy and him being publicized. It would put her at too much risk. In the worst-case scenario, they would have to flee the country if Connor killed everyone in sight. In this case, modern technology was more of a hindrance than ever. Back in the day, Connor could slaughter a village and go into the next town without drawing attention. Nowadays, a stunt such as that that would put him and Samantha on the world news. How irritating!

"I have had enough of this!" Torin yelled. "Samantha, you are coming with me, away from this pedophile!"

Connor flared up, ready to burn down all of New Hampshire if he had to. Sammy screamed as Torin took a step towards her. Before Connor could react, Buddy jumped free from Sammy's grip. Teeth bared, the heroic dog chomped down on Torin's extended hand. The man screamed in pain, but the dog wasn't releasing his grip. Even Connor was shocked. Buddy had always been so calm, never showing an ounce of aggression. As Torin screamed and flailed around to get the dog to let go, Connor watched Sammy. She didn't seem surprised at all. On the contrary, she had a look of hatred as she calmly watched Buddy ripping apart Torin's hand. Finally, Torin had had enough and kicked the dog in the side as hard as he could. Buddy yelped and rolled a couple of feet away.

"Buddy!" Sammy screamed as she ran over to her best friend.

Connor stood between Torin and Sammy. His green eyes grew darker as he growled at Torin. "Get away from here now! I will pay for the medical bills for your hand, but otherwise you are never to see or talk to Sammy again."

Torin looked angrily at Connor as he cradled his bloodied hand. "I'll see you in court, you snake!" Then Torin ran off, with his shredded hand tightly hidden beneath his jacket. Connor surveyed the witnesses, who went back to their business as if they hadn't seen anything.

As Connor turned back around to Sammy, his eyes resumed their green color. Tears flowed down her face as she softly petted Buddy's head. Buddy was in far too much pain to move, but didn't whimper. Connor quickly knelt down next to Sammy and stroked Buddy once from head to tail. This time Buddy did whimper as Connor passed over his rib cage. From what Connor could tell, Buddy had suffered a couple of broken ribs, but it was difficult to tell if there was any internal bleeding.

"Is ... is Buddy going to be okay?" Sammy cried.

"I sure hope so, Sammy." Connor grabbed the keys out of his pocket. "Go run to the car and open the back door."

Sammy ran to the gun-metal Subaru WRX and opened the door as

Connor swiftly picked up the whimpering dog, ran with him to the car and carefully set him down on the back seat, Buddy licking his face in gratitude. Then Sammy climbed in to accompany Buddy. Connor hopped in the driver's seat and took off. At this moment, the traffic laws meant nothing to him, but he kept a far-ranging eye out for police, who would only get in his way. Using his incredibly fast reflexes and knowledge of the streets, Connor raced around other cars, drove on the wrong side of the road and ran four stop lights without incident. Occasionally he would glance at Sammy, who was whispering praise and encouragement to Buddy. Within six minutes, they were at the closest emergency veterinarian's clinic.

Urgency propelled Connor out of the car. He flung open the passenger door to pick up Buddy, as delicately as if he were a baby bird. Once in Connor's arms, Buddy licked his face affectionately. It seemed to Connor that Buddy wanted to say his last goodbyes, but he was refusing to accept goodbye. The death of this dog would be catastrophic to Sammy. Closing the car door with his foot, Connor sped towards the clinic, where Sammy was already holding open the door. Tears silently streamed down her face as she watched Buddy lying injured in Connor's arms.

Bursting into the clinic, Connor created a sense of urgency akin to a hospital emergency room. Seeing the situation, one of the two vet techs ran to fetch the vet while the other asked: "What happened?"

"He was kicked in the rib cage. There are definitely broken ribs, but I'm more concerned about a ruptured organ," Connor explained, as the other tech and a veterinarian came out with a gurney. Connor gently laid Buddy down.

The vet was a tall man with broad shoulders, peppered hair and glasses. It gave Connor some comfort that this man appeared to have a serious concern for Buddy.

Connor repeated what he'd told the vet tech.

"Why is there blood in his mouth?" the vet asked accusingly.

Connor looked at Sammy, hoping she wouldn't say anything, then turned back to the vet. "A dog was going to attack her. Buddy jumped in and saved her. The owner of the other dog came running over and kicked

Buddy in the rib cage to stop the dog fight. Please, do whatever it takes to save his life."

The vet and a tech disappeared into the back with Buddy on the gurney.

The other vet tech stayed put. "Sir, I will need to you fill out some paperwork. Your daughter can take a seat over there," she said, pointing to a row of plastic chairs.

"I'm her guardian, not her father," Connor corrected.

"Oh, I'm so sorry. Um …" she looked around awkwardly and then went behind the desk to get the papers ready.

Connor turned and knelt down to Sammy's level.

"Is Buddy going to be okay?" Sammy sniffled, the flow of tears slowing.

"Buddy is in good hands," Connor said with a smile. He rested his hands on her shoulders for comfort.

Sammy ran into Connor's arms and hugged him around the neck. Her tearful face buried in his shoulder, she sobbed, "I don't want him to die."

Connor was putty in her hands. He embraced her tightly and rubbed her back. This was a moment he would treasure despite the horrible circumstances. As he held her, Connor whispered in her ear, "Buddy will be fine. He knows he needs to come back to you. Buddy will be hurting for a few days, but he will be all right."

It took several minutes for Sammy to calm down and stop crying. Connor didn't mind. It was as if holding her was his entire life's purpose: to be there for her whenever she needed him. As Connor held her, tears and snot soaked his shirt, he felt a deep warmth that could only be described as love.

Finally, Sammy pulled away and smeared the snot on her face.

"Eww," Connor laughed in a way that made Sammy laugh as well. "Why don't you go clean up in the bathroom while I sign papers with this nice lady over here."

Sammy nodded her head and slowly walked into the bathroom.

"I need you to fill out a few forms and designate your method of payment," the vet tech repeated cheerfully.

"Don't be so cheerful that her dog is dying," Connor said in a menacing tone. This woman was really getting on his nerves. It isn't ethical to ask for payment before securing the life you are trying to save, he thought. Nonetheless, Connor filled out the papers while Sammy cleaned up in the bathroom.

Several minutes later, Sammy came out of the bathroom and joined Connor in the waiting area. Although there were multiple magazines on the table near the chairs, they did little to entertain her for long. Sammy perked up at every sound that came from the other room. Every time the door opened, she would begin to get up as if she expected Buddy to come running out. For two hours, Sammy watched the door, hoping Buddy would come out all right. A little past five o'clock, the vet finally came out, a serene expression on his face.

The vet drew out the intense moment until it was too much for Sammy to bear. Releasing a deep exhale, he said, "Buddy is going to be all right. Two ribs are fractured and there are some torn muscles, but no ruptured organs nor internal bleeding."

The good news elevated Sammy to her feet, followed by triumphant bounces.

"When can we bring him home?" Connor asked calmly.

"I want to keep him overnight for observation. If nothing goes awry, then you can take him home in the morning," the vet replied.

Sammy's triumphant bounces stopped. "You mean he can't come home with me tonight?" Sammy asked woefully.

"If anything bad were to suddenly happen to Buddy, then he will be much safer here, where we can immediately treat him," the vet explained.

Connor stood up and turned Sammy's chin to face him, "Buddy will be perfectly safe here. Why don't we go out to eat tonight, to get your mind off things. What do you say?"

Sammy looked down, disappointed. "I guess."

The rest of the evening passed in silence. Even eating at Sammy's favorite diner did little to brighten her mood. She hardly spoke, and when she did, it was only about Buddy. When they finally got home, she silently went upstairs to get ready for bed.

Giving her some space, Connor went about his business, getting things cleaned up and preparing for tomorrow morning. After several minutes, he heard the distinct sound of a light switch followed by the rustling of covers. Concerned, Connor went upstairs into her bedroom.

He lightly knocked on the door and waited for her to say "Come in" before entering. Sammy was lying in bed, wrapped tightly in her covers, with her back to the door.

Without permission, Connor turned on the light and came to sit down on the edge of the bed. "Sammy, talk to me. Why are you feeling so down?"

Sammy turned over so Connor could see her tear-stained face. "It's all my fault that Buddy got hurt!" she cried.

"Hey," Connor said softly as he wiped the tears away. "None of it is your fault. Buddy was protecting you, which he will happily do again because he cares deeply for you."

Sammy seriously looked into Connor's green eyes. "But I told Buddy to do it. That strange man was frightening me and saying he was going to take me away from you. I was scared so I told Buddy to attack."

While it was true that *she* had a special connection with animals, he never quite grasped to what extent. Connor consoled her, "Sammy, I didn't hear you say anything and I have really good hearing. Buddy attacked that man to defend you and would do it again if it meant your safety."

Sammy sat up and yelled, "No, Connor, you aren't listening to me. I told Buddy to attack the man and then I told Buddy to hang onto the man and bite his arm harder. Buddy obeyed me like he always has … just like that tiger did. I am the one who got Buddy hurt. It was all my fault!" Sammy fell into Connor's lap and cried harder.

"Sammy, how long have you been talking with animals?" Connor asked curiously while Sammy clutched onto his shirt and cried into it.

"Since the tiger," Sammy sobbed into Connor's chest.

"Well, then, you are a very special young lady, aren't you?" Connor said with a smile.

Sammy looked up into Connor's sparkling green eyes and asked, "Am I not normal?"

This moment seemed so pivotal in her development. He knew that her destined signs would appear sooner or later. He had just hoped they would be later. The nightmares hadn't started yet, which was a huge blessing. So far, Connor was proud that he had been able to shield her from the horrors of the world that would seal her fate— a fate he hoped to permanently stop this time. Still, the matter of the animals was compelling. On one hand, Connor could foster this ability and make it grow into a strength that could save her life. On the other hand, it might cause even more trouble for her if she couldn't control it.

"No, Sammy, you aren't normal. But then again, there is no such thing as normal. I'm definitely not normal. Your dad wasn't normal, nor your mom. Normal is something everyone strives to be, yet there is no definition or model to guide them. I suggest you be happy with all the wonderful things you have in your life. Such as a dog who would be willing to put his life on the line to save you," Connor explained.

Sammy wiped her tears with her pajama shirt. "And I have you, Connor. You make me happy as well."

"And I am willing to go to the ends of the earth to make you happy," Connor added.

"Don't do that, Connor," Sammy said, beginning to cheer up. "I would much rather you stay next to me."

"I can do that," Connor said with a warm smile. Wrapping his arm around the girl, he gave her a big hug that she gladly reciprocated. "Do you still want to hear the story of Pearl Harbor? It might help take your mind off things."

Sammy's eyes lit up. She always loved it when she could hear a new story for the first time. Snuggling up in her blankets and grabbing a pillow to hold, she enthusiastically commanded, "Tell me a tale of Pearl Harbor."

Getting into the role, Connor's green eyes glistened as he leaned in. "Let me tell you a tale of bravery!"

* * *

195

OAHU, HAWAII

DECEMBER 6, 1941

The sun shone brightly on a warm, humid day in Honolulu. A large battleship cast its shadow on a group of young adults. Lazy puffs of smoke drifted up from their cigarettes. Three candy-stripe nurses were giggling at the crude jokes four naval officers were making at the expense of the Germans.

"Oh Rob! You're terrible!" An auburn-haired young woman with green eyes giggled in a flirty sort of way.

"Yeah, well, you love it, Shirley! Otherwise you wouldn't love me the way you do," a buff navy officer laughed, then leaned in close and gave her a kiss on the lips.

Shirley pulled away and wagged a finger at her boyfriend. "Now, now, Rob. Love is a strong word. What makes that big head of yours think I love you?" The other two women laughed and added support to Shirley's claim.

"That depends on which head you're talking about, Shirley," Rob said smugly, smoothing back his blonde greased-up hair with a comb. The other three officers laughed and stood behind him. "Shirley, I already know that you *love* my big head. You've moaned it several times," Rob continued, making crude sexual gestures. The other officers laughed in their own immature manner.

"These navy brutes are all the same," a blonde nurse by the name of Denise said. "Why do you put up with this bum?"

Shirley looked at her boyfriend, knowing she could ruin his reputation if he kept pushing it. "Because I know something the rest of you don't … that he is actually a softie pretending to be all tough for his crew."

Instantly the tide turned against Rob. Eager to jump to any conclusion that would give them a good laugh, the other officers made jests at Rob's expense.

Intolerant of disrespect, Rob instantly pulled rank. "Stop your hollering or else I'll demote you all to seamen scrubbing the decks!" Instantly the men stopped and assumed their saluting positions.

"Come now, Rob, enough with the games," Shirley said as she wrapped one of her arms around his, "Will you walk me to work?"

Switching to a more gentlemanly tone, Rob replied in a suave voice, "It will be my pleasure."

Shirley winked at the girls. The other nurses giggled. As they all walked over to the hospital, half a mile from the naval base, Shirley put on her white tri-tipped hat. While pinning it in her hair, she noticed a young man no older than herself. He appeared to be another naval seaman: sharp blue service dress uniform, slicked-back black hair tucked beneath a blue navy cap, and a robotic walk. However, his eyes made him stand out: they were purple. At an opportune moment, the wind caught the edge of her flimsy nurse's hat and sent it flying.

"My hat!" Shirley called. She'd be in big trouble if she came to work without her full uniform.

Frantically, she ran after the hat, fearing it would end up in the water and be ruined. The young seaman with the strange eyes leapt up and caught it.

He dusted its edges and returned the hat to a relieved Shirley.

"Thank you so much! I would have been in deep trouble had I lost the hat," Shirley graciously said.

"No trouble at all, Miss Shirley. I'm glad I could be of assistance," he replied.

A blush appeared on Shirley's cheeks as she approached. "How did you know my name was Shirley?"

He chuckled. "I overheard you talking with your friends." Friends who were quickly advancing towards them.

Shirley flirtatiously twirled her skirt. "What's your name, seaman?"

He could see his superior quickly approaching, yet made no move to walk away. "I'm so sorry, Miss Shirley, my name tag was actually damaged a couple of days ago. I'm a new recruit— sailed in last week. My name is Clarence Roberts."

Shirley held out her hand. "Nice to meet you, Clarence."

Instead of shaking it, Clarence bent down and kissed the top of her hand, as his captivating purple eyes looked intently up into her gorgeous green ones. A small gesture, but enough to make Shirley swoon and Petty Officer Rob to pull rank. As if in slow motion, Clarence could see a fist flying through the air, an attack he normally would have easily evaded. Yet there was something more gratifying about letting Shirley see her boyfriend's true colors, so Clarence stood his ground and let the fist catch him right under the cheekbone. Dramatically, Clarence turned his head at the right moment to turn the punch into a glancing blow, making it look worse than it was. To add to the drama of the hit, he twirled and fell to the ground.

"Don't you ever lay another fucking hand on my girl," Rob shouted as he pointed menacingly at Clarence, who was adjusting his jaw back into position, purposely biting down on his tongue to release enough blood to spit on the ground in front of Rob.

"Rob!" Shirley said in a shrill voice. "What was that for? He didn't do anything wrong."

Rob turned on Shirley, casting a shadow over her with his bulk. "Shirley, he kissed your hand. He was trying to seduce you." Then Rob turned towards Clarence, who was standing up, "This *freak* was trying to find some way to get into your dress!"

Clarence remarked, "They say a jealousy is a reflection of one's own failures."

"You fucking freak! Boys, grab him!" Rob commanded. Instantly, the lower-ranking officers bolted forward to restrain Clarence, who made no move to defend himself. Two of them grabbed each of his arms, pulling them apart, while the third got behind Clarence and held him in a choke hold. Shirley screamed at Rob to stop as he advanced as if he were a steaming bull, delivering punch after punch into Clarence's stomach. Offering no resistance, Clarence made sure to react as a normal human would, even though the blows felt more akin to light taps. She screamed for Rob to stop, but he paid no heed. Not today. What Shirley didn't know was that Rob had been Clarence's superior for the past week and had instantly grown to hate him. He hated Clarence's ability to pass every test with flying colors, beating some of Rob's old records. The higher ranking officers admired Clarence and had expressed hopes of promoting him as fast as possible, which threatened Rob.

Shirley had enough of Rob's behavior. Determined to stop his bullying, she ran up behind her boyfriend and pulled hard enough on his shirt to make him fall backwards. "Stop it right this instant!"

Rob pivoted on his elbow to look up at her. "He's a purple-eyed freak, Sugar!"

Shirley pointed a sharp finger right at Rob's nose. "You are not to use that word, Robert. He can't help the eyes he was born with. You are being a schoolyard bully while he was being a gentleman. Say you're sorry!"

Rob glared venomously at Clarence, weighing the consequences against the satisfaction he would get from pulverizing this lowly freak. Clarence smiled bemusedly at the petty officer. The other officers released their grip, but as soon as Clarence had his arms free, Rob gave him one last upper cut that clipped the edge of his chin. Replicating the reaction of a normal human being, Clarence rotated in the air and smacked the ground hard.

"I'm sorry," Rob stated mockingly.

"Rob!" Shirley growled, hitting his chest with weak little slaps. "You are such an egotistical brute! I swear to God if—"

Before she could finish, Clarence pushed himself off the ground. "No, please," —Clarence looked directly into her green eyes with his swirling purple eyes— "I am sorry. I didn't mean to cause this much trouble for you."

Thinking Clarence was apologizing to him, Rob puffed out his chest. "On your way then. We will talk about your behavior in the morning with the senior officer."

"Yes, sir," Clarence responded in a depressed tone as he walked away from them with his head hung low. A show of defeat, yet a strategic move to win Shirley over. Knowing her personality, she wouldn't stand by while someone was beaten into submission.

Several hours later, Clarence sat on the edge of the pier, facing the bow of the warship. In his lap, he held a large drawing pad and charcoal. Even with little more than moonlight, he could clearly make out the details of the ship and recorded them on the drawing pad. Over the years he had gotten pretty good at drawing. They were merely replications of real life, after all.

"Hello, Clarence," a soft, feminine voice said from behind him.

Clarence smiled and turned around. "Good evening, Miss Shirley. What are you doing here so late?"

Hands held behind her back, it was evident that she was shy to approach him. She still wore her nurse's uniform, minus the hat, which she'd stuffed into her pocket. "When I got off work I could see you sitting here from the lobby windows up at the hospital. I wanted to come down and apologize for Rob's behavior. He's not here, of course."

Clarence gave her a warm, welcoming smile. "Would you like to join me?"

"Sure," Shirley responded, her eyes twinkling similar to the stars above.

Shirley was careful to tuck her dress underneath her before sitting down on the salty pier.

Watching her cute mannerisms, from the way she nibbled on her lower lip to the gentle gestures of her hands, Clarence couldn't help but be smitten by her. "You didn't need to come and apologize. None of that was your fault."

"I still feel awful that he treated you," Shirley said, as if she'd been the one punching Clarence's stomach earlier.

Lightly pressing his finger on the opposite side of her chin, Clarence made her look into his mysterious purple eyes. "None of this is your fault, okay, Shirley?"

"You're only human, Clarence. And so is he. It is not his job to bully you, and it is not your job to take it." Her wisdom, he thought, was more reminiscent of a schoolteacher than a nurse.

A warm, tropical breeze wafted around them. The clear water reflected the moon in her eyes and illuminated her face. She was breathtaking to behold. Clarence found it near impossible to pull away, as if he were caught in some snare he was eager to stay trapped in. By the way Shirley started to lean in, he could tell that she was also captivated by his magnetism.

"Do you believe in soul mates?" she whispered, her lips a mere inch away from his own.

Sparks flew as the two inched closer. Time itself seemed to stop ... or at least stop long enough for Clarence to gather his thoughts. It was all far too easy, almost as if fate were setting a cruel trap for him. Every other time, it had taken much persuading and reconnaissance to get this close to her ... to get her to want him. Yet this time it was effortless. Her question echoed in his head. Did he believe in soul mates? Of course he did, because she was his soul mate. Yet if this happened too fast, especially under these circumstances, her guilt would pull them apart. He had been patient for so long, and now it required a little more patience. Clarence pulled away from her kiss he wished to taste so badly. It was a kiss that was offering itself to him— a kiss that would have to wait.

Shirley opened her eyes in surprise and then quickly resumed her original seated position. Even under the dull light, a deep blush could be seen on her cheeks.

"I'm sorry," Clarence explained. "It would be dishonorable to kiss you right now. I have too much respect for you to allow you to cheat."

Shirley didn't respond, muted by her own embarrassment.

"I do believe in soul mates, though," Clarence continued. "But how could you know if I'm your soul mate? We barely met."

Shirley smiled, "Well, let us fix that, then." She extended her hand. "My name is Shirley McCloud. Nice to meet you."

"McCloud?" Clarence raised an eyebrow as her shook her hand. "Are you Scottish?"

"Yes, my father brought me here to America when I was a wee lass. Scottish born, American proud!" she said in a quite convincing Scottish accent.

"That makes sense," Clarence mumbled under his breath.

"What makes sense?" Shirley asked, confusedly.

Clarence waved away the thought with his hand. "Oh nothing."

"Hmmm," —Shirley gave him a curious glance— "Where are you descended from, Clarence Roberts?"

"From a long line of nobodies that no one ever seems to remember," he joked.

They both laughed in unison. The connection was effortless.

"What are you drawing?" Shirley asked.

Clarence pulled out the sketchpad and handed it to her. She flipped through the white pages full of charcoal pictures of navy guns, planes and ships. Each of which was drawn perfectly to scale, almost as if she were seeing a black and white picture. The drawings also had a variety of numbers written very minutely in pencil, the current one of the ship showing numbers as well.

"These are very well done, Clarence. You should be an artist instead of a seaman. What are these numbers for, though?" she asked.

Clarence sighed as if he had said this a million times. "Some are simple measurements, such as the side of the ship here. Others are calculations for how much heat or pressure something can withstand."

"Are you a spy or something?" Shirley joked as she handed the drawings back.

"Not at all. I'm proud to serve in the U.S. Navy. I simply find these engineering achievements fascinating. Only a few decades ago, humans were building wooden ships with sails and oars. Now they are moving through the power of steam and coal." —Clarence redirected his attention to Shirley— "Why are you so drawn to the military? Why aren't you married with kids already?"

Shirley laughed. "There's something sexy about a strong man willing to fight for something bigger than himself. Also, I'm only 21, thank you very much. Kids can wait," she said, staring down at her candy-striped skirt with flushed cheeks.

"Shirley..." Clarence said with longing.

Shirley looked deep into his purple eyes, her green eyes sparkling with a strong desire to be with him. This was everything Clarence wanted. This was his goal, but he didn't feel right about how easy it seemed to be to achieve. He couldn't accept the simplicity of this moment. Nothing was ever this simple.

"You should get home, Shirley. We can talk tomorrow after you have rested," Clarence said woefully.

"Why are you pushing me away?" Shirley asked, seemingly hurt from the rejection.

"Because you have a boyfriend," Clarence stated bluntly. "Goodnight, Shirley. This was the best night I have had in a long time."

A toothy, almost childish smile popped on her face. With quick precision, she kissed him on the cheek and stood up. "Well, perhaps the next time we meet, I will be available for you to court me. Goodnight, Clarence."

Clarence put a hand up to the kissed cheek, now stained with a lipstick mark. He watched her skip away with a light heart. He felt a similar elation, even if he didn't show it.

The next morning, Clarence was completing his daily tasks on the ship. Though it was nearly impossible to focus on the task at hand. Clarence was on cloud nine thinking about Shirley. Their instant attraction was effortless. Quite a relief to Clarence who had been spending weeks mulling over how he was going to win her affection. Even now he could hear her voice as clear as silver bells.

Clarence paused in the hallway and waited. Her voice wasn't only in his head. He could actually hear her. Following her voice, Clarence made his way down the hallway and listened in at Rob's door.

Shirley adamantly announced, "We are breaking up, Rob!"

For a moment, Rob was speechless, then he laughed. "Shirley, Shirley, Shirley, is this about that seaman? I already apologized to him."

"Doesn't matter anymore. We are breaking up!" Shirley repeated stubbornly.

Getting serious, Rob asserted his voice the same way he would discipline a seaman. "What if I assign him to the Atlantic fleet? Carrying supplies to the war with German U-boats prowling around? What say you then?"

Shirley was now the speechless one.

"We aren't breaking up, Shirley. You are going to be my wife. Do you know why this is going to happen?" Rob threatened.

Shirley mumbled, but otherwise had no voice. All the power she had was gone.

"You are going to stay with me, otherwise I'll send him to his death. If you want to stand up for the little guy … the *freak* in this case … then you will be loyal, by my side," Rob commanded with a slight snarl. Suddenly his voice morphed to a softer tone, "Now, Sugar, why don't you go back home? Go doll yourself up the way I like. Then tonight I will take you out for a very special date. A wonderful evening you will remember forever."

Shirley didn't speak.

Impatiently, Rob grabbed her arm and pulled her out of the room. "Come on Shirley, you know you can't be here. You are going to get me in trouble," he said lightheartedly, but his grip was rough and forceful. This gave Clarence an opening.

"Ow, Rob. You're hurting me," Shirley winced as she tried to undo his vice grip on her upper arm.

Clarence's blood boiled. Without warning, he slammed Rob against the wall so forcefully it caused the metal to indent. Shirley was jolted to a stop and noticed that Rob's grip had loosened and his feet were slightly elevated off the ground.

"It is not gentlemanly to bruise a lady," Clarence growled. "Let her go."

Immediately, Rob let go of Shirley, who rubbed her sore arm. Then Clarence let go of Rob's upper arm. The heels of the petty officer's boots clicked against the metal-grate floor as he regained his balance. Rob imitated Shirley and rubbed his own arm.

Rob shoved Shirley back into his room. "Get back!"

Shirley fell sprawled on the ground. The heavy door shutting with an audible click.

"How dare you interfere and injure a superior. You will be punished for this insubordination!" Rob growled.

"Do you honestly think I fear you at all?" Clarence hissed, sizing Rob up as if he were a predator analyzing its prey. "I have no respect for bullies who flex their muscles against the vulnerable."

"I'm going to teach you a lesson, you purple-eyed freak!" Rob threatened as he chambered a punch and uncoiled it right onto Clarence's cheek. The effect was unexpected. Rob's fist crumpled against Clarence's immovable face. Not even a mark was left from the blow. Rob's heartbeat quickened as he threw another punch.

This time, Clarence caught the punch with an open hand, then crunched down on the fist as though juicing an orange. With his hand bent backwards and threatening to break in several places, Rob went down on his knees in pain.

"Ah yes, you want to know why I have purple eyes? Let me show you," Clarence said with a maniacal smile. With an open clawed hand, he swept down to bash Officer Rob's head against the side of the wall. Not enough to kill him, but definitely enough to knock him unconscious. Right before his hand made impact, Clarence heard footsteps behind him, and stopped his strike inches from Rob's face.

"What is going on here?" a lieutenant asked sternly.

Anger rolled deep in Clarence's chest. It was an inconvenient interruption. He knew that attacking his commanding officer in full sight of the lieutenant would get him shipped immediately to another post—a risk he couldn't afford. Clarence turned on a dime to salute the lieutenant.

Rob scrambled up. "Lieutenant Bryan! This seaman attacked me!"

The lieutenant's shoulders remained wound tight with authority and his chin high. All it would take was a snap of his fingers to put both men in the brig. "Seaman, why did you attack your superior?" he said, his face inches from Clarence's.

Standing at attention, Clarence answered robotically, "After being held down and beaten by Officer Stillman and his fellow officers, I have lost all respect for him, SIR!"

The lieutenant asked Rob, "Petty Officer Second Class Robert Stillman."

"Sir!" Rob responded in a salute.

"Why would you beat down a seaman?" the lieutenant asked calmly.

"He made disrespectful comments. I was punishing him for mouthing off to me, sir!" Rob replied robotically.

"You do realize we have different protocols for a mouthy seaman, correct?" the lieutenant asked.

Rob didn't answer. He didn't need to, because he knew the rules.

Clarence spoke up again, "Officer Stillman called me a purple-eyed freak, which he believes gives him the excuse to beat me up, sir!"

The lieutenant turned back to Clarence. "Although I will agree that your bizarre eye color causes alarm in some, you are still an excellent seaman nonetheless. You were assigned to Pearl Harbor because you hold promise. We expect great things from you, Seaman Roberts. I know that you will quickly climb the ranks because of your advanced skills. Maybe that is why Officer Stillman feels threatened by you." Lieutenant Bryan looked over at Rob briefly before turning back to Clarence. "That being said, in the military, respect for authority is a necessity. Punching your superior will hurt your progression, regardless of the reasons. I'm willing to waive further punishment for this outburst if you are willing to accept a reprimand."

"I will accept the consequences, sir!" Clarence responded.

Lieutenant Bryan nodded, then addressed Rob again. "What do you feel is a proper punishment?"

Rob glared at Clarence. "One hundred push ups with one hundred lashes."

The lieutenant rolled his eyes. "Twenty-five will be enough."

"Yes, sir!" Rob said, a little smugger as he sharply saluted the lieutenant again.

"Follow me," lieutenant said to both of them.

"Sir," they responded in unison as they marched behind him to the deck of the ship.

The sun was blindingly bright as it reflected off the water below. Clarence wondered how long Shirley would sit in Rob's quarters before growing restless and walking out. The usual chaos ensued around him as the ship's personnel went about their morning drills and tasks. Most would be done soon, but Clarence still had a long list to accomplish. This distraction was not helping him with his workload. He walked out to the middle of the deck where they did their morning exercise drills as a unit.

Before Clarence could get in a push up position, Rob commanded, "Shirt off!"

Without giving him any eye contact, Clarence yelled out, "I would prefer to keep my shirt on, sir!" He didn't want them to see his scar. That could cause more trouble than it was worth.

"Will you accept financial responsibility for buying a new uniform shirt if this one is damaged?" Lieutenant Bryan asked calmly.

"Sir, yes, sir!" Clarence said as he got down into a push up position. He noticed Rob smirking.

"One!" the Lieutenant called out. Clarence performed a perfect push up, followed by a whip to his back, but he didn't falter.

"Two! ... Three! ... Four! ..." Something in the distance caught Clarence's attention: the distant sound of planes. They didn't sound like US Air Force, though; there was a different pitch to the engines, a more exhausted, noisy tone.

"Five!" The planes were getting closer and there was a growing unease deep in the pit of Clarence's stomach. He craned his neck to look behind and possibly catch a glimpse of the oncoming planes. Out of the corner of his eye, he barely saw them. At the moment, they were tiny little specks in the sky. Too far for the average human eye or ear to detect, yet Clarence was starting to make them out.

"Five! Pay attention!" Rob screamed the order. Obediently, Clarence performed another push up and the whip came crashing down.

"Six!" This time Clarence did the push up with advanced speed. He could hear the planes coming closer. Now he was sure they weren't American.

"Seven!" Clarence couldn't care less about the order. The planes were getting dangerously close. By now everyone heard. Everyone that is, except Rob.

Before Rob could call the next, aerial gunfire rained down upon the deck. Chaos erupted on deck; no one had been prepared for this sort of attack.

As the other sailors scattered, Clarence maintained the push up position as the assault continued. Three bullets hit him, rapid-fire, with the velocity to tear right through his femur, kidneys and scapula. All three ripped right through his body into the wooden floor of the deck. Overwhelmed by the sheer power and velocity of the bullets, Clarence fell flat on the deck. Rob, who'd taken shelter from the aerial onslaught, appeared horrified as blood poured from Clarence's body.

It only took a few moments for Clarence to heal. These wounds, he had to admit, hurt worse than any other bullet or knife, but he had a mission that drove him to find and save Shirley.

Now the sound of answering fire was blasting into the sky. Clarence peered up and saw the insignia on the planes swooping low overhead: the Red Sun of Japan. Rob had disappeared from the deck. That made Clarence's decision easier. He jumped off the ship, making a perfect swan dive into the warm waters of Pearl Harbor, seconds before a huge explosion vibrated through the water. Swimming as hard as he could, Clarence found himself dodging large chunks of debris—torpedoes must have hit the ship docked next to his. Time was running out. Clarence finally understood: the Japanese were entering the war on their own terms, trying to destroy a Pacific fleet ill-prepared for a brazen daylight attack. It wouldn't be long until this ship was also struck.

Panic seized Clarence's throat as he swam along the side of the ship, calculating where Rob's quarters were. When he swam up to the surface, he turned his hands into claws and dug his hands into the thick steel. Every grasp left the metal red from the heat he was generating. His eyes swirled a dangerous red as he used his powers.

Finally he was outside Rob's quarters. Holding onto the ship with one hand and supporting himself by pushing hard into the ship with his feet, Clarence focused all the heat into his hand until a large purple flame swirled around his fist in a fireball. Then he punched the ship, melting a large hole in the steel. Shirley screamed on the other side as Clarence ripped away at the metal, making the hole big enough for a human to climb through.

Shirley, cowering in the tiny quarters from the roar of the bombing, appeared terrified of this monster melting away the steel wall. Clarence could understand her fear ... he was a horrifying sight to behold. Although he couldn't make his eyes return to purple from their currently vibrant red, he could withdraws his claws at the very least.

Extending a hand to her, Clarence begged, "Shirley, come with me if you want to live." She stood back, her eyes wild with fear. *There's no time for this*, Clarence thought, so he pulled out his wild card. "Shirley, I do believe in soul mates. You are different from other girls, just as I am different. I want to save you, but you have to trust me."

Explosions continued to thunder all around the harbor: ships going down and anti-aircraft guns seeking their targets in the sky. Time was running out. Rob came bursting in the door, then stared uncomprehendingly.

"Shirley," —Rob stretched his hand out to her— "Get away from him! He's a monster!"

Those words solidified her decision. "No, Rob, you are the monster." Before he could react, she ran toward Clarence. Rob tried to grab her dress to stop her, just as an explosion rocked the ship violently. Rob fell to the ground, and Shirley fell out of the hole. Thanks to Clarence's quick reflexes, he managed to catch her before she plunged into the water.

More explosions erupted within the ship. It was leaning toward the side where Clarence was clinging with one claw, holding Shirley with the other hand. Clearly, the ship was about to go down, too.

"Take a deep breath!" Clarence commanded.

Shirley took a large breath and down they fell, hitting the water and swimming fast away from the ship. Clarence feared the suction from the sinking ship. It was slow going for Shirley, with her heavy dress weighing her down, and they couldn't stay underwater long. Although he couldn't die, not even from drowning, Clarence still needed air to stay conscious. Clarence knew he could hold his breath for twelve minutes before succumbing to the darkness, but she couldn't last more than two. If he could get her past the pier, she had a high likelihood of survival.

Time was running out. Clarence realized a shadow was coming over them, fast. The ship was sinking, turning over faster than anticipated, and with the fall came the suction as water poured into every doorway and hole in the ship. There was no time to swim away.

Shirley's eyes widened in horror when she saw death looming.

"As the ship falls, we are going to climb back on as fast as we can," Clarence shouted, strategizing. "The ship will trap air initially, which we can use to survive for a short period of time."

"Are you crazy?" Shirley asked.

"Trust me!" Clarence yelled over the explosions.

Propelling her along as fast as he could, Clarence pushed her while paddling madly himself. *At least she's a strong swimmer,* he thought. The closer they got, the more it appeared they were going to be crushed by the ship. But this was the point of no return. Clarence hoped they could make it into an opening on the captain's deck. Desperately, he flung Shirley into an open hatch. Before the ship crushed him, he saw her get inside safely. If he calculated correctly, she would have thirty minutes of air minimum before the windows cracked. As the world went black, he was content at least knowing he had given her thirty extra minutes to plan her escape.

Light filtered in. The first sense that returned to him was the sensation of soft lips pressed against his own. Then he felt the pressure on his nostrils, closing them off. What made him wake up completely was the sudden burst of air being pushed into his water-filled lungs. Clarence jolted awake to Shirley resuscitating him with her years of nursing experience. She had held him above the water level in this small room and breathed air into his lungs. Clarence gasped and coughed the rest of the water out of his lungs.

After regaining full consciousness, Clarence looked around and noticed that the water level was far higher than he originally anticipated.

"How long was I unconscious?" He looked back at an exhausted Shirley and quickly rephrased: "Thank you Shirley, but you should have saved yourself."

Shirley blushed, "You saved me, so I figured it was only fair to save you. Honestly, after your head was busted open by the edge of that metal door frame, I was surprised when you healed before my eyes. I figured the least

I could do is see if I could get you to breathe."

"Shirley ..." Clarence said.

"Yes?" Shirley asked with dreamy eyes, hoping for a last, romantic moment.

Clarence wanted to tell her that he loved her. He wanted to hold her in his arms and kiss her passionately. He wanted to be with her more than anything. But he couldn't give her these things ... so instead of telling her his deepest desires, he said, "You're bleeding, Shirley!"

Shirley put a hand on her left side. She already knew this. "I got cut on a piece of metal when I was pulling you into the cabin to keep you from being crushed by the ship."

That was when he noticed how pale she was and how blue her lips were. Clarence kicked himself for not noticing the decline of oxygen in the room.

"Shirley, how much blood have you—" But before he could finish his statement, the windows finally cracked and water came rushing in. Shirley didn't have a chance to take a breath. In her weakened state, Clarence knew she wouldn't last long. Already her heart was racing fast and her lungs were stressed for oxygen. Grabbing her around the waist, Clarence pushed off the ship and jetted for the surface. But there was still another thirty feet to go.

Shirley could hold on no longer. Opening her mouth reflexively only caused water to fill her lungs. Clarence watched her clutch her throat as she drowned. In desperation, Clarence put his lips to her blue ones and tried to breathe the air from his lungs into hers. But, once again helpless to save her life, Clarence watched the light fade from her beautiful green eyes.

Lost in despair, Clarence held onto her for a few precious moments as her heart finally stopped. Then her body burst into a million purple wisps that glowed under the sea in a breathtaking array of light. Very slowly, they floated to the surface of the water as Clarence fell back down to the sunken ship, with a handful of grindylows, vile bottom-feeders, latching onto his flesh to begin their feast.

The deeper he fell, the greater his rage grew. The water grew hot around him as heat radiated from his body. Unable to withstand the heat, the grindylows fled, looking for easier prey. Soon, the water boiled around him as his eyes turned blood red. Not being able to contain himself anymore, Clarence furiously screamed through the water.

On the surface, things were calming down. The anti-aircraft weapons had brought down or chased away the Japanese air fleet. Twenty-one ships had been hit, either sunk and lying on the ocean floor, or badly damaged and billowing up black smoke. The search was on for survivors as the full scope of the horror became apparent. The pier they had been trying to reach was in splinters, floating in the wreckage.

A handful of navy personnel scrambled to the scene and saw a miraculous glow amid the tragedy. Millions of tiny purple lights drifted out of the water, drawing attention as these delicate and surreal wisps danced in the air and swirled upward.

Once the beauty was gone, the horror followed. The emergency crews stepped back from the boiling water. Before they could vacate the area, a huge torrent of steam erupted into the sky. Purple fire and smoke swept around the region, catching all survivors in its wake. The heat was so intense it had evaporated straight to the sea floor, burning the coral, crustaceans and fish. Any human caught in this hurricane of fire and steam was quickly disintegrated to ash. The fire raged and reached to the sky with a frightening array of power that ate up Pearl Harbor and the surrounding quarter mile around the harbor.

As quickly as it had appeared, it suddenly vanished. A great torrent of burning-hot rain poured down within a mile radius of the explosion. The sea took back its burnt and dead land with a fury that only Mother Nature could unleash. The water broke the blackened sea floor, pushing the hardened earth onto the beach, and swallowed up the town. People and buildings were swept into the sea as it pulled its water from the island. Screams of loved ones lost to the disaster were washed away by the vengeful sea, leaving behind a chilling silence. This explosion would forever be remembered as the first, unprovoked attack by the Japanese imperial regime. The atomic bombs the U.S. unleashed upon Japan, although horrific, were never quite satisfying for Americans who suspected Japan to have been the first to drop a nuclear warhead, in Hawaii.

Three days later, as the debris washed upon the Hawaiian beaches, a body was discovered. As the naval patrol came to claim and tag it, they were astonished to find the dead man was actually alive. He was reported to be the only living survivor in the attack on Pearl Harbor. Although his clothes were burnt beyond recognition, he was identified as a seaman and immediately promoted. According to the records, his story was published all over American newspapers as a hero who defied the worse scenarios and came out on top. Days later, he disappeared, further adding to the mystery of the lone survivor.

* * *

Connor walked towards the bedroom door and glanced over his shoulder at Sammy, who was almost asleep. It was midnight, after all, much too late for her to still be awake. Yet she was far too entranced by his story to fall asleep earlier. "Goodnight, Sammy, sweet dreams."

Right before he closed the door, he heard her soft voice mumble, "Goodnight. I love you, Connor."

He was speechless. After all these years of caring for her, love had always been expressed, yet rarely spoken.

Reciprocating her words of affirmation, Connor whispered, "I love you too, Sammy," and shut the door noiselessly.

Walking down the hall suddenly became more difficult. The burden of responsibility weighed down on him, creating a heaviness, simply from a word he hadn't heard spoken to him in centuries. Simultaneously, he was elated from hearing the word *love*. His conflicting emotions made it a struggle to walk down the hallway to his bedroom. Once hidden behind his bedroom door, Connor fell to the ground. Rattled by these foreign feelings, he put his fingers to his cheek and was surprised to find them wet from tears. There was no reason for these tears, because love could not be reasoned with. Love was illogical, yet a basic necessity for humanity.

Except he wasn't human…

Connor had felt love before, of sorts. Love of another's body. Love of self-preservation. Love of a friend. Love of the kill. Love for power. A love that would drive him to the ends of the Earth just to make *her* smile. A love that would persistently keep him on the same path to save *her* … no matter the cost … no matter how many times he failed.

Yet this sort of love was different. He no longer possessed the love, but rather felt possessed by it. It was this feeling of love that had control over him, over his emotions and over his reactions. It was much deeper than the love for a companion, friend, or a lover. It was a love that ripped away his free will and subjected him to servitude. He was a slave to her love.

Connor felt surer of himself and knew that he would do anything to make her happy, but now he had developed a new love, a new loyalty. Connor would do anything she asked of him, even if it went against his own moral code. He knew what he had to do, even it meant trading his human green eyes for his monstrous red ones.

Determined to head down this set path, Connor pulled out his cellphone and picked the most trustworthy contact he knew.

"Morgan," he spoke into the phone, "I need you over at my place immediately!" Before she could answer, he hung up. Two hours later, there was a knock at the door.

Connor ran downstairs soundlessly. Using a speed technology couldn't keep up with, he put in the alarm code, which disarmed the house instantly. Then, after releasing three more deadbolts, he opened the door.

Morgan stood on the porch, a seductive yet curious expression on her face. It was apparent by her blue-sequined dress and expensive diamond jewelry that she had been at some sort of social gala event.

"I'm sorry to pull you away from your event," Connor lied.

Morgan instantly noticed the drastic change since she had last seen him. "Connor, you look so … so …"

"Different? Weak?" Connor said to fill in her blanks.

"Human …" Morgan said as she reached a hand out to caress his face.

Connor chuckled and greeted, "Morgan, it's good to see you."

214

A smile softened her face. "It's been a few years. What's with the green eyes?"

Connor glowed and felt a warmth in his heart. "I'll explain while I'm preparing. Come upstairs with me."

"You know, in this day and age, it's proper to buy a girl dinner first before taking her up to your bedroom," Morgan teased, but still followed him upstairs.

"How is Peter doing?" Connor sidetracked the conversation, refusing to acknowledge the comment, which made him feel more awkward and uncomfortable than it normally did.

Morgan sighed, "Peter is eccentric, as always. The distance does us good. We truly are amazing for each other, in small doses. Any longer than a year and we start attacking each other."

"Sounds adventurous," Connor replied, unsympathetically.

Morgan collapsed on the bed. "You mind telling me what's going on?"

Connor stripped off his white shirt and jeans. "You are well aware that my eyes are predominantly purple most of the time. When I use my powers, they turn red. The duration of which depends on how much power I use. If I use too much power or give in too much to my evil side, then my eyes turn black for a spell. Well, turns out that happiness— pure happiness— turns my eyes back to their original color."

"You mean?" Morgan asked, leaning forward.

"Yes, this is my true eye color." —Connor stood up to give her a long gaze into his true green eyes— "The same green I was born with. My eyes didn't turn purple until *her* fate and mine were sealed that one fateful day. There's something about her this time. Maybe it's the fact that I have been able to live by her side for much longer than ever before. Maybe it's because she pulls the human side out of me."

"That is wonderful to hear, Caspian. Although I must say it is a bit creepy that you are head over heels in love with an eleven-year-old."

"Call me Connor when in proximity to Sammy." —He gave Morgan a reprimanding look, then resumed putting on his black pants— "When you are as old as I am, age and time mean little. I by no means am sexually

215

attracted to her at this age. The love I have for her is stronger than that … it feels as if I'm a slave to her love."

"Yeah, still creepy." Morgan watched Connor button up his pants and put on some black socks and black combat boots. Along his back, from shoulder to hip, was a long skin-colored mark that could easily be mistaken for a scar. Yet upon closer look, it shone in the light similar to scales. "Do you know what your mark means? I've only ever seen it glow once. That was one of the most terrifying things I have ever witnessed."

Connor paused and peeked over his shoulder, then took a deep breath as if the mark troubled him. "That is not a tale I wish to ever repeat. She has a similar mark on her body. That's how I usually identify it is her when I'm uncertain."

"No," —Morgan shook her head in disagreement— "I've seen *her* bare back on a couple occasions throughout history. It isn't marked."

"Its not on her back," Connor snapped, annoyed by the intrigue. Quickly he put on a black, long-sleeved shirt and then some black leather gloves.

"Who are you hunting this time, Caspian?" Morgan asked.

"There is a man who threatens Sammy. No one gets away with such a crime," Connor said, as he finished pulling a black hoodie over his head.

Morgan paused for a moment, then said disdainfully, "I'm the babysitter …"

"Yes." —Connor turned around to face her— "I know you can keep her safe in my stead. I'll only be gone a couple hours."

Morgan looked down at the ground, giving this some thought. "You know that I will always do my best to serve you in any way I can. I am concerned, though. You finally have this slice of happiness with Samantha. If you give in to your demons, won't you lose these green eyes? Why don't you just send me to do the job instead?"

Connor came over and gave Morgan a hug. A small gesture that startled her for a moment, but she quickly melted into his embrace, grateful for the rare affection. Then Connor pulled away and gave her a genuine smile. "Thank you for your concern. That means a lot to me. I'm sure you can conjure up another outfit while I'm gone. Sammy doesn't know who you are, so tell her the code phrase: 'Butterflies are gentler than ladybugs, but vampires are more unique.'"

"That's an odd phrase, but okay," Morgan said, confused.

"I'll be back before sunrise. Sammy should stay asleep until eight because she stayed up so late." Connor grabbed his car keys off the dresser. "You can watch TV downstairs, just no porn, please."

"Aw, you ruin all my fun, Caspian," Morgan joked.

"Lock the deadbolts behind me," Connor instructed as he raced out the door.

"Happy hunting," Morgan said with a nostalgic smile.

* * *

Torin grumbled to himself as he shuffled over to his crappy cheap room at the very end of the crappy motel complex that literally had a zero-star rating. It was a perfect location to stay without drawing any unwanted attention from the authorities. It had been a shitty day full of disappointment. Somehow, he had found a guy who sold painkillers, which were wrapped several times in a black bag. He'd already taken enough to numb his pain and give him an extra edge. With his hand still injured and poorly wrapped in an ace bandage stained with blood, Torin struggled to get his hotel key out of his pocket and into the keyhole. Finally, after some fumbling, he was able to get the door open.

Torin stumbled in, finding it difficult to regain his balance. Then he threw the package down on the floor and turned on the lights. That was when he saw Connor calmly sitting in a chair with Torin's entire cache of opioids, heroin, meth and marijuana laid out in a very organized manner on the bed.

"What are you doing here? This is breaking and entering! Get out!" Torin screamed.

"I'm here to talk business, Torin. I'm pretty sure that you are not going to call the police," Connor said as he waved his hand over the drugs as if he were a game-show hostess.

"W-w-what kind of business?" Torin asked, clearly afraid. "Do you s-s-see something you like?"

Soaking in Torin's fear, Connor stayed where he was so as not to spook the addict. "How much do these drugs cost nowadays, Torin?"

"Well, um, you see," Torin started, then cleared his throat. "The marijuana is top grade quality so—"

Before Torin had time to register it, Connor was at his side, injecting him with a double dose of heroin. The drug worked faster than normal, riding the painkillers already coursing through Torin's bloodstream. Overwhelmed by the high, Torin fell in a lump on the floor. As he did so, Connor breathed in deeply, as if he were also getting a high.

"Ah! That's the stuff, isn't it, Torin?" Connor asked as his eyes grew darker. "I do miss the hunt."

"What?" —Torin swallowed with difficulty— "What are you going to do to me?"

"Patience, dear Torin, patience," Connor said as he bent down and grabbed Torin's arm. As though he were flinging a rag doll, Connor threw Torin onto the bed. A wet popping sound went off as his shoulder was pulled out of its socket. Torin grumbled, but he was too numbed to offer any other response.

"Now you see, Torin, you threatened Sammy's happiness. I will assume by your past history and your present obsession that you were after her money. I'm a nice guy,"—Connor gestured towards himself, then shrugged— "these days. I would have been more than happy to pay you off to never show your face around her again. However, that would be a risky call on my part. After all, addicts can't get enough of their sweet, sweet drug." Connor picked up another syringe full of heroin. "And you want to guess what my drug of choice is, Torin?"

"Don't hurt me," he mumbled as drool dripped out of the side of his mouth.

Connor leaned in. "Don't worry, Torin, I'm amazing at finding the right target. I can get this needle into your vein with my eyes closed. A man such as yourself has probably built up a tolerance to these drugs, so I've added an extra kick to this one that you might like."

Connor injected the heroin into Torin's injured arm for the second time. As he did so, Torin mumbled, but could no longer make out any words.

"Oh, that's right," Connor said playfully as he picked up a third syringe, "I never told you what my drug of choice is. Silly me!"

Placing the needle into his injured arm for the third time, Connor leaned over Torin. He wanted to watch the light fade from eyes.

Torin watched Connor's eyes as they swirled from a green into a devilish red. "My high comes from killing pathetic souls such as yourself," Connor said venomously. "This is for Sammy." Using the energy from his hand, Connor heated the liquid until it was boiling in the syringe, then, before it could burst, injected the boiling hot liquid into Torin's arm.

Connor watched intently as Torin shook and seized. Blood oozed out the side of his mouth, followed by a mixture of foam and vomit. Connor watched until the seizing stopped and Torin's body lay still. The light disappeared from his eyes. Connor stood up and arched his back, breathing deep the addictive release he received from killing. Connor's eyes swirled a dangerous red, and then turned pitch-black. "Oh yeah ... that's the stuff!"

Connor walked towards the door, addressing the corpse one last time. "The next fun I'll have is to see whether the coroner will report your death as an overdose or a suicide. Toodles!"

* * *

At 9:47 a.m., Sammy came into the kitchen, rubbing the sleep out of her eyes. She wore her purple kitten pajamas with pink fluffy slippers. She'd slept in late, which was no surprise.

"I've never seen a moose look so frightened in its life," Morgan laughed hysterically. "I thought you were going to kill it from fright."

"Well it's your fault for getting me drunk on absinthe!" Connor laughed along, until he noticed Sammy standing there. "Good morning, sunshine!"

"Who is she?" Sammy asked sleepily.

"Do you remember the zoo lady who helped us with the tiger?" Connor asked.

Morgan smiled while sipping her home-brewed cappuccino.

"Well, she is a really good friend of mine and has agreed to stop by every now and then to give you some girl time," Connor said happily.

"Okay," Sammy replied sleepily. Her eyes finally adjusted to the light of the kitchen. Noticing Connor's purple eyes, Sammy pointed directly at his face, and asked, "Connor, why are y—"

Connor quickly interrupted, "You notice my eyes, but you don't notice your best friend who has been patiently waiting for you all morning?"

Snapping out of her sleepiness, Sammy saw Buddy lying on a new, super-fluffy dog bed. He had some white bandages wrapped around his stomach to give his broken ribs extra support as they healed. Although injured, he appeared happy to see Sammy. His tail beat madly against the floor as he whimpered for permission to run to her.

"Stay," Connor commanded, not wanting the dog to injure himself worse.

"Buddy!" Sammy screamed as she ran over and showered him with affectionate pats, gentle hugs and facey kisses. "Oh, Buddy! I'm so glad you are okay!"

While Sammy devoted her affection to Buddy, Morgan and Connor continued to sip their morning cappuccinos and enjoy the heartwarming scene. Being too distracted by Buddy, Sammy forgot about Connor's purple eyes. He knew she would eventually demand an explanation, but for now, he was content seeing her happy.

8

THE NATURE OF VAMPIRES

ORLANDO, FLORIDA

MAY 4, 2009

The sound of Sammy's scream was drowned out by the chaotic environment. Sammy lifted her hands up into the air, the bright blue sky behind her, as adrenaline rushed through her bloodstream, fear and excitement in her eyes. Connor put his hands in the air, too, as they heard an ominous clicking.

"Here we go!" he yelled, over the roar of screams. Suddenly, they were catapulted down the steep slope of the roller coaster's biggest drop. They screamed in excitement as their stomachs floated up to their throats on the new wild ride at Disney World. Strapped in tightly to the cars, they were spun in tight loops, then hung upside-down. They raced along the track until at last they came to an abrupt stop, right where they had started.

"Woooo! Again! Again!" Sammy exclaimed joyously. Her two braided ponytails hung behind the headrest, and the little wisps of hair in the front remained windswept back in a humorous fashion.

Connor chuckled. "Again?! We've ridden this ride almost two dozen times in the last week. Why don't we go see a show, or we can try Universal Studios? We haven't checked that out yet."

Sammy corrected him as if she were a lecturing adult. "Connor, we still have three more days here. Let's spend our time wisely. And ... I want to ride again!" The bored acne-faced ride attendant released them from their harnesses and lazily ushered them off.

"All right, but then afterwards, I want to win you a new prize!" Connor said excitedly.

"Wooooo!" Sammy screamed, throwing her hands up in the air. Eager to ride again, she ran to the back of the line, which would presumably eat up another thirty minutes of their time.

Connor's green eyes sparkled with happiness as he watched Sammy being a kid. It was surprising that she was already twelve. She was growing faster than a weed. He somehow wished he could slow down times such as these, knowing they went by far too quickly. This was a much-needed vacation and long overdue. Each year had grown more complicated than the last. Her uncle's return was minor compared to other challenges he'd had to overcome. Sammy's nagging about wanting to go to a real school was wearing on him. It didn't help that it was difficult for her to maintain friends— Connor took the blame for that. After all, it was the parents who kept their kids indoors when Sammy begged them to come out to play. Their distrust of Connor was warranted but not beneficial for Sammy's happiness.

It was the end of another long day at Disney World that had adequately exhausted both of them. Sammy was so tired she was almost falling asleep in the elevator on the way up to the penthouse suite. Luckily, the elevator opened directly into the suite, so Connor didn't have to open any additional doors with his arms full of sweets and souvenirs. At this point, the living room was almost covered in Disney merchandise. Yet this didn't stop Connor from buying her whatever her heart desired. He was, after all, wrapped around her little finger, ready to oblige her every whim.

"I'm tired!" Sammy yawned.

"I hear you," Connor said, stretching. "Why don't you get ready for bed and I'll tuck you in?" It had been such a long day. It didn't help that he was constantly scanning the crowd for anyone with ill intent towards him or Sammy. With the number of people passing by every minute, it quickly became a draining exercise. Connor was grateful to be in the tranquil penthouse suite he had carefully chosen for its increased security measures.

"Okay," Sammy replied as she sleepily rubbed her puffy eyes and zombie-walked into her bedroom.

The couch was covered in stuffed animals from Disney movies and television shows. Connor took a moment to survey them before finally picking up a Winnie the Pooh. "Which stuffed animal do you want to sleep with tonight?"

Sammy didn't answer. Connor assumed she was in the middle of brushing her teeth in the bathroom. While he waited, he picked up Beast from *Beauty and the Beast* and weighed which one she would prefer more.

"Sammy?" Connor called out again.

A soft breeze blew through the open door to the patio. Alarms went off in his head as Connor snapped to look at the curtains blowing from the open door. He distinctly remembered locking that door before they left this morning. He also remembered disarming the alarm system to the penthouse when they returned, but hadn't reset it. He was too busy putting away her merchandise from the day. Dropping the stuffed animals, he sped over to the door at his god-like speed and looked out. Behind him he heard the cold sound of a pistol being cocked.

Checking the reflection in the glass door, he saw the attacker: a woman with waist-length white-blonde hair that flowed similar to silk in the wind. Her pale complexion was accentuated by the black business suit that jutted out around her hips. It complimented her breasts, their curves visible in the opening slit of the suit that cut down to her flat stomach. In her hand was a military-grade handgun with a silencer attached to the barrel. Connor didn't know how she had avoided setting off the alarm system. Judging by the fragrance emanating from her, he was sure her stealth was related to her vampire gift.

"Don't move a muscle, Caspian," she warned in a voice as seductively smooth as honeyed whiskey.

"If you know who I am, then you surely know that won't kill me," he replied, frozen in place, watching her reflection.

"I know you recover quickly from bullets, which is why I have prepared a tranquilizer powerful enough to kill five elephants within five seconds. It won't kill you, but it will at least subdue you for a while." Her cold, suggestive voice sounded closer to a lover than an assassin.

"You've done your research. … Who accompanies you?" Connor kept her talking as his mind calculated the best plan of attack.

"My partner. Who is currently holding your ward captive," she replied, her red lips twisting into an evil grin.

Connor growled. "If you so much as harm one hair …"

"Ugh … don't be so dramatic!" —the vampire rolled her eyes— "We won't harm her if you do exactly what I say."

"I will follow your exact orders, so long as she is unharmed." Connor raised his hands as a display of surrender. Reflexively, he saw her step back and tighten her aim on his heart. She bought his ploy, but he would still need to strategize to eliminate the threat. "May I turn around? I want to speak with you face to face."

"You may turn around slowly. If you make any sort of quick movements, I'll shoot you in the heart," she stated coldly.

"Of that, I have no doubt," Connor responded, as he slowly turned around to face the vampire. Her fair skin and hair were full of sexual intrigue, but her blood-red eyes reflected the ferocity of a hunter. Although she appeared as firm as a rock, Connor could see her red eyes dilating— a sign of fear. It was as if her body knew what her mind refused to acknowledge: that she was staring death in the face. "Are you one of Veronica's?"

At a speed comparable to Connor's, she drew out a second gun that pointed directly between his eyes. "Why do you ask?" she asked, her voice quivering.

It suddenly became clear how she had entered undetected. Her speed was greater than that of a normal vampire. It would have been easy for her

224

to enter without his detection for the few precious seconds she needed to secure her plan of attack. Years of peace and happiness had left him rusty—a flaw that could end up being detrimental to Sammy. Nevertheless, before he could attack the vampire, he first must secure Sammy's safety. The only solution would be compliance—at least until another opportunity presented itself.

Connor remained calm, refusing to reveal his unease. "I wouldn't live up to my reputation if I didn't know my allies and, in this case, enemies. There are only three vampire lords in the world. The first was Vlad Dracula, but he keeps his vampire legion in Transylvania. His days of conquering are over, which pleases my contract with him. Ruling over Asia is Zhian Ghao II. Even though I do not have a contract with him due to a lack of common ideology, we still maintain enough respect for each other to not step across our given boundaries. Last is my treasure, Veronica, who rules over the Americas. Even though she gives her small legion of followers a great deal of freedom, they still abide by her strict rules. Given your act of rebellion, you must be one of hers. Please give me credit for basic deduction, nameless vampire."

Refusing to put down either gun, she replied, "Your reputation does precede you, Caspian. You may call me Brittany Gledhill."

Connor tsked as he reprimanded, "Now Brittany, it is rude to demand so much from me at gunpoint. I am assuming you want a contract with me, so help me feel more at ease about this relationship we are going to build." He watched as her grip relaxed slightly, though both firearms remained aimed at his vitals.

"These are for my own safety, if you don't mind. Once we have sealed a contract, then I will put them away." Brittany's red eyes remained firm in their resolution.

"Tell me what drives you to threaten me." —Connor gave her a lustful look— "You could have had a greater payout if you would have approached me another way. I am, after all, a giving individual."

For a moment there was silence. It was clear that Brittany hadn't rehearsed her speech. After a few moments of silence, she explained,

"I need power— as much power as you can give me. You have been around since the dawn of time. Some legends state that you are the father of all creatures that wander the night. Many have sought your power throughout the centuries, and many have been destroyed by you. This is because many do not understand your primary weakness: your ward. You follow around red-haired, green-eyed women who remind you of your first love. When they do not live up to her character, then you kill them. Currently, you follow around a young girl named Samantha Valda. Using her now is my greatest asset at getting what I want ... and I want a lot.

"Veronica has grown weak over the years, yet she refuses to give up her title. We tire of catering to the humans. We believe it's time to overthrow Veronica and lock her away. Humans were meant to serve vampires and be our food. My fellow brothers and sisters are ready to strike. All they wait for is me.

"That is where you come in, legendary Caspian. You are the sole reason that Veronica rules the vampires in America. With her extraordinary strength, day walking abilities and invincibility, she has been able to create devoted followers in America. I want the same abilities so I may fight and overthrow our weak and pathetic leader. I will lead my vampires into a new world of dominance!" Brittany ended with a vision of triumph clear in her eyes.

"A coup, then?" Connor asked as if the whole idea bored him.

"Yes," she snapped with authority.

Connor put his arms down, which prompted Brittany to sharpen her aim. "I applaud your overarching vision of the future. You did your homework well, dear Brittany. Unfortunately, you also made several errors. The most important oversight you made was making a contract with you would be in violation of my contract with Veronica. Your second greatest error was telling me your plans, including giving away that this is your only option for success. Without my bestowed powers, you will fail."

"That is not true!" Brittany appeared to be getting heated.

"Isn't it?" Connor responded suavely.

"No. Because I still hold the life of your ward, Samantha Valda! If you don't give me what I want, then my partner will run far away with her. Then you will have two hours to make a contract with me before we end her life." Brittany held her head high, knowing she now held the high ground in this negotiation.

The purple mist appeared from Connor's corneas, swirling around dangerously in anticipation of the fight to come. "It appears as if you have me in a corner. Not a good start for what should be an ongoing relationship. Tell me what you want, and then I will tell you what I want in this contract."

"You are to give me day walking abilities, invincibility, and strength greater than Veronica possesses," Brittany stated.

A flippant sigh escaped his lips. "Due to the constraint you have put me in, I have no other option but to concede. However, you must meet my own demands!" Connor could feel his heart quicken in anticipation. He was about to put her in checkmate.

"What are your demands?" she asked.

Connor smiled and leaned in slightly. "My demand is that your partner must bring Sammy out here so I can ensure her safety. I also demand that with your new vampire army, Sammy must have constant protection from the war that will ensue."

"Seems reasonable," Brittany concluded before yelling, "Brian, bring her out!"

The two waited in silence as the bedroom door opened. Out of the corner of Connor's eye, he saw a large male vampire enter the living room. In his arms dangled an unconscious Samantha, still in her day clothes. Connor growled with displeasure at her present condition.

"She is not harmed, only put to sleep. You can see she bears no fang marks and still has a heartbeat," Brittany said, trying to put him more at ease.

Connor glanced over as the large vampire grunt gently moved her head around to ensure no bite marks.

"Lay her on the couch!" Connor barked. Brian snarled in response, so Connor added, "To make her more comfortable. You may still stand over her."

"She will be gently placed on the couch the second our contract is finished," Brittany commanded. "You ask for too much. We will only be pushed so far!"

Despite his best efforts, Connor had accomplished little to create a safer battlefield. Keeping Sammy safe in the enormous arms of this vampire brute was going to be difficult. "Fine!" Connor growled, "to make the contract, I need to get close to you."

"How close?" Brittany asked skittishly.

"Uncomfortably close," Connor replied with a glint in his eyes. "What I'm doing is imprinting a part of my soul into yours to share my power with you. For most, this is but one ten-thousandth of my soul. However, for your demands, I will have to give you five times that amount. To imprint this in your soul, I need to reach up into your rib cage and manually place it on your black heart. This will be the most excruciating pain you've ever experienced in your abnormally long life! Which is why I don't need muscles over there tackling me when you scream bloody murder. Do you understand?"

Brittany nodded, noticeably giving herself the mental preparation needed.

"This is what you want, isn't it?" Connor asked, his eyes shifting mischievously.

"Yes," she agreed.

"Then lower your weapons," he said calmly. He turned to the grunt. "And don't hurt Sammy when you hear Brittany scream, because she will scream!"

The tremors worsened in her hands as she slowly lowered her guns. "Is there no other way?"

"No," Connor replied, as he approached her slowly, his green eyes now dangerously consumed by purple and red mist. By the time he was within kissing distance of her, his eyes had turned a hellfire red. "Do not resist me. You must remain strong, if you want to survive this."

"Okay," she said, her voice shrinking.

Moving at lightning speed, Connor thrust his clawed hand up her rib cage, forcibly enough to reach up to her heart. With his other hand, he held the back of her head as one would caress a lover. Brittany screamed in pain as Connor thrust his clawed hand deeper and deeper. His eyes swirled dangerously red, the same eyes that glanced over at the grunt, Brian, who watched helplessly in awe.

A long, sinister smile crept across Connor's face as he whispered in her ear, "Shoot Brian." With involuntarily quick reflexes, Brittany whipped the gun up and shot her partner in the forehead. The second the trigger was released, Connor ripped her heart out through her rib cage. The fluid motion with his clawed fingertips incinerated her heart to dust, and reduced her body to ashes. Connor leapt to the stunned grunt and drove his clawed hand deep into the grunt's throat. His swirling red eyes, snarling lips and monstrously sharp teeth revealed the truth about the monster that lay dormant within Connor. It took no more effort to remove the head of the vampire than removing the lid from a glass jar. A column of dust exploded from the mangled body. Before Sammy could fall to the floor, Connor caught her with his black clawed hands and gently laid her on the couch.

It had been far too long since Connor had released his darker side. This monstrous side that tempted him daily tasted freedom once again. Unstable with his tremulous power, Conner felt it safer to step away from Sammy for her own protection. Adrenaline pulsed through his veins as he stormed to the balcony with blazing red eyes. It took a few moments of pacing and calming his deep, growling breaths before Connor could command his hands to return to normal. Only at that point was he able to use his cellphone to call Veronica.

Veronica answered on the first ring. "**Caspian! Is she all right?**"

"Sammy will survive another day. Brittany, on the other hand…" Connor growled into the phone.

There was a brief pause, then the caller flatly surmised the outcome. "**You killed Brittany Gledhill.**"

Connor found himself shifting into a deadly calm. "Brittany threatened

Samantha's life. Would you expect anything different?" he asked.

"**No**," Veronica stated unfeelingly, "**I am sorry to get you mixed up in this, Caspian.**"

"You do realize there is a coup forming around you. Brittany was the leader, but I'm sure there are others ..." Connor said, in a threatening tone.

Veronica sounded worried. "**I knew of the coup and was ready to diplomatically arrest and execute Brittany and her followers. I just needed more evidence.**"

"Veronica!" Connor snapped, "Clean up your mess!"

There was a long pause. Then her meek, subservient voice answered, "**Of course, Caspian. I'm sorry to have inconvenienced you. I will send in a few of my closest and trusted advisors to clean up the mess in your hotel. This insubordination will never occur again.**"

"If this does ever happen again, I will choose someone else to fill your place. Do you understand, Veronica? Sammy means far too much to me, and I will not stop until the entire world has been made safe for her." A surge of emotion rose into his throat, choking out his cruelty in the threat.

"**I will always be here for you. Just tell me how to serve you and I will follow your every command,**" Veronica replied, with warmth in her words.

Sammy was starting to stir, so Connor took a deep breath and quickly picked up the two guns that lay in Brittany's ashes, tucking them away in his belt line. "Goodbye, Veronica. I will call on you soon." Before she could respond, Connor ended the phone call and walked over to Sammy.

Sammy stirred as Connor picked her up off the couch and carried her to the bathroom. At first, Sammy's eyes fluttered open, and then suddenly shot open in shock. "Connor! Your eyes are purple!"

Connor turned away, ashamed of his monstrous side. Sammy then saw the living room, where piles of ash were covering the carpet and furniture.

"What happened? Who was that man in my room?" Sammy was starting to hyperventilate and panic.

Once in the bathroom, Connor set her down on her feet and held her shoulders steady, "Sammy, I must apologize to you for not protecting you from this danger. It was my fault that this man was able to make it into your room. I let my guard down, which could have cost me you. I am so, so sorry!" Connor hugged her and was surprised to feel her hand rub his back.

This seemed to calm Sammy down significantly. "I forgive you, Connor. What happened to him?"

The cold steel returned to Connor's purple eyes. "No one threatens you and gets away with it. When the monsters go bump in the night, rest assured that I always bump back. Fear not the monsters in your nightmares, for I am *their* nightmare!"

"Is that why your eyes are purple again? Because you killed another monster?" Sammy was smart. Not only did she catch on quickly to school work, but she learned so much from the stories he told her. It would only be a matter of time before she finally connected all the dots.

Connor thought it best to give her a small explanation, even though it might connect a few dots a lot earlier than he had planned to reveal to her. "Sammy, I am not normal … we are not normal. I have the strength to kill monsters. When that happens, my … strength can be seen through my eyes."

"I don't want you to kill, Connor. Please don't kill people," Sammy begged.

Connor dusted off Sammy's shoulders and replied, "I only do what I do to protect you. If you don't want me to kill people, then I won't. Though I will kill monsters who threaten you."

"I don't know … I like your green eyes much better than your purple eyes. Your green eyes don't scare away my friends," Sammy remarked childishly, and then smiled to lighten the mood.

Connor chuckled, "I will do my best, Sammy. Now, it's nearly midnight. Why don't you take a shower and then I'll tuck you into bed?"

"Okay," Sammy agreed with a yawn.

"I'll be right outside the bathroom." Connor stepped out and stood guard in front of the door. While Sammy washed up, he could hear movement in the living room. Silently, he walked over and peeked out. He wasn't surprised to see four of Veronica's most loyal vampires cleaning everything better than new. It did surprise him that they were so quick to get here with supplies. It was little things such this that he appreciated in his contract with Veronica. Leaving them to their work, Connor closed the bedroom door and locked it. As he did so, he could feel the cold steel of the guns pressing against his back. Pulling one free, Connor inspected the model. A *Fang,* the most powerful gun in the market, designed by vampires for killing werewolves. Unloading the cartridge, Connor pulled out one dart and held it close to see the manufacturer's detail: "Ryuu Corp." Connor reloaded the cartridge and tucked the gun back in his belt. He had hoped the militarized tranquilizers would have come from somewhere he knew and could send Peter to investigate. Unfortunately, he didn't know what to do with this information. He had never heard of Ryuu Corp. or its connection with the American vampires. It might have been a black-market deal.

When Sammy was done, Connor helped her dry her hair and tucked her into bed.

"Can you stay with me tonight?" Sammy asked as she hugged her Winnie the Pooh stuffed animal tightly.

"I was already planning on it," Connor replied, as he sat down with his back against the wall. It was the perfect tactical position for him to be, between the door and Sammy.

"I love you Connor," Sammy said sleepily as she drifted off.

A warm smile appeared on Connor's face, "I love you too, Sammy. Now go to sleep."

As Sammy fell deep into an exhausted sleep, Connor's mind drifted. He worried that as the years passed, he would struggle to keep his inner demon contained. The release he got from *the kill* was most akin to what a drug addict feels when shooting up. It was a deep craving that felt necessary for his existence.

Connor's mind drifted to Veronica and his initial meeting with her. Veronica was the embodiment of the release of *the kill.* How strange it was that both he and she have grown tamer over the years, a stark contrast compared to how they lived upon their initial encounter.

* * *

VENICE, ITALY

MARCH 13, 1485

He lay upon a lumpy mattress in a quiet room filled with a musky smell. None of this bothered him, for the requirement to sleep did not apply to him. It was peaceful to simply lie still and pretend to sleep and listen to the noises made by drunkards as they walked the narrow lanes of Venice or drifted by on the canals enjoying their stupor. The men of Venice didn't need reasons to celebrate other than the act of celebrating—such an oddity, one he never really understood. What interested him more was the shadow that was creeping into his room through the open window. Fully aware of this presence, he continued to feign sleep while listening to the figure's movement toward the bed. The figure hovered over him threateningly.

"I see you found the courage you needed," he said with a smirk. This particular figure had been following him for about a week, always keeping to the shadows. Seeing no harm in it, he allowed the stalking to continue, hoping the mystery person would find the courage to approach him.

Hissing as if she were an angry cat, the figure jumped away. She rescinded to the darkest shadows in the far corner of the room.

He sat up in his bed, languidly supporting himself with an elbow. He was able to see his red-haired stalker, despite the darkness. This woman wore tight black pants, tucked into boots that went up to her mid-thigh. She wore a red velvet corset trimmed in black lace over a loose black long-sleeve shirt that covered her arms and shoulders but left a large opening in front, revealing her cleavage. She had a mysterious beauty about her that would bewitch any man, as long as that man didn't see the terrifyingly long vampire teeth she now bared. He was curiously drawn to her and couldn't explain why.

"I'm not going to hurt you. Come closer, so we can talk," he said, easing himself to the edge of the bed until his legs dangled.

Cautiously she tiptoed closer, asking in a strong Italian accent, "What are you?"

"Is that any way to introduce yourself? You're the vampire that's been stalking me for the past week." he interrogated her calmly.

As she approached, he was able to better see her detailed features and found her even more attractive upon closer inspection. Finding her bravery, she firmly planted her boots in front of him and introduced herself. "My name is Veronica Vladimirescu. I was determining what sort of threat you would be to my clan. Now, introduce yourself."

He sighed and formally introduced himself, "My original name is Caspian. I am no threat to you or your clan. In fact, I find vampires quite fascinating."

Veronica relaxed her stance. "You think we are fascinating?"

"Yes, I find your primal drive to feed quite animalistic," Caspian responded.

Veronica laughed. "You find us animalistic? I'm afraid you are mistaken."

"No, I'm not," Caspian said with confidence. "Vampires are purely driven by their need to feed. That is their entire existence."

Insulted, Veronica put up a slender finger in objection. "We are not animals existing to feed. We are much more complicated than that, which you would know nothing about. By what means do you live, since you think you know it all?"

Caspian thought about all the heartache the centuries had given him. At this point, it was a repetitive torture that he had grown numb to. "I live to serve," he finally answered in a flat voice.

Pity was transparently expressed on Veronica's face. "What a pathetic existence. Whom do you serve?"

Numbly he stared out the window, as if his master was standing right outside. "A woman I fear getting too close to. I have this irritating repetition of killing her."

"Problem solved. Kill her and you are a free man! Live up to your freedom and be who you were meant to be," Veronica said with a coy smile.

"You know nothing of this. Whether she dies by my hand or another, I am still bound to her. I'm an uncontrollable monster who is feared by all and loved by none. It is best for me to remain hidden. Worry not about what I will do to your clan, for they shall never be aware of my existence. All I have left is my own numbing existence among the swine who plow their way through this world yet make little impact on it." Caspian felt lost at this moment, as though he was losing his purpose without *her*.

"You are a peculiar man. I have yet to meet a monster who rejected his innate nature. Come! Let me show you the life you were born to live. I want to help you feel that adrenaline rush you get when you indulge in your own pleasures." There was an excitement in her voice and a twinkle in her red eyes.

His interest increasing, Caspian prodded, "Why would you go out of your way for me? For all you know, I could kill you the moment you turn your back."

Taking a more seductive approach, she took a step forward, allowing some of the moonlight to illuminate her face and bosom. "Well, I pity you. You remind me of a bird who locked itself in a cage, fearful of how far it could fly. If you are who I believe you to be, then it would be my honor to give you back the purpose you lost long ago."

Caspian wasn't convinced. "Who do you think I am?"

Annoyed by his reluctance, she responded, "A conqueror. A king. The prophesied one. If I am correct, then it would benefit me to have a powerful friend. Yes?"

Caspian didn't know why he was opening up to this vampire. It could be that loneliness had finally taken its toll. It could be that Caspian had always wanted to exercise his powers to their full potential but had been too scared to unleash them. Perhaps it was simply just that Veronica seemed so similar to *her* in appearance and personality ... almost as if they were blood relatives. Either way, Caspian was hooked by her charm and felt he had no choice but to say, "Show me your ways."

Her face lit up as she ran over to the open window and stood on the sill. "Come with me. The night is still young!"

A curious smirk on his face, he obeyed.

They ran along the rooftops of Venice. The moonlight lit up her fiery red hair as she ran. Every now and then she would glance back at Caspian, as if they were schoolchildren playing tag. She ran fast, too fast for a human to follow, yet Caspian had no difficulty keeping up. The night air was refreshing and the moon was energizing.

No one knew they were up there. No one could hear their silent steps nor their leaps from one rooftop to the next. The public went about their debauchery while Caspian followed Veronica, having fun of their own. They perched similar to ravens upon a balcony and peeked inside a grand room filled with gold, jewels and fine art. Downstairs was a brothel where whores lent themselves out to desperate men. Veronica pointed inside the room where three men in satin clothes were getting liquored up while making fun of the women they whored. A current whore was filling up another pitcher of wine to serve to them. She wore nothing but jewels and a small cloth wrapped around her hips.

Veronica leaned in to whisper in Caspian's ear, "These men steal women from distant lands, bring them back here and force them to sleep with other men. Not to mention, they beat them senseless. You should have no reason to not kill these men."

Caspian observed his potential prey for a moment. One of the men beckoned the whore over. She obediently filled his cup with wine. Another man bumped her elbow, causing her to spill wine on the table. Instantly, the man smacked her across the face and sent her spiraling to the ground, the jug of wine spilling into the far corner of the room. The three laughed while the whore tenderly touched her cheek where she had been struck.

The glass doors to the balcony shattered in a powerful array that flung glass in all directions. One of the shards flew into a man's throat. He reflexively smothered the mortal wound with both hands, as if he could stop the bleeding with pressure. The other two stood up in shock and watched Caspian casually stroll into the room. Venomous red eyes glared at the villainous men.

"So you like to hit women, do you?" Caspian asked, poising as if he were a viper coiled to strike.

"Get back, you monster!" yelled one of the men, who picked a knife off the table and pointed it threateningly.

Caspian flicked the knife aside into the adjacent wall. Both men gawked at him in horror, one loosening his bowels in fear. Faster than the eye could register, Caspian grabbed the man's throat and tore his jugular out, spraying blood everywhere. The whore screamed but made no move to get away. As the first man bled out, Caspian took the head of the other man and bashed it against the table hard enough to crush his skull. The table fell to pieces on the floor, while the man's brains spilled out on the stained wood.

Caspian then walked over to the man with glass in his throat. Blood had soaked his shirt down to his belt line, yet the man held onto his throat for dear life. His eyes widened in terror at the monster who had ripped apart his comrades. Caspian looked into the dying man's eyes and watched as they widened and twitched. With the delicate touch of a lover, Caspian reached for his neck and pulled the broken piece of glass free from between the man's fingers. The blood rushed out in a similar flow as a river. Finally, the man's heart gave out and he died in a pool of his own blood.

Adrenaline rushed through Caspian's veins, giving him that pulsating, sweet release. Killing always gave him a thrill nothing else could replace.

Terrified that she might be next, the whore screamed a battle cry and ran at Caspian with her own knife. Caspian heard Veronica call for him to watch out but disregarded the warning. As the knife was falling towards his skull, he turned around and evaded the blade. The whore froze when she realized the monster had won, her eyes trying to register what her body already knew. Caspian's hand plummeted so deep within her stomach that his arm disappeared up to the elbow. In one fluid movement, Caspian ripped her still-beating heart out of her chest. The whore remained alive long enough to see this monster shove her heart into his mouth, biting a large chunk out of the middle. It was only after he swallowed that the whore fell dead upon the floor.

Veronica stepped out of the cover of darkness, showing great admiration for her new ally. Disgusted by the taste, Caspian threw the remainder of the heart on the whore's chest.

"I didn't want to kill her. Stupid whore should have run," Caspian spat.

"Wouldn't have done her any good," Veronica said, approaching the monster who had ripped apart four people with no mercy. Lustful hunger propelled Veronica forward, twisting her fingers through his bloody ones. One by one, she licked his fingers clean, maintaining eye contact with Caspian. Once all the blood had been licked clean, Veronica added, "I would have sucked the whore dry if you hadn't so sexily torn her heart from her chest."

Caspian smiled, happy he had met someone with such a deliciously dark mind. "I'm sorry I wasted her blood, then."

"It's all right, Caspian. I ate before I confronted you, just in case I needed my strength. However, I could use a snack. Would you like to go downstairs to the brothel?" she asked.

He felt a strong appeal in the way her red eyes met his now black ones. "What is of use to me downstairs?" Caspian asked curiously.

"Did you enjoy the kill?" Veronica asked seductively, circling around him, a hand exploring the chiseled muscles hidden by his black shirt.

Caspian remembered the adrenaline and thrill of spraying blood upon the floor and walls. Feeling the life fading from his victims as their hearts stopped and souls wandered. The adrenaline gave him the feeling of being whole again. It was as if his life existed to end others. Killing these scums had reawakened the hunger to kill— a hunger that had been dormant for decades. It demanded higher death counts each time, but left him with an empty void in the aftermath of destruction. Rarely did he allow himself to lose control, but part of him still wanted to learn how to regain that control.

Finally, Caspian responded, "I enjoy the kill ... a little too much. You should fear me more than you do."

Veronica was so overcome with lust she couldn't help but explore his muscular body with her fingertips. "It brings me great joy to watch you kill, especially since you get so much release from it. I know that feeling, because I feel it with every kill I make. I can already tell that you were born to rule over the swine that fill this forsaken land. I actually find it incredibly sexy when that alluring red shine to your eyes glows in the midst of tearing apart your enemies." Veronica came closer, until she was mere inches away from Caspian, her moist lips hovering close to Caspian's. "Now, let us go down there, so you can feel the ultimate pleasure of several women at once. They will be so pleased to hear that you freed them from their slavers."

Caspian felt drawn in by Veronica's seduction. "I have no desire to allow whores to rub themselves upon me."

"Come now, don't jest. No man can deny his own sexual nature." She glanced down at his crotch and then back up to his eyes with a raised eyebrow. "Unless you no longer have anything to give a woman."

Drawn in by the rush of adrenaline and a glowing vampire, Caspian pulled her in closer until her leg was intertwined between his and her stomach was pressing against his own. "I have much to give a woman … but not a whore."

Veronica bit her lower lip and then opened her mouth as if she wanted to taste his lips, but she instantly changed her mind and teasingly pulled away from him. Instead, she grabbed his hand and pulled him towards the door. "Let us at least go play around with whores, then. Even whores have something to offer."

Caspian begrudgingly followed her down the stairs and into a large, musky room. The room was lusciously decorated with pillows, cloth hanging from the ceiling, and many Persian rugs. Some customers were smoking from hookahs, while others were drinking heavily. Most were being entertained by scantily clad women. Veronica pulled Caspian over to a set of cushions that enveloped him.

Instantly there was a whore at her side, young, with a delicacy about her. Though she appeared quite frail, her bust was exaggerated, with small jewels strewn across her breasts. Her long black hair was pulled out of her face, so as not to get in her way of pleasuring customers. Still, she did nothing to arouse Caspian.

"How can I be of service to you?" the whore asked.

Looking as enthusiastic as if she had inherited a fortune, Veronica happily requested, "The masters said we could have whatever we wanted. So I want seven girls over here immediately." Veronica winked at Caspian, then turned to face the whore again. "We also want a private room, my dear!" Veronica threw a heavy bag of coins at the whore, who eyed the money hungrily. Little did she know that it was her dead master's money satchel that Veronica had stolen.

As if this was an emergency that demanded immediate attention, the whore ran off and gathered seven others with prominent, bare breasts, all ready and eager to please. Together, they walked back into a luxurious Persian-decorated room with a large four-poster canopy bed. Four of the girls led Veronica over to the bed and pampered her with exotic massages. Caspian watched out of the corner of his eyes as the women stripped down the vampire, kissing her pale white body. Three other women sat Caspian down in a chair and slowly undressed him as well. Unmoving, Caspian watched them as if watching a scene from far off. The whores did not hold his interest, and he instantly grew bored.

One of the whores looked up at him from below, noticing his lack of interest. "Do we not excite you?"

Another whore asked him, "Is there something else you would prefer?"

Caspian didn't answer them. He watched Veronica, who was slyly feeding on one of her moaning whores. The other three didn't even notice that their friend was slowly dying. Instead, they maintained focus on pleasuring Veronica's body until the first whore passed out. Then Veronica drew in the second whore and started feeding on her as well. Veronica was so gentle and sexual about it that her bite felt orgasmic to them. This held Caspian's interest much more than the whore currently trying to get him hard. Caspian had never seen a vampire able to disguise its kill so well. Normally, the vampires he had come across in the past would bare their layers of teeth and stretch their mouths wider than what is humanly possible to terrify their prey. The vampires he had known would tear open a throat with their teeth and shower themselves in blood. Veronica was a new breed of vampire— or simply an evolved vampire who could hide among humans undetected. This lured Caspian to her.

Out of nowhere, Caspian felt a hand whip across his face, leaving a red mark for a moment. There was fire in Caspian's eyes as he glared at the frustrated whore who had delivered the slap. "Pay attention to me!" she said.

Eyes glaring a deep red, Caspian responded, "I can pay attention to you." Before the whores could respond, Caspian grabbed all three of them and threw them to the floor. Then he pounced on top of them and, without spilling any blood, crushed their bodies while muffling their screams. Any sounds that escaped their lips were covered by the moans of Veronica's whores, who were also dying in orgasm. Caspian stood up and watched Veronica consume her third victim. Reaching her full point, she stopped, and settled for breaking the whore's neck.

The last whore started screaming in horror as she surveyed her fallen sisters, all dead on the floor. Caspian reached the screaming whore first and wrapped his hand around her throat. It was over in a blink of an eye. The whore fell to the ground, her head bent at an unnatural angle.

"How interesting," Veronica said, her pale, naked body splayed upon the bed. "You desire killing more than sex."

Caspian could hear a commotion outside the door. "Get your clothes on. We have been found out."

"Ugh … doesn't anyone know how to leave well enough alone?" she complained, but still went about dressing.

The men outside the door banged hard enough to crack the wood. "Don't come in here," yelled Caspian, as he put on his pair of boots. Clearly not listening, a handful of half-intoxicated men with red cheeks burst through the door. Their eyes instantly went to the pile of dead whores. In unison, they looked over at Veronica, who was tying up her corset as fast as she could. Then they laid their eyes on the ominous, bare-chested man, prepared for battle.

The mob advanced on Caspian with knives and bludgeoning weapons. Caspian took a deep breath, expanding his chest, then put his hand to his mouth and exhaled a brilliant spray of purple fire. The fire ravenously consumed the men. There wasn't even time to release a scream before the purple fire disintegrated them to ash. Veronica observed the magical purple fire she had only ever heard about in stories. She kneeled before Caspian, showing respect to the mightiest warrior.

To Veronica, he seemed almost a god. Without giving it a second thought, she grabbed his outstretched hand and followed him through an open door without getting burned. When they re-entered the large room, half of the people there were cowering and the rest in a drugged stupor.

The fire was quickly spreading, but Caspian remained calm as he led her up the stairs to the master's room. They stepped over the fallen bodies and out the shattered balcony doors. Lithe as cats, they jumped from the balcony to another roof, and on to a tall building nearby, where they finally stopped to sit and relax.

The purple flames consumed the brothel in waves, obeying the master who conjured it. Caspian could hear people in the neighboring palazzos coming out, sounding the alarm and trying to extinguish the legendary purple fire. It was a pathetic attempt. Only Caspian could command the flames to diminish. No remorse in his blood-red eyes, Caspian watched the building burn to ash that drifted into the canal below. Onlookers whispered that this was an act of God, destroying the house dedicated to sinful desires.

All the while, Veronica couldn't take her eyes off of Caspian. She watched in utter amazement as his eyes slowly returned to their dark black pits. "I have heard the legends of your unstoppable power, but never in my life imagined I'd be honored to see it with my own eyes. The legends do you no justice, Caspian. It still begs the question: What are you?"

His black eyes fixed upon the dying fire, Caspian responded emotion-lessly, "I honestly don't. Others have called me monster, demon, the devil ... yet I know none of those are true. A demon doesn't mourn those he has murdered. A monster devours its victims for sustenance, but I require none. And at least the devil believes in a God, which I do not."

"Yet you took a bite out of that woman's heart," Veronica said, skeptically.

"Nothing more than blood lust. Blood, food, water, alcohol, sex … none of these sustain me." Caspian watched as the last licks of his fire died down, coals falling into the water.

"Then how do you survive?" Veronica asked, easing closer to him, not wanting to miss anything that he might say.

"It is my curse," Caspian said as he looked into her vampiric red eyes with his vacant black ones.

"Your curse?" she asked.

Caspian told her the bare basics of the cursed life he lived. How he was forced to live forever with full memory of everything he had ever done and seen. The curse made him madly hunger for death and destruction, but he had the morals of a human. Guilt and shame mixed with blood lust and violence was as difficult as mixing oil and water. The only cure to this perpetual curse seemed to be to save one woman whom it was impossible to save, no matter how much he tried. It was a woman he was constantly drawn to, yet could never have. She was the key to unlocking his prophetic potential and ending his curse. She was his promise of peace, yet he failed her time and again. Now it had come to a point where Caspian had all but given up trying. He told Veronica he was close to his breaking point and would try to stay away from her this time if it would help prolong her life.

Caspian sat in silence as Veronica took all this in. He didn't know how a vampire would react. Veronica was the first woman he had ever spoken to about his curse. He was starting to fear that he would have to kill her for it very soon.

"Thank you for confiding in me," Veronica said sweetly. "The sun is about to rise. I must go. I shall see you when the sun sets and the moon graces us with her presence."

Veronica then leaned over and kissed Caspian on the cheek. A cold kiss, but a kiss nonetheless. Shocked by the random act of affection, Caspian held his cheek as he watched Veronica disappear into the vanishing shadows.

Caspian sat upon the building, watching the people below, fretting and whispering about the mysterious fire. The sun passed over Caspian while he contemplated the possible reasons for his continual failure. He wasn't able to pull himself out of it until the sun was setting and he sat in its orange glow. Realizing the time, Caspian quickly got up and ran back to his bare room.

The room was dark, just as he had left it the night prior. Except for one difference: Veronica was sitting calmly on his bed, wearing a lustful expression.

"You came back," Caspian commented.

"Are you surprised?" she asked with a sly smile.

"No," Caspian lied.

Veronica stood up and took a couple of steps towards Caspian. "I thought about what you told me yesterday. It is a secret that I promise not to tell anyone, on one condition."

"What is that condition?" Caspian asked, intrigued.

Veronica took another step forward and laid her hand on his chest, where a little skin was currently showing. "Allow me to be your companion, dark prince. You have been alone for so long and constantly failing at the one task you were assigned. Let me be your companion and help lift your loneliness. Perhaps I can even show you the pleasure of living a life you believe is cursed."

Caspian removed her hand. "You do not want my company. There is a reason I walk alone. Not only can you compromise everything I have worked so hard for, but you also won't survive at my side."

Forcefully grabbing his shirt, Veronica pulled Caspian closer and said through gritted teeth, "I am not a weak mortal. We both wish to learn from each other." She lessened her grip and said, a little more lightheartedly, "Besides, what have you got to lose? You don't have anyone to protect right now. Come and have a little fun with me."

Once again, Veronica reminded Caspian of *her*. There could be some benefit to a companion. If nothing else, it would be nice to have someone to talk to after centuries of talking to the wind. "I guess it doesn't hurt anything for you to tag along."

Happy as a cat with a mouse in its paw, Veronica jumped for joy. "Excellent! Shall we go on another adventure? This time we must venture farther away. You did create quite a stir last night."

Caspian watched her for a moment, entertained at how she could switch so easily between sexual goddess and ferocious woman. Veronica reached the window and turned around to beckon Caspian to join her. He followed with a smile.

The next two months went by in a blur. Every night, Veronica would come to Caspian, only to pull him on a far-off run to a distant destination where their own brand of chaos would ensue. Mostly this involved ending the lives of evil men who took everything from the weak. The sort of evil men that you wished would die but who were too rich and highly guarded. At the beginning, that was Caspian's ideal target: corrupt bankers, abusive military commanders, slavers, tax collectors and even some cruel rulers. As Caspian's moral compass continued to slip, his targets grew vast. Prey no longer consisted of the evil and the sinful, but also the weak and the poor souls who happened to be in the wrong place at the wrong time. Caspian enjoyed the freedom his powers gave him and the fun that Veronica added. As his control grew, his powers and abilities reappeared from lost time.

It was true that Caspian was finally free to unleash all that pent-up energy and anger out onto the world, yet it still felt as if something was missing. During the daytime, when Veronica would be hiding away and sleeping for the next gallivanting adventure, Caspian occupied his time so he wouldn't have the urge to search for her. If he truly was the reason for her agonizing deaths, then saving her would mean staying far away.

One day, after busying himself with menial tasks around the town, Caspian returned to his bare room as usual to meet up with Veronica. Not surprisingly, she was already there, barely beating him. Surprisingly, she was lying naked on his bed.

Caspian froze, caught completely off-guard. Veronica's pale body glistened in the dim light of the room. A few flickering candles had been placed on the floor, the dancing flames playing with her curves. The red of her hair glowed akin to embers in the candlelight. Those two red eyes sparkled with desire as she lustfully peered down at his crotch, which was starting to respond uncontrollably.

Quite beside himself, Caspian walked forward and grabbed a blanket to wrap her up in. "Veronica, what are you thinking?" His heart was pounding, his blood racing. All of his senses honed in on her luscious body, which was waiting patiently for him. This was the first time in centuries that his body had acted out for the purpose of sex. Caspian wanted to taste the skin of a vampire. The desire to unload all of his tension, aggression and passion on this woman was too strong to resist. Yet Caspian felt he must resist the temptress. Nothing good would come from this.

"I see the way you look at me, Caspian. You have been curious for quite some time. How long has it been since you have felt a woman's touch?" Veronica asked, adjusting herself so Caspian could get a better view of her.

Caspian held up the blanket so he couldn't see the temptress' seductive body. His physical desires were clashing with his already shattered moral compass. He knew what he wanted. Yet he knew that what he desired now wasn't what he wanted in the long term. Every fiber of Caspian's being was screaming out to take her. To pull her close to his chest and rip his own clothes off in a terrifying fit of passion. To give into the physical sensations and pleasure that he knew would be forthcoming. Every fiber of Caspian's being was screaming out and telling him to pursue the carnal pleasure and physical sensation he was craving. It was as though five million years of evolution and human history were screaming at him to do one thing, and that one thing was to take her completely … to dominate her. But an annoying voice was telling him not to. In a furious battle between body and soul, Caspian chose to listen to that voice, even though his physical body wanted to slap him in the face for denying such a beauty.

His arms quivered as they tried to hold up the blanket. Caspian had denied hundreds, if not thousands, of women over the years. Why now was it so difficult to reject the sexual nature of this vampire? The trembling increased when he saw her stand up behind the blanket.

The vixen pushed it away with hardly any resistance. Now Caspian found himself within inches of the naked vampire. Her erect nipples triggered a reaction in his body he had not felt for a long time. Veronica looked deep into his black eyes and licked her plump, soft lips as if preparing to devour a meal. Then she leaned in and kissed him ... and he did not resist her.

The kiss was cold and forceful, yet strangely addictive. Her sharp fangs grazed his lips without cutting them. That long, articulate tongue of hers found its way into his mouth, where it started twisting with his own. He could smell her sweet pheromones draw him in, as they shared the same breath. Caspian wanted to consume her in that moment, to draw the life out of her through the breath that lingered in her throat. As the kiss grew more passionate, one of her fangs made a slight incision in his lip. They both could taste his sweet, metallic blood.

Barely a taste, but it was too much. Caspian threw her naked body off of him.

Completely caught off-guard, Veronica was thrown to the floor. She responded with a playful, animalistic look in her eyes. Caspian could tell she wanted more. Putting a hand out, as if that would stop her, Caspian commanded, "Get your clothes on, Veronica. This is not a good idea."

"Your blood! There is so much power. So much ... I cannot describe it," she said, with wild eyes.

"Stay down," Caspian commanded again.

Veronica started to stand up but stayed slightly hunched over, as if she were a predator ready to pounce. "I promise to give you more than you ever thought possible. I just want another taste."

Caspian took a step back, his black eyes reflecting in the candlelight. "You may have aroused me, but you cannot seduce me completely."

Veronica smiled as if accepting the challenge. Faster than the human eye could perceive, she pounced on Caspian, throwing him against the wall. Still not wanting to hurt her, Caspian attempted to gently push her off. It was at that moment that she scratched him across the face, causing his head to smack the wall and leave an indentation. Blood beaded from the small scratches down his cheek a moment before the wound quickly healed. The air grew heavier and Caspian whipped his head back at her with red eyes. When everything pulls violently in one direction towards incredible pleasure and ecstasy, it is easy to tell those morals to fuck off.

In response, he grabbed her throat and drove her to the ground. For a moment, they stared at each other, her vampiric red eyes reflected in his own swirling red eyes. Adrenaline surged through both of their bodies. In one fluid motion, Veronica ran her sharp nails across his back and down his arm. The black shirt tore in half as her deep scratches caused streams of blood to flow down his back. The deep gashes she created healed as fast as they were made. Yet the blood remained.

Caspian growled as his own demon came out. Before she could taste the blood on her fingertips, Caspian ravenously lowered himself and kissed her passionately. Their tongues intertwined as her fangs cut into his lips, tasting his pure blood. The pure, addictive blood filled both of their mouths. It didn't end their kissing, but it did cause Caspian to punch the floor right next to her head, making a hole. Caspian ripped himself away from her to allow his mouth to heal. Taking advantage of the moment, she rolled over on top of him and tore off the remainder of his shirt, along with a few more scratches on his chest that were already healing. Desiring more, she bit into his chest, getting another mouthful of his sweet blood. Completely aroused, Caspian grabbed the back of her red hair and slammed her down on the ground, quickly rolling on top. She made quick use of her hands and tore off his pants. Caspian's eyes burned a fierce red. Lust overcoming all thoughts, Caspian mounted her, holding her down by her hair. Overcome with blood lust, Caspian bent low and bit into her neck. She moaned as he fed upon her. Reciprocating, she bit into him. Their animalistic passion continued on for hours into the night, each scratching and biting the other, then quickly healing after.

After eight hours, they finally stopped. The room was a complete disaster. Blood was smeared on the walls, floor, bed and ceiling. Walls were broken; floorboards cracked. They both lay upon the broken bed, blood smeared all over their bodies, yet no wounds to show for it—at least on Caspian. A couple of wounds were still healing on Veronica, as she was not as fast a healer.

Her tangled hair complemented her satisfied expression. "I have never experienced sex that mind blowing. Your blood is so intoxicating. So much power surging through your veins."

Caspian locked onto Veronica's eyes, which still held red sparks. He was surprised her eyes would do that just because of drinking his blood. He was also surprised that he had tasted so much of hers. Panic traveled up his throat as he felt his teeth. Relief washed over him when he felt their blunted and softer edges. Caspian didn't expect to turn into a vampire by drinking her blood, the way normal human beings did. Still, it calmed him down to confirm it.

Noticing him checking, Veronica asked, "Why did you not turn into a vampire? Are you immune to our venom?"

Caspian replied in a sarcastic tone, "I guess it means that I am a far superior creature."

Veronica laughed and gave him a light slap. Then she relaxed and stared up at the ceiling. "Does that mean that I'll become like you?"

"Why don't you go out into the sun and let me know?" Caspian teased.

Veronica startled as she noticed the rising sun. "I'm too late! How will I get back to my clan?"

Caspian looked at the sun without feeling threatened. "Well, I guess you could always stick a finger out and see if it gets burned off."

In horror, Veronica watched the sunlight grow brighter. Shaking in fear, she stuck a finger out of the window, exposing it to the sun, then gawked at her finger in amazement. It was neither smoking nor turning to ash. Bravely, she stuck her arm out in the sun, then the rest of her body. Veronica's jaw dropped. "I can't believe it! I can finally stand in the sun!" She danced and twirled in the sunlight.

"You are now a day walker," Caspian commented light-heartedly.

At that moment, Veronica suddenly realized something different on her body: long, twisting purple markings deeply embedded into her skin. Victorian spirals and sharp spikes weaved from her inner thighs. The purple markings wove up her stomach similar to ivy, squeezing between her breasts, and traveled up to her neck, where Caspian's deep bite was still dripping blood from an hour ago.

"What is this?" she asked in terror, as she tried scratching it off her body, to no avail.

A maniacal smile twisted across Caspian's face. "I marked you while you ever-so-willingly rode me. It's the most intimate blessing I can offer you."

"I don't like it! Take it off!" she screamed, once again tearing at her flesh without effect.

"If I take it off, it will kill you. You see, you wanted to be my companion. Well, now if I ever need you, I will know right where to find you." Caspian spoke calmly, with the ease of a snake.

Panicking, Veronica asked, "What sorcery is this? How do you do this?"

Caspian looked at her as if she were his prey. "In order to mark you, I need to put a part of my soul into you. Which is why you are able to now stand in the sun. For normal humans, it prolongs their life unnaturally until I finally take that part of my soul back."

Veronica gave him a curious look, "Doesn't that make you a lich?"

Caspian snorted at the absurdity of the question. "Of course not! I only put a fraction of a fraction of my soul in you. The only reason liches exist are because I taught one person how to do this, and the fool halved his soul into inanimate objects until there was very little remaining of the man. Yet he taught others, and so began the growth of the lich population. Those hollowed-out souls that are more beast than human. Most get lost in their own beast forms so that they forget where they placed the rest of their souls. That's why they are so dangerous."

He whispered to himself, "I really need to exterminate the lot before they do further damage."

Veronica's voice quivered as she asked, "So one day you will kill me?"

Caspian looked earnestly into her red eyes, "Yes."

Veronica's brow furrowed and she rescinded from him, "So what am I to you? Something for you to use?"

Once again Caspian said, "Yes."

"And I offered myself to you," Veronica said, choking up.

Caspian blatantly replied, "You did. But since you gave me so much and taught me to feel again, I thought I would give you the greatest ever: sunlight."

"Am I still a vampire?" she asked, a bloody tear smearing down her right cheek.

Caspian smiled. "Yes. You still require blood to survive and still need to rest during daytime to replenish your strength. Everything remains the same, but now you don't fear the sun."

Veronica looked down at her marked body as if it were a disease.

"Go back to sleep," Caspian instructed, reclining on the bed, "Your clan will understand if you couldn't race the sun." He could tell she was torn up inside, yet she still walked over and crawled under the sheets, her naked body pressing against his own. After she was fast asleep, Caspian's own restlessness pulled him from bed.

While she slept, Caspian cleaned up the room as best he could. It took incredible self-control not to stare at Veronica sleeping in his bed. This rare vampire had not only seduced him but also reawakened his inner demon he had locked away. Part of him wanted to abandon his pointless mission and stay with Veronica forever. She was not so fragile and understood him in ways that *she* never could. He didn't have to worry about saving Veronica, especially now that the sun wouldn't kill her.

Yet that same emptiness ate away at Caspian's soul. He wasn't complete without *her*. Veronica might satiate him for short bursts, but it was *her* who actually filled his soul … if he even still had a soul. Restless and unable to stop himself, Caspian went out to search for *her* once again. A far-off whisper told him that he was close.

Caspian found himself wandering thirty kilometers south of Venice in a town called San Marino. The large, bustling town was filled with people going about their busy lives, not stopping to noticing a dark stranger walking in their midst. Caspian could feel *her* pull and knew he was getting closer.

Scaling up the side of a building, Caspian peeked through a window. The interior was open, with high, vaulted ceilings and large windows. An artist was fast at work on his next masterpiece. In the center of the painting was a depiction of Venus, being born from a shell upon the waves— a goddess of beauty.

"How much longer, Sandro?" asked the model. She was stunningly beautiful, with long, billowing auburn hair tied in a Greek style that cascaded over her left shoulder, where she held it up to cover her nakedness. Her green eyes radiated the glow of the evening sun as they glanced up to the window. An angelic light appeared to radiate around her, which was why Botticelli had selected her to serve as his model for such an important piece of art.

"Hold still, Seraphina," the artist said. "We only have about an hour of sunlight left. Lorenzo de Medici wants to see this tomorrow. I just need to get the last details on how the sunlight radiates off your skin and then you'll be done."

Seraphina gave the artist an impatient look.

Seeing her glare, the artist responded, "Oh, please. They are paying me handsomely for this painting. I have compensated you more than most models in appreciation of your fine beauty. Stand still for one more hour."

"Can I see it after it's done?" she asked optimistically.

The painter exaggerated his flip of the brush stroke in the air, landing paint in his messy hair. "Of course! You are, after all, my muse. Without your stunning beauty, I would not be able to paint such a breathtaking Venus. It will be done tomorrow morning. Please come back early before the buyers, so you can view it in peace without others gawking at you."

"I'm excited," she giggled in anticipation.

"As you should be, my dear. Now hold still!" he reprimanded.

There she was. The one woman he had been both distancing himself from and searching for. A part of him desperately wanted to run away from her to keep her safe. Simultaneously, he wanted nothing more than to hold her in his arms. Her beauty was unmatched. Not even this Sandro could replicate her beauty. As Seraphina was finishing with her last hour of modeling, Caspian wishfully watched her, settling on the one fact that he should not be this close to her. Accepting his torturous decision, he leapt down from the window to the streets. This initially caused a slight commotion as the locals glared at him for his unruliness, then went on their way. Caspian shrugged this off and walked in the opposite direction of Seraphina and Sandro Botticelli.

It wasn't long until he sensed a familiar presence approaching from his rear.

Veronica approached from behind in an attempt to surprise him. "Did you miss me?" Before he could respond, she continued, "The sun feels so incredible, yet it makes me weak and tired."

Disgruntled by the interruption, Caspian responded bluntly, "Just because I marked you doesn't mean you have to follow me around like some lost mutt!"

Veronica recoiled, the sting of his words whipping her in the face.

Caspian sighed. He only slightly regretted what he said, but still rephrased, "You should remain in the shadows so the sun doesn't drain you. Besides, with your pale skin and red eyes, you stand out in the crowd."

"Well, that is unfortunate," she said as she latched onto his arm, as though they were a couple. "Let's go burn down a building. I want to see smoke billowing up into the air as the sun sets. I bet it will create a beautiful array of colors."

Caspian feigned a laugh, but continued to resent her clinginess. "I suppose." It would help him release some of his self-hatred for choosing to stay away from Seraphina. Plus, it would get Veronica away from Seraphina as well. There was no telling what Veronica would do if her place at his side was challenged by another woman.

Some time later, Caspian's patience began to run thin. "Will you pick one already? I bore of gawking at houses and shops."

Veronica rolled her eyes, then lazily pointed at the largest building around. It was an older building full of family businesses and smaller homes. Caspian shook his head. Of course she would pick that building, he thought to himself, but I might as well give this to her, since it will be the last one. Caspian quietly followed her into the building.

"Light this place up while I find a good meal or two," Veronica said ecstatically, then ran off down the hallway to find her victims.

Deep down, Caspian's conscience was yelling at him to not burn the building down. Unfortunately, his need to feel powerful again consumed all other conscious thought. Pressing his finger against the wall, Caspian drew spiral patterns. Purple sparks and fire trailed from his fingertip. The purple fire trail spread as if it were a virus on the wall, slowly devouring the paint and plaster. A poor, panicked soul, smelling smoke, ran out into the hallway, only to run into Caspian wearing a wicked smile and red eyes. Caspian swooped down on him as if he were an eagle snatching its dinner from the water. His fingers hooked inside the man's rib cage. He felt an odd yet familiar energy. The man in his grasp was screaming in pain, but Caspian was too distracted to torture him. So, Caspian merely broke his neck and calmly searched the burning building to find the source of the energy.

As Caspian walked past a window, a glimmer of red, flowing hair caught the corner of his eye. Taking a step back, he gazed out the window and locked onto the girl approaching the building he was destroying. Little did he know in that moment that she was returning home to her father. The money she had made for the modeling job would have helped support her father in his old age. How foolish he was to be so naïve to her whereabouts. This woman that he searched for, this Seraphina, had been thrown into the fiery pit of hell he had created with his own hands.

Seraphina approached the building where her father worked and lived. When she noticed the building was on fire, she clutched her heart, panic propelling her towards the building. In front of the building she saw a man lying on the ground. Kneeling, Seraphina shook his shoulder and asked, "Sir, are you all right?" When she rolled him over, she saw puncture wounds in his neck and his shattered skull, which was oozing blood and brains onto the cobblestones. Seraphina screamed and moved away from the body, making the sign of the cross, as if that would protect her. Her terror was compounded when a woman screamed from the burning building. That familiar brave resolve in her eyes was a sign to Caspian. Seraphina ran over to the street water fountain, decorated with cherubs, and jumped in, soaking her clothes, and then burst through the building's burning

254

door.

Caspian ducked back into the building and frantically checked every room he passed, trying to find her. He or Veronica had already been through most rooms, leaving a path of dead bodies. While searching, Veronica came up behind him, rubbing her hands under his shirt and licking the back of his neck. Caspian shrugged her off.

"We need to go, Caspian. Let's go find a rooftop to sit on while we watch the building crumble with all the victims inside," she said, her devilish smile repulsing him.

"Veronica, you get out. Sit on whatever rooftop you'd like," Caspian snapped.

She took a step back, confused by the change in his demeanor. Veronica didn't appreciate his new attitude. "Aren't you coming with me?"

"Not anymore," Caspian held both of Veronica's shoulders. "Our time together is over."

He could feel Seraphina somewhere in the building and desperately needed to find her. However, Veronica appeared to be the jealous lover type, and Caspian worried that he would have to rip the vampire apart if the two were to meet.

"No, I refuse. We will spend an eternity together, you and I. We were made to wreak havoc together!" Veronica shouted. Then something that Caspian didn't expect: a tear—a lone tear of blood ran down her face. Caspian knew he had no choice.

The air grew dense around them as the flames destroyed everything they touched. "Get out of here! If you continue to stalk me without my permission, then I shall end your pathetic existence," he yelled with menacing pitch-black eyes. Bloody tears were now running down Veronica's face as she ran out of the building to escape the monster and his purple fire.

Caspian heard it: *her* all-too-recognizable scream that haunted his memories and turned his stomach. Knowing exactly where Seraphina was, he brought his fist down on the floorboards, instantly smashing through to the second level.

Relief washed over Caspian when he saw her. She was the same as ever: a heavenly body, long, flowing auburn hair and sparkling green eyes. Yet something was terribly wrong. She wasn't seeing him as her savior, here to rescue her from the burning building. She saw him as a terrifying monster. At that moment, Caspian realized that he was a monster, and nothing else— a monster dedicated to the death and destruction of everyone who got in his way. He was a merciless beast who didn't kill for food, but for pleasure. Caspian was devoured by his own destruction as he saw the terrified eyes of the woman he had come to save. He felt as if he were a demon cringing away from the light of an almighty angel. He wanted to console her and explain away his actions, but he knew that words could not fix it.

Trying to show he meant no harm, Caspian stretched out his hand to her, hoping she would take it so he could carry her away to safety. Too focused on this moment, he didn't realize that by cracking through the floor, he had also weakened the structure of the building. It all happened so suddenly. The ceiling cracked and dust fell down on her head. Before she had a chance to look up, everything came crashing down. Purple flames rode the debris as if they were projectiles from hell. A beam fell on her first, followed by floor boards and furniture. Her back was broken. Her ribs snapped, rupturing her lungs. Caspian, helpless to save her, watched in horror. All he could see under the rubble was a soft, petite hand. As he reached out and grabbed the hand, it burst into thousands of tiny purple wisps. The wisps floated up through the opening of the burning building into the dusk.

Refusing to accept what had happened, Caspian sat in a slump and stared at the spot where she had died. Broken beams covering that spot, as though to hide the fire he had created for selfish enjoyment. The man she had tried to save—her father, he thought—murdered by Caspian's hands. Staring absentmindedly at his claws, Caspian was able to finally see all the blood his hands had spilled.

Caspian hated her for always being so reckless and dying so easily. He blamed God, if there was one, for creating a monster with urges to kill, yet a conscience to tear him apart when he did. More than anything, Caspian

256

hated himself. Being trapped in his own despair and anger for all eternity was hell. In fact, Caspian would almost prefer the Catholic hell, where there was no hope and he could enjoy his sins for eternity, not be burdened by them. The flames grew higher and higher. Caspian could hear the building groaning and cracking, yet wouldn't move. The weight of his guilt was far too great to bear. At last, the building fell upon him in a great heap of stone, wood and debris.

Caspian had hoped the fall would kill him, but it couldn't. He lay underneath the rubble for what felt like an eternity, its weight pressing down on him even harder than his guilt—a relief, in a way.

Numbly, he climbed out, uncaringly refusing to dust the ash off his body, letting it mark him so that all could see his monstrousness. In despair he walked to where the end of a pier met the sea. Caspian could feel Veronica watching him from afar, but he never looked back. Wishing for death, yet knowing it might never come, he stepped into the sea. The cold waters embraced him and pulled him to the bottom. On the long descent, Caspian looked up at the glistening surface and watched as the air escaping from his lips floated in bubbles to the top.

This was the first time he tried to drown himself. He wondered how long he would remain down here. Would he eventually sleep? Would he start to decay? All these things he didn't know and didn't care. Caspian softly landed at the bottom, uncaringly watching the sea life above him. Numbness tingled at his fingers and toes as oxygen left his lips. Finally, he was soothed by the weight of the water and fell into a deep sleep.

9

FAITH IS NOT FAIRNESS

LONDONDERRY, NEW HAMPSHIRE

AUGUST 8, 2011

Connor looked down with thoughtful green eyes at the computer screen in his study. From the screen, a room full of top executives in suits stared back at him, sitting at a long oval table in front of a wall plaque that read *Valda Enterprise, CORP*. As representative for the owner of the company, Connor was tasked with making major decisions until Samantha came of age. Though he had put much time and energy into helping her company flourish, he found these board meetings burdensome. He refused to don the corporate uniform of a full suit for these gatherings, preferring a simple button-up light blue shirt and jeans. Still, members of the board and the top executives respected him and his decisions, after a period of adjustment when he first took a virtual seat at the table.

"I'm telling you that it's too risky!" the CIO banged his fist down on the table.

"Well, it's never really been done before," the R&D director commented, preferring to stay neutral.

"Exactly my point! It's never been done before, which is why Valda Enterprise will profit beyond its wildest dreams if we can pull it off," the CFO remarked optimistically.

"Listen, gentlemen," Connor interrupted, "I have given you DNA samples from twenty different humanoid species with extraordinary abilities. If these DNA strands can be used to boost vaccines and cure the most lethal illnesses, then why don't we try it out? There could be a Nobel Prize if we unlock the genetic code for accelerated healing."

The R&D director leaned in towards the camera. "It is risky. This was tried before with vampire blood, and all three test subjects died as a result. Plus, it is an enormous investment."

Connor leaned back in his chair, deeply thinking about his options. "How much of an investment?"

The room of men discussed it quietly among themselves, then the CFO answered, "Well over two million in startup costs, to begin with, then—"

"Done!" Connor stated, startling the entire room. "I will personally donate the money to research. In return, I get full control over the process. For instance, I want a new laboratory built in Canada where we will partner with V-Laboratories." All the men in the boardroom reacted as if they'd been slapped across the face with a dead fish. Just as the CEO was about to object to partnering with a vampire company, he was interrupted.

"Oh, Connor!" Sammy called out from the kitchen.

"Is that Miss Valda?" the COO asked.

Connor chuckled and replied, "Yes gentlemen. Give me a moment. You may continue discussing this opportunity to expand R&D efforts while I see what it is she needs."

As Connor was rising from his chair, Sammy came in with a bright smile and glistening green eyes. Already fourteen years old and growing so quickly. Her wavy auburn hair still hung down to her mid-back, despite the numerous times Connor had cut it to keep it from tangling. She wore black patterned leggings with layered green and white tank tops that were fairly low cut. Connor assumed that it would be headache to fight with her to put more clothes on. Heaven forbid the boys start coming around

259

early, acting as if they were hungry little puppies, wanting her to give them a bone.

"Connor! I made you lunch! Come on out and we can talk!" Sammy said. She appeared far too chipper to be up to any good.

"Miss Valda! Is that you? It has been so long!" the CFO called out from the computer screen.

"Oh! Are you having another conference call?" Sammy asked as she started to walk closer.

Quickly, Connor held her shoulders to keep her from getting in front of the camera, "Sammy, you are not in professional enough attire to present yourself in front of the board."

"Uh-huh, and you are?" Sammy asked with a lot of sass, eyeing his jeans and blue shirt.

"Go ahead and eat without me," Connor prompted.

Sammy pouted. "Connor, I made you lunch so we could talk."

Connor sighed, knowing where this was going, "Fine. Fine. Go set everything up and I'll close the meeting for today."

"Excellent!" Sammy clapped her hands together and then bounced out of the room.

Going back in front of the computer screen, Connor addressed the board members. "Well gentlemen, it appears as though the meeting will adjourn early today. Please talk to Ms. Sommers for the assignments of each department and make sure you are prepared for the follow-up meeting next Wednesday. Miss Valda apparently wants something from me, because she has created her own lunch meeting."

The men all laughed and said their goodbyes as Connor turned off the camera and ended the meeting.

The smell of food drifted into the study from the kitchen. Following his nose, Connor made his way to the dining room, where Buddy sat ready to greet him.

"Hello Buddy, has Sammy put you to work?" Connor was referencing the black bowtie around Buddy's neck.

Buddy barked in response and pulled one of the chairs at the head of the table out for Connor.

"Thank you, Buddy," Connor said as he sat down in the chair and scooted in closer to the table.

Sammy had gone out of her way to decorate the table with their fine china and antique place settings. Buddy ran out of the room to the kitchen while Connor took a sip from his wine glass. "Ah! Grape juice!" Connor chuckled to himself.

Buddy came into the room backwards, his jaws clenching a rag that helped him pull a serving cart into the room. Sammy came in directly after, with a crystal pitcher of more grape juice. "Thank you for joining me for lunch!" Sammy said with a smile too big for her face.

"Thank you for inviting me to lunch," Connor replied professionally. "What have you made today?"

Once Buddy had pulled the cart close enough, Sammy excused him to lie down in the corner with a simple hand gesture.

"You really have done an excellent job in training him," Connor commented.

"Well, I do have a *special* connection to animals," Sammy said with a wink.

"Yes, you are quite bright," Connor commented as he put his napkin in his lap.

Pulling the lid off the serving cart, Sammy displayed a wonderful array of food that she described as she served it onto his plate. "Here we have filet mignon, rosemary red potatoes, lemongrass steamed vegetables and, for dessert, chocolate covered éclairs!"

"Ah, magnifique! And you made all of this in the last couple hours?" Connor asked.

"Everything except the éclairs. Those were thawed from the freezer," Sammy said, her head held high.

"So that's why you asked me to buy these ingredients last time we went grocery shopping. It wasn't so I could make them for you, but so you could bribe me," Connor said, with a clever glint in his eyes. He took a bite of the filet mignon and savored the flavors. "Well done, chef! You have really outdone yourself!"

"Thank you!" Sammy said as she started to eat. "It took me all morning."

Connor swallowed his food before interrogating her. "I'm assuming all your algebra is done."

"Last night!" Sammy waved her fork at Conner as if it were a wand.

"And your essay on the comparisons between Mark Twain and Charles Dickens..."

"Just needs to be edited. It's not due until next week anyways."

"And what about your paper on the witch crusades?"

"Crap!" Sammy cringed. "I thought that wasn't due for another two weeks."

Connor gave her a mischievous smile. "It is. I just wanted to see if you had started on it yet."

Sammy laughed as she took another hearty bite of potatoes.

"So, I'm assuming you are wanting something from me," Connor said in a business tone while putting down his silverware.

Making sure to swallow first, Sammy also put down her own utensils, "Oh, Connor. What if I wanted to be nice? Just because I make you an award-winning meal doesn't mean I am wanting something from you."

"Oh! All right then!" Connor shrugged as he cut another bite of filet mignon.

Realizing her mistake, Sammy quickly added, "But if you are willing to have an open-minded conversation while enjoying the fruits of my labor, then let us talk."

Making sure to take one more bite, Connor rested his hands in his lap and gave Sammy his full attention. He already had an idea what she was going to ask about.

"So, as you know, I am now fourteen," Sammy started. "I have been brilliantly taught by you through home school methods. Since traditional high school starts in a couple weeks, I figure now is a perfect time to start my registration."

"Thank you for that straightforward introduction. Now give me your reasoning to your argument. Why should I let you go to high school?" He flicked his fork to make his point.

Sammy held up her first finger to clarify the next set of objectives she wanted to cover. "First, I am of age to start high school as a freshman. Second, I have high scores on all assignments and have never fallen behind in my studies. Third, I promise to also take some college courses while in high school, which you have envisioned me to do. Fourth, I want to join some clubs and play in some sports. Lastly and most importantly, I need friends and the best way to make friends is in high school." Sammy wiggled her five fingers as a reminder of her strong arguments.

"Brilliantly put. Now let me make my counter-proposal." —Connor imitated her finger counting— "First, although you are physically of age, you surpassed your peers academically five years ago. Second, you will grow bored of the assignments in high school because you have learned at a much higher level than your peers. Third, you should be able to take online college classes next year after testing for your GED this year. Fourth, I can have you do some volunteer work in the community to substitute for clubs. You are also much more physically skilled than your peers and would outclass them with your agility, which would instantly cause you to be outcasted. Finally, you have Buddy as your friend. The so-called friends you would make in high school would be cruel and back-stab you the moment they got the chance."

Sammy stood up and firmly palmed the table, "Why do you have to be so mean, Connor? Why won't you let me go to school?"

Connor remained seated despite the aggravation he was feeling. "Because there is nothing for you at school. The kids are mean and the teachers don't care! Besides, you'll be safer being home-schooled."

"This is so unfair!" Sammy threw her hands up in the air. "Stop treating me as if I'm a china doll for you to keep locked away in a glass case. I need to make *real* friends at a *real* school. I need to eat lunch in a cafeteria, have my own locker, use my backpack for books, slip notes to my best friends, play sports, go on dates ..."

"Absolutely not!" Connor raised his voice. "You are not going to high school just so you can date a boy whose prerogative is to get into your pants!"

Sammy stepped back in shock. Connor had never raised his voice to her before. It surprised Connor enough to prompt an immediate apology. "Sammy, I ..."

"I hate you!" Sammy shouted as tears ran down her face.

This stabbed into Connor's heart. He almost would have preferred a spiked sword over these hurtful words.

"Sammy, I'm sorry," Connor said, trying to made amends before it worsened.

Sammy stormed away, shouting, "Leave me alone!"

Her stomping could be heard through the house, followed by a loud slam of her bedroom door. Once the angry violin music started, Connor knew there was no use in talking to her until she had calmed down. Defeated by his own temper, Connor put his plate down on the ground. Buddy immediately came over and started eating the fine meal. Connor instructed him, "Stay close to Sammy. She will need a friend shortly."

Licking his chops, Buddy obeyed and went romping upstairs to sit by the door. It took several minutes before Connor heard Sammy open the door to let Buddy in and slam it shut.

Exhaling a deep sigh, Connor cleaned up the beautiful arrangement Sammy had taken so much time to prepare. Then he went into the kitchen, which was piled high with dishes and garbage. With nothing else to do but wait, Connor cleaned the kitchen for her as his atonement. After the kitchen was finally clean, Connor went upstairs, surprised to see that her bedroom door was open.

Deciding this was an invitation, Connor let himself in. Looking around the room only made Connor realize how much of a teenager Sammy was now. All of her princess posters had been replaced with boy bands. The stuffed animals on her bed were now mostly in the closet, save a couple that she still cherished. The small table and chairs she once studied at was now a professional black desk with a study lamp. What used to be beginner language books and educational learning material was replaced with documentaries and advanced books on philosophy and literature.

Sammy was sitting on her built-in window seat, with Buddy resting his head on her lap. She softly petted his head and gazed out of the window.

"Sammy, I'm sorry for raising my voice. That was impulsive on my part and I apologize." Connor hung his head low in submission.

Sammy didn't look at him as she responded. "You're scared of losing me, aren't you?"

Connor inhaled sharply, not prepared for this conversation. He took a seat at her desk to be closer to her. "Yes, I suppose I am."

"Why?" Sammy looked down at Buddy but refused to look at Connor.

"I suppose ..." Connor started, took a breath and then continued, "I suppose it's because I love you, Sammy. My fear is that when you go to high school, I won't be able to protect you as I have been."

"What makes you think I'll be in danger?" Sammy's eyes wandered down towards Connor's feet.

"You have already seen a couple of examples. You are extremely special. Because of that, there are others who wish you harm. We were far away in Disney World when we were attacked. If you went to school on a daily basis, it would be all too easy to be targeted there. I couldn't protect you there as I can here."

Finally, Sammy looked Connor in the eyes and tears flowed down her face. "I feel so trapped here sometimes. I look at other kids and wonder why they get to have normal lives while I can't ... because I'm *special*. It's just not fair."

Needing to comfort her, Connor came over and hugged her. Reflexively, Sammy clutched onto the back of his shirt and cried into his chest. "I know life isn't fair, Sammy. I understand why you would feel trapped. Please try to understand why I'm hesitant to let you go to high school."

"Why am I cursed to live this life, Connor? Why must I be kept at a distance from everyone else?" she sobbed.

Connor pulled her from him and lifted her chin until her bright green eyes met his own forest green eyes. "Sammy, I understand and have been in your shoes many times. I know this doesn't make you feel better right now, but it will get better. Okay?"

Sammy hugged him tightly. "I'm sorry, too. I don't hate you."

"It's okay," Connor said. "I know you didn't mean it."

"Will you tell me a new story?" Sammy looked up at him again, "To get my mind off this matter."

"Of course," Connor said as he sat back down at the desk to get comfortable. "I actually have a fitting story. You may feel confined right now, but this is very slight in comparison to that of a nun."

"Is this supposed to teach me a lesson?" Sammy smiled a little.

Connor nodded. "Hopefully, yes. If you pay close attention, you might learn something for your paper on the witch crusades as well."

Sammy settled into her window seat. "All right, Connor. Tell me a tale of a nun."

The smile that appeared on Connor's face right before he started every story showed up again. "Let me tell you a tale of a witch hunt."

* * *

TRIER VILLAGE, GERMANY

AUGUST 11, 1593

White clouds drifted across a perfect blue morning sky. Barely a wind stirred the trees on the mountains surrounding a small village. The townsfolk went about their daily chores to keep food on the table. In the center of the village stood an ancient church with steeples that reached up into the heavens. The architecture was complex and pleasing to the eye, with its mixture of round and square towers that gave the cathedral the appearance of a fortress. Simple archways added to the welcoming and pleasing nature of the church. Other than the castle that looked down upon the village, this cathedral was the pride of the Catholic faithful who worshiped there.

Within the cathedral, underneath the ribbed, vaulted ceilings, sat a multitude of pews normally filled at services with everyone in town. At this moment, there were a few priests listening to the confessions of tormented souls; nuns attending to daily chores, and head nuns answering questions about the good word. A handful of villagers sat in the pews, praying about their troubles and seeking forgiveness for their petty sins.

There was, however, one man who stood out. This man, clad in black with dark eyes, was not praying, but instead admiring the domed ceiling. It was a beautiful display of artistry. Set against a dark blue background was a battalion of angels who appeared ready for war. Which war they prepared for was uncertain. Some said it was a war of artists from different time periods trying to add their artistic flair to the dome and hoping to surpass the last artist. Others claim the angels congregated here purely to help children of God fight off sin. This particular man believed none of that as he stared up at the heavenly host of angels who surrounded Jesus, the savior of all Christianity.

As he gazed upon this incredible work of art that took centuries to complete, the man could feel the watchful eyes of a nun standing far back in the shadows. Eventually, curiosity got the better of her as she approached the man in black. The man pretended he didn't see her coming, though he'd been long aware of her presence.

The nun lightly stepped beside him and looked up at the dome as well. "It's beautiful, isn't it?"

Not startled in the least bit, he responded as if he was expecting her to converse with him. "I appreciate the complexities that have been added over the long years this cathedral has been standing. Unless I am mistaken, this is the oldest Catholic cathedral that is not in Rome."

This nun had an expression of pleasant surprise, but her intrigue guided her eyes up and down his cloaked figure, as if trying to decide whether he was appropriate to be standing in this cathedral at all. Her eyes lingered on the handsome features that he was quite aware of himself, though he was humble about acknowledging his own physical perfections. Finally, she asked politely, "You are indeed correct, sir. Have you come here on a pilgrimage to find a closer relationship to God?"

"No." He had been waiting for this moment for hours and could finally admire the young nun's beauty the way it was meant to be seen: up close and in person, just like the dome. Even though her body and hair were completely covered by her black and white habit, he could still appreciate her elegant face and breathtaking green eyes. A small smile twitched in the corner of his mouth, as he confirmed mentally that he had found the beauty he had been searching for.

The young nun looked into his eyes and took a half-step back. It is rumored that the eyes are the gateway to the soul. If this was true, then his black eyes showed only darkness. Instinctively she grabbed at the rosary in her pocket, as if it would protect her. She took quiet comfort in the belief that evil couldn't walk into the house of God and gaze up at its glory. "Then, are you here for confession? God always forgives his children who ask for redemption through Jesus Christ, our Lord."

A coy smile popped upon his princely face. How adorable he found her stone-solid faith. God was a myth man made up to enforce loyalty to the *godly elite*. That rosary wouldn't protect her from evil. Not even witches bat an eyelash at the crucifix, nor should they. A false God holds no power over them. Yet men have held fast to the belief in one God and have slaughtered masses in the name of that God.

Which is what brought him to this town of Trier in the first place. Rumors had spread through the land similar to a thick fog that a powerful presence was ridding the world of witches. One man should not possess such power, unless that man was himself. Putting his ambitions aside, the young man cloaked in black flirted with the young nun. "Yes, I have something to confess to you."

Having such a beautiful face, it was no great stretch to imagine that this particular nun has been the subject of similar advances from other men. True to her age, the nun rolled her eyes and redirected him. "Oh, I am not able to receive confession, but I shall tell our next available priest who may …"

"I won't confess to a priest," he interrupted.

The nun went silent, not knowing how to respond to this request. The man turned his body to fully face the young nun. Then he surprised her by bending down on one knee while taking her hands in his. "I have come to confess that I have fallen head over heels in love with you, Sophie."

The nun's face went completely white as she pulled her hands away. "How do you know my name?"

The young man calmly smiled up at her, his charming, princely features glowing. "I noticed you when I entered this town. It would appear you do not fit well in this role, seeing as you are constantly scolded by your mother superior. Let me save you the heartache of nunnery life and whisk you away to a land of milk and honey, where you shall not be burdened by the unfairness the religious life has offered you."

Sophie tried her hardest to cover the blush rapidly spreading on her face. She snatched up a Bible and held it up as if it were a shield to guard her from both evil and embarrassment. "I am sorry, sir, but I only have love for God. The sins of carnal love cannot sway me from my faith." She abruptly turned and sped down the aisle. She cast a quick glance over her shoulder, startled to see him following her. Walking as fast as she could without running, Sophie finally made it to the door that would lead her to the sacristy, where only clergy and nuns were allowed. Pulling on the large iron handle, she found it impossible to open. Then she noticed a hand above hers on the door. Slowly, her eyes traced the owner of the hand and was alarmed to see the man dressed in black, wearing a smile.

"Sir, please let me go," she requested, still desperately hiding her red-hot blush.

"I did not mean to scare you, Sophie. Can we please talk outside, where our voices won't echo as much?" he whispered. Peering around, he noticed a couple of nuns and a priest watching her. He could hear the quickened beating of her heart and knew she didn't feel safe in her own parish.

Maintaining a soft whisper, he continued, "I can tell by the marks across your knuckles that you would prefer to not draw attention to yourself. Can we please talk outside, Sophie?"

In a loud voice, she asked, "Would you be interested in learning about the history of the church, sir? Our garden has many historical features in it and gives you a lovely view of Trier Castle." She was still being observed, but the onlookers' curiosity was diminishing.

Copying her tone, he replied, "Thank you. I would love to talk more about the foundations of this cathedral." The onlookers finally lost interest and went back to their fervent prayers.

Quietly and calmly, she led him to the garden outside. The garden was beautiful in its simplicity. The view from the cathedral was a spectacular panorama of the quaint town over to the castle looming above on the mountain.

"What is it you wish to talk to me about? I do have other things I must attend to," she snapped rudely.

Before he could speak, an older nun stuck her head out of a door and called out, "Sister Sophie, did you forget that you are supposed to assist in preparing the meal tonight?" Then she saw the young man wearing all black, "Who is this?"

"Um," —Sophie paused as she looked at the man in black— "this is Brother Caspar, from Bramburg Cathedral. He made a long pilgrimage to our cathedral to get closer to God."

The old nun seemed suspicious for a moment, and then dismissed the odd visit from a friar who was not wearing a traditional robe. "Well, hurry it up. You are needed in the kitchen." She disappeared behind the door to go reprimand another nun.

"Caspar, huh? From Bramburg?" he inquired with a raised eyebrow.

"I'm sorry I didn't ask your name. It was the first idea that popped into my head." Sophie looked up him, and then shied away to hide the blushing. "What do you know of love? You know nothing about me."

There was a slight pause as he gazed across to the mountains. A darkness rustled the trees, forewarning of danger to come. While he had to admit that his initial introduction to her had been on the brash side, it certainly got her attention, though it wouldn't be enough to get her to leave this wretched town before death fell upon it. She was far too beautiful to become a victim of the cruelty that was on its way to Trier. His next words had to persuade her to follow him far away from here. In truth, he didn't know much about her but could make some pretty solid guesses. "I know more about you than anyone in this parish. I know you have long, auburn hair, which you hide under that habit. Your mother died giving birth to you. Your father, cruel to you, flung you into the servitude of a convent, knowing it to be an easy way to rid himself of you. For the most part you keep your nose clean, but your stubbornness gets you in trouble. Hence the whip marks across your knuckles. You dream to be rid of this place, yet fear holds you here because it is the only thing you have ever known. Oh, and right now, you are terrified of me for knowing far too much about you. At the same time, you feel a magnetic draw to me, which only makes you curious to get to know me more. I would even guess that you are wondering what it would feel like to kiss me right now."

At this, Sophie smacked him across the face. The sound echoed through the valley. Caspar looked at her almost playfully as he rubbed his cheek, which now had a red hand print on it.

Sophie pointed an accusing finger at Caspar. "I don't know how you know so much about me, but I do know that you need to stay away from me."

Caspar stopped rubbing his cheek where the hand print was fading. "Then I was right," he said, pride swelling in his chest.

There was a stubborn fire in her eyes that Caspar loved, because it meant she was a fighter. There was a chance he could convince her to leave this cathedral that she would otherwise die in.

"You're very observant, Herr Caspar, but you are wrong about one thing. My father didn't give me to the parish to be rid of me. He died. The parish took me in, fed me, clothed me and taught me the Lord's love. That is why I stay here." A small twinge of sorrow glimmered in her eyes as she turned around to head back inside.

"I'm sorry," Caspar called out to her.

She paused at the door and asked, "Sorry for what?"

"I'm sorry for your loss. I'm sorry for upsetting you. I am also sorry for making you feel uncomfortable. That was not my intention." Caspar took

271

a step forward, hoping that she would turn around and start talking to him again.

"You are forgiven," Sophie said.

As she was opening the door, Caspar quickly called out, "Can I see you again?"

There was a pause as she thought about this for a moment. "No," she replied curtly as she went inside and closed the door. All alone now, Caspar took a deep breath as he accepted the challenge.

The next morning, Sophie was straightening the hymn books after mass. For the moment, she was alone, allowing her the freedom to hum her favorite hymn. Caspar silently walked the aisle, drawn in by her beautiful melody. Distracted by her current task, she didn't notice as he sat down a pew back from where she stood. When she saw Caspar, she startled and almost tumbled down in the pew adjacent to him. Habitually, she clutched her rosary.

"Why do you believe that will protect you?" he inquired curiously, picking a hymn book from the back of a pew. "It's just beads and string."

Turning her nose up at him while continuing her task, she replied, "It is a symbol of my faith. My faith is what protects me."

"From what? The devil? I hate to disappoint you, but he doesn't exist," Caspar said nonchalantly while flipping through one of the hymn books. These ancient songs made no sense for modern woes.

"Are you not a religious man?" Sophie asked as she forcefully snatched the book away and put it in its proper place.

"I used to be, a very long time ago. Yet in all my time, I have never seen evidence of a god nor a devil. I have seen both evil and good in the world, but never the embodiment of either." Caspar paused and watched Sophie fixing the books. "Do you believe in the devil?"

"I believe in God," she said without looking at him, a trick that was helping her not to blush. "Therefore, I believe there is a devil. My faith protects me from the devil."

"Yet your faith can't protect you from bodily harm," Caspar added.

"I have no threat of bodily harm," Sophie responded curtly.

Concern washed over Caspar's face. Whether out of naivety or arrogance, this air of feigned invincibility would surely throw her to the pits of hot fire that were inevitably getting closer to this cathedral day by day. The long silence drew the nun to finally look at him.

"As long as there are evil people in this world, you will always be in danger," Caspar said, understanding a difficult truth he thought she couldn't accept as long as she believed in her Catholic God.

For a moment, Sophie was caught in his dark eyes, which had lightened slightly from yesterday. Aware that she'd been staring at him, she broke her gaze and rudely asked, "What are you even doing here? I told you to not come back to see me."

"I'm allowed to be here and you can't tell me what to do." Caspar offered her a playful grin.

"So, are you going to stalk me forever?" she said. Sophie's voice carried through the vaulted cathedral, causing a passing nun to glance in their direction. "Stop following me," she followed up in a whisper.

Caspar stood up and walked over to her. "I can't. You have bewitched me with your beauty. Now I have the responsibility of protecting you from harm."

Frustrated, she glared into his eyes, which were swirling a dark purple. "Why?"

"Because a beauty such as yourself should be saved from the darkness that shrouds this land," Caspar whispered, his eyes pulsating into a richer purple.

Sophie's cheeks burned red hot, prompting her to tear her gaze away. "Repent and serve thy Lord." Not caring about finishing her task in the last two rows, she left a stray book and escaped to the back.

Later that night, during evening catechism class, Sophie sang from the choir to pews full of people trying to follow along off-pitch. Not everyone could sing, but in times such as these, all were eager to display their faith in God. The hymn was soon over and the bishop bid everyone sit. As they obeyed in unison, Sophie's eyes locked onto Caspar, in the dead center of the rows of pews. The people around him didn't notice his oddness, because they were so focused on their devotions the pulpit, where the bishop preached. Caspar mimicked the faithful townsfolk and occasionally glanced over at Sophie, who sat with her mouth agape. Over the course of the catechism class, Sophie was so distracted by Caspar's audacity that she kept losing her place in the prayer book and was late to stand or sit or recite prayers she had spoken thousands of times. An older nun sitting next to her noticed and surreptitiously smacked Sophie on the top of her head. Sophie gritted her teeth as she glared at Caspar, who could sing along to every hymn without glancing at the hymn book. The same man who had told her he wasn't religious.

After the class was over, a few people stayed to talk to the bishop and priests about their concerns. The nuns left to finish their nightly chores before going to bed. Sophie watched Caspar linger for a moment until most of the congregants had left. Then he stood up and calmly went outside, baiting her to follow him. He walked much faster than normal, testing her determination. She practically had to run to keep up, verifying the impact he had made on her in such a short amount of time.

Finally, she caught up to him and grabbed his arm, turning Caspar around to face her, "What are you doing in my church? I told you to leave me alone!"

Caspar admired the way the moon brought a gorgeous glow to her delicate face. "Pardon me, Sophie, but you did instruct me to repent. So, I decided to attend the catechism class. Also, it is not *your* church. The church belongs to your God, who I thought accepted all sinners into His house."

"I told you to leave me alone," she said again, stubbornly.

Caspar looked around at the night sky and the trees, then made his point. "I believe I was leaving the church when you followed me out here. Correct me if I'm wrong, but we aren't in your sanctuary right now, are we?" A cunning glint shone in his purple eyes.

When it dawned on Sophie that she wasn't in the safety of her church, she hunkered down warily as if something might jump out and get her. Caspar continued towards the forest as he nonchalantly called back, "Go home, Sophie, I'll see you tomorrow."

"Wait a moment," she said stubbornly as she followed him. "Why are you playing these games with me? First you confess your love to me in my own church, then you stalk me, and now you won't talk to me." Caspar kept walking without explanation. Sophie, not willing to be ignored, grabbed his arm tightly and turned him around. "Stop and answer me!"

Caspar replied with an authoritative tone, "Go home, Sophie! It is not safe for you out here."

The insult brought a pout to her lips and a flare of anger. "Yet it is safe for you? You have got some nerve, coming to my—"

"Shhh." Caspar tried to quiet her, a snapping twig drew his attention towards the ominous forest.

"Don't you shush me as if I'm some child in church," she continued her rant.

"Be quiet," Caspar whispered as he peered into the trees with his acute night vision.

"Will you just—" she began.

Caspar put his hand forcefully around her mouth and pressed hard enough to muffle her voice. His eyes scanned the dark forest as he whispered to her, "There is something out there. Will you please stay here, low to the ground? I need to go check it out." Caspar waited until she nodded before letting her go. Soundlessly, he ran into the trees until Sophie could no longer see him.

Standing alone in the dark next to a forest that everyone was encouraged to avoid, Sophie was skittish and vulnerable. She wrapped herself tighter in her cloak. The sounds of the night spooked her, similar to a deer listening for a wolf's howl. When she could take the isolation no longer, Sophie called out, "Caspar … Caspar …"

No response.

"Caspar?" Her timid voice grew smaller when the bushes rustled nearby.

"Caspar?" she asked hesitantly.

In the blink of an eye, a dark mass lunged at her from the darkness. Reflexively, Sophie put up her hands in defense as the creature knocked her to the ground. As she was holding the small creature away in fear, Sophie saw her attacker through the moonlight. The creature's dark skin glistened as if it were some sort of amphibian. Its face was grotesque, almost demonic. Its long-yellowed teeth gnashed towards Sophie as she desperately tried to keep them from gnawing her face off. The creature's screeches were unbearably high-pitched, to the point where Sophie thought she would go deaf if they continued. The creature's long, spindly arms reached out to her with razor-sharp talons that ripped at her arms as she deflected them away from her face. It had no back legs, but instead a tail that whipped around one of her legs to keep her from standing back up. Saliva dripped from its large jaws and landed on her shoulder, burning the fabric down to her skin. Losing strength, she called out one last time, "CASPAR!"

Stepping into his heroic moment, Caspar lunged forward and flung the creature off. Sophie rolled over towards the direction the creature had been flung and held her sizzling shoulder in pain as her auburn hair was released from her habit. She watched Caspar run over to the snarling creature. Angrily, the creature flew at Caspar with what appeared to be hideous bat wings. Evading the body, Caspar caught the tail and pulled it from the body as if pulling a sword from its sheath. The entire spine ripped clean from the body, leaving Caspar with what appeared to be a grotesque whip. What remained of the creature fell to the ground in a bloody heap. Disgusted by the tail, Caspar dropped it to the ground and wiped his hand off on some nearby foliage.

Immediately after, Caspar turned towards Sophie and asked, "Are you all right?" Before she could answer him, Sophie, exhausted from the fight, succumbed to sleep. Caspar grimaced when he saw her wound. Perhaps he had gone a bit too far with his staged heroic display.

She awoke inside a tiny, simple room, with a bed and a cross on the wall. Caspar was leaning over Sophie as she lay in the bed. Her gorgeous green eyes fluttered opened to a new reality, one that had shaken her awareness of the dangers in the world.

"How are you feeling?" Caspar asked tenderly.

To show how well she was doing, Sophie sat up but then grabbed at her shoulder where the monster's saliva had burnt through to her skin. She winced as Caspar coaxed her back down. When his calming touch lingered upon her bare skin, it initially calmed her—until she realized that her habit had been removed, leaving her exposed to this man. She panicked at the predicament he'd put her in. A nun, skin exposed, lying on the bed of a man. If anyone were to find out, she could be burned at the stake. She was desperate to cover herself.

Caspar laid a blanket over her upper body, leaving her shoulder exposed. "Stop struggling or you'll make the damage to your shoulder worse," he reprimanded.

Sophie inspected her shoulder and saw it was caked with a green and brown mixture. "What happened? Where am I?" she asked in a rush.

Caspar put his hand on her forehead and brushed her auburn hair out of her face. "You are safe, Sophie. Don't worry, I haven't taken your honor. Please lie still while your shoulder heals."

"What was that … *thing?*" she asked, still terrified.

Caspar poked at the mixture caking the wound on her shoulder, "That was a Llamhigyn Y Dwr …" —he paused and noticed her confusion— "Some call them water leapers. They are more common along the coast of the sea, yet some have evolved to be out of water for longer periods of time to hunt. For some reason, it seemed to think you were easy prey. I have to say, that is the biggest one I have seen."

"What did it do to my shoulder?" Sophie asked.

Calmly, Caspar replied, "Its saliva is acidic to help it digest its food quickly before it gets hunted by something bigger."

"There are other things out there?" she asked, frightened.

Caspar answered, "There are a lot of creatures out there that you know nothing about, Sophie. That was why I told you to go back to the cathedral."

Sophie craned her neck to see her wound again. "What did you put on my shoulder?"

Caspar glanced at it, then back at Sophie. "It's a mixture of herbs and different types of mud that will expedite the healing process. Luckily, I caught it before it went to your bones, but it will still leave a nasty scar."

"How long will it take to heal?" she asked hesitantly.

"Maybe a couple days, if you keep refreshing the herb mixture on it. I will give you some to put on it every night. Otherwise, keep it covered during the daytime. Sunlight might cause any residue acid to react. Allow me to refresh the mixture and wrap it up, then I'll escort you to the cathedral. Everyone is probably wondering where you went." Caspar scraped off the mud mixture.

Sophie winced in pain as the mud mixture was removed. "Thank you for saving me ... and healing me ..." —she blushed— "and ... I'm sorry I was mean to you."

As if mocking her, Caspar said in her same tone from earlier, "You are forgiven ... now go repent and serve thy Lord."

Sophie laughed and watched him spread a batch of gross fresh mud on her wound. "Can you teach me?"

"Teach you what?" Caspar asked, his focus on her shoulder.

"Teach me about how to heal myself from the creatures that could harm me?" Sophie shyly looked up into his purple eyes, scared he would reject her.

"I would love to teach you!" he said warmly. "When would be the best time for you to escape from the abbey?"

Sophie thought on this for a moment before answering. "Nightfall," she finally decided. "You can teach me at nightfall."

Caspar shook his head. "That is awfully risky, Sophie. That is when creatures come out to hunt."

"Don't think me weak, Caspar. I am strong, because the Lord is with me," she said, with fortitude.

"Your Lord does not protect you from the darkness," Caspar responded.

Sophie grabbed his hand, "Then teach me how to protect myself ... please ..." Sophie longingly looked deep into Caspar's dark purple eyes. He looked back into her green eyes and seemed for a moment to get lost in them, as if hypnotized.

Sophie broke the long silence. "Your eyes … they frighten me."

Caspar tore his gaze away, ashamed of his appearance.

Sophie pulled him face to face with her again. "Your eyes are not of this world. There is a beauty in those terrifying eyes of yours. Please don't hide them from me. I wish to look upon them."

"Are you falling for me?" Caspar suggested with a suave smile.

Sophie let go of his face and stubbornly turned away. "I am a nun. The only love I have is for our Lord, Jesus Christ."

Caspar chuckled. "If you say so. I'll teach you how to protect yourself from monsters that go bump in the night."

"But what about the others? Are they safe from danger so long as they stay in the parish?" Sophie inquired.

A grim reality pulled on his face. "I'm afraid that not all creatures follow the laws of your God. Holy water doesn't work the way you think it does."

"That is nonsense." Sophie turned up her nose. "Only the devil creates monsters, and everything holy repels the devil."

A small red glint flashed in Caspar's eyes. "Whoever said that everything that dwells in darkness is of the devil? The devil is not responsible for all the evil in the world."

Sophie shivered from a chill that ran down her spine from the truth in his words.

"Luckily, you have me. I will teach you to see the darkness that lies in even the most pious man's heart." Caspar finished bandaging her shoulder to keep the herb mixture in place. "Let me escort you back now."

It was only a five-minute walk, but he was determined to not let her walk the night alone, no matter how short the trip. Instead of walking her to the convent door, he walked her to an open window. Acting his part as the gentleman, he opened the window and escorted her inside.

"I shall send for you tomorrow night," Caspar said, then kissed her hand and disappeared.

The next night, a black cat escorted Sophie outside, past the boundaries of the cathedral gardens. Every now and then the cat would turn around to make sure that she was following. From afar, Caspar watched Sophie talk to this cat as if she thought it was Caspar. Little did she know that Caspar sent this acutely intelligent cat to be by her side and watch her when he could not. This shadow cat had won his favor many times over and would continue to do so, so long as it concerned *her*.

"Where are you taking me, Caspar?" The cat meowed in response and continued towards the forest. The moment they reached the edge of the forest, Caspar came out from behind a tree. Sophie appeared relieved he wasn't the black cat in disguise.

Caspar leaned down and fed the black cat a piece of meat, which it eagerly ate. Then Caspar turned to Sophie, "Are you ready? We will be going into the forest. I have already laid out a safe foundation for us to work in."

"I'm ready," she said eagerly, adrenaline squeezing her stomach in a knot.

Caspar took her hand. "Please try your best to be quiet. We don't want to attract anything before we reach our destination." The cat meowed as it followed closely behind.

The forest was dark and terrifying at night, with many unfamiliar sounds Sophie had never heard. Her eyes searched the darkness, fearful about spotting another pair of eyes looking back at her. Her fingers weaved tighter through his and her eyes kept shooting back to the black cat that tailed them.

At last, they reached a small clearing in the woods. It was nothing more than a slight parting of the trees, enough room for four people to lie down without touching. In this small clearing, a couple dozen candles had been lit and placed in a circle. Their unique scents would keep creatures of the night at bay; even vampires would give this clearing a wide berth. Hanging from the trees were various flowers and herbs commonly seen around the borders of Trier village. In between the candles were small leaves and branches broken and assembled to form a small barrier.

"What is all of this?" Sophie asked with a sense of wonder, as she stepped into the circle. The black cat followed and started twining itself around her legs.

Caspar let go of her hand and checked the candles to make sure they were still burning. It was at this point that Sophie realized there was writing carved into the sides of the candles. Not German nor Latin, but something archaic that she didn't recognize.

Caspar turned to face her. "All of this is for your first lesson."

The black cat purred against her leg, so Sophie knelt down and pet its silky fur. "What is the cat's name?"

Clapping his hands together and giving them a quick rub, Caspar answered, "Um ... I haven't given her one yet, but I did instruct her to stay close to you. I do hope you can have cats in the convent."

Sophie scratched her under the chin, which the cat greatly appreciated. "I shall name her ... Midnight! Unfortunately, she can't come into the church, but she could stay outside in the garden. I'm sure she could catch some field mice." Sophie glanced curiously over at Caspar. "Why did you instruct her to stay close to me?"

Caspar smiled, "Cats are considered guardians of the underworld ... or the spirit realm, depending on the religion. They keep harmful entities at bay. Plus, they are normally great indicators of approaching danger. If you see the cat suddenly spook or hiss, then I would suggest you follow the fleeing cat to safety."

"That's odd," Sophie stated.

Caspar tilted his head. "What is?"

"It's odd that other religions would know anything about what happens after life," Sophie said.

Caspar smiled. "Despite what the Catholic church teaches you, there are other religions in the world that know a few legitimate things. Some even have useful practices."

"What else can you teach me?" Sophie asked, still petting her black cat.

Caspar smiled as he went on to tell her about the simple herbs and plants he had scattered about. Mostly she listened to his lessons, but would occasionally ask questions. Caspar was surprised at how open-minded she was, despite her education and upbringing. As the night went on, the two talked for hours while the cat lounged about.

"Sophie, it is now time for me to escort yo to the cathedral," Caspar said sadly.

"Aw, really? I was having fun learning from you," Sophie whined.

"Do not fret. You shall see me tomorrow, and you now have Midnight to comfort you throughout the day," Caspian said optimistically.

Sophie scratched the top of her cat's head and told her, "So long as you stay out of the cathedral. Last thing I need is for one of the elder nuns to beat you for wandering into the kitchen."

Midnight meowed in response.

"Come along, Sophie." Caspar held out his hand to her.

Sophie blushed slightly as she took his hand. Both remained quiet as they ventured through the forest, the cat ever present at their feet. Caspar wished they had more time together but knew the dangers if she were missing for too long. Disappearing at night was risky enough.

"This is where we part," Caspar said sadly as they exited the forest.

"Can't you escort me to the abbey window?" she begged.

"I am sorry, Sophie, but it is too risky for me to be seen in public with you. The last thing I want is compromise your safety by making others suspicious of our activity— especially with the escalation of witch accusations."

"*Witch accusations?* We have been completely cleaned of the witch plague. Unless … you are one …" Sophie eyed Caspar suspiciously.

He chuckled. "No, I am not a witch, though I do have a vast amount of information about creatures that lurk in the darkness. Please be careful. Many innocent people have lost their lives due to the plague of fear that has consumed towns searching for hints of witchcraft."

"Well, as I mentioned, Trier has been completely rid of witches," Sophie said confidently and then instructed her black cat, "Come along, Midnight."

The cat meowed and followed her the last stretch to the cathedral.

A deep, uneasy feeling settled in Caspar's stomach. He wondered and hoped that Sophie was not responsible for any of the deaths from the witch trials. With her innocence and love of life, he doubted she would accuse anyone of something that would lead to a pyre. Still, her naivety and trust in the church worried him. Caspar sighed as he gazed up at the moon and noticed it was only a few hours until dawn. He needed to hurry and dismantle everything he had built, in case someone wandered through the forest during the day.

The next three weeks went the same every day. Sophie would wake up and do all of her chores and assigned tasks. Then, late at night, her cat would wake her quietly. Only then would she get dressed and sneak out to meet up with Caspar. The real fun would begin when he led her through the forest into her mystical circle of protection for a couple of hours of learning.

Caspar could tell that Sophie, despite her stubbornness, was showing a stronger attraction to him every day, almost to the point where she found it unbearable to part with him at the end of the night. Sophie had become confident enough to plant little herbs that drive away evil in each windowsill, just in case. Her cat, Midnight, stayed with her during the night and would sleep in the garden throughout the day. Every day was better than the last.

Until one day, something unexpected happened.

Caspar lounged in a wagon, blending in as a merchant selling herbs. Similar to the rest of the townsfolk, he feigned ignorant curiosity and gawked at a parade he regarded as the epitome of evil. The procession traveled up to the front of Trier cathedral, where resident nuns and priests formed two lines awaiting its arrival. A carriage emblazoned with golden crosses and pulled by two strong horses pulled up to the cathedral doors. Behind it came wagons bearing large cages full of women in rags. Judging by their shredded attire, they were women from different villages accused of witchcraft and now awaiting their prosecution. The despair on their faces revealed that they knew what fiery hell was awaiting them. Caspar's eyes hung on one poor soul with fierce hazel eyes and brown hair. She was far too young for such a fate. However, there wasn't much he could do for her without drawing attention to himself and Sophie.

The bishop came forward and opened the carriage door personally. "Welcome back to the Cathedral of Trier, Archbishop Johann von Schonenberg!"

The archbishop was a man with a terrifying presence. Others gave him plenty of room to avoid being sucked into his darkness. The man didn't stand very tall, but his mitre towered above all others. He was draped in red silk robes embroidered with gold thread. The man might claim to be humble and godly, but his appearance told quite a different story. Everyone averted their eyes as he passed by.

"How were your travels, Archbishop?" the bishop asked, trailing the man even he feared.

"They were long," Archbishop Johann von Schonenberg bluntly noted. "It disgusts me to find so much filth in our beautiful kingdom. Far too many witches practicing their foul craft, turning the minds of the innocent toward evil. Such a dreary job cleaning our holy towns, yet someone has to do it." —the archbishop glanced at the wagons— "Please put this scum in proper shackles, separated from one another. Don't want them getting any bright ideas. The sooner we can dispose of their corpses and expunge this town of the devil's progeny, the better."

The bishop tried to keep up to the Archbishop, but struggled to do so. "As you wish! I will send several of our best men to take care of those arrangements. You should be pleased to know that we haven't found any witches here since your last cleansing. We remain a holy city."

Ignoring the bishop's comment, the Archbishop commanded, "Get me a private room where I can review my notes."

"Yes Archbishop, of course Archbishop!" the bishop said, bowing several times in quick succession.

Sophie was one of the last sisters in the welcome line. In the past, when Archbishop Johann von Schonenberg had been ridding the town of witches, the nuns were frightened to look upon him, but she was different. Sophie stubbornly refused to avert her gaze, and so got a good look at the man who had condemned hundreds to die under the sentence of witchcraft. Although the man was threatening, he just seemed like any other old man, but with a fancy hat— except for those cold-stone eyes, which seemed to care little for any living thing upon this planet. This was not a man to listen to begging and unlikely to offer absolution for your sins. He was a man hardened by the death he had wrought on others. While Sophie was sizing up the archbishop, Caspar was cringing and shifting from side to side. How stupid could she be? There was only one man to avoid, and she was challenging him with her brazen stare. Unluckily, Archbishop Johann von Schonenberg caught her gaze and zeroed in on her. Though she quickly averted her gaze to the floor, it was too late.

The Archbishop stopped promptly in front of Sophie and squared up his puffed-out shoulders to her slumped ones: "What is your name, Sister?"

"Sister Sophie," she replied, eyes glued obediently to the floor.

"Hmmm, you are much bolder than the rest, aren't you, Sophie? Why do I not recognize you?"

"I am not sure, Archbishop. I have lived here at the parish my entire life and served the Lord with my every breath," she responded, eyes still glued to the floor.

"Hmmm, right ..." the Archbishop pondered while glaring down on this lowly nun.

"Archbishop, your room is prepared for you," piped up the bishop, who appeared much braver than the rest, despite his tremors.

"I'll keep an eye on you, Sister Sophie," warned the Archbishop. He followed the bishop to his room and the congregation dispersed to their chores. Caspar was terrified for Sophie, the fear squeezing his heart. Caspar growled under his breath and ran off to make a different kind of preparation for tonight.

Later that evening, Sophie raced out a little earlier than normal to see Caspar. Midnight ran after her, meowing a warning. Heedless, she continued on. Unbeknownst to her, the Archbishop saw her sneaking off into the woods with a black cat. Caspar looked up from the seclusion of the woods and could feel the cold, calculating eyes of Archbishop Johann von Schonenberg narrowing in on his next target. It probably didn't help that a black cat was following her around; Caspar regretted his poor decision with that cat now. He knew she couldn't afford to be seen with him at this moment and retreated deep into the forest. By now, though, she'd grown bold enough to look for him at the circle in the forest. Caspar tucked himself into the trees, hoping that if she came and found the circle empty she would give up and return to the convent. But when she arrived, her haste sent her tripping over a rock. Instinctively, Caspar lunged in and caught her before she could fall.

"What do you think you are doing, Sophie!" he scolded, unable to hold back. "I instructed you to never wander in here alone. Who knows what could have attacked you on the way!" Midnight meowed with him.

"I couldn't wait any longer, Caspar—"

"Have you finally fallen in love with me?" he interrupted, sounding more sarcastic than hopeful.

"I told you that the only love I have is for God," she lied.

"Then why did you decide to brave the forest alone?" he inquired.

"It's Archbishop Johann von Schonenberg. He has returned," she said, worry written all over her face.

Caspar's face fell. He knew this danger more than she did, but this was not the time to go into a long tale. All he could think to say was, "Oh."

In disbelief and frustration, Sophie retorted, "*Oh?* Is that all you are going to say? Oh? Do you know who he is?"

Caspar helped Sophie to her feet and stared longingly into the forest, the only true shelter from the Archbishop. "Unfortunately, I know him all too well. You must go back to the convent immediately so as not to raise suspicion. I don't want him to have reason to investigate you for witchcraft."

Suddenly, Sophie appeared guilty.

A red flare flashed in Caspar's purple eyes. "What did you do, Sophie?"

She twiddled her thumbs as if she were a child who had been caught misbehaving. "He already knows me. I ... I looked him in the eyes."

Caspar flung up his arms and weaved his fingers through his hair. He already knew this, but it was impossible to hold back the fear and frustration he felt for her sake, "For fuck's sake, Sophie! Do you have a death wish? Now you really must go back, before he becomes more suspicious of you."

"But can't you teach me to protect myself from him?" she asked hopefully.

"Sophie, I'm afraid I can only teach you to protect yourself from creatures of the night. He's just a human. It'll be best if you didn't come to see me for a while." The bluntness of his statement would surely sting, but it was necessary to keep her safe. "It is the only way I can protect you, Sophie … to make you appear normal again."

Sophie stared into his deep purple eyes. "Will you at least escort me back?"

"Of course," he said with a smile.

As always, they walked hand in hand out of the forest. When they made it to the edge of the forest, Caspar turned around to face Sophie, the moonlight glowing on her face. "Alright Sophie, this is where I leave you. Please go about your normal day and do not do anything out of the ordinary. The last thing I want is for the Archbishop to set his targets on you."

"Thank you, Caspar … I … I think I might …" She couldn't say it— the "L" word.

The awkward waiting passed, and Caspar sighed. "Please be safe today. I can't stand the thought of losing you," he said, his eyes swirling a light shade of purple.

"I will be safe," she promised. Midnight meowed again, which prompted them to part. Sophie returned to the convent, much earlier than usual, with the black cat on her heels.

Caspar's resolve hardened throughout the day until he finally committed to leaving Trier to draw the witch hunt away. Which meant he had to make some sort of appearance. However, he had to say goodbye; she at least deserved that courtesy.

He arrived while she was performing her midday chore of harvesting and weeding the garden. Relieved to find her completely alone, Caspar approached her from behind.

Sophie wiped the sweat off her brow as Midnight rubbed up against her leg. "What are you doing here? I thought it wasn't safe for us to be seen together."

"I came to say goodbye," he said seriously as he came closer.

"And I suppose you will whisk me away with you, kicking and screaming?" she jested as she stood up to face him.

"No. I will go alone, pulling the attention off of you and forcing Archbishop Johann von Schonenberg's hand to hunt me away from Trier," Caspar said quickly, an urgency to his voice.

"Caspar, I'm safe. No one has even noticed anything different about me," she interrupted.

Caspar grabbed her shoulders and said, "Sophie, this is very important. You must not venture into the forest until I return. Do you understand me?"

Sophie smiled at him as if he were just being silly. "Why can't I? I did last night and was just fine. Midnight helped to protect me. I can eve—"

"No Sophie," he interrupted her. "You must not go into the forest. Tell me you won't go into the forest without me!"

Putting up her hands and waving the white flag, she submitted. "Fine, fine. I won't go into the forest, but when will you return? I worry for your safety, not mine. It's foolish to tempt the Archbishop to hunt for you when you've done nothing wrong."

"I do not know when I'll return, Sophie. Rest assured I'll be safe. Unfortunately, I've had to do this a couple times with the Archbishop, to get him to leave others alone. Promise me you won't go into the forest until I return!"

"Okay," she agreed.

Before she could say another word, Caspar quickly disappeared from her view. Then he headed back inside the cathedral. Caring little for common decency, he pushed past two friars and glared up at the Archbishop, who was seated on the dais in the sanctuary.

Archbishop Johann von Schonenberg looked down at this young man, his lips curling in a hideous snarl. Next to him stood a dark and terrifying man, wearing thick black furs and multiple crosses. Several rosaries were wrapped around his wrists and hanging from his belt. Secured to his belt was a flask of holy water and various blades. Although his face was shadowed by a heavy black beard, his chin and lips remained visible, revealing the crucifix tattooed into his lower lip. There was a dense heaviness around this monstrous man, who clearly knew more war than peace.

"Now you know what your target looks like, Hexenjager," the Archbishop said, pointing directly at Caspar, "the devil himself walks among us. Seize him!"

Immediately, the guards surrounded them, their armor, emblazoned with a crucifix, glistening in the sunlight cascading through a stained-glass window.

A mischievous smile grew upon Caspar's wicked-looking face. "Your familiarity with the devil astounds even me," he told the Archbishop. "Your handiwork must be impressive to such an evil entity." Before the guards could react, Caspar threw down a tight ball of compressed powder which exploded, creating a smoke screen that stifled the breath of those around him. Those unlucky enough to be present doubled over, coughing up the irritant, as Caspar made his escape.

Once the smoke had cleared, the Hexenjager stated his claim. "I have seen this devil before. I would gladly dispose of him for you ... at a price." The witch hunter's deep voice cracked with hardship and cruelty.

"Land or gold?" Archbishop Johann von Schonenberg clarified, clearing the last remains of powder from his own throat.

"Both," the Hexenjager said with a greedy smile.

"Done."

Caspar trekked through the forest in the comfort of the night. Creatures moved around the trees, giving him a wide berth—too smart or too frightened to attack him. What did startle him was the rustle in the trees ahead. At first, it appeared to be no more than a gentle breeze. But soon the trees were shaking as if a hurricane had hit. Soon enough he was surrounded by creatures of the night, screaming at first in a chaotic and painful way that soon became synchronized. That was when he heard it:

the old language, one he had not heard in several hundred years. It spoke of a warning. Caspar's eyes widened as he finally understood the message. Feeling a strange presence behind him, he ducked down and rolled away as a long arrow passed by where his head had been a moment ago. Crouched low to the ground, Caspar removed his large pack, knowing he would soon be initiating combat. Another arrow flew, but this time he caught it and sniffed the roughly made tip, which smelt strongly of holy anointing oil. Then he knew what he was up against.

The Hexenjager stepped through the trees and into view. In his hands was a massive crossbow with a crucifix carved into the weapon. This monstrous man stood taller than most and was clothed in layers of crude black furs and crucifixes. "Finally, I meet the devil himself."

"I was wondering when you would show up," Caspar mocked with a sly grin.

Bringing up his loaded crossbow, the Hexenjager shot Caspar at close range. Far too close for any mortal to dodge, yet this was child's play to Caspar, who avoided the arrow with ease. He ducked below the crossbow and struck it out of the Hexenjager's hand, splintering it into a million pieces with a deafening crack. The Hexenjager barely avoided getting hit himself, as Caspar swiped at his knees with clawed hands.

Bounding backwards, the Hexenjager unsheathed his curved knives with crucifixes burned into the handles. Crouching, he began chanting the exorcism ritual, through lips emblazoned with a cross.

None of his words affected Caspar, who advanced upon the Hexenjager with full intent to destroy him. Caspar knew hundreds had died by this Hexenjager's hands— not only the witches, but also the innocent who were wrongly accused of witchcraft. The world no longer had need for a blood-hungry Hexenjager.

Seeing that his words had no effect on his prey, the Hexenjager changed tactics and slashed his knives at the oncoming threat. Caspar evaded those, too, and grabbed the Hexenjager's right arm. As Caspar curled his fingers into the Hexenjager s arm, a wet crunching sound could be heard as the bones were shattered.

Blindly lashing out, the Hexenjager slashed Caspar across the face with one of his blades. Caspar let go and dabbed at the blood on his chin. The Hexenjager watched from the ground in horror as the cut magically healed and disappeared.

Retreating on all fours, the Hexenjager tried desperately to get away from this monster's reach. Caspar's eyes glowed a deep red as he quickly advanced on him. Panic rose and choked the Hexenjager's throat.

Caspar reached down and grabbed the pathetic, war-torn Hexenjager by the front of his garments. One of the rosaries fell into Caspar's hand, with no effect. Caspar then held up the Hexenjager until his feet hovered above the ground, and pinned him against a large tree. In a last attempt, the Hexenjager threw holy water in Caspar's face. Caspar paused and licked the water dripping over his lips.

"What sort of demon are you?" asked the Hexenjager, fear constricting his pupils to tiny black dots.

Caspar smiled, his red eyes glowing menacingly. "Whoever said I was a demon? I'm something much worse!"

The Hexenjager screamed out to the heavens, praying to God to protect him. Meanwhile, Caspar built the heat in his hand. The heat grew so intense that the Hexenjager's clothes singed and caught on fire around his face and throat; it boiled his blood within his veins. The heat was so agonizing the Hexenjager seized. Then, spreading faster than wildfire, purple fire consumed the Hexenjager and blazed up the tree. Untouched by the fire, Caspar watched hungrily as the Hexenjager screamed his last. The red in his eyes glowed in the dark of the night as the fire died away. Sweet adrenaline running through his system, Caspar flexed every muscle, enjoying the thrill of the kill. For a moment, his fingers grew into sharp claws before receding back into their normal human state. Instead of returning to purple, his eyes darkened to black.

Returning to a calmer state, Caspar suddenly remembered Sophie. Leaving his pack behind, he set off at a run towards town.

Sophie woke groggily, her head pounding. Instinctively, she tried to raise her hands to her head, but found that her arms were restrained. It was then that she noticed she was no longer wearing her habit. She had been stripped down to her white slip. Her body was bound tightly to a pyre. Panic dilated her pupils as she took in her surroundings. A mob was screaming, spitting at her, throwing tomatoes, she realized, to her disgust. She made out the word "witchcraft," repeated over and over. She managed to turn her head and saw behind her several cages imprisoning a dozen other women, gazing upon Sophie with forlorn and pitying eyes. They understood her fate better than she did. One woman in particular, with hazel eyes and dirty brown hair, watched her intently, as if recording this memory in her mind.

Panicking, Sophie pulled at the twine keeping her fastened to the wood, which smelled of pitch.

Archbishop Johann von Schonenberg approached, his servant holding a torch. He had a wicked smile upon his lips. "Sophie, Sophie, Sophie ... how did you get into this predicament? Were you seduced by the devil or did you search him out?"

"What? I am not a witch!" she cried in fear.

"Nonsense! We caught you not only fraternizing with the devil himself, whose head should be brought to us shortly, but also casting a spell with the help of your minion!" the Archbishop shouted venomously.

"No! I'm not a witch!" Sophie cried. She pulled against her restraints but found it impossible, so she hung limply. "You are a monster!"

Archbishop Johann von Schonenberg leaned in close enough to cast his putrid breath on her, "That devil is the monster!"

"What did you do to him?" she asked with red hot anger in her eyes.

"You'll find out when you meet him in Hell, you filthy witch whore!" spat the Archbishop, taking a few steps back.

The mob cheered as the Archbishop signaled his servant to light the pyre. Instantly, the fire spread, with heat so intense it drew all the moisture from her throat and eyes. Sophie screamed out in agony as the flames licked her bare feet hungrily.

Caspar ran as fast as he could. His heart was racing as he pushed his body as hard as it would go. Even at a speed five times faster than a normal human, he worried it would not be enough. His strategy to pull the Hexenjager away from Sophie had failed, for a greater monster remained lurking amidst the sanctity of the cathedral. As he looked up at the glow in the sky surrounding the village square, he worried he might be too late. Sophie's screams were echoing through the town, triggering something primal within Caspar. His eyes turned red and he sprinted faster. The smell of cooking flesh wafted through the air, which sickened Caspar, knowing whose it was.

Caspar burst through the crowd surrounding the pyre, trampling anyone who got in his way. It was too late. Above the fire, so intense and thick, a million tiny purple wisps were floating upward and flying away on the wind.

From afar, he could hear panicked orders being called out, but he didn't care. Caspar fell to his knees as three men lassoed him with ropes and sprayed him with holy water. None of this mattered. Caspar didn't even care that the terrified crowd was demanding that he be thrown into the fire next. What did matter was that Archbishop Johann von Schonenberg sat in a plush chair, screaming orders to his holy soldiers. Caspar stood and forcefully walked over to the archbishop, dragging along the hapless men trying to keep him under control. He stopped a mere five steps away.

The Archbishop shakily held a crucifix out in front of him, shouting, "May the power of Christ compel you, devil. Return back to Hell, where you belong!"

The crowd grew quiet as Caspar glared at the Archbishop with red, glowing eyes, "I am not the devil, but I am in hell. Here, father, let me show you hell."

Caspar pounced on the Archbishop as if he were a cat catching a mouse. With sharp-taloned fingers, he drove his hand into the Archbishop's chest, breaking through all the ribs. Archbishop Johann von Schonenberg watched in horror as his still beating heart was ripped from his chest and then caught fire in Caspar's hand. The Archbishop died watching his own heart cooking to a crisp, which Caspar took a carnal bite out of it and then threw the rest on the corpse. Satisfied, Caspar turned around, his eyes glowing redder than the blazing pyre. The crowd fled, screaming in horror. Caspar brought his clawed hands up as if raising a great load above his head. Instantly a purple fire wall trapped everyone in the town square.

"Let me show you what I really am," he growled. As if in a dance, Caspar swept his hands around in three large loops as purple fire burst from his fingertips. The purple flames formed into a great dragon that towered over Caspar, yet didn't burn him. The crowd screamed in terror as the purple fire dragon breathed hot flames down upon them. Men, women, children. It didn't matter. All who lived in this cursed town would soon perish in the purple flames.

The purple dragon faded away, leaving Caspar to walk the flames unscathed. Even his clothes remained intact as he parted the flames to survey his kill. The fire didn't stop or die down until the entire village of Trier was nothing but a pile of rubble and ash. No one made it out alive that night ... no one except ....

Caspar walked over the piles of rubble and burnt skeletons, frail enough to be crushed to dust by his boots. What he saw next surprised even him. That girl with the hazel eyes and brown hair, probably no older than eighteen, lay curled up in a ball on the ground. Some of her hair and white tattered dress had been singed, but she otherwise remained unharmed. As Caspar gazed down upon this girl, curled within a circle she had drawn with her own blood, he wondered how such a young and simple thing could have survived his flames.

Wanting to wake her, yet not caring enough to do it gently, he kicked the sole of her foot. The girl stirred, her long brown hair shifting as her hazel eyes opened and stared up at Caspar.

"How interesting," he said with a curious tilt to his head. "No one has ever survived my flames before."

* * *

"Wow!" Sammy instantly connected the dots. "That was Morgan! That was Morgan! She told me about that day! The day that she was saved!"

Connor scratched the back of his head, wishing Sammy could connect more than just Morgan's origin story. "Yep, that was the day that Morgan was saved by the devil and dubbed Morgan la Fae."

Sammy's proud posture slumped as she came to her next conclusion. "Don't you think Caspar overreacted?"

"Well, how would you feel if someone burned Buddy alive?" Connor retorted defensively.

Buddy instantly appeared alarmed, shifting his trusting eyes from one to another. Sammy patted his head reassuringly, which calmed him back to sleep.

"Yeah, I guess I would overreact, too," Sammy shrugged. "But Sophie was being taught how to protect herself from monsters. Caspar didn't teach her how to protect herself from humans."

"That," Connor bopped her nose, "was his greatest downfall. Well, that and leaving her alone to fend for herself."

Sammy collapsed on the floor. "But you have taught me how to defend myself! I'm ready to join special ops with how much sparring we've done in the past year."

"I would say more like basic army boot camp ... or reserves ... neither of which I expect you to join." Connor shook the horrifying image from his head.

There was a long silence. After chewing on the words he didn't want to say, Connor finally gave in. "I will look into high schools for you to go to. Only when I find a suitable match will I let you go and tour around the school. Deal?"

Sammy popped up from the floor, nearly rocketing herself into the air. "Deal!"

They shook on it, leaving Sammy to bounce around the house for the rest of the evening.

10

BLURRED LINES OF MORALITY

LONDONDERRY, NEW HAMPSHIRE

SEPTEMBER 29, 2012

The sharp sound of a whistle pierced the air, followed shortly by a referee's call. "Sportsmanship misconduct!"

Connor stormed onto the soccer field, "Are you kidding me?"

"No parents on the field!" the referee called, which instantly made the coach run over.

"Sammy didn't trip that girl. She tripped over her own clumsy feet!" Connor yelled over the roar of the crowd.

The coach, a plump, middle-aged woman, was trying to pull on Connor to get him off the field, with no luck at even budging him. Seeing the struggle, Sammy ran over in her bright green soccer uniform. Her Auburn hair was tied up in pigtails wrapped about her head to not get in her way. Always the mediator, Sammy jumped between the referee and Connor.

"Connor! It's okay. You aren't helping," Sammy whispered while trying to hide her embarrassment and then turned to the referee. "I'll take the penalty. I'm sorry about my guardian. He's a touch protective."

The referee sniffed, apparently not satisfied. "If you make another move like that, then I'll take you off the field."

"I understand, thank you, sir." Sammy apologized as she pushed Connor off the field.

Connor sulked back to the stands. "What does that ref know about soccer? It is meant to be aggressive! Sportsmanship misconduct, psht."

Sammy laughed, and replied, "Connor, I'm grateful for the opportunity to play soccer for Hopkinton High School. Please don't get me kicked off the team so early in the season."

Connor took a deep breath. "Fine. I guess I can watch from the benches."

"Thanks." Sammy gave Connor a high-five.

"Now, obliterate the other team!" Connor yelled.

Sammy waved as she ran onto the field. As a front liner, she was quite talented. No surprise to Connor, she was faster than the rest of her team and could play for longer without exhausting herself. Her greatest strength was that she could kick the ball the hardest, to the point where goalies hated blocking her ball. It was all because Connor had slowly been conditioning her strength, agility and speed for the last three years without her even noticing.

It was agonizing to let her go to school. That first week had been the hardest for Connor, much harder than he anticipated. It became so painful to watch her leave for school and wait at home all day long. Conner was beside himself. So, he cleverly got a job as a counselor at her school. Sammy wasn't thrilled but got over it, knowing it reduced Connor's anxiety.

Despite all his resistance, Connor was glad to have registered her for high school. Sammy appeared much happier to be in school, even if three-quarters of her classes were college classes—a concession she'd made in their negotiations. She was just happy to be able to compete in sports.

The whistle blew as both teams fought for the ball. Sammy stole the ball away and headed toward the end of the field. With her other front liners protecting her from both sides, she was able to kick in another goal. The team cheered and high-fived each other before lining up again.

Connor saw a familiar expression from the lead front liner on the other team. His heart skipped a beat as he heard the whistle blow. The opposing team bunched closely around Sammy, who freed the ball to another team member. Connor saw what most didn't: the lead opponent stomped down on Sammy's ankle hard enough to make her fall to the ground. The opposing team stole the ball and bolted down the field. Sammy was left curled up on the ground, holding her ankle and grimacing in pain. Before they could make a goal, the whistle was blown.

Connor rushed onto the field, following the coach and the nurse on site. Sammy's team already surrounded her. Bursting into the huddle, Connor leaned over Sammy and ignored the nurse's reprimands against lightly touching her injured ankle. Sammy winced in pain. Sighing with relief, he said, "It appears to be sprained. Nothing was broken."

Then he turned to the referee with fire in his eyes. "Why the hell aren't you penalizing that girl. She played dirtier than Sammy!"

Realizing he was right, the referee turned around and hounded the guilty party.

"She should be taken to a doctor," the nurse chimed in.

Connor picked Sammy up carefully and cradled her in his arms as he had done so many times before. "Thanks for saying the obvious, nurse!"

While they walked away from the field, Sammy moped, "I guess I'm done for the season, huh?"

"Not at all," Connor replied optimistically. "We are going to go to the hospital to get you examined. Then, after we get a nice brace for your ankle, we will have Auntie Morgan use her own herbal remedies to make you heal faster. You should be back on the field in a week."

Sammy giggled and then winced. "Thank you, Connor."

As Sammy was getting x-rays, Connor sat in the hallway, holding his head. He couldn't deny that he had wanted to rip out that girl's throat for daring to harm Sammy. How petty girls were, willing to hurt their peers to win one game. Humanity disgusted Connor. All the more reason to put humanity in its place.

"Kids sure do grow up fast, don't they, Caspian?" said a familiar voice.

"She's fifteen now, right?"

Startled, Connor looked up to see an old friend, "Dorian..."

"It's been a while." Dorian smiled. The gentleman appeared as if he had stepped out of a GQ magazine: stunningly gorgeous blonde hair, a suit designed by an esteemed fashion designer, a face so charming it made women melt and men envious, and he smelled of Parisian cologne. Overall, Dorian was a catch!

"It has been a while," Connor replied, nostalgia returning to the forefront of his mind.

* * *

LONDON, ENGLAND

APRIL 4, 1888

Londoners went about their day in the normal fashion of Victorian England on a cloudy, gray day. Women wrapped their shoulders in thick shawls and men bundled against the cold in long wool coats and top hats. In a peaceful park, couples wooed on wooden benches, sitting close for warmth, while children played hide and seek.

Up above, in a large willow tree, sat a gentleman wearing the customary black overcoat, black pants, a black button-up shirt beneath a dark purple vest, and a tall black top hat. Comfortably nestled in the crook of some branches, the gentleman was calmly carving a chunk of wood he had broken from the tree. The hat shadowed his eyes as he diligently worked on his carving. Every now and then he would glance over at a particular couple lounging next to the pond. A beautiful girl in a voluminous white dress with purple bows on her hat was sitting upon a checkered red blanket with a young gentleman wearing brown and beige. She tossed her auburn curls back over her shoulder, giggling flirtatiously at the gentleman's cautious advances. Her green eyes fluttered as her cheeks grew rosy. The blonde, blue-eyed man sweetly fed her a piece of fruit, which she ate from his hand. The two were so adorably affectionate that they were making the hidden gentleman sick. The man focused on his carving for another minute until their cuteness passed.

At least she looks happy, he thought.

"Hello there, Caspian!" called out a voice from below. Caspian had to lean partially off his branch to see who had so rudely interrupted his peace and quiet. Below stood a wealthy aristocrat wearing the finest of Victorian fashion. His hair was smoothed back and his beard was full, yet craftily groomed. A man of impeccable style, he could buy anything he wanted, no matter how immoral the rest of society might perceive it to be.

Caspian settled into his original position and glanced at the couple before returning to his carving. "Hello, Henry," he greeted flatly. "What do you want?"

"I'm having a masquerade ball tonight!" he said exuberantly.

Caspian remained silent.

"The wealthiest and most beautiful people of London will be there!" Henry added.

"Thank you for the heads-up," Caspian grumbled, while concentrating on his carving. "I'll make sure to be somewhere else tonight."

"No, no, no, Caspian, I was inviting you," Henry said quickly.

Caspian finally looked over at the young lord and said with deep irritation, "Just because I live with you in your manor doesn't mean you get to parade me around as your pet."

Henry came closer to the tree, but then thought better of possibly soiling his suit. "No, Caspian. Not my pet. I am eternally grateful for the abilities you have graced me with and want to repay you in kind, with fantastic connections to the London elite."

Caspian didn't say a word, but instead glanced over at the flirtatious couple, who were now watching clouds.

Lord Henry caught Caspian's gaze and realized why he had perched in a tree. "If you would prefer, I can invite the young lady to accompany us.

Her name is Sally Stanbury, correct? I can easily add her to my guest list."

"No," Caspian responded flatly.

"It's a masquerade ball, so you would be able to talk to her without her knowledge of who you are," Henry suggested, with eyebrows raised.

"No!" Caspian snapped, "I do not wish to engage with the young woman."

"Just watch her from afar? Life is meant to be lived to its fullest potential," Lord Henry said, with much exaggeration in his voice. When Caspian remained quiet, he continued, "You are the most powerful being I have ever met, Caspian. Go take what you want."

"Henry, you are the last person I would take advice from," Caspian said as he finished carving his figurine of a woman in a large dress with long hair tied up in ribbons.

"That is quite a fine piece there, Caspian. I didn't know you could be so artistic." Lord Henry watched as Caspian admired his handiwork for a moment. He then held it up in the palm of his hand so the small woman was looking out toward the pond. Without warning, the small figurine instantly burst into purple flames, which incinerated into ash. Lord Henry jumped back and put a hand to his heart. Caspian dumped the ash onto the tree and clapped his hands together to get rid of the remains of the ash. He then jumped down as lithely as a cat.

"Do you hate her?" asked a startled Lord Henry.

For a moment, Caspian turned towards the young woman's direction as if he had trouble deciding whether he hated her or not. "Sometimes I do ... most of the time it's merely self-loathing."

Readjusting himself, the young lord followed Caspian to the edge of the park. "Well, how about if I give you something else to think about. Please attend my party tonight. I truly wish for you to meet one person. Please Caspian, I beg of thee."

"Fine!" —Caspian rubbed his temples— "If you will stop pestering me about it, then I will *briefly* meet with *one* person."

Lord Henry looked overjoyed. "Excellent! You may even find this young man to be quite fixating, with an addictive personality."

"Another one of your proteges?" Caspian asked, clearly annoyed at this point.

"Except I guarantee that this one will not fail me. He has far surpassed my own expectations and blossomed into exquisite flower. He is a man of fine tastes that hungers for the extraordinary." Lord Henry said as he beamed from ear to ear.

Caspian kept his hat brim low over his purple eyes as he passed by Sally and her suitor, who were now gazing deeply into each other's eyes. "I'll speak with him then, but don't fault me for finding him too eccentric. You, Lord Henry, are far more than I can handle already."

Lord Henry didn't shy away, but instead tipped his hat towards Sally. "You shan't be disappointed."

Later that evening, Caspian leaned on a gilded balcony as he gazed down on the masses of people entering the grand doors of a manor. All these wealthy guests were lavishly dressed in London's latest. Though their faces were covered, Caspian knew most of them from previous events. Lord Henry Wotton enjoyed throwing luxurious parties, because it was one of the ways he stayed so high on the social ladder. Caspian himself refused to wear anything extravagant but did agree to dress up. Lord Henry picked out a simple yet sharp black dinner jacket for Caspian to wear, with a simple gold trimmed black-velvet mask. Caspian calmly waiting upstairs for the majority of the crowd to pass into the ballroom.

Finally, after the crowd had packed itself into the luxurious ballroom, he went downstairs. Most guests were dancing in the center of the room, while others stood along the edges drinking champagne. Waiters weaved between guests, offering them the finest cuisine that Lord Henry Wotton could offer. Caspian weaved silently among the guests as if he were a lion quietly stalking through tall grass.

Caspian hated aristocrats and high society. They would snobbishly rub shoulders and then talk venomously behind each other's backs— a tendency Caspian had seen repeated throughout the ages. Now he was forced to be meshed within this world of finery and deception. A while back he had seen promise in Lord Henry. Perhaps it was his refusal to believe what the general public believed. Perhaps it was his manipulative nature. Or perhaps it was simply that he secretly sought to watch the world burn—a compulsion easily understood by Caspian. So, Caspian had a crawling desire to use Henry's wealth and prestige to his own advantage. In exchange for Lord Henry Wotton's unlimited resources, Caspian gave him a taste of his own immortality— an arrangement he had made with only a dozen other people. At times, Caspian regretted his decision, and one of those times was right now as this extravagant party the eccentric Lord Henry was obligated to throw.

Tiring of the crowd, Caspian made his way over to Henry, who was currently laughing in a small group with four other men. Two of the men were new owners of the opera house and the third was a wealthy shareholder in America. Rumor had it that America was growing exponentially more prosperous, rivaling Europe. The last was a young man dressed completely in white from head to toe, including a white mask in the shape of a lion's head, with a golden mane. Unlike the other aristocrats, he did not push his nose in the air as though he was sniffing out gossip. Instead, his amber eyes intently watched everyone around him, as if they had something fascinating to offer. The aroma that drifted off this young man drew Caspian in like the call of a dying animal to a predator. As Caspian approached, the young man fixed his gaze on him.

"Ah! Carl! How pleasant of you to join us!" Lord Henry called out, opening his arms in a welcoming gesture. Caspian nodded, grateful that Henry was still keeping his name secret from the rest of the aristocracy. "I'm sure you remember Arnold and Fredrick from the opera house."

Caspian shook their hands and greeted them.

"Then of course you have met Brewer, our American entrepreneur," Henry continued.

"And this must be the gentleman you told me so much about," the young man said. He removed his mask to reveal his flawless skin and sparkling amber eyes. "My name is Dorian Gray. It is a pleasure to meet you," the young man said, as he held out his hand.

Caspian shook the hand, but didn't let it go. "A pleasure, I'm sure. How much has Lord Henry told you about me?" There was a strange energy flowing from Dorian's body. Its signature felt familiar, yet the way it pulsated was strangely foreign. There was something to this young man that could not be seen with the naked eye.

"Enough to still let me be surprised when I met you," Dorian said, fascinated. "What a surprise, too! Your eyes are the most extraordinary color of purple, Carl."

Caspian finally let go of his hand. "Why, thank you Dorian. Unfortunately, at this point in my life, I no longer see them as extraordinary, but I appreciate that others still do."

"Yes, I can appreciate that. I also bore easily with the mundane. Yet you seem to be a man whom I would not easily tire of." Dorian's amber eyes sparkled with the curious fascination of a child.

"Yes, Dorian has been quite the little hell-raiser lately," Henry interrupted, "breaking the hearts of many beautiful women as well as indulging in many of his own pleasures."

"What can I say?" Dorian defended. "I always try to experience something new and extraordinary every day."

"Hear, hear!" agreed Brewer.

"Enjoy it while you are young," Caspian added, trying to fish something out of the strange young man.

"Yes," Arnold interrupted, "Before you get fat, old, wrinkled and have a wife nagging you over every little thing."

All the men laughed in unison.

"I have no intentions of growing old," Dorian said with a mischievous smirk. Caspian caught that slight smile and instantly knew what caused Dorian's strange energy.

"You might not have intentions of growing old, but it happens to everyone. Isn't that right?" Lord Brewer asked in a deep voice. The others laughed in unison.

"It was a pleasure to meet you, Dorian, but I have another matter to attend to," Caspian excused himself politely.

"Oh, please don't go," Dorian begged.

"Yes, you only just arrived," Henry said, his eyebrows raised.

"Will we meet again? I would love to go on an adventure with you, Carl," Dorian begged again.

Caspian glanced over at Henry, then responded to Dorian. "I'm quite positive that we will meet again." Then he turned back to Henry. "Henry, may I please have a private word with you?"

Putting on a jolly smile, Henry excused himself. "Gentlemen, I need to take a moment with Carl here. Enjoy the masquerade." This time he winked at Dorian, who smiled flirtatiously.

Caspian grabbed his upper arm with enough force to bruise him to the bone.

"You're hurting me," Henry said through gritted teeth.

"Be quiet," Caspian whispered.

Henry smiled and greeted his guests as he was pushed through the crowd. Others desperately wished to share their gossip with their popular host, but the pain in his arm forced him to decline their conversations for the moment. When they made it into the empty billiard room, Caspian shoved Henry in and locked the door.

"What did you do?" Caspian growled, his purple eyes swirling with anger.

"I was lonely and you are so distant, despite how much I lavish you in luxury," Henry spoke with an air of arrogance.

"Henry, so help me I will rip you apart and end your selfish life right now if you don't explain yourself!" Caspian pounded his fist against the wall, leaving a hole in the wood panel.

Henry gulped. "I was fascinated by what you did to me,"—he paused to pull off his suit jacket, revealing twisting purple marks on his shoulder that led down his right arm— "so since you wouldn't tell me how you did it …" He took a deep breath, not wanting to say it. "I had to do some investigating. It took much of my resources to find a man who knew a man who had a book on ancient magic. Turns out you are a lich …"

"Ha!" Caspian mocked him, "I'm not a lich. I once taught a man how to divide his soul so he could live forever. Knowledge that I never passed on to others for a reason. Liches become demonic and quickly lose their human side. Once they no longer remember where they left that piece of their soul, they wither away and die. Hence the cursed life of a lich."

"What makes you different from a lich, then?" Henry asked curiously.

"Liches are dumb enough to halve their souls up to five times, not knowing that once could be the end of their humanity. I was the original one who possessed the talent, so I never cut off more than a percentage of a percentage of my soul. Liches harbor their souls in inanimate objects. I always put my very minuscule percentage of a soul into living beings. I only ever do this to keep that living being as an asset for my own needs in the future, such as yourself. Liches rip apart their souls for the selfish reason of living forever." Caspian sighed at the stupidity of his new follower. "What is the object?"

Henry blinked a couple times.

Gritting his teeth, Caspian asked again, "What is the object you put Dorian's soul into?"

"Oh, um, yes. You see, that was how we met. He was getting a painting done by a good friend of mine. The painting captured his flawless body and naive innocence. I grew attracted to this young lad who had so much potential, and I thought the painting was a symbol of his eternal youth."

Frustrated at the stupidity of humans yet again, Caspian massaged his temples. "Does your painter friend know what you did to his painting?"

"Oh, er, yes … about that …" Henry said, fidgeting.

"What?" Caspian could feel his anger rising again.

"Dorian killed the painter," Henry said meekly.

"Of course, he did," Caspian said, now pacing the length of the billiard table. "What other damage has he done?"

"Well, he has been more of a wild card than I expected. He's completely adopted my philosophy of hedonism, brilliant lad. That also means that he is constantly searching for some new pleasure to enjoy. Whether that be beauty, the opera, food, fucking, drinking, opium or even killing … that lad is exploring it all. Which is why I was hoping you could help him level out. Maybe fix the painting, which has increasingly grown distorted." Henry looked expectantly at Caspian.

"You really are turning out to be nothing more than a headache, Henry." Caspian continued to pace. "Let me talk to the boy in private."

"Brilliant! Let me go get him!" Henry said joyfully.

"Not now! I can't handle anymore of your shit today!" Caspian quit pacing and glared at the confused lord. "Bring him back here tomorrow for tea. I shall talk to him then."

"Excellent!" Henry said, his eccentricity returning.

"Alone!" Caspian shouted at him as Henry enthusiastically returned to the masquerade.

The next morning, Caspian sat in the sunlight cascading from a window that reached from floor to ceiling. The vaulted room was filled with similar windows, which created wonderful lighting during the daytime. There were four small tables for the pure use of quiet socializing. Caspian calmly watched a bird flutter outside the window as he waited for Dorian Gray to arrive.

Soon enough, Dorian arrived, escorted by one of Henry's servants. Caspian excused the servant as Dorian removed his black overcoat and straightened his navy-blue suit with purple accents. He wore no hat, which only made his youthful amber eyes stand out even more. Dorian stretched out his hand, which Caspian shook.

"Thank you for coming to meet with me again, Dorian," Caspian greeted.

"The pleasure is all mine. Who wouldn't want to spend the afternoon with a handsome devil such as yourself?" Dorian started pouring tea from the blue china teapot.

Caspian smirked. "Interesting choice of words."

"Is it?" he asked with a raised eyebrow.

"Are you flirting with me?" Caspian also raised an eyebrow.

"Maybe I am, Carl." He paused and looked mischievously deep in thought. "*Carl* doesn't quite fit you, now does it?"

"Hmmm," Caspian was intrigued by Dorian's mind games. "That is my name."

"But not your only name," Dorian said as he poured Caspian a cup as well. "I have heard Lord Henry call you *Caspian* ... a surname?"

"Perhaps." Caspian continued to play Dorian's game, wondering where it would go.

Dorian smiled as he subtly shook his head once. "No ... not a surname. Sugar?"

"My surname isn't sugar," Caspian said as he leaned back, arms crossed.

"I was asking you if you wanted sugar in your tea." Dorian motioned towards the sugar cubes.

"One, please." Caspian watched as Dorian plopped a cube into the small china cup and stirred before handing the teacup to Caspian.

"How many names do you have?" Dorian took a sip, keeping his brilliant amber eyes fixed on Caspian.

"Many." Caspian also took a sip of his tea and kept eye contact with Dorian.

"Well if Henry calls you Caspian, then I shall call you Caspian as well." Dorian took another sip.

Now it was time for Caspian to turn the tables. "I know about your painting."

"Do you?" Dorian smirked.

Caspian smiled and put his teacup down. "I do. I also know about the trouble you've been getting into recently."

Dorian leaned over the table, a dangerous glare in his eyes. "That was a secret."

Caspian could see Dorian tensing as if ready to pounce. This young man harbored no fear—if only he knew what sat across the table from him. "You endanger yourself."

Dorian laughed and loosened up. "Apparently, you don't know about my painting."

Caspian seriously explained, "I know that your painting harbors half of your soul. You don't age because of that painting, which Lord Henry Wotton so graciously set up for you. I know that you have been out of control and have been doing the most foolish things to attract unwanted attention to yourself. I also know what will happen to you if you don't heed my advice on this matter."

Suddenly Dorian went pale. "How would you know what will happen to me?"

Caspian leaned forward to keep Dorian's attention. "Because I have lived long enough to see it happen to others. You will ignore that painting because you don't want to see the ugliness that you have become. Little do you realize that by doing so, you will lose yourself completely until you no longer have a grasp on your humanity. Then, and only then, will you become a monster that will be hideous and unrecognizable. After a long time of aimlessly attacking those around you while feeling empty and worthless, you will finally wither away and die. Is this the fate you seek?"

Tears rolled down Dorian's face as if he could see it all happening before his eyes. "What do I do to stop that from happening?" He dabbed the tears with a handkerchief and attempted to recompose himself.

Caspian leaned back in his chair and sipped his tea. "You must routinely interact with your painting, no matter how hideous you find it. You must also keep it safe. Any damage to that painting will also be damage to you."

Dorian had managed to compose himself again and smiled at Caspian. "This was indeed a very fortuitous meeting. Thank you, Caspian. If you are correct, then I am indeed in your debt." Dorian paused and put on an almost childish smile. "Would you like to go on an adventure with me?"

"An adventure?" Caspian chuckled, caught off-guard.

Dorian's eyes sparkled. "Yes, I do love a good adventure. There is one I would like to share with you."

"Show me the way."

A short time later, Caspian found himself walking side by side with Dorian in a graveyard. The weather was gloomy enough that Dorian popped the collar of his jacket up to keep the chill out. Since temperature never affected Caspian, he left his jacket alone.

"Why did you bring me to a cemetery?" Caspian asked.

Taking a step closer and putting an arm around his shoulders, Dorian pointed out an elderly woman approaching a gravestone with a fresh bouquet in her hand. "Isn't it an extraordinary thing, love?" Dorian asked, pausing to observe Caspian's expression.

Caspian watched the elderly woman take great care in removing wilted flowers from the vase next to the marker and replace them with fresh, beautiful flowers. In all his life, Caspian had never visited a graveyard. There was never anything for him there. All the countless times he had watched *her* die, he never had a body to bury. The sight of the woman so lovingly attending to the grave stung him deeply. "Is it her husband?"

"I would assume so," Dorian responded, watching Caspian's face. "I never bothered to ask. I find it extraordinary that some people can love so deeply that they would remain loyal even after death. Have you ever loved someone so deeply that you would remain loyal after they were buried?"

Painful memories of watching *her* die flashed through his mind. Caspian couldn't bear to look at the old woman any longer. "Love is miraculous. Have you ever loved that deeply?"

Dorian watched the old woman leave with the handful of dead flowers. "I have felt many kinds of love: love of a woman's voice, love of a woman's touch, love of a woman's body, but never a love that would bind me to her for eternity. I guess that is why I am so fascinated by such a love." Dorian glanced at Caspian, who stared vacantly at all the tombstones.

Caspian finally popped the collar of his coat up. "Dorian, you are blessed to never have felt the pain that associates with love. Love is by far the worst curse. Love is without reason and can cause you incredible pain—worse than death."

"It is apparent that you have felt such a love. Will you show her to me?" Dorian gazed directly into Caspian's swirling purple eyes.

"Not today, Dorian." Caspian meandered to the cemetery entrance.

Dorian took a couple of quick steps to catch up. "I do apologize if I brought up bad memories. How about I make up for my curiosity by taking you to the opera tonight. They are currently showing *Carmen*. My treat."

Caspian didn't know why, but Dorian intrigued him. It was true he had a charisma that drew people in. Dorian had a level of mystery to him, along with a hunger for knowledge. It was almost as if Caspian was drawn not only to help Dorian explore the world, but to explore it with him. For too long his world had been in shades of gray. Different eras. Different people. Different places. It was all the same to Caspian. After living for centuries, it was difficult to find the beauty in anything. Dorian gave Caspian a glimpse of color, a fresh chance to see the world as if it were new and wondrous.

Caspian responded, "Dorian, I would enjoy experiencing the opera with you tonight."

"Shall I send a tailor your way? My treat?" Dorian asked with a raised eyebrow.

"That will be quite all right, Mr. Gray. I have a black suit that shall work fine for the opera. I'm not a man of high demands nor extravagance." Caspian smiled. "Thank you for the adventure. I enjoyed hearing your viewpoint on love."

"I will be by Lord Henry's manor to pick you up at five o'clock sharp." Dorian gave his charming yet mischievous smile— a smile Caspian was growing fond of.

Caspian flashed his own mysterious smile, which Dorian was also growing fond of. "I would much rather meet you at the opera house, if you wouldn't mind. There are a couple of errands I need to attend to."

"Then I shall meet you at the Opera House at six." Dorian smiled and went on his way.

A few hours after their meeting, Caspian was reclining at the top of a building, keeping watch on a restaurant across the street where Sally was eating an expensive meal with her boyfriend. He could tell it was a special occasion by the beautiful white dress she wore and how much preparation she had put into her hair. The gentleman was also wearing an expensive dinner suit, with his hair slicked back. Caspian was satisfied keeping his distance from her, though watching her was always a cruel torment. While he watched her eat and flirt, Caspian captured her happiness on paper.

"Figures I would find you up here. You are becoming rather predictable," Lord Henry said as he climbed on the rooftop by a ladder at the opposite side of the building.

"I'm impressed that you found me," Caspian commented.

"Well, your fixation with the lass makes it a little easier." Henry stood next to Caspian.

Caspian ignored the snide comment and stayed intent on his drawing.

Henry peeked at the portrait of Sally's face. "That is a really good representation of her, though it's creepy how you stalk her. Why don't you go talk to her?"

"Henry,"—Caspian put down his pencil— "you know very little about my situation. Nor do I want you to know anything about her."

Caspian was suddenly distracted by a commotion in the restaurant. Sally was flapping her hands and squealing with joy as her boyfriend was sliding a large diamond ring on her left hand. The waiters clapped in celebration. Such a joyous occasion—and how Caspian hated all of them. Caspian crumpled up the drawing, which he had nearly completed, and threw it off the building.

Henry put his hand on Caspian's shoulder. "I'm so sorry, Caspian. That is a spot of bad luck."

"I'm happy for her," Caspian lied.

"Do you hate her now?" Henry asked.

Caspian didn't respond as he walked away from the ledge of the building. He didn't want to say it. His love for her was deeper than any mortal could understand. Yet he remained true to his word; he wouldn't interfere in her life this time. Still, deep down, Caspian wished that he was the one kissing her— that she would gaze into his eyes while the rest of the world rushed around them. The torturous part was he would never be that man. He would never walk her down the aisle. Never would they hold each other's hands as they grew old together, watching their children and grandchildren grow. That was not their destiny. That was their curse.

"Caspian, you might want to see this ..." Henry said with concern. Caspian joined Henry's side and saw the happy couple leaving the restaurant, holding hands and giggling. Lurking in the shadows were two men in dark clothes. "I wonder how happy their night will turn out

… if you don't intervene."

Gritting his teeth and growling under his breath, Caspian jumped off the roof and landed soundlessly on the sidewalk. Henry followed via the ladder to the side of the building. Being the ultimate predator, Caspian stalked his prey, who were stalking theirs. Their intentions were obviously to rob the young rich couple of all they carried, including her new ring. Caspian feared that if the newly engaged couple offered any resistance, the predators would use the knives they were unsheathing.

"The moment I attack, you are to distract any onlookers … including Sally and her fiancé," Caspian whispered, so only Henry could hear.

"As you wish," he said, quickening his pace.

The cloaked men were a few steps behind the naïve couple, blinded by their bliss. Caspian silently approached and grabbed hold of the the men's collars. He threw both into a alleyway. Though stunned by the attack, they were quick to scramble to their feet to defend against a lone wolf blocking their exit.

It was all over in under a second. Both men lunged into an attack, knives bared. Caspian ran between them faster than their eyes could register. They died simultaneously, clutching at their ripped throats as Caspian stood behind them with glowing red eyes and blood dripping off his sharpened claws. They fell into pools of their own blood. Caspian returned his claws to his normal hands. His eyes burned red, which took a few moments to fade to black.

"Excuse me, would you two happen to have the time?" Lord Henry asked Sally and her fiancé, who turned to look at the speaker. Before they could respond, Henry added, "Oh my word, were you the two that just got engaged in that restaurant? Congratulations!"

"Why, thank you. I'm still rather surprised," Sally blushed.

"We were going to meet with my soon to be father-in-law so he might share in the good news," added the young man.

"What a glorious occasion for both of you!" Henry clapped the young man on the back with a little too much force, causing him to take a step forward. "Allow me to hail a carriage for the two of you."

313

"Oh, you really don't ..." started the young man.

"I insist. It doesn't put me out any!" Henry interrupted with a smile.

After the couple were on their way home in a carriage, Caspian finally came out of the alleyway. "Maybe I should use your talents more often," he said with a smirk.

Henry handed him a handkerchief. "Clean yourself up. We have an opera to go to, dear Caspian."

"Oh, you are going too?" Caspian had hoped it would be only Dorian and himself.

"Who do you think pays for Dorian's balcony seating?" Henry asked with a laugh. "Come along."

Waiting outside the opera, Dorian was clad in a white tailcoat with a matching top hat accented in purple, as if that were his new favorite color. The second he saw Caspian and Henry, he beamed and jogged towards them with a bounce in his step. "What a pleasure to see you both!"

"Great to see you too, my lad," Henry greeted.

Dorian was startled by the change in Caspian's eyes. "Dear Caspian, your eyes ... they are black!" he exclaimed.

"Yes, they tend to do that from time to time," Caspian responded flatly. He blinked a couple of times, returning his eyes to a dark shade of purple— the best he could conjure up currently. It would take them another day to return to their normal vibrant shade of purple. "Is that better?"

Dorian took out his own embroidered handkerchief and dabbed it on Caspian's lower jawline. "You're bleeding." Dorian studied him quizzically after realizing there was no wound that would have caused the splash of blood on his face. "Was that your blood or someone else's?"

Henry laughed, "Probably from one of the poor blokes that—"

Caspian stepped on his foot to shut him up. Henry took a step back and kept his mouth shut, knowing that the next one would break the bones in his foot.

"Errands," Caspian responded vaguely.

"Absolutely extraordinary," Dorian said in utter amazement. "Not a dull moment goes by once you are near, Caspian."

"Please call me Carl in public," Caspian requested, nervously scanning the people passing by.

"Well then, Carl, shall we go inside?" Dorian offered with a hand extended.

Part of Caspian felt impelled to take the hand offered, but then suddenly realized how emasculating that would appear. He straightened his coat and followed Dorian. Similar to Henry's parties, everyone was dressed in their best, glittering with jewels and overwhelming perfume. The interior of the opera house glowed, with gold-framed mirrors and glistening crystal chandeliers. Patrons were in a hurry to reach their seats, eager to see one of the most famous operas. Caspian followed Henry and Dorian upstairs to a closed-off balcony section with eight seats, all of which were for them thanks to Henry's gracious donations.

The opera was nothing like Caspian had ever experienced. It was evident that much time and energy had been put into the production, and he was awed by the artful acting and powerful singing on stage. He was moved by the delicately intertwined stories, the fragility of the characters, the heightened emotions expressed by the orchestra, and the intricacies from the broadest scenes to the littlest props. Caspian's eyes were fixed on the stage as the drama unfolded in the vibrant story of Carmen. For the first time in his long life, Caspian forgot about his turmoil and anguish over his constant failures. When the opera was over, Caspian stood with the rest of the crowd and applauded the incredible performance of the actors and crew. Caspian finally understood why so many people, such as Dorian, were drawn to the opera. He also understood why others, such as Henry, were willing to give donations to support such productions.

"I dare say, you seem happier than I have ever seen you," Lord Henry observed as Dorian curiously inspected Caspian's expression.

This brought Caspian back to reality, his heart sinking again.

"It was a nice change of pace to see excitement in your face when you were watching the plot twists," Dorian added with a smirk.

"I quite enjoyed the opera, Dorian, thank you for inviting me," Caspian said politely.

"Such a treasure the opera is, yet sometimes I grow more bored of it than Dorian here does … and that is saying a lot," Henry added with a chuckle.

Caspian bowed. "Thank you both. Now, I must be off." He excited the box.

Dorian ran to catch up with him, with Henry on his heels. "Oh, please don't leave yet, Carl," Dorian interrupted. "Why don't you come back to my manor? We can drink wine, or scotch, while talking about the opera in more depth."

Caspian responded with a sly smile, "I barely met you this morning and yet now you invite me to your place for liquor. You move fast, don't you, Dorian?"

The three continued through the crowd.

"I'm sure you can handle it. Don't be afraid," Dorian whispered in his ear as they exited the opera house.

Caspian turned around to face both of them as he replied egotistically, "I fear nothing."

"Everyone fears at least one thing," Dorian said.

"Then what do you fear?" Henry asked.

Dorian rolled his eyes, "Don't you know me well enough? I only fear boredom."

A cool evening breeze blew past the crowd while the three stood in the middle, parting the waters. Lord Henry and Dorian pulled their coats tighter around their necks to keep out the chill. Caspian enjoyed the wind, which felt akin to a gentle caress against his skin.

"Well, gentlemen, I shall see you both tomorrow. I need to get to bed; I have an early meeting tomorrow morning." Henry bundled up tighter and gave a short wave before departing.

"So, what do you say, Caspian? Would you be interested in picking my brain while I pick yours?" Dorian asked with a mischievous smile.

"It doesn't hurt anything, I suppose," Caspian agreed and followed Dorian through the windy streets.

It wasn't long until they found themselves inside Dorian's manor. The walls were covered in a clutter of paintings. In fact, there were more paintings than there was blank wall space. What wasn't covered by paintings was covered in gold paint and family crests from different eras.

"You know, they say that a man's house is similar to the constructs of his mind," Caspian said sarcastically as he removed his jacket to hand it to the waiting butler.

Dorian ordered drinks to be brought before turning around to respond. "What does my house tell you about my mind, then?"

Taking another look around, Caspian could see that Dorian had spared no expense. The chandelier sparkled, its light glimmering on the gilded moldings. The furnishings were upholstered in velvet. If it wasn't already evident in his behavior, it was clear from the house that Dorian enjoyed the finer things that life could offer. "That you have much to hide. Where is your painting?"

Dorian extended a hand toward the gilded staircase. "Right this way. Tell me, Caspian, what do you hide?"

Caspian followed Dorian up the stairs. "I hide a lot."

"Such as your age?" Dorian turned around with a smirk, then continued up the stairs.

"If I told you I was well over a thousand years old, would you believe me?" he asked, as they reached the top.

Dorian paused to give this some thought. "Several years ago, I would say that is impossible. Now, the prospect fascinates me." Dorian showcased a flirtatious smile and continued down a long hallway to a revolving bookshelf. Caspian followed, observing how the interior changed. There were no longer pictures on the wall nor gold trim. The windowless walls were now bare gray brick and the stairway was dark.

"How many women have you been with in the last thousand years?" Dorian pried.

"In which way?" Caspian clarified. The air was growing denser, as if they were going downstairs into a cellar instead of upstairs into an attic.

"Sexually," Dorian answered, with a grin that could be heard yet not seen. They finally reached the top of the staircase, where Dorian opened a heavy door that screeched loudly as the hinges complained of the weight.

"In the last thousand years, a couple dozen. Though most of those occurred in my youth, when I was much more brash and bullheaded," Caspian replied flatly as he entered another dark room.

"Is this because of the woman you love?" Dorian struck a match and started lighting candles around the small, circular room. The room was as bare as the staircase. The walls, ceiling and floor were all cold gray brick. Other than the candle sconces on the walls, the only thing in the room was a large portrait in a golden frame, propped on a sturdy easel.

"Perhaps," Caspian evaded the question, as he walked around to see the painting.

Dorian stood facing his painting in contemplation, then shifted his gaze to Caspian. "Does sex no longer interest you, Caspian?"

"The desire is no longer there. Maybe someday—" Caspian started.

"When you are with your true love?" Dorian interrupted.

"Sadly, that may never happen," Caspian said with remorse. He finally stood in front of the painting. What Caspian saw was much more grotesque than he could have imagined. All that humans have created in the name of art, religion and politics, never quite captured pure inhumanity as this painting did. Although it stood still, the painting seemed to have a life of its own. The colors seemed to be constantly moving and changing. It was easy to see the demons that that lay beneath Dorian's skin. He understood what no one else would ever understand about Dorian: He would lead an abnormally long life, suffering loneliness and torture, an agony that no ordinary person could bear. The only salvation granted to Dorian was that he had a way out, that there were ways for Dorian to finally end his life when he had had enough. There would never exist such a saving grace for Caspian, which brought a pain no one else could ever understand.

"Reflecting upon this painting every day will not only save you from becoming a monstrosity, but might even humble you," Caspian advised. "Does the painting allow you to suffer injury? Can you still bleed?"

Dorian's demeanor changed to intrigue. "Want to find out?"

"Of course," Caspian said with a smirk.

318

"Don't hold back," Dorian said, pulling his shirt down to reveal his neck.

Caspian smiled, knowing there would be two possibilities. Either Dorian would die and Caspian would have to explain to Lord Henry how he killed another of his little social experiments. Or Dorian would indeed prove to be a lich and heal. The real question was: how long would he take to heal? For some liches Caspian had encountered, it took months to recover from a substantial injury. Others would heal in a matter of minutes, while the scar might take a couple of weeks to fade.

Allowing only one of his fingers to grow into a sharp, hideous talon, Caspian slashed Dorian's throat. Blood squirted briefly as the heart worked harder to push blood to all the limbs. Then Dorian fell to the floor, blood pouring from his neck. Caspian watched with fascination as the picture moved and changed. Blood poured down the creature's neck until there was a large puddle underneath the creature and its cheeks became hollowed, the lips and eye sockets purple.

For a moment, Dorian lay motionless on the floor, making Caspian almost wonder if he had indeed killed him. Then Dorian coughed and said in a raspy voice, "My turn." Quite fast for human speed, yet relatively slow by Caspian's standards, Dorian popped up with a knife. The first slash was aimed at Caspian's throat, which he easily dodged. The second strike came immediately after and barely nicked Caspian on the cheek with the tip of the blade.

The scratch healed immediately. Caspian wiped the small trickle of blood off his cheek and smiled. Before Dorian could respond, Caspian pinned him against the wall by his bleeding neck. Caspian's eyes glowed red.

Completely unaffected by being choked against a wall, Dorian took a finger and wiped it across the smear of blood on Caspian's face. "Tell me, Caspian, have you ever been with a man before?"

As Dorian put his finger in his mouth, tasting the sweet, rich blood, Caspian lowered Dorian to the ground and saw how his blood made Dorian heal faster. Soon, the wound was practically gone.

"Not yet," Caspian answered, his eyes fading to black, as his intrigue grew.

The next morning, Caspian gazed at his reflection in Dorian's bedroom. Somehow, he didn't feel right wearing Dorian's clothes, even if they fit. It had been a very long time since he had worn white. The sight of it actually disgusted Caspian. Wearing all white practically publicly proclaimed him as innocent and pure— two words that did not describe him.

"I have to say, it suits you," Dorian said from behind, wearing a white suit with purple undertones.

"Then you don't know me at all," Caspian said out of spite.

"Your clothes were torn to shreds during our passionate tussle last night, and I couldn't very well have you walk home naked?" Dorian said with his mischievous little grin.

"Did you really have to dress me in all white, though?" Caspian asked disdainfully.

Dorian smiled and turned Caspian to face him. "Yes!" Then Dorian casually kissed him, as if this was a normal occurrence.

Though Caspian kissed back, and thoroughly enjoyed tasting Dorian's soft yet firm lips, he had to interject, "Please don't kiss me in public, though."

"Are you ashamed of me?" Dorian asked, clearly taking offense.

Caspian now gave his own mischievous grin and pulled Dorian into him, "Not at all. I appreciate your talent. Especially because you are the first person to actually make me feel something in a while. However, if you kissed me in public, it would draw far too much unwanted attention. That is something that I cannot risk, for reasons that I shall keep to myself."

"Fine, fine, let us go meet up with Henry." Dorian waved him off.

The next week was bizarre. Every day, Dorian would drag Caspian off to a public function— or rather, Caspian followed along willingly. It fascinated Caspian to see Dorian's wondrous world through his eyes. In a way, it opened up part of Caspian that he had kept locked away— not out of fear or hatred; that wasn't it at all. Rather, Caspian never had a use for exploring personal enlightenment. The only time Caspian needed to observe his surroundings was to search for danger or hunt down his enemies. Yet now he found himself using his observational skills to manipulate people to his advantage, simply by gathering information for future use. These lessons were never free, though. In return for Dorian's elite skills, Caspian had to dote upon Dorian. Although he claimed to get bored easily, Caspian never ceased to amaze Dorian. Often Dorian would ask for anecdotes from the past or simply to hear more about the store of knowledge Caspian had developed over the years. It was a give-and-take relationship, both of them equally teachers and students.

Henry was motivated to keep Caspian close to Dorian's side. Neither of them minded, since Henry paid for their activities to keep things interesting. Henry was always hovering, but never really interfering. This started to raise Caspian's suspicion that he was up to something.

The evening was chilly, with a fall breeze that suggested winter was coming sooner than expected. Caspian found himself joining in Dorian's favorite pursuits.

Gambling had never interested him much, but since it was Lord Henry's money he was playing with, Caspian saw no harm in it. The young lord was off at another table, more content smoking his cigar and trading gossip with fellow gamblers than actually playing cards. Dorian sat next to Caspian, intent on helping him actually win a game. Though he understood the rules, Caspian couldn't care less about the game that had other gentlemen in London hooked. These cards, it seemed, had provoked a rare phenomenon of addiction among the social elite within the past year, and Caspian couldn't understand why. To him, it was a boring counting game where you were not allowed to count the cards. A silly rule, yet Dorian didn't want to get thrown out, so Caspian played what he was dealt and didn't focus on the numbers remaining in the deck. The accumulating smoke in the room didn't seem to bother Caspian; neither did the crowd of intoxicated men, who were growing louder by the minute. Even though Caspian couldn't quite shake the feeling that something deep down was warning him, his recent apathy was making the message difficult to decipher. Caspian didn't even know why it was so important, yet he felt compelled to leave immediately.

"Are you even paying attention?" Dorian chided.

Realizing he was staring towards the exit, Caspian shook his head and looked around at the table. All of the players were waiting for him to place his bets. Peeking down at his cards, Caspian knew he would win this round based on what everyone else was holding. Yet that mattered little to him. "Um, I'm out for the next game, gentlemen." Quickly he stood up to go to the door.

As Caspian straightened his black suit, Dorian pulled on his sleeve. "Where do you think you are going?" he asked flirtatiously.

Out of the blue, Caspian realized that this young lich no longer mattered to him. "I need some fresh air away from all this cigar smoke," Caspian lied.

"Well, don't be too long." Dorian waved him off.

Without another word, Caspian politely excused himself and made a beeline straight for the exit. The cold night air greeted him with a refreshing, cleansing. Everything was starting to clear in his mind as his senses grew acutely aware of his surroundings. No longer did he feel tied to Dorian and his wild desires. Something much more important pulled him forward. Following an innate sense of direction, he ran at full speed down dark streets, the fog evaporating from his mind.

Then he felt that urgency reach down and squeeze his heart fiercely—the cruel feeling of losing all hope. He finally understood what his instincts were trying to tell him: *she* was in danger. Fear drove him forward. Anger cracked every stone he stepped upon in his desperate attempt to reach her before it was too late.

A newer Victorian house stood quietly on the dark corner of a street. Despite the calm, Caspian kicked open the door. The wood shattered, projecting pieces of the door down the hallway. Though he had never set foot in this house, he knew it to be Sally's. Caspian went into the elegantly decorated living room, which would have been lovely except for the two dead bodies on the floor. Their throats had been brutally mauled, and their blood sprayed all over the furniture. One of the bodies Caspian recognized as Sally's fiancé. The surprise on his face, coupled with the enormous gash in his throat, made it clear the attack happened in a flash. The other body was that of the father, his gun tightly grasped in his cold hand. A creak upstairs was followed by a painful moan. Caspian raced up the stairs, casually jumping over the maid's slain body.

Following his instincts, Caspian crashed into the second door to the left of the hallway. The room, with its lacy décor and feminine necessities lying about, was obviously Sally's bedroom. Standing behind the bed and closest to the window was a slender, pale man in dark Victorian clothes, bloody fangs protruded from his stained red lips. Opposite and closest to Caspian was another male vampire, whose fangs were bared at Caspian. A hissing akin to a cat's resonated in the vampire's throat. Clutched tightly to his arm, wearing a white nightgown, was Sally, who appeared pale, with purple tints around her eyes and lips. With her hair pulled up in a bun, it was easy to see the multiple bite marks on her neck, which were no longer bleeding despite the size of the holes. Greedily, she sucked the blood from the vampire's arm as if it was her only choice. It *was* her only choice if she wanted to live. Clearly, the vampire's objective was to change her into one of them.

Caspian didn't know why they wanted her and didn't care. He had never sought to understand the logic of vampires— not even with Veronica. His body heating up, Caspian struck fast at the vampire feeding Sally. One swipe of his claw was all it took to decapitate the vampire. Bits of skull and brain flew through the air and splattered half of the bedroom. The vampire didn't even have time to scream before his remains turned to dust. Filled with rage, Caspian then turned his attention to the other vampire, who had fled from the window. A sob was all it took to stop Caspian from chasing the vampire.

Crumpled at his feet, Sadly appeared so sickly and frail. Her skin was pale from the blood loss. Drops of blood and ash had tainted her beautiful white nightgown. Her body trembled and beaded with sweat. Anger vanished as Caspian was overcome with sorrow and love for the woman he had watched from afar.

Carefully, Caspian knelt down and tenderly pulled her into his arms. The temperature of her skin was steadily dropping. Her green hollow eyes trembled and her lips quivered fiercely.

"Do I know you?" she asked tremulously.

"No," he said sadly. Caspian knew the vampire toxins were quickly working their way through her body. There was no stopping it now. The best he could hope for was her own transformation into a vampire.

"Then ... why are you ... so familiar?" she asked between small body spasms. The vampire venom would shut down all of her secondary organs and then spread to every muscle in her body.

A single tear ran down his face as he spoke the unbearable truth, "Because I know you ... very well."

Sally winced again. "Am I going to die?"

He couldn't say it. The first part of becoming a vampire was for the body to die. There was no way around it. It was an ugly truth ... and Caspian didn't know how it would turn out. Would she stay a vampire and live? Or would her cursed existence cause her to instantly die and start the whole cycle all over again? He had never run into this before.

Suddenly, he remembered how Dorian's body healed faster once he tasted Caspian's blood. Hoping it would save her, Caspian bit his wrist and tore a chunk of flesh off, exposing his main capillaries. "Hurry and drink, it might save you!" Caspian commanded as he thrust his already healing wrist into her mouth. The second his blood touched her tongue, her body seized so violently that Caspian had to hold her head to keep it from hitting the floor. Blood and vomit erupted from her mouth, showering her and Caspian. Then her body abruptly stilled. Tears rolled down Caspian's face and splashed down onto hers. The vampire venom had taken its toll, and there was no going back from this curse. Now was the moment of truth, and it terrified him. Caspian drew her in and used all of his heat to warm her body.

The corners of her lips turned upwards slightly. With her last bits of strength, she was able to make out one mumbled word, "Caspian ..." That was it. Sally's head rolled back as her green eyes closed. Her delicate hand, the fingertips purple, flopped to the floor.

Caspian cried out in agony as he pulled her body tightly to his own. The pain returned. Tears flooded down his cheeks as he screamed as loud as his lungs could go. Sally's frail body disintegrated into millions of purple wisps, lighting up the room and giving it a mystical glow. Caspian silently watched with a tear-stained face as they floated out the window and up into the sky.

At that moment, he realized something vitally important. Even though he had tried so desperately to not influence her life in any way, she still died. There was no avoiding it. He wasn't the curse, but he might be the solution to it. If only he wasn't so fixed on his own selfish whims, he could probably have saved her. She wanted him to save her. Those green eyes knew deep down that he alone was the key to ending her curse. Which meant that she was the key to ending his— as it always was.

Sorrow turned to vengeance as Caspian remembered the true monster tonight. Red eyes glaring, Caspian walked to the window and deeply inhaled the vampire's scent. An evil smile spread across his face as he hunted the vampire who murdered Sally.

"Please protect me!" the vampire groveled at Lord Henry's feet.

Henry kicked the vampire's hands away from his new shoes. "You were supposed to turn the bitch. Why didn't you follow through as I ordered?"

"I'm sorry, my lord, I truly am. We should have taken her far away from London, but we thought we could be quick enough," sobbed the vampire, still begging on hands and knees.

In a sympathetic tone, Lord Henry bent down. "That was your mistake, for not knowing your enemy." —then his tone chilled— "Now you shall pay for your arrogance."

The vampire clutched Henry's legs. "Please protect me from that ..." but he never finished. A broken piece of a gilded railing flew through the air and penetrated the vampire's heart into Lord Henry's leg. The vampire screamed in an unnaturally high pitch as his body burst into ash.

Unable to fall down, Lord Henry screamed at the bloodied piece of railing projecting from both sides of his leg.

Falling from a three-story-high window into the ballroom, Caspian landed softly on the hard marble floor. He was a terrifying sight, with bloodied clothes and glowing red eyes filled with blood lust and vengeance. "It's odd that I didn't see it," he said casually.

Henry firmly held his profusely bleeding pierced leg. "Caspian, I can explain!"

Caspian circled the lord in predatory fashion. "How long have you been plotting to kill her?"

"Caspian ... please, I never tried to kill her. I simply thought if she were more indestructible, then maybe you could actually be with her," he said, trying to buy time.

Caspian continued as his circles tightened. "That is a lie and I know it, Lord Henry Wotton. What benefit does her death give you?"

"Caspian, know that I only wanted to free you from all the pain that tortured your soul. I am your loyal servant. I would never do anything against you," Lord Henry argued his point as silver-tongued as a politician.

"Lies! You were obtaining leverage over me." Caspian watched as Lord Henry pulled a gun from beneath his petticoat and pointed it at Caspian's face. He dodged the bullet and swiped the gun from Henry's hand. To display his power, he broke the metal barrel clean in half. Lord Henry's eyes widened in horror as Caspian's eyes burned a piercing red. He then discarded the remnants of the gun, lunged forward and tackled his foe. Henry screamed loud enough to rattle the chandelier above. Caspian growled menacingly, then quickly snapped Henry's other leg so that it assumed an odd angle.

Henry screamed in pain and begged Caspian to stop, "Please heal me, Master. I have learned the errors of my ways. Just make the pain stop."

Caspian remained calm and almost jokingly replied, "Oh, no, Henry, you shall pay for your arrogance."

"Then just kill me and get it over with!" Henry spat.

Caspian's voice dripped with venom. "You are guilty of many unforgivable acts. The worst thing you did, though, was hurt Sally. She suffered,

Henry … she suffered more than I had seen in a long while. For that, you must pay. I will keep you alive until you have adequately suffered ten times more than she did. Then maybe once I bore of you … then I will finally take back what is mine and leave you to die in a pool of your own blood." A sinister smile spread across Caspian's face from ear to ear.

The mansion echoed with Lord Henry's blood-curdling screams throughout the long hours of the night. If they ceased at all, it was only momentary for Caspian to wake him back up. The torture was never ending until the sun finally broke over the horizon. The police reports which would follow were so horrific they were never published in the newspapers. This grisly crime would never reach the public's ears. A few coppers even quit after seeing the horrors that could befall one man whom society had deemed a true gentleman. What did leak to the press was evidence of all the illegal activities and cruel blackmail that Lord Henry had kept locked away. Soon, no one cared about Lord Henry Wotton anymore.

Dorian Gray sat calmly on a park bench in the middle of the afternoon. A newspaper was opened in front of him, blocking his view of the fall leaves sprinkled around the edges of the pond. "I was wondering when you would show up," he said.

Caspian discreetly sat down next to Dorian. "I had to let off some steam."

Dorian folded his newspaper and placed it in his lap with a certain article face-up, about a man found dead whose fiancé had mysteriously vanished. Taking a deep breath, Dorian flirtatiously admired Caspian. "I see you are making good use of Henry's suits."

Caspian tugged on the collar of his expensively tailored black suit, which he had indeed taken from Henry's house, along with a couple of expensive items he had traded for a hefty sum of cash. "He didn't need them anymore."

Silence sat awkwardly between them.

"Tell me the truth. What did you know about Sally?" Caspian gazed intently into Dorian's eyes.

Dorian replied earnestly. "I knew she was an extraordinary woman to have stolen your fixation, possibly even your adoration. I was saddened to hear of her disappearance."

Caspian broke his gaze. Though he knew Dorian was telling the truth, it hurt deeply that she was gone. It hurt even more to verbally replay the account. "Lord Henry Wotton planned and ordered her death. She died in my arms."

Dorian suddenly displayed something Caspian had never seen before: sympathy. "I am truly sorry to hear that, Caspian. I assume that also explains dear Henry's demise."

"Yes," Caspian replied simply, as if this were a casual conversation, "I tortured him for nine hours and then brutally stole his life."

Dorian sighed and stared at the pond. "He deserved every second of it."

Caspian handed Dorian a thick envelope. "Lord Henry left everything to you, his protégé."

Confused, Dorian took the envelope as if it were foreign to him, then laughed. "I suppose that is fortuitous for you, then. I have written off everything in my will to you. So, you will end up with a large inheritance!" Once again, an awkward silence fell over them before Dorian spoke, somberly this time, "Are you going to kill me, too? You know how to do it."

Caspian stood up and stretched. "No, Dorian. At this time, you are an asset to me, so hold on to that large inheritance and enjoy your operas."

Smiling, Dorian stood up in front of Caspian. The wind blew back his locks of hair. "I shall be at your beck and call, then."

The two men embraced as friends, then stepped back to admire each other one last time, knowing it would be a while before they saw each other.

"What adventures do you have in store, my friend?" Dorian asked.

Caspian smiled and gazed off into the distance, "Unknown at the moment. What adventures do you have planned today?"

Dorian's eyes glinted with the excitement of discovery. "I am to meet with a man who wishes to hear my story. Have you ever heard of the writer Oscar Wilde?"

"I haven't heard of him, but I shall be sure to check into his works. Ensure not to mention me in your story," Caspian requested.

"Of course, my friend," Dorian smiled. For a moment, there was nothing but the sound of the wind blowing through the trees. As Dorian reached out his hand in a gesture of friendship, a tangle of purple swirling patterns wrapped around his wrist, reaching to the ends of his pointer finger and thumb, glistened in the sunlight. Smiling at his mark, Caspian knew he would always be able to track Dorian down, just in case he was in need of his unique skills. Caspian grasped the purple marked hand. The two men gave each other a firm handshake and then departed, each going their separate directions in life and knowing that someday they would meet again.

* * *

Back at the hospital, Dorian looked at Connor with wise, amber eyes. They didn't sparkle as much as they used to. The deceptive appearance of youth in his rich brown hair, handsome face and sculpted body were somehow faded by the age in his amber eyes. Still, this didn't stop him from dressing as a billionaire.

"Dorian, your eyes age you. Why is this?" Connor asked.

A deep sigh left his lips as Dorian stared blankly at the ground. "I'm tired, old friend. I have traveled the world and seen all the wonders it holds. None of which could hold my interest for long. Even the fascinating people I come across do little to hold my interests for longer than five years before I tire of them, too. The longer I live, the more your words ring true. How they circle around my mind—like a fly with the sole purpose to irritate."

"What words of wisdom did I share with you that have you so caught up in your eloquent mind, Dorian?" Connor asked, with a hint of egotism.

The chaos of the hospital rushed past the two men lost in reminiscence. Not bothered by the chaos, Dorian closed his eyes and repeated the words that haunted his existence:

"Of all the beings of this Earth,
Death is a blessing, save you.
Beast and Man shall find their peace,
Surrendering their bodies to ash,
Save you.
Love burns hotter in a finite time,
While yours will only smolder.
All others may lay down their fears,
Their hopes and their doubts,
And yours shall attach to your skin,
As unwanted boils,
Haunting reminders impervious to senility.
It is you, who shall remain
Ageless, Tireless, Fadeless,
Alone.
However…
Your ambitions will age.
Motivations that drove you will tire.
The ability to connect will fade
Like a muscle atrophies from sedentary life.
An eternity without love,
Without connection,
Surrounded by a world that doesn't care about you.
On that day, the dawn reveals unto you
That you are now like them,
Beautiful and dead,
Just like that perfect portrait of yourself.
That is the Secret Curse of the Immortal."

"I did warn you, Dorian. I have suffered this curse much longer, until it feels that it has eaten my very soul … if I ever had a soul to begin with." Connor felt the weight of his words and the hopelessness that had carried them through the centuries. "You speak of feeling tired. I hope that is not a plea for death, Dorian."

"What if it is? What then?" Dorian asked seriously.

Connor put his hand on Dorian's shoulder. "It would give me great honor to give you that eternal rest. However, I need you now more than ever. Please help me, my dear friend."

Dorian looked inquisitively into Connor's new green eyes. "You are different this time, Caspian."

"Connor ..." Connor corrected.

"You are so much more ... more ..." Dorian rotated his hand as if this would help him think harder.

"Human?" Connor filled in the blank.

"Yes," Dorian shared an enlightened smile.

Also smiling, Connor continued, "I've been getting that a lot recently."

Dorian laughed and said, "You are full of surprises, Caspian!"

"Connor," he interrupted.

Dorian continued without noticing, "I mean, your exquisite purple eyes were mesmerizing. While your red eyes were adrenalizing. Then your black eyes were terrifying. Yet I have never seen your breathtaking green eyes. I have never seen you so happy!"

"She makes me happier than I have been in a very long time," Connor responded, his genuine smile softening.

Connor changed the subject. "So, what brings you to New Hampshire, Dorian?"

Brightening up a bit, Dorian leaned back. "I thought now was the best time to check up on my adorable goddaughter living in my getaway house."

"You're not her godfather," Connor corrected, with some irritation.

"Then can I be her uncle?" Dorian suggested.

"No," Connor said bluntly.

"You steal all my fun away, don't you." Dorian made it theatrical, with the back of his hand pressed against his forehead. "So how is my house treating you? I haven't been to it in decades."

Connor said, "Well, I had to burn all your pictures for Sammy's sake. Your fascination with portraits still confounds me. I thought you would have grown bored of collecting them decades ago." Connor stood up as the door opened, but was disappointed by the nurse who walked straight past him on her way to another patient. Impatiently, Connor sat back down. "Thank you again for letting us use your house in New Hampshire. Its secrecy and lack of paper trail has aided in keeping her under the radar."

"But now she's in school. That's gotta attract attention from unwanted sources." Dorian started to unwrap a Snickers bar he pulled out of his pocket.

"Yes, I know, which is why I need your help," Connor said, as Dorian raised an eyebrow. "I have won many battles and conquered many foes, but I must say that raising a teenager is the most difficult trial I have ever been put through. Hence why I need your guidance and strength to keep me from killing all these other obnoxious high school students."

Dorian burst out laughing.

It was apparent that Connor did not appreciate being mocked. "Yes, well, let's see if you're still laughing after helping me for a week."

Wiping away a fake tear, Dorian apologized. "I'm sorry, old friend. I find it so comical that you struggle with a teenage girl, even though you have successfully seduced women and men with a mere glance."

Annoyance and embarrassment prompted Connor to quickly change the subject. "Have you—"

"Mr. Roberts," the nurse interrupted. Eagerly, Connor stood up while Dorian craned his neck to see her. "You may now come back to the room."

"Thank you!" Connor said with a slight nod of his head to Dorian. "Stay here a moment." Then he turned back to the nurse. "What is the diagnosis?"

Typical of an ER nurse, she flippantly described Sammy's condition, "Just a sprain. No bones were broken. No ligaments nor tendons torn. You'll need to sign the discharge orders and then you are free to go."

As they were entering the room, the nurse added, "She does need to wear her ankle brace for three weeks. Use ice packs and ibuprofen for the pain. No exercise or strenuous activity for a month. Come back in …"

"What?!" Sammy yelled and then flopped back on the bed, "Ugh! Why can I never have any fun?!"

The nurse raised an eyebrow, then handed Connor a clipboard of papers to sign. "As I was saying, schedule an appointment with your primary care provider in three weeks to have the ankle reassessed. Maybe she'll be able to resume her activities at that time … if she takes care of her injury."

"Ugh!" Sammy grunted as she dramatically put a pillow on her face.

"Thank you." Connor smiled at the nurse, signed the paperwork and handed it back to her. "May we have a moment in here to talk? Then we can free up the room?"

"Sure," the nurse said uncaringly as she walked out with the clipboard.

Connor approached Sammy and pulled the pillow off of her face. "Do you have to be so dramatic?"

"It's not fair!" Sammy pounded her fists into the mattress. "I finally get to play soccer with kids my age and *this* happens! I think God hates me."

"He doesn't hate you," Connor said in an overly sweet voice, "He is probably just annoyed with you."

Sammy pouted.

Connor couldn't help but laugh. "Oh, don't pout like the teenager you are. We will talk with Morgan about getting your ankle healed in time for your next soccer practice."

"But that's in three days," Sammy whined.

Connor shrugged, "Yeah, you'll probably be healed in two days."

Sammy grunted again.

"Anyway, I have someone I want you to meet," Connor said. On cue, Dorian walked into the room. "He is an old friend of mine and will be hanging around for a while."

"Why?" Sammy asked.

"Because, my dear, you prove too much of a handful for poor Connor to handle," Dorian cut in. "My name is Dorian. It is a pleasure to finally meet you!"

Curious about the new stranger, Sammy sat up to get a better look at him. "You look like you are in a boy band." Then she collapsed back on the bed.

Connor rolled his eyes. Dorian perked up, "Hmmm, I am not, unfortunately. However, that does sound interesting to pursue."

Sammy sized up Dorian as if she didn't quite trust him.

Dorian winked at Connor and said, "Ca— Conner, you never told me what a rare jewel Samantha is." He walked over to Sammy's bedside. "It is no wonder he has been so protective of you for so long. You are an exquisite beauty, my dear. There is a uniqueness in you that shall bring men to their knees. If it would be all right, it would be my honor to help keep you safe from harm and from boredom." Leaning in with an intense gaze, Dorian kissed her hand.

Sammy blushed. "I suppose it's okay if you stick around."

"Cool down there, Casanova," Connor said with a smile as he pulled Dorian away by tugging on his collar. The three laughed together, no longer paying attention to the chaos of the hospital around them.

11

UNRELENTING ADDICTION

NEW YORK CITY, NEW YORK

JULY 12, 2013

If music were visible, hundreds of colorful ribbons and stars would have been bursting out of the limousine from the pop music pounding in the speakers. Sammy and three of her new high school friends stood up in the limousine, their heads popping through the sunroof. Their eyes bulged with awe at New York City's lights in the bustling city that never sleeps. Dressed to the nines, the girls squealed and giggled at the passing city in all its wonder.

Inside the limousine, Connor and Dorian calmly drank their bourbon on the rocks. The colorful lights that blinked inside the limousine glistened in their drinks, reflecting off the ice cubes. Dorian appeared to be enjoying the new adventure, surrounded by teenage girls. Since Dorian maintained a youthful appearance of eighteen, it was easy to see why Sammy's friends had a crush on him. Sammy behaved in a way that suggested she, too, had a crush on Dorian. Connor was grateful that Dorian had the maturity to redirect their suggestive advances.

"Wasn't this a fantastic idea?" Dorian asked excitedly as he eyed a pair of long legs exposed all the way to the bottom of the girl's butt.

Catching his gaze, Connor commented, "Remember that sex with a minor is considered a felony these days."

"It's their fault they choose to wear clothes to lead men on. Back when I was young, a woman only showed skin when she wanted sexual attention. Times have changed significantly from petticoats to belly shirts." Noticing he wasn't being listened to, Dorian glanced over at Connor, who was staring absentmindedly into his drink. "What troubles you, old friend?"

Readjusting, Connor plastered on his fake smile and replied, "I can't believe she is sixteen already. It seems only yesterday she was five, holding a teddy bear while we drove in a limousine from New York to New Hampshire." Connor drifted off again and watched Sammy freaking out over some of the iconic neon signs.

"There is something more on your mind. I can tell," Dorian said in observation.

Before Connor could answer, Sammy and her friends popped back inside. "Connor, this is the best sweet-sixteen ever!" Sammy screamed.

Connor chuckled, "And your birthday has only begun, Sammy!"

"What could be better than a private jet and a limousine in New York City?" one blonde friend asked with sass.

"Not to mention the Hampton penthouse suite tonight?" another friend squealed.

The third rubbed her stomach. "Can't forget the most expensive meal I have ever eaten in my life!"

"I thought Sammy would enjoy authentic French food. However, the rest so far are compliments of Dorian," Connor added, with a slight bow in Dorian's direction.

"Oh please," Dorian said with a hand flip, "I am merely supplying transportation and hotel accommodations. The real treat is the event we are heading to right now." Dorian made sure to end his statement with a suggestive look that made each of the girls swoon.

The girls flapped their hands in excitement.

"What adventure are we off to now, Connor?" Sammy asked excitedly.

"Let me show you," he said, right on cue. The limousine stopped in front of a plain building with a bright purple door. The limousine driver opened the car door and escorted the ladies from the limousine. As the two men exited, Connor handed the driver a heavy tip. "Please be back here no later than 10:30."

"Yes, sir," the limousine driver responded professionally.

As Connor turned towards the group of giggling girls, he smiled slightly before the smile fell off his face. Dorian ushered the girls inside the building while Connor silently took up the rear. The interior was dimly lit, but Dorian went on without fear or hesitation. The girls skittishly followed. Their clicking heels echoed on the cement floor as they entered a large room.

"Connor, where are we?" Sammy asked.

On cue, lights flashed and fog crawled in. A concert stage lit up in a glorious display of red and orange lights. Standing on the stage were three men and one woman with black hair and pale white skin. The lead guitarist strummed his guitar, which resounded loudly in the concert hall.

All of the girls, including Sammy, squealed in excitement as the female singer spoke into her microphone, "We are the Night Reapers here to tell you: Happy Birthday, Sammy!" Sammy and her friends ecstatically screamed even louder as the band immediately rocked out their most popular song. Dorian rocked out with them as if he were a teenager again.

While Connor watched Sammy and her friends dancing to their favorite band, he got lost in his own thoughts. It had been a long time since his last kill. A few years ago, he defensively killed two vampires that had threatened Sammy's life. Before that, he killed her uncle. All together, that was two times in the past ten years. For a monster that lustfully killed a hundred living beings every year for two thousand years, this dry spell was taking its toll.

It was true that Connor needed very little to survive. Sleep wasn't required to revitalize his body and heal his mind. Nourishment was unnecessary to keep his body strong. His body remained hydrated even

337

after months without water. Oxygen was only ever required to keep him conscious, but it had been proven many times that he could survive without oxygen for long periods of time in an unconscious state. Yet there was one desire his soul craved. This insatiable craving was a necessity for his vitality and kept his skills sharp. Without the rush of the kill, Connor was losing touch with his dark and powerful side. That monstrous side sang to him from deep within.

The human he had become heard a deadly whisper from his internal demon— the whispering of his true power that begged to be unleashed. For years he had subdued these urges and locked away his monster, so as not to reveal his dark side to Sammy.

Now it was overwhelming. The internal demon whispered to him sweet temptations, as if it was a lustful lover. How glorious it would be to smell fresh spilled blood. How adrenalizing it would be to hear the heartbeat of his victim quicken before he ultimately silenced it forever. How relieving the sound of his victim's last breath as the soul left the destroyed body.

Temptation haunted him now more than ever. Connor could hear the roar of the street around him. He knew this location to have many potential victims who preyed upon the weak of New York. One in particular stood out in his mind right now: a corrupt crime lord who currently hid only one street away. The temptation was as irresistible to him as a drug in the palm of his hand.

Sammy continued to dance, distracted by her birthday gift. It wouldn't take long for Connor to sneak away and dispose of the filth— possibly only fifteen minutes, given how rusty Connor was. No one would notice. One more release was all he needed.

In the middle of the chorus of the Night Reaper's song, Connor ducked away into the shadows. Before he could reach the door, he felt a presence lurking in the dark.

"Where are you running off to, Caspian?"

It was unfortunate that Dorian had been able to detect Connor's absence. This was an obstacle Connor knew would be difficult to overcome. With a large smile on his face, Connor turned around. "I was just going to the bathroom."

Dorian scowled and responded, "Bullshit. I know you better than that, Caspian. You always know the layout of every building before you even enter. Since Sammy is here with us, I have no doubt that you have a full mental map of the surrounding ten-mile radius. This would include the infamous crime lord who is rumored to be situated three buildings away."

"Dorian, you are being ridiculous. Besides, you are supposed to be watching Sammy," Connor stated with a sarcastic smile.

"You have been acting odd all day. I assumed you were up to something," Dorian added, "A hunting trip, perhaps?"

A low growl rumbled deep in Connor's throat. "You should understand why. Dorian, it has been so long since I have had the thrill of the hunt. I won't be gone long."

"I understand your addiction to the hunt. It feeds your inner demon. Which is why I'm afraid I can't let you do that, Caspian," Dorian said with mournful eyes.

The growl grew louder in Connor's throat.

"Besides, you are much happier in your human state," Dorian added. "Why would you throw away this happiness for one more release? What would you tell Sammy when your eyes turn purple?"

"That I protected her from intruders during the concert," Connor replied automatically.

"She is too smart for that, Connor, and you know it. You've raised her to be more intuitive than to believe simple lies," Dorian said softly.

Connor's heart raced as his ferocity rose. It was almost uncontrollable. "You can't stop me! I can command you to stand down!" Connor found himself shouting unnecessarily; luckily the concert music drowned him out.

"No," Dorian said, sounding much more authoritative, "You won't make those commandments, because your human side knows this is wrong."

"Then maybe it's time to release my beast," Connor growled, swirls of red mist clouding his pristine green eyes.

The strong bass of the concert music created a rhythm of vibrations on the ground that hid the monsters in the dark. Faster than the eye could perceive, Connor lunged forward. Dorian spun around his attack and clutched onto Connor's neck. Irritated with this new encumbrance, Connor dug his clawed hand into Dorian's forearm, which snugly fit across the front of Connor's throat. Though the pain was intense, Dorian maintained his grip. Connor lifted his feet, forcing Dorian to bear his entire weight. Using gravity's momentum, Connor bent over and flung Dorian, sending him rolling down the hall. It didn't take long for Dorian to come flying back in with a double kick to Connor's chest. Connor was pushed back several feet, but didn't fall. Instead, he morphed his hand into a black claw. Succinctly after, Dorian pinned Connor against the wall. Hastily, he secured Connor's clawed hands with his whole body weight. Dorian's purple mark glowed upon his hand and up his arm. "Caspian, no! You don't want to do this!"

"I control you! How dare you attempt to get in my way!" Connor roared loudly.

"Connor?" asked a small, scared voice. Sammy stood in fear, the music still booming behind her. Her sparkling green eyes widened at the horror she was seeing.

Immediately defeated by her presence, Connor's red swirling eyes darkened to a deep black. The demonic claws softened into normal human hands. The purple marks on Dorian's arm dulled to a mellow purple.

Sammy took a frightened step back, anticipating running away from the monsters she now saw for the first time.

Faster than a blink of an eye, Connor was wrapping his arms around her in a tight hug. "I'm sorry, Sammy. I'm so so sorry. You were never meant to see me like this."

"Wha … what … what?" Sammy was in too much shock to process anything. Dorian stood up without any wounds or blemishes, despite his battle-torn clothes.

Connor pulled away from her and held her face firmly so she couldn't look away. "Sammy, it's okay. You are safe. I promise. No harm will come to you."

340

Sammy watched as Connor's eyes went from black to his swirling purple hue. Then her courage returned. In a knee jerk reaction, she slapped his face hard enough to throw Connor's head to one side. Connor accepted the reprimand.

Riding her confusing surge of emotions, Sammy slapped him again. "It is my birthday!"

Upon the third slap, Connor caught her hand. "Okay, that's enough." The two red marks on his face were already fading.

Sammy teared up, truly seeing him for the first time. "You are not human, are you, Connor?"

Shamefully, Connor didn't know how to answer that question. Not this time.

"Tell me!" Sammy screamed, as tears ran down her face.

"Okay!" Connor yelled back, then broke free of her and walked a couple of steps away towards Dorian. The monster inside threatened to rise again, but he knew he had to suppress it. He fought his instincts, squeezing his eyes shut to force them back to green, with little hope of instantly doing so. "I can't tell you everything. I will, however, answer three questions … and only three."

"Connor," Sammy squeaked.

This time Connor commanded Dorian, "Call a separate limousine to take the girls to the hotel after the concert. Sammy and I will take the first one early. We have much to talk about."

"What if the girls ask about Sammy?" Dorian asked.

"Tell them she got food poisoning," Connor answered. He turned toward Sammy, who was sitting on the dirty floor in her glittery expensive dress with a mascara and tear-stained face.

Defeated, Connor went over to pick Sammy up. At first Sammy flinched from him, then relaxed in his familiar, gentle hold. Connor carried her in his arms outside to the limousine. The limousine driver dutifully opened the car door and shut it behind them.

The short ten-minute ride to the five-star Hilton was filled with a heavy awkward silence. They remained silent as they rode the elevator up to their penthouse suite. But once inside, Sammy burst out, "What are you?"

Connor took off his suit coat and put it in the closet before replying, "Is that your first question?"

"Yes!" Sammy demanded with pursed lips.

"Let's go sit down at the table," Connor directed.

Sammy stomped loudly in her heels over to the dining area, elaborately furnished with a full crystal chandelier and a gold-rimmed, polished wood table. She sat down in a huff and crossed her arms. Before Connor could get fully seated, Sammy blurted out again, "Tell me what you are!"

Not appreciating her attitude, Connor sharply responded, "You mean your guardian and protector who has selflessly raised you?"

Sammy maintained her firm glare.

It took another breath for Connor to cool down enough to answer. "Although I cannot truthfully tell you *what* I am, I can tell you things about me."

"Like what?" Sammy snapped.

Connor's eyebrow twitched slightly into a scowl and then was forced to relax. "Sammy, you know about some of the other beings on this Earth who are different than humans or animals. There are vampires, werewolves, changelings, mermaids and witches. There are hideous creatures of the night that haunt nightmares. However, I am the monster all these creatures fear. I have abilities that others envy. I am as invincible as a god, yet feared by most as a demon. Alas, I am neither. Even after two thousand years on this Earth I cannot be categorized because there is nothing to compare. Hence I remain alone."

"Then all those stories you have told me …" Sammy started, too scared to finish her thought.

"Yes, all those stories are of my past. Each are recounting my many adventures and failures throughout the years," Connor finished her sentence.

Sammy gulped, trying to process this information. "What about Veronica? Dorian? Or even Morgan? Are they like you?" Sammy asked with a tremor in her voice.

"That is your second question," Connor reminded her. "Veronica is a vampire. Dorian is a lich. Morgan is a witch. Each are under my service. Part of my ability is that I can put my mark on others to permanently freeze their bodies in time. That way they don't age and cannot die. In return, they must loyally obey my commands. I can end their contracts, and thus their lives, at any time. Hence why they respect me so."

"It didn't seem like Dorian respected you today," Sammy said doubtfully. "Why were you two fighting? Why did your eyes change color?"

"That's two questions, Sammy," Connor started tensely, then relaxed. "However, they both receive the same answer."

Connor paused for a moment, struggling to admit his own failings. "Dorian was trying to stop me from leaving—"

"You were going to leave me on my birthday?" Sammy screamed in outrage.

Shooting her a stabbing glare quickly silenced her and then he continued. "—leaving on an errand." Connor paused, gulping down his own pride. "This is my fault, Sammy. It is my own weakness getting the best of me. Because of my cursed nature, I crave the hunt and the kill that comes shortly after. I was leaving to rid the world of scum— an errand that would have taken me no longer than fifteen minutes if Dorian hadn't intervened." This appeared to scare Sammy quite a bit, so Connor added, "It is the monstrous side of me that craves the kill. When the monster inside of me comes out, my eyes turn red. My human morality gets lost along the way, then my eyes turn black. What I assume is my neutral state is purple."

"But your eyes have turned green around me," Sammy added, trying desperately hard to understand.

A small smile grew on Connor's face and his heart grew lighter with each word. "For reasons I cannot explain, you have the powerful ability to bring me back to my human state. The green eyes you have seen have been hidden for over two thousand years. I didn't believe they would ever come back until that one Christmas Day. You are the most influential person in my life. You help me subdue my inner demon."

For what seemed like hours, but was merely a few minutes, Connor sat in anticipation as Sammy silently mulled over all the new information. She was thinking so long and hard that Connor could almost hear the gears turning her head. Finally, she spoke, "Thank you for finally telling me the truth, Connor. I had known for a while that you were hiding something from me. Now that I know, I'm both relieved and overwhelmed. It's strange. I should be terrified of you, but I feel much safer and happier, now that you have confided in me. Since you have finally opened up to me, it's only fair to open up to you." Ashamedly, Sammy kept her gaze focused on the table—opposite from what she had been displaying mere minutes ago.

Connor was suddenly on edge, caught off-guard to learn that she had the ability to hide things from him. Throughout their time together, Connor had spent almost every waking moment with her. Perhaps he had been too consumed by his belief that their relationship was so tight that she would talk to him about anything. Apparently, he was wrong.

"I will tell you three things, since you shared three things with me," she started, "First off, I know your real name is Caspian. I have heard Morgan and Dorian call you 'Caspian' many times. It didn't take me long to figure out that you had two identities."

Connor was floored. He had been certain she had no clue about his real name. In past lives, she only said his true name when her memory returned. It was his one assurance that he was bringing her memories back. Now he had lost that assurance. "Well, when you live as long as I have, then you have to keep changing your name to cover the trail. It's a way for the government to leave me alone. Morgan and Dorian met me with my original name. I didn't tell you because I didn't want to confuse you at such a young age." Partially a lie, but he still felt the cold grip of anxiety as he waited to see if she bought it.

"Don't worry, I'll still call you Connor. It is the best name I have known you by," Sammy smiled reassuringly. "Secondly, I knew you had other abilities. You haven't aged, not even one gray hair. Plus, you used to never sleep or eat, which is not normal. Now you do. I knew you were different. Which is why I believed you clung onto me so tightly, because I am also different. I never knew how different you actually were, which makes me feel insecure about my own differences. Am I just like you?"

"No," Connor responded sympathetically, "You will never have to carry the same curse I must carry. Think of your differences as a blessing, whereas mine are a curse. Your blessings are starting to bloom. I'm sure with some patience and time, you will grow into a breathtaking flower the world has never seen before."

"Yeah …" Sammy fidgeted with her hands a bit. "That goes to my third point. I don't feel like I'm blessed, Connor. I feel like I'm cursed."

"Why?" Connor couldn't help but grab her anxious hands with his comforting ones.

A few small tears ran down her face as Sammy stifled her emotions the best she could. "I feel so confused, Connor! It's not maturation, like Morgan says. My emotions are out of control and foreign to me. Not only can I talk to animals, but I can control them as well. Not in a mind-control way, but in a friendship sort of way. That is not normal, and at times is difficult for me to hide at school. Especially during science class."

Connor rubbed Sammy's hand to soothe her tears. "That's a blessing Sammy, not a curse. You have an incredible bond with animals that no one else will ever understand. I can pull you from classes that have animal dissection to make it easier on you."

Tears continued to fall down Sammy's face. "I also have dreams, or rather nightmares, of fire. Lots of fire. It doesn't burn my flesh, but I can hear screams of those around me. Am I dreaming of the future? Am I going to kill people with fire?" Bursting into tears, Sammy collapsed on the table.

Reflexively, Connor stood up from his chair, knelt before Sammy and lifted her chin. "Samantha Valda, you will never kill another person if you don't want to. Your heart is too pure for such evil acts."

"Connor, I want to know more about you and your past, but I can barely wrap my head around what you have already told me. It is all too much and I hardly even know what is real anymore." Sammy still appeared afraid, but at least the tears had stopped.

The elevator into the penthouse dinged, which prompted Sammy to wipe the tears from her face.

"We can talk about this more later. Just let your mind settle on what you have heard today," Connor said, ending the conversation.

"Sammy!" yelled the girls as they came running into the room. Closely following them was Dorian and two bellhops, dropping off their many bags and suitcases. Immediately, the girls spouted off their concerns.

"Oh my god, are you okay?"

"Food poisoning? That blows!"

"Literally! LOL!"

"How are you feeling?"

Putting her hands up to silence them, Sammy cut in, "I'm glad you are so concerned about me. I'm fine, though! Just felt a little sick for some reason and Connor WAY overreacted and brought me back here, away from the loud music."

The trio of girls chorused: "Girl, you had me worried!"

"Aw, that was sweet."

"You missed the best grand finale EVER!"

"I got it on my phone though! I'll show you."

"You would!"

Sammy laughed. "Like totally, girls, give me room to speak. I would love to see the recording. But first let's get into our pj's. I hope none of you wore lacy thongs. Cuz girls, you ain't impressing no one here!" The group of girls giggled as they all shoved their way into the master bedroom suite where they would be sleeping together. Or rather, where they planned to watch horror movies on the big screen TV until they fell asleep.

While the girls scurried off to get ready for bed, Dorian went over to the kitchen to prepare two drinks. Connor watched from his seated position as Dorian poured the rum. Drinks in hand, Dorian motioned towards the balcony. Before following Dorian outside, Connor set the lock on the elevator door and quickly scanned the room for any open doors or windows. He didn't want a repeat of Disney World.

Outside on the balcony, Dorian sat in one of the lounge chairs, with his feet propped up on the railing. The Manhattan view was spectacular, with all of its twinkling lights and tall buildings. It was no wonder so many paid through the nose to live in such a lively and unique place. Connor sat next to Dorian and, without saying a word, nursed his White Russian.

The two sat there for a long time, listening to the buzz of the city and the giggling inside. Finally, Dorian broke the silence. "Do you want to talk about what happened tonight?"

Connor preferred to stare into his glass instead of at Dorian. Several minutes of silence passed while Connor gathered his thoughts enough to answer. "Below us right now are thousands of people. Some are getting ready for bed. Others are working. Others are playing. While some others are up to no good. I can hear their heartbeats. I can feel their energy shifting around me as if I'm lost in a tidal wave of their blood. The temptation to spill their blood and burn the city down calls to me. It whispers in my ear. It tingles at my fingertips. It quickens my heart in anticipation for the kill. This addiction to the kill lingers in my soul."

"Yes," Dorian replied as he took a sip of his drink. "I understand the pull of addiction as well."

Staring down at his drink, Connor realized he no longer had an appetite for alcohol or any food at all. Defeated, he put down the drink and rested his head in his hands. "Samantha brought out the human side of me, which has really shown me the wonders of happiness in these past years. Years I wouldn't trade for anything. Although I have strongly embraced this newfound human side of my soul, the inner demon still lingers, still hungers. My daily challenges to suppress the demon have grown pressingly more difficult as the days go on. I need to feel that rush again. Yet the need to be happy by Sammy's side is much stronger. Dorian, I'm torn."

"Stay strong, Caspian. If you can't stay strong for yourself, then stay strong for Sammy. Even during your mishap this evening, you stayed true to what you want to be for Sammy. It is that reason that you didn't go full throttle on me. You want to be the hero Sammy sees in you— so be that hero. That is the best advice I can give you." Dorian smiled.

"I do love her … with a love that continues to grow in the infinite vastness of space and time. Yet I fear she will reject me. A blackened and sinful soul such as mine has no place next to a pure soul such as hers. This struggle has tortured me for centuries, and now it is at its climax of impossibility."

"Connor?" Sammy spoke up softly.

Connor startled by her sudden appearance, "Sammy? Is everything all right?"

Nervously, Sammy rubbed her arms as if she was cold despite the midnight summer heat. This too made Connor nervous, as he wondered how much of this conversation she had heard.

Avoiding the awkward tension, Dorian stood up and made his exit. "I'll give you both some space to talk. I'll go watch the girls watch a horror movie."

As he passed by Sammy, she nodded to him in acknowledgment, "Mr. Gray."

Delighted, Dorian chuckled and went inside.

Motioning towards the chair that Dorian had vacated, Connor said, "Would you like to sit down?"

"Yeah," Sammy replied weakly as she took the seat next to him on the balcony.

There was a brief pause and then Connor filled the silence. "You wanted to talk to me?"

Sammy smiled and pulled her knees into her chest. "Connor, I know you have given up a lot to take care of me. Even with your undivided attention, I know it hasn't been easy."

"Even with some of our difficulties, I still wouldn't trade these years for anything. I treasure spending time with you and helping you grow into a strong woman," he responded honestly.

They both smiled.

Sammy gazed out over the New York City landscape. "It's been a long time since I've been back here."

"It has," Connor agreed. "Do you miss it?"

"I miss my dad ... a lot," Sammy replied.

Silence.

Sammy held onto her knees tighter. "I remember the day my father died, when the towers fell. You stayed by my side and helped me when I was at my most vulnerable. I distinctly remembered the way my night light lit up my room with princesses and castles. You told me a story to help distract me from my grief— a story you have now told me over a hundred times. Your stories became a special gift for me; I just never knew they were stories about your life. Still, they helped me cope with my own struggles, such as missing my dad."

"I'm glad." Connor felt the warmth returning to his heart. Even his eyes were melting from a swirling purple to a deep green.

"I want to help you cope with these challenging thoughts you now face. Can you tell me another story, Connor?" Sammy asked.

"What story would you like to hear?" he asked, touched by her compassion.

"Tell me a tale of a time you struggled with this killing urge," Sammy requested.

Connor chuckled, "All right, let me tell you a tale of addiction."

* * *

JACKSON, MISSISSIPPI

MAY 4, 1975

An army major sat on the bus with arms crossed tightly over his chest. His pressed brown uniform was as creased as his furrowed brow. His black buzz-cut hair was conveniently hidden beneath his hat. Small patches across his bicep and on his chest read "Jackson" with his accelerated rankings above it. Ten years ago, he was Private Cody Jackson, but he'd quickly risen through the ranks. Rows of medals and ribbons adorned his dress uniform, but these meant little to him. He cared nothing for the decorations of war nor the reasons he earned them.

What he really cared about was being on the battlefield. Nothing adrenalized him more than the strategic challenge of keeping his men alive while simultaneously destroying the enemy. Throughout the Vietnam War, he was the only officer in active combat who had kept all his men alive. Even when given nearly impossible missions, he was able to meet objectives and bring all his men back to base with intel.

Now, the war was over, and not in victory. No. The U.S. had pulled out, leaving the South Vietnamese to their fate, a pathetic disgrace that disgruntled Major Cody Jackson. If he wasn't so constrained to appear normal in front of the humans, he could have won that war on his own. The death toll he could deliver invigorated him. Yet now it was all for nothing.

His men had cheered their departure as they discussed what they'd do on their first night home. Their celebration also disgusted him. There was nothing to celebrate. Just an end to the war that had given him so much freedom to release his anger and frustration.

Trying to put the men and their celebratory plans out of his mind, Major Jackson stared out the bus window as the bustling city of Jackson rolled by. Two more hours until they returned to Camp Shelby to debrief, then released to return home. It was easy for the other men to rejoice. They had a home to return to.

A small crowd of protesters formed around the bus as it stopped at a light in the center of the city, holding signs about peace. Impatiently, the bus driver honked at them. Major Jackson wanted to ignore them, despite the disrespect they were showing his soldiers. All of a sudden, a large bucket of red paint was thrown on the bus. Some of the soldiers inside sitting next to open windows got red paint splattered on their uniforms. Instantly, there was a ruckus as the soldiers stood up and shouted at the protesters, who were now throwing eggs as well.

"Sit down!" Major Jackson shouted. "Roll up your windows and don't say a fucking word!"

Respecting their leader, the soldiers obeyed, smirking at the poor souls who were foolish enough to disrespect Major Jackson's men.

Furiously, Major Jackson stepped off the bus and into the mob, which continued to scream. One young man with round yellow glasses, long hair and bell bottom pants threw an egg directly at Jackson. To the shock of the crowd, Jackson caught the egg without breaking it and hurled it back, hitting the shooter right between the eyes.

"Whose brilliant idea was it to throw red paint at my bus!?" he screamed into the crowd, which instantly quieted.

The sound of a megaphone being turned on drew his attention. "You murderers are a disgrace to our country! Make love not war!"

Faster than the crowd could react, Major Jackson cut through to the megaphone and smacked it to the ground so hard it shattered into pieces. The woman holding the megaphone wasn't frightened. Quite the contrary, she had a unique fire in her eyes.

He grabbed her brown, tasseled vest and pulled her in close enough to lift her off her feet, "Yes, I am a murderer, but my men here were forced to follow orders. Most were sent to war without much say in the matter. Men died to protect your freedom. They come back with their heads held high, knowing that America remains home of the brave, and you disrespect them! YOU are the disgrace!" He paused as he closely inspected the woman. Held back by a flowered headband was her straight, auburn hair, which fell to the waist of her bell bottom pants. Behind her round, rose-colored glasses were strikingly familiar green eyes.

"They fired those guns all the same," she spat in his face, showing no fear.

"What is your name?" Jackson growled as he slightly released his hold on her.

Her fierce green eyes stared at him. "I'm not going to ..."

"Tell me your name right now!" he demanded.

"Martha Green!" squeaked another female protester to the side.

The name disappointed him, especially because this woman appeared to be a mirror image of *her*. He sighed and pushed her back into the crowd. "Go home, Martha Green! The war is over. And as for the rest of you," he said, turning around to see the whites of their eyes, "If I ever catch any of you disrespecting a soldier again, then I will demonstrate the murdering

I did in Vietnam. Now move aside, so my soldiers can go home to their families!"

Terrified by his presence, the crowd gave him and the bus a wide berth as he stepped on. "Drive," he commanded aggressively as he took his seat.

Upon their return to Camp Shelby, the troops received a much warmer welcome. Families were there to greet the soldiers with relieved hugs, kisses, pictures, and happy smiles illuminated by the golden glow of a setting sun. A few soldiers even held their child for the first time. It was a beautiful reunion, except for Major Jackson. Keeping his head low, he cut through them all and made his way to the solitude of his assigned quarters.

Jackson stood in front of a large window, staring at the night sky. A crumpled-up letter sat on his bed, congratulating him on another promotion. None of that mattered, though. For some reason he couldn't get Martha Green out of his head. He knew she was the wrong girl, but it nagged him. After all, it wouldn't be the first time that *she* had a pretty convincing doppelganger. He had two weeks of leave time to kill. What better way to spend it than to learn more about this Martha Green?

The celebrations at the bar were winding down when a stranger wearing an army cap and trench coat entered. Two of the most loyal patrons bobbled their attention over to the stranger. Losing interest, they redirected their gaze to the television airing the latest updates on the withdrawal from Vietnam.

"Take a seat sir, and I'll be right with you," Martha Green greeted as she continued to clean up behind the counter. The stranger took a bar seat right in front of where she was cleaning. An empty whiskey glass with two cigarette butts sat on the counter from the last patron. Ignoring the grungy bar that matched the grungy establishment, the stranger removed his hat out of respect.

Martha dragged herself over, tired after a long shift, "What can I get for—" she paused, suddenly recognizing the stranger. *"You?"* Her green eyes sparkled in the dull light of the bar and her auburn hair was pulled back into a messy bun.

"Good evening, Ms. Green," Major Cody Jackson greeted.

Slamming a dish rag down, she pointed an accusatory finger between his black eyes. "How did you find me, Mr. ..."

"Major Jackson, ma'am," he replied curtly.

"Well, I refuse to call you by your military title. What's your real name?" she asked as she cleaned a glass with a worn out rag.

"They call me Cody," he responded.

"Cody, huh?" she asked as she filled a glass with beer and placed it in front of him. "How did you find me, Cody?"

"I asked around. Not too difficult to find a little lady throwing up protests against the war." Cody peered into the glass as if it was poisoned. "I didn't order this."

"It's on the house," she said with a nod. "I'm sorry for throwing paint and eggs at your soldiers."

"Perhaps you can apologize to them in a couple weeks, when they get rewarded for all their hard work," he suggested, without touching the beer.

"Now you're pushing it! I said I was sorry, not that I wanted to enlist," she stated, continuing to clean.

Abruptly, a young man with sandy colored hair and stoned eyes popped his head out of the kitchen, "Yo, Martha! I'll close up if you want to run off to your party."

"Thank you," she called to him, then nodded her chin at Cody. "Enjoy your drink, man." Martha removed her apron and headed out the back door.

Thinking on his feet, Cody stole a pen from behind the counter, scribbled something down on a napkin, then spilled beer all over it.

"Yo man, it's time for me to close up shop," the young man announced as he came out.

"Goddammit!" Cody yelled, as he stood up so the beer didn't drip on him.

"Chill out, what's the trouble?" the boy asked, getting a rag and cleaning up the mess.

Cody delicately picked up the napkin, which was clearly illegible.

"Martha wrote down the address to the party she invited me to. And, well, look at it." Cody held up the napkin, which was already disintegrating and falling apart.

"Oh, no worries, man. Let me write down the address for you. It is going to be a wild party!" The young man laughed as he pulled over a napkin and started writing on it. He paused as he looked at Cody's perfectly pressed army uniform. "Huh, I wouldn't figure you'd be the type to go to one of these parties. But hey, no judgment, man."

"Thank you again." Cody dismissed the young man, who was rounding up the other two patrons so he could close up. Looking at the address, Cody deduced that it was only about five miles away. With a light jog, he could get there in about ten minutes.

Cody found himself at the door of the party house, which was bursting with college students drinking and dancing to records. He wasn't sure why he was here. At the bar, he had confirmed that Martha was not *her*. Yet some nagging thought in the back of his mind kept pushing him to find *her*.

No more hesitation— Cody entered the house. The first thing to hit him was the strong odors of weed, booze and nag champa incense. Hippies were everywhere in this house, with their long necklaces and flowers braided into their hair. Most were half-naked and high as a kite. Cody slowly navigated through the house surveying the occupants. After confirming that she wasn't in the living room, he went to the kitchen, where a group was currently shooting up. Ignoring their illegal activity, Cody went upstairs to where the bedrooms were.

The first room was full of naked bodies sharing a bowl after what appeared to be a sweaty orgy. The second room had two men and a woman who were currently in the midst of their activity. Moving on, Cody opened the third room, which had only two occupants. The man's back was facing Cody. Judging by the hastily way he was removing his pants, Cody could only surmise that he was about to be in the midst of fucking. The girl's pants were discarded to the side of the bed, along with her ripped pink panties. Her legs hung limply over the sides of the bed. An alert went off in Cody's head as he realized that she wasn't making any sounds.

The man was too stoned to hear Cody enter, let alone see him come around the bed to check on the girl. Once she came into view, Cody saw that it was Martha Green, completely unconscious. The injection site in her arm was fresh, too.

"Stop! Can't you see she has passed out!" Cody yelled at the man.

Finally noticing Cody, the man smiled with glazed eyes, "Hey man, you can have a go at her after I'm done."

Rage bubbled up in Cody's chest and face. Without considering the consequences, Cody grabbed the man's head in his hand. With one quick squeeze, the head crumpled and burst under the intense pressure. As the headless body fell to the floor, Cody grabbed Martha's pants and found her wallet in the pocket. He opened it and saw her Mississippi driver's license.

Martha's true name was Shannon Green.

To confirm his suspicions, Cody rolled her head to the side. Sure enough, her auburn hair hid a dark orange birthmark that trailed down her neck to the top of her shoulder blades. Cody's rage burned hot as he gently pulled her pants back on. Picking her up, Cody quickly scanned the room, noting the spreading blood from the corpse. Wanting to destroy the evidence, Cody whipped his hand out as if he was throwing a card. Purple sparks flew from his fingertips and immediately set the room ablaze.

Without delay, Cody ran down the stairs and out the front door. Before leaving for good, he melted the handle of the door so no one could escape his flames. All who saw his face tonight would surely die. He would make sure of that.

Laying her down gently in the grass, Cody pulled the car keys out of her pocket. Hastily moving from car to car, he finally found which was hers: an old, beat-up blue Ford pickup. As he ran over to pick her up, something in the house exploded and the people inside screamed. While the house went up in flames, Cody carried her to the truck.

Turning the key to the ignition, Cody put the truck in drive and quickly fled the scene of the crime. As he did so, one word escaped Shannon's lips: "Caspian."

Under a crisp blue sky and wafting clouds sat the epitome of Americana: a white farm house nestled in forty acres of farmland. A red barn with black doors and white trim sat to the side. Wrapping around the property was a white picket fence that did little more than establish the boundaries of the farmland.

The smell of bacon and biscuits wafted over to Cody from the barn. Wiping his forehead off on a small bandana, Cody dropped his task of fence repair to check on Shannon. No doubt she would be hungry after last night. Food would do her hangover some good. While he traveled inside, Cody wiped his dusty hands on the bandana. The smell of food was even stronger from within the house, tempting a recollection for the savory enjoyment that food used to give him. Ignoring these primal reactions, Cody marched up the stairs to the bedrooms. Inches away from rapping his fingers on the door, he paused to listen at the conversation ensuing inside. He cracked the door and peered in.

"Ah! You're awake!" exclaimed a short, plump woman with graying blonde hair and a dirty apron. "I was worried you would sleep through breakfast. My goodness, you were so dead asleep that not even the devil himself could have woken you."

"Mama?" —Shannon held her throbbing head— "How did I get home?"

"A friend of yours drove you home. He felt this would be the best place for you." A mother's concern washed over her face. Compulsed to comfort her child, she walked over and gave Shannon a tight hug. "Oh baby, it has been so long since you've been home! We are so glad to have you back!"

"Where is he?" Shannon asked, struggling to sling a sentence together.

She pointed to the window. "Oh, he's out helping Papa with the farm. It's nice to have the extra help."

Shannon held her head with enough dedication to whiten her knuckles, "What about Roger?"

"Oh, your brother is in town fetching supplies. This nice young man offered to help us fix up the place while you recover," she replied happily. "Now, come downstairs and let's have breakfast as a family."

"What? Wait!" Shannon said, stubbornly holding her hands out. "Recover?"

The stern face of a scolding mother appeared on her face. "Shannon Martha Green, don't you give me that lip. Your friend told us what you have been up to in the city: smoking weed, drinking alcohol, all kinds of sins. Some nice country air and perhaps some church-going would do you good. Lord knows you have confessions to make to Father Dave."

Shannon stood speechless.

"See you downstairs, sweetie," her mother said lovingly again.

Instantly aware that he was about to be caught eavesdropping, Cody pulled away from the door and raced downstairs to the dining room. Luckily, Mrs. Green was unaware of the snooping.

Down at the breakfast table, Shannon slunk into her chair with her arms folded. She appeared miserable with her messy hair and sunken face. Mrs. Green was bringing food to the table while Mr. Green sat at the head of the table rubbing his round gut in preparation for a country breakfast. His jolly blue eyes made him appear quite approachable and kind, even with his thinning blonde hair. The son, Roger Green, sat down next to his father. Although strong from working on the farm, he had a baby face with patchy facial hair that matched his messy, thick blonde hair, which desperately needed a comb. Cody quietly sat down after washing his hands, noting that he stood out in this light-haired, blue-eyed family. But he noted that Shannon stood apart as well, with her abnormal auburn hair and green eyes. Even her sour attitude stood out in this happy family. She wouldn't give Cody so much as eye contact. He couldn't blame her.

Mrs. Green kissed her husband on his thinning hair before sitting down. "So, Cody, I hear you fought in the war."

"Yes, ma'am, returned from Vietnam the other day," Cody replied, as he served himself bacon.

"Oh! You were an officer! What rank?" Mr. Green asked.

"Major, sir. However, I just received a promotion to Lieutenant Colonel.

There's a ceremony in two weeks," Cody replied, keeping his respectful formalities.

Intrigued, Roger leaned in closer and asked, "Do you have any medals?"

Cody smiled at Roger's enthusiasm. "I do have some honorary medals and ribbons, but I don't brag about them. It was an honor to serve my country."

"Ugh!" Shannon rolled her eyes in disgust.

Ignoring her, Roger looked at Cody wistfully. "I wish I could have served in the army."

"Yes, well, that is all good and fine for Major Jackson over here, but we couldn't stand losing our only son to war," Mrs. Green chimed in.

There was an awkward silence that hinted at an argument that had taken place at this table many times. Shannon was obviously against the war. The parents were neutral on the war, but patriotically supportive of America. If Roger wasn't their only son, he most likely would have been drafted regardless of the deferment. Feeling a touch mischievous, Cody poked the bear, "You would have made a fine soldier, Roger, I'm sure. Mrs. Green, is he your only heir?"

There was another awkward silence. Before Mrs. Green had the chance to politely answer, Shannon burst in, "God, it's because I'm adopted! Okay? They didn't want to lose their only child and not be able to see their pure bloodline passed on! Why the hell are you sitting at our table, anyway? You love causing trouble, don't ya? Well, fuck off!"

"Shannon!" Mrs. Green yelled to reel her child in.

"Go to your room!" Mr. Green shouted.

"Gladly," Shannon stomped upstairs.

"I am so sorry!" Mrs. Green apologized. "She has been quite temperamental for the last couple years."

"No, I apologize, Mrs. Green. I didn't know she was adopted," Cody said, with his head hung low.

"It's not your fault, son. It is no secret that we adopted her, but it isn't discussed very much. You see, her mother died in childbirth and her father was a soldier who died in the Korean War— a touchy topic for her, as you can tell." Mr. Green sighed.

Cody smiled at being called *son*, especially because he was centuries older than Mr. Green, but the sentiment was appreciated. "I understand she is going through a difficult time. I want to help her through it as much as possible. Thank you for the breakfast, Mrs. Green. I'm going to continue working on the cattle fence if that is all right."

"You are such a dear," Mrs. Green said affectionately.

Roger stuffed some bacon in his mouth and grabbed a roll. "I'll join you!" Running after Cody as if he were a duckling keeping up with its mother, he started hammering more questions about the army.

Several hours later, after Cody had finished with the cattle fence, he found himself fixing a tractor in the barn. Roger and his father were bringing in the cattle for the night, leaving Cody alone with a calico cat. By this point his jeans and white tank top were stained beyond repair. Roger had already offered to let Cody wear some of his clothes until they could make it to the store. There was some mild satisfaction in using his hands to fix and repair things. He was so used to destroying things that it was a nice change of pace. These small fixer-upper projects also helped him to keep his mind off his own cravings. Being back in the civilian world, it would be challenging to curb his appetite for killing. Sooner or later he would have to find some avenue for hunting before he lost control again.

In the middle of working on the fuel line to the engine, he heard someone approach. The cat meowed a greeting. "How are you feeling?" Cody asked without looking at Shannon.

At first, she startled, but then brushed it off. "My head hurts from last night, but I've been worse."

"That's good to hear. Keep drinking plenty of water. The worst is yet to come," he forewarned. From his peripherals, he noticed her lingering eyes on his bare chest and forearms. Normally he would reciprocate the attraction, but judging her sickly and disheveled appearance, now was not the optimal time to ignite a spark.

"You are determined to sober me up, aren't you?" she asked angrily, tears of frustration forming.

"And you are determined to kill yourself with drugs, aren't you?" Cody finally looked at her with his heartless black eyes.

Shannon shivered, a sign of detox. It was getting worse. "Where did you hide my stash?" she asked, tears of frustration streaming down her face.

Cody put down the wrench and towered over her. Her first reaction was to take a couple of hesitant steps back, but then she firmly held her ground. They glared at each other with unflinching resolve.

Unsympathetic, he answered, "Your marijuana. Your liquor. Your cocaine … I destroyed them all."

Unable to restrain herself, Shannon beat on his chest with her fists, which had little effect. "You monster! How could you!? You don't know me at all! Why are you doing this to me?" She sank to the floor in a puddle of her own self-pity.

Noticing her shaking, Cody knelt to the floor and started to pick her up. Angrily, Shannon slapped him. He grabbed both of her hands and planted them on the ground.

"I'm going to tell my family about you. That I don't even know you. That you basically kidnapped me to bring me home. You have no right to be here!" she spat in his face.

While still holding her hands down, Cody wiped the spit off his face with his shoulder. "If you do that, then I will tell them how I found you."

Shannon's eyes widened in horror. "How did you find me?"

Cody's black eyes were hard as steel as he recalled the party. "In that party house, there were drugs— marijuana, cocaine, meth, alcohol, orgies. You were located in the back room. Whether it was your choice or it was forced on you, it was obvious you'd taken too much cocaine. You were unconscious, drooling. A man was readying to have his way with you while you were passed out. When I came in the room, he offered to let me have a turn on you once he was done. I took it upon myself to rescue you. I didn't kidnap you, Shannon Martha Green. I brought you home, because it is obvious that you need help."

Shannon broke down and wept uncontrollably. Cody picked her up, and this time she didn't resist. Instead she hung on to his neck and cried into his oil-stained shirt. To reassure her, he added, "I only told your family that I am a friend of a friend who saw you struggling with drug abuse. So, as a friend, I brought you home to sober up away from the temptations of the city."

Shannon didn't reply and continued to cry into his shirt as he carried her to the house.

Mrs. Green watched Cody remove his shoes and carry Shannon upstairs to her bedroom. "Is my baby all right?"

"She'll be fine," he said soothingly as he went up the stairs. "She needs rest and some water."

Cody laid her down on her bed. Refusing to show her face, Shannon turned around and buried her head in her pillow. He knew the cruel hand of addiction and how it can cause a large array of emotions to surface that normally would have been suppressed. Cody proceeded to tuck her in and exited the room.

A half moon hung in the sky. It's heavenly glow was accentuated by the bountiful stars that kept it company. Cody watched this crescent moon from his lounged position on the bed of the truck. Fingers woven to support his head, he listened for Shannon. All had been quiet and calm until he heard the front door handle give off a high pitched squeak. Silence followed as Shannon listened for anyone stirring awake. The door then screeched loudly as it swung closed. Silence again. Shortly after, Shannon was sprinting across the grass towards her truck.

Cody sighed and continued to listen as she swung open the passenger side door. Her fingers worked fast as she searched the glove compartment, which was obviously empty. Although her shaking fingers made it difficult to unscrew the back two screws, Shannon was finally able to get them out. Once she pulled the glove compartment free, where her stash had been duct-taped, it took her a moment to recognize that it was gone. Frantically Shannon patted down the area and banged around deeper.

"I told you I destroyed all of it," Cody calmly informed.

Shannon bumped her head and then fell backwards out of the truck into the dirt. "Where are you?"

Cody sat up from the bed of the truck, "I knew you would come back to your truck to find your hidden stash," he said with a proud smile.

Shannon shifted in the dirt to angrily glare at him, "God, why are you torturing me?"

"God isn't doing this to you. You did this to yourself," Cody replied, as he jumped over the side of the truck bed.

"No, *you* are doing this to me." —Shannon pointed angrily at him— "Why can't you let me have a little?"

As Cody started to pick her up, she instantly fought him. Having zero patience, he threw her over his shoulder.

Shannon pounded on his back, weakly screaming, "Aargh! Why are you doing this to me? Give them back! You are so mean!"

Ignoring her tantrum, Cody carried her to the house, where lights were coming on. Mr. Green met them at the door, which he held open for Cody to carry a screaming Shannon to her room. Mrs. Green walked out in her nightgown, worried for her daughter. Roger opened his bedroom door for a minute, rubbing the sleep from his eyes. Once he saw his screaming sister, he groaned and went back to bed.

Cody plopped Shannon on her bed, which groaned from her weight.

She glared up at him with fire in her green eyes. "Do you really think you can stop me?"

Cody pursed his lips for a moment before making the decision to threaten her. "When I was serving in Vietnam, I was given soldiers with high AWOL risk. For a month, two of my soldiers tried to run away on a nightly basis. I caught them and dragged their heavy asses to base every time. And they were much more stealthy than you. If you want to keep playing this game with me, then bring it on. I'll just keep bringing you back to the safety of your bedroom."

Shannon growled in frustration and threw her pillow at Cody, who caught it and placed it on the foot of her bed. Then he exited the bedroom to let Shannon continue throwing her tantrum alone.

Mr. and Mrs. Green stood outside the door, expecting an explanation.

"She thought she had a stash of drugs hidden away in her truck," Cody said with a shrug. "She is quite upset that I already destroyed them."

"Mmmm, all right then," Mr. Green said, nodding. "See you bright and early in the morning then, son."

Cody sighed and went out to the barn to find something else to fix. He already knew this act of defiance would only be the beginning.

And he was right.

The next day, Shannon's detox symptoms proved to be more severe. Shannon slept through most of the day but complained of her head hurting every waking moment. She woke with shivers but had a fever spiking. Mrs. Green sat by her daughter's side throughout the day while Cody completed her house chores. To keep his mind off of the agony Shannon was experiencing, he found things around the house that needed fixing—save the front door, which he left squeaky on purpose.

That night, after everyone had gone to bed, Shannon made her way downstairs to the key rack next to the door. It took several minutes of jingling through all the keys before she realized that none of them belonged to her truck.

"Dammit! Dammit! Dammit!" she screamed as she hit the wall with her fist and then slid to the floor in defeat.

"Come on, let's get you back to bed," Cody sighed as he strolled over to her.

"Did you hide my keys?" she asked as he knelt on the ground.

Wrapping her up in his arms, Cody once again carried her to bed. "No, your brother thought it would be a good idea. You're in no condition to drive." Lacking all strength, Shannon beat on his chest with a weak fist while he carried her upstairs.

"Again?" Mrs. Green asked. Mr. Green stood behind his wife with a relaxed grip on his rifle.

"Yes, ma'am. Not to worry. I'll get her back in bed," Cody responded. The parents returned to their bedroom, exhausted by their daughter's escape attempts.

This time, he gently placed her in bed and covered her up with the sheets. Before he left the room, Shannon feebly asked, "Have *you* ever been denied your greatest desire?"

"Yes, too many times to count. Now go to sleep, Shannon. You need your rest to recover." Cody closed the door, and stood outside in the hall for a moment. He had many answers to her question. Throughout the centuries he had been denied *her* many times over. Fate had not been kind to him. Cody understood the pull of addiction all too well. However, the addiction he felt was not for substances, but for the hunt. It was an addiction that no mortal man would ever understand or justify in times of peace. Shannon would recover from her addiction in time, but he could never escape his. The whisper of death called to him as if it was a lover in the dark. Although it never called for his own death, no. Death was greedy and insatiable in its requests of him. Oh, the adrenaline rush and sense of release he got from the kill—how easily it equated to her own drug-induced release. Thinking about this only made his hands tremble as he listened to the steady breathing of the house's inhabitants as they fell asleep. The desire was creeping in, and there was no one in this small town he could morally dispose of. Cody walked outside to find something else to fix and occupy his mind.

The next day proved devastating to Shannon, who screamed in agony. She hadn't eaten in days and could barely keep water down. Her shakes and tremors had gotten worse and her fever had spiked. Mrs. Green finally called a doctor in, who was happy to write a few prescriptions for controlled substances to help ease the detox process. These pills seemed to do the trick to calm down Shannon's symptoms, but only increased her whining for more pills. Still, the love of a mother kept Mrs. Green at Shannon's side throughout the day.

During the night, Mr. Green now felt it necessary to sleep in Shannon's room with her, so she wouldn't escape, but Mr. Green was a heavy sleeper. Still woozy from the prescriptions, Shannon snuck out of bed. Tiptoeing lightly, she walked around her snoring father in his rocking chair and over to her bedroom door. After wiggling the handle for a moment, she realized it was locked from the outside. Another fixer-upper job by Cody. Feeling invincible and desperate, Shannon tiptoed over to her bedroom window. Carefully she lifted the window, trying not to make too much noise. Once there was enough room, Shannon ducked down and crawled out of the window. Overconfident that she could easily make it around the side of the house to the window of the bathroom—where her prescriptions were kept—she paid less attention to her footing. Before she got there, she lost her balance. Shannon screamed in fear and shut her eyes.

Waiting for this exact moment of stupidity, Cody caught her in his strong arms.

"Ugh! There is no escaping you!" she groaned.

Cody chuckled, "I warned you, didn't I?"

Shannon groaned and then asked, "Since we are down here, is there any chance you can get me more pills? My headache is getting worse."

"According to the doctor, your next dose is in four hours. However, your mother did make some delicious porridge," Cody suggested as he carried her into the house.

Mrs. Green was waiting at the top of the stairs, clearly exhausted. "How did she get out this time?"

Mr. Green shuffled out of her bedroom and scratched his thinning blonde hair.

"Seems she thought she could fly off the roof," Cody joked.

Shannon scowled at him, but a slight smile could be seen at the corner of her mouth.

"No snarky remark?" Cody asked in surprise. "All right then, off to bed with you."

Mrs. Green shook her head as she returned to her bedroom. Again, Cody tucked Shannon into bed, only this time she didn't turn away from him. Instead she watched him leave the room.

The next night, Cody knocked on Shannon's door after a day of quiet rest.

"Come in!" she answered.

When the door opened, she appeared surprised to see Cody arrive with her medications and a tall glass of water.

"Where's Mom?" she asked.

For a moment, he didn't answer and admired her sitting at the window sill. The orange sunset sky cast a warm glow on her hair that stilled his heart. Quickly brushing this off, Cody entered with her medications and answered, "Your mom is thoroughly exhausted from caring for you. She is sleeping at a neighbor's with your father. Your brother is also exhausted, but is sleeping in the next room. I volunteered to watch over you tonight to give the rest of the family a break from your med-seeking behaviors."

Guilt hung over Shannon in a dark cloud, slouching her shoulders and upturning her brow. Shannon glanced up at Cody inquisitively as he held out her medications and water.

"I'm letting you know right now that this is the only medication you will get until dawn. Are you sure you want to take all of them right now?"

"Yes, I'm sure. My head is pounding and the chills have started," she made her excuses, before ravenously swallowing her pills.

"It will go away over time," Cody said, watching her take the pills. "The doctor says that you should be done detoxing in another four days. That's when the medicine will run out and you'll be back to aspirin for the headaches."

After handing back the glass, Shannon asked suspiciously, "What are you getting out of this?"

Instead of answering immediately, he set the water glass down on her bed stand and surveyed the room. Drawing out the silence, Cody pulled up a chair near the window and sat down next to her. "I'll answer your question only if you answer one of mine."

"All right," Shannon agreed.

Leaning forward in his chair, Cody asked, "Why did you start doing drugs?"

Now it was Shannon's turn to draw out the silence. For a while she gazed out the window at the full moon. "I used to have nightmares, terrible nightmares. In most of them the world burned around me in a hellish fire that consumed every living soul. In every nightmare, I died in the most

366

horrific ways. I felt pain and anguish, as if I had lived many tortured lives over centuries. I couldn't stand waking up, hearing screams and feeling the fire licking my skin. The drugs numbed me from the pain."

Shannon wiped a couple of tears from her face. "Since I've been here, the nightmares have started again. I need the drugs to get a release from the agony. Haven't you ever been consumed by an unhealthy habit just so you could avoid all the pain? Surely with war you've wished for release."

Cody focused on his muscular hands, clasped together. Right now, they were clean, but he could envision the blood that had dripped off them countless times. He knew exactly how she felt— they just had different drugs. The adrenaline rush from killing revitalized him and helped him forget about the painful memories.

"I understand the need for release, Shannon," he finally replied. "However, what gives you a release is slowly killing you. What gives me the release is ... different."

"Hmmm," Shannon nodded. "So why are you doing all this for me?"

A warm smile spread over Cody's face. "Do you believe in fate?"

Shannon tilted her head to the side, "I suppose I could believe in fate."

Cody's black eyes glistened with a purple shine. "Well when I first saw you, throwing red paint at my soldiers, defiantly holding your head high, I was struck. I can't explain why I was so drawn to you. I even tried to dismiss the feeling altogether. Yet still I was pulled towards you, similar to a paper clip to a magnet. The longer I am around you, the more the world makes sense. The need to satisfy my own cravings subsides and I start to feel a hint of what peace could be."

A single tear rolled down Shannon's face. "I've been resisting it, but I have to admit I feel the same way."

Cody's heart skipped a beat as euphoria washed over him. Perhaps this time he had actually broken through her strong outer wall and into her heart and memories. But his elation was instantly broken by a blood-curdling howl that rose up to the moon.

Shannon peered out the window curiously to see two large wolves dart across the field towards the shadows. "Wolves?"

Cody leaned over her close enough that he could smell her intoxicating aroma. The stink of drugs and detox had mostly gone, allowing her blossoming natural scent to dominate.

Cody's blood ran cold when he recognized, "These are not mere wolves."

"What?" Shannon asked, confused.

Too preoccupied to bother with her questions, he darted out of the bedroom, slamming the door shut behind him.

Roger was already in the living room, loading his shotgun. "Damn wolves won't get our cattle today," he grumbled.

Much to Roger's surprise, Cody grabbed the shotgun out of his hand and emptied the shells. "This will do nothing to them."

"What?" Roger asked, baffled.

Another howl cut through the night, lifting the hairs on the back of Roger's neck. In response, Cody ran over to his military rucksack, left leaning against the staircase, and rifled through it. "Those are werewolves, and they are not after your cattle. They are here for you and your sister." Cody pulled out a pistol and loaded it with silver bullets.

"But … but … werewolves are banned from America! They're illegal!" Roger objected.

"All it takes is one to wander in, and then it is far too easy to create a pack from there," Cody explained coldly as he finished loading the pistol and spun the barrel closed.

"Cody, what's going on?" Shannon asked, peeking her head around the corner from the top of the staircase.

"Get back in your room, Shannon!" he yelled up the stairs. In response, Shannon quickly ducked into her room. Cody walked over to Roger, each heavy step emphasizing the seriousness of the situation. Cody handed the pistol to Roger, who shakily took it. Before letting go of the pistol, Cody grabbed Roger's arm and pulled him in closer. "It is your duty to keep your sister safe. Don't let anything enter. Shoot for the heart or head, and shoot true."

Shakily, Roger nodded.

"And don't let them bite you, otherwise you'll have to be put down as well," Cody warned before letting go of Roger and heading towards the front door.

"W-wait! Where are you going?" Roger asked in a panic.

Pulling out a silver machete that glistened in the light, Cody answered, "I'm going hunting for werewolves, of course!"

Too stunned for words, Roger watched mouth agape. As Cody stepped off the porch, common sense returned to Roger, who immediately started shutting all the windows and barricading the door with the living room sofa. Shannon's green eyes peered from the window in her room.

The silver machete grasped tightly in Cody's white-knuckled hands gleamed in the moonlight. Shadows darted around the barn, drawing Cody's attention. Then a shadow padded out of the dark woods toward Cody.

A naked man approached Cody with his hands held up in a nonthreatening manner. He had long black hair tied up in a braid and a dark complexion, with a long scar across his eye that marred his face.

Down on the field, the naked man called out to Cody in Algonquin, "There is no reason for you to wield a weapon against me. I come to speak with you about peace."

"Do you remember me, Dark Moon?" Cody asked in the same language, refusing to let go of his machete.

"Of course I remember you, great one! We first met in the woods behind Legna Manor many moons ago," the man replied, "You are the alpha of those who may change their skin regardless of the moon."

"If you know me, then you must understand the dangerous ground you now tread," Cody said coldly.

"Let us make an exchange. I see no reason for blood to be spilled on this night. We already know you protect a valuable soul that would give us insurmountable power if it were not so precious to you. My pack will respect you by not harming a hair on the one you protect," Dark Moon explained.

"That was not a bargaining chip for you. What is it you want?" Cody asked with a slight snarl.

"As you may know, our numbers dwindle. The human menace has slaughtered our kind without mercy, just as the white man slaughtered my peoples. We seek to rebuild our numbers, our culture, and our defense against the human menace," Dark Moon said, with a sinister glint in his good eye.

"How many?" Cody asked.

"We require all the young and healthy in this town, including the young man in the house you currently protect," Dark Moon requested.

Cody chuckled. "Let me clarify. How many are in your pack currently?"

"That should matter not to you, for we wage no war against you—" Dark Moon responded.

"You waged war with your presence here. Now you have two choices, and only two. Either you all run off to another town that I do not care for and leave this small farming community in peace. Or you all will die by my hands."

"How dare you threaten me!" Dark Moon growled. "You are not in a position to make such threats against us!" On cue, eleven pairs of yellow eyes glowed from the darkness.

"I like my odds," Cody said with a smile. Without warning, he slashed the machete toward Dark Moon's chest.

Dark Moon jumped away in time to save his own life, but not fast enough to avoid the blade entirely. The tip of the machete drew a line of blood across Dark Moon's muscular pectorals. The silver caused the wound to sizzle and smoke. Before Cody could swing again, Dark Moon turned to run to the safety of the forest, ripping out of his human skin as he did so.

Cody ran after the alpha only to be cut off by three others. The first, a white werewolf, leaped onto Cody with claws and fangs bared. Spiraling down, Cody was able to slice through the werewolf's stomach as it flew over his head, spraying blood down on him. The white werewolf fell to the ground, whimpering, its bowels spilled onto the grass, smoking.

Meanwhile, a brown werewolf snapped at Cody's arm, barely missing it. Another black werewolf lunged at Cody's back. In a rapid coil, Cody elbowed the brown werewolf in the jaw as he decapitated the black werewolf and then continued to spin towards the brown werewolf, planting the machete deep in it's heart. As the two werewolves disintegrated, Cody calmly stepped over and plummeted the machete into the injured white werewolf's heart, finishing the kill.

The other eight werewolves circled him ominously, forming a new attack pattern. Dark Moon hung back, instructing his pack during the hunt.

"Who is hunting whom?" Cody smiled devilishly as his eyes burned red. He was ready to ignite the world in a tornado of purple fire, but he felt watchful eyes upon him. Peeking towards the house, he remembered that Shannon and Roger were watching his every move. He couldn't afford to reveal his ultimate powers.

The werewolves took his hesitation as their chance. The largest ran at full speed towards Cody while the others hung back. Cody smiled, ready for the challenge of the pack's best fighter. But as he lunged forward, Cody sensed danger on his left flank. The champion werewolf feinted as the werewolf to his left lunged. Cody spun around in time to catch the gnashing jaws of the hidden werewolf and throw it to the ground by its muzzle. Simultaneously, he was attacked from behind by another werewolf—an immense blow that took Cody to the ground as his machete went into the heart of the first. Heavy claws dug deep into his back. Out of the corner of his eye, Cody saw a black werewolf coming in, its massive jaws wide so as to clamp his head.

Cody poured on every ounce of his immense strength to push off the ground and roll over the werewolf. As he rolled, he brought up the machete he had primed with heat in time to cleanly slice off the advancing black werewolf's head. Then he spun around on the other werewolf, planting the burning-hot bloody machete deep into its throat, slashing deep until the machete pierced its heart.

The dead werewolves smoldered and disintegrated. Before Cody could get back up, a gray werewolf bit down on his shoe and dragged him by his foot. Reflexively, Cody swung his machete again. In the middle of his swing, another gray werewolf jumped and bit down on the handle of the machete. Cody tucked in all his limbs, freeing his hand, but losing the machete. The gray werewolf ran away with the machete into the forest, closely followed by a smaller white werewolf. This left Cody alone with one gray werewolf still dragging him by the foot, and the champion werewolf who had evaded him earlier. Panic rose in his throat as he realized he was missing one. Reeling around, Cody saw the last white werewolf sprinting towards the farmhouse.

"Roger!" Cody called out the alarm, hoping beyond hope that Roger was ready to protect the household.

Meanwhile, Cody splayed his fingers, allowing his claws to pop out. Pulling his legs in tightly, he raked his clawed fingertips across the attacking werewolf's eyes. Letting go, the gray werewolf whimpered. Enraged, the champion werewolf leapt onto Cody.

Cody waited for the split-second when the champion werewolf was over him. In the blink of an eye, he pierced the chest of the champion werewolf with so much speed and power that his clawed hand came out the other side, bloodied and holding the werewolf's heart. The champion werewolf sunk its fangs into Cody's shoulder as it died.

Roaring out more in frustration than pain, Cody heaved the heavy, disintegrating body off of him just in time to face off the gray werewolf, which was now half blind.

Cody heard Roger scream and hoped that the white werewolf hadn't won. Anger escalating, Cody pulled the silver tip off one of his shoelaces and threw it at high speed directly at the gray werewolf. The silver tip pierced through the werewolf's eye socket at such velocity that it exited the other side of its skull. For a moment, the werewolf stood there in shock, as remnants of smoking brain escaped the entrance and exit wounds. Finally, it fell dead to the ground.

Dark Moon, one of the oldest werewolves in America, had already mastered a speed capable of sinking his jaws successfully into Cody's throat while he was distracted with the gray werewolf.

"You will regret killing my pack," Dark Moon growled as he chomped down harder on Cody's throat.

From far away, Cody could hear Shannon screaming out for him, believing him to already be dead. *Not today my dear,* Cody thought, as he drove his burning, clawed hand deep into the belly of the beast. Dark Moon loosened his grip as Cody's clawed hand burned him from the inside out. Soon, Dark Moon was ablaze in a glorious purple fire that reached up toward the full moon.

Cody rolled over and coughed up the blood trapped in his throat as it quickly healed. Realizing he was a bloody mess, Cody ripped off what remained of his shirt and tried to wipe the blood off his healed body as he ran to the farmhouse, yelling, "Roger! Roger, are you okay?"

Stunned to be alive, Roger held the gun tightly in his shaking hands, still pointed at the disintegrating corpse of the white werewolf. Roger was in such terrible shock he didn't hear Cody call. He did hear the sofa barricading the front door being slammed out of the way. Terrified, Roger shot at the doorway, expecting another werewolf.

"Woah, woah, woah!" Cody called out, "Don't waste all my silver bullets! They are a pain to make."

"Sorry," Roger replied, still holding the gun out.

"Put the gun down, Roger," Cody commanded.

Roger, trembling, dropped it.

Slowly, so as not to spook Roger further, Cody bent down and picked up the gun. As he secured the gun in his side pocket, he asked, "Are you okay? Did you get bitten or scratched?"

"No, no," Roger replied shakily as he continued to stare at the disintegrating werewolf.

"You did good, Roger. You would have made a fine soldier, judging by tonight." Cody took another step forward to rest a reassuring hand on Roger's shoulder.

At first, Roger flinched away at the sight of Cody, still bloodied, then relaxed. "Did you get hurt?"

"No, I—" Cody began, before being interrupted by Shannon, who ran over and wrapped her arms around his shoulders. At first, this act of affection startled Cody, but then he relaxed and rested his arms around her.

"I was so scared that you got hurt!" Shannon cried as she clung onto him tightly. "How are you not hurt? I saw the werewolves bite you!"

Both set of eyes were on him, expecting an explanation. So, he told the truth. "If you kill the werewolf that bit you before the next full moon, then the curse of the werewolf goes away." —and then he lied— "Killing the werewolf that bit you will also make the wound disappear."

For a moment, the brother and sister exchanged glances questioningly, but then accepted the explanation. "Thank you, Cody, for protecting us," Roger said, with a slap on the back.

"I couldn't have done it without your help, Roger," Cody acknowledged with a smile.

"Seriously, I'm glad you are okay," Shannon said again as she hugged him tightly.

"I will always come back to you," Cody said warmly. "Now you need to get back to bed. It is important for your recovery."

"Where are you going?" Shannon asked anxiously.

Cody tenderly touched the side of her cheek. "I need to hunt down those other two werewolves before they get the clever idea to come back for revenge."

"Please return safely," Shannon begged.

"I've battled worse things than werewolves," he chuckled— a joke only he found amusing. Realizing they didn't share in his humor, Cody turned to Roger, "I'll give you another loaded gun, just in case."

Roger nodded nervously.

"Now go get some sleep," Cody prompted. He waiting for Shannon to reluctantly head up to her room, and then he bolted outside towards the forest.

In the morning, Mrs. Green was cooking bacon next to the broken window. Mr. Green and Roger were outside, discussing what happened last night. When Shannon made it outside, Cody was sitting on the porch, sharpening his silver machete.

"You're back!" Shannon said excitedly. "By the looks of it, I assume you found the other two werewolves?"

Cody looked up at her with pitch black eyes and a warm smile. "Yes, unfortunately for them. How are you feeling?"

"I'm really tired, but otherwise I feel much better," Shannon said truthfully.

"Well, I'm sure you'll get plenty of more rest today while your brother, father and I go into town to get new window panes," Cody replied, peering down the edge of the blade to check for a smooth cut.

"Can I come with you?" Shannon asked hopefully.

Cody eyed her suspiciously.

"Ugh, I'm not going to run off. I just really need to get out of this house. I'm getting cabin fever in here," Shannon complained.

Cody chuckled, "All right. You can join us. Why don't you go get dressed?"

"Okay!" Shannon exclaimed as she ran back upstairs.

Hours later, she was eating ice cream outside in the warm sun. Her father splurged on some tougher windowpane glass than they currently had. Shannon appeared much happier now that her detox symptoms were wearing off.

Cody enjoyed seeing her smile— a smile that not only lit up a room but also lightened his heart. Watching her smile and laugh gave him a pure joy he couldn't find anywhere else in the world. He wished moments such as these would go on forever. Even Mr. Green smiled in approval of this simple but joyous occasion.

"Martha?" asked a strange female voice, in a surprised tone.

Shannon turned towards the woman who had called her name. She wore a large, floppy sun hat and a tie-dyed long dress with a brown, woven belt. Judging by her many bags, she had come here to do some shopping as well.

"Linda?" Shannon asked. "Linda! It's good to see you!" She ran to hug her old friend.

"Oh my God! I thought you were dead!" Linda said in shock.

Shannon laughed and waved away the thought. "No, just trapped back home in the middle of nowhere. I'm fine, though."

"No, seriously." —Linda held Shannon's shoulders— "How did you survive that?"

"Survive what?" Shannon asked.

Worried about where this conversation might lead, Cody stood up and took a couple of steps towards the two women.

"Didn't you go to Johnny's party?" Linda asked.

"Well, yeah. What of it?" Shannon asked with growing concern.

"How do you not know?" Linda asked in a way that bordering on offensive.

"I think it's time we headed back," Cody cut in.

"What happened, Linda?" Shannon asked again, ignoring Cody.

"Everyone died in that house. Something went wrong and the whole house went up in flames. The fire burnt so hot that barely anything was able to be identified. They couldn't get an accurate body count, but no one who went to that party has been found alive until I found you." Linda hugged Shannon. "I'm so glad that you got out and survived!"

Shannon finally turned to confront Cody. "Did you know about this?"

Not having the strength to lie to her face, Cody remained silent.

This enraged Shannon, who stomped forward and yelled, "Tell me the truth! Did you know about this fire?"

"Yes," he replied through gritted teeth. Both Mr. Green and Roger stood up and backed up toward the truck to give them some space.

"Why didn't you tell me?" Shannon yelled. "Why didn't you tell me that my friends died the night you kidnapped me from that party?"

Cody didn't answer. He couldn't answer. How could he tell her that he didn't bat an eyelash as he killed all of those worthless druggies? How could he reason with her that it was the right thing to lock them in a burning house. He couldn't answer her, because what he did was monstrous.

"Did you ... did you cause that fire?" Shannon asked with disgust on her face.

"You were being taken advantage of by all those people, Shannon!" Cody attempted to defend himself. "I saved you."

Furiously, Shannon pushed him as hard as she could. It frustrated her even more that he didn't budge, so she smacked him hard across the face.

"I would rather be in that house being fucked by every drunk than eating ice cream with a murderer like you! I hate you!" She slapped him across the face again and screamed, "I HATE YOU!"

Cody continued to stare at the ground as Shannon left with her friend, Linda.

"Shannon, come back here," Mr. Green shouted.

"Leave me alone! I'll live my life the way I want! Without murderers like him!" she screamed as she hopped into Linda's car.

Cody didn't move a hair as she drove away. It was true, what she said. He was a murderer who would go on killing. It was his drug of choice, after all, with a craving much stronger than cocaine. If she wanted to kill herself with drugs this time, then fine. He wasn't going to interfere anymore. It wasn't worth it to fight this battle with her, time and again. She was already too far gone this time around. In a sense, he was giving up on her. Maybe next time she won't be such a pain in the ass.

Defeated and angry at himself, Cody returned to the truck with his head held low and hopped in. "Take me back to the farm to gather my things."

"Aren't you going to run after her?" Roger asked incredulously.

"No, he isn't going to," Mr. Green spoke for him. "He already lost the battle."

Without saying another word, both of the men climbed into the front of the truck and drove back to the farm. Cody watched the trees and houses pass him by. In a way, this is how his entire existence had felt. The whole world and all the people in it went about their lives without any conscious thought of him. After all, he was nothing more than a lingering mist. These people lived and died without knowing him or understanding the danger he was to them. No one took the time to question his existence or why he lingered as he did. None, except for *her*. *She* was the only one who even cared about his existence. *She* alone could understand that he meant more to this world than anyone had yet to realize. It was *her* alone that understood how dangerous he could become. Perhaps it was by *her* doing that he would someday meet his own death. One could only hope for such a day when he would be knocking upon death's door, but today was not going to be that day. Today she would probably die, and then be reborn again.

When they finally approached the farmhouse, Cody jumped out of the truck without saying a word and walked over to the barn to gather his things.

"You know, son, we really appreciate all that you have done for this family. Not only helping our stubborn daughter, but we appreciate all the help you have given us around the farm, the money you paid for Shannon's medications, and the repairs to the house. My son also told me how you saved him and Shannon from werewolves. All these reasons and more are why you will always be welcomed."

"That is very kind of you, sir. Where is the nearest bus station?" Cody asked as he quickly tied things together in his military pack.

"A mile and a half down the road. I can drive you down there," Mr. Green sighed. "You know, I said you lost the battle, but that doesn't mean you can't win the war. Shannon is a stubborn one, and I can understand why you wouldn't tell her. Especially if she was struggling to sober up. I have faith that you would have told her at the right time."

Cody remained still as he listened.

"All I'm trying to say is that you shouldn't give up. I can tell there is something special between you two. It requires patience to get to the point where you will both love each other in the way you are hoping. Have some faith, son." Mr. Green walked over and put his hand on Cody's shoulder.

Looking at the hand on his shoulder, Cody said, "She doesn't want to see me. I'm not going to ruin her life, no matter how messed up it is."

"But if you don't interfere, then she'll probably kill herself, won't she? If she keeps going down this path?" Mr. Green added, with concern etched into his brow.

Cody tried to sort out the obstacles in his path and wondered if it was worth it.

"Listen, I know you have been through much more than I have ever known. I can't make you go, son, but I know that you will regret not going to her right now when it means the most. Her friend lives in the Capital

Tower Apartments in Jackson, if you choose to make up with Shannon before she ruins her life further." Mr. Green waited for Cody to respond and appeared disappointed when he didn't. "Well, son, I'll meet you at the truck to drop you off at the bus stop." Mr. Green jingled his keys and walked to the truck. After a few minutes, Mr. Green went back to check on Cody and was shocked to see that Cody had already disappeared, leaving all his belongings behind.

Pushing himself harder than he had ever pushed before, Cody raced as fast as he could through the blur of woods and streets towards Jackson, Mississippi. Fear and guilt struck his heart as he tried to get over his own failures, stubbornness and pain. He should have never faltered in his resolve to keep her safe. For now, she was an incredible danger to herself. This morning, she had taken a heavy dose of detox medications. If she were to take an illegal drug on top of that, it could easily cause an overdose. Now it was a race against fate.

After a few hours on the road, Cody burst through the doors of the Capital Tower Apartments.

"Excuse me, sir! What do you think you are doing?" a greasy, fat security guard barked, standing up from behind the counter. Although he had a night stick on his belt, and pepper spray, it was obvious he had never seen real combat.

Making a beeline for the guard, Cody quickly intimidated the fat man into dropping his pepper spray. As it fell underneath the desk, Cody slammed his hands on the counter and demanded, "I need the apartment number for Linda."

"Linda Barkley?" the guard squeaked. "I can't tell you that. She should have told you the number if she invited you."

Losing what patience he had left, Cody grabbed the guard by his collar and pulled him up onto the desk, ruthlessly pressing the guard's head into the desk. "If you don't tell me that room number, then so help me, I will crush your head on this desk. It'll be as easy as cracking an egg!"

"1512. 1512! Please don't hurt me!" the guard begged.

Cody pushed him behind the desk, where the guard tumbled onto his bag of chips. "Thank you," he said politely. "Where are the stairs?"

Trembling, the guard pointed down the hall. Cody nodded and raced up the stairs.

Fifteen flights later, Cody was bursting through the door of 1512. Much to his surprise, the inhabitants of the room didn't appear the least bit alarmed that a strange man had busted down their door. On the contrary, one of the men, a guy with greasy black hair, merely giggled and pointed, while the two girls chuckled along. The other guy, seemingly the least drugged-up of the lot, kept quiet.

Cody stomped over to the quiet young man and grabbed him by the collar. "Where is Shannon?" The young man didn't respond. His eyes looked dead, as though he was asleep and only appearing awake.

"Who?" said the other man, still giggling.

Throwing the young man to the ground, Cody asked one more time, "Where is Martha?"

Linda, whom Cody recognized from earlier, started to giggle and lolled her head back so it was hanging off the bean bag to invert her view of the world, "She went to the roof to see the stars. I bet they look groovy with all that acid she took."

Cody's heart stopped. Shannon was five floors up. It was dangerous for her to be up there, but he wasn't going to lose her this time. Without a moment to lose, Cody darted to the stairwell.

Shannon's face was wet with tears. The vodka bottle she'd taken up to the roof slipped from her numb fingertips and shattered in a crystal crescendo, the shards lying in psychedelic rainbows that glittered in the sunlight. Shannon bent and picked up one piece of the rainbow glass and walked with it in her palm, listening to its whispers of happiness to come. In her psychedelic state, she heard it promise her glorious rainbows and glitter if she were to merely slide it across her skin.

"Okay," she agreed to the piece of glass cutting her hand as she held it tightly. Suddenly, something hard hit her foot. Woozily, she looked down to see she was at the edge of the rooftop. Finding some comfort in this thought, Shannon stepped up on the ledge. Then, taking the shard of glass, she dug it deep into her arm and ran it from wrist to the crook of her elbow. As the glimmering glass promised, beautiful ribbons of glittery rainbows flowed out of her arm, similar to a magician pulling colored handkerchiefs from his sleeve. Dropping the glass to its death twenty stories below, Shannon watched it with a tearful face as it shattered on the concrete sidewalk.

"Don't do it," Cody said from behind her.

The rainbows faded, revealing the ugly concrete jungle that surrounded her. A look of confusion crossed her face as Shannon's eyes searched nearby buildings, wondering where Cody was.

Cody's heart beat ferociously as he inched closer to her. She was so near the edge that he didn't want to spook her. The image of *her* falling into the volcano in such a manner flashed vividly in his mind. The torment he felt in that volcano was more than he could bear. This time had to be different. "Shannon, stay still," he said in a low voice. "You don't want to jump."

"Caspian?" she asked as she looked over her shoulder, "Is that you?"

His heart stopped as he heard his birth name uttered from her beautiful lips. The wind picked up enough to flutter her long auburn hair toward him. Her sweet aroma called to him, until he smelled the alarming scent of blood. The iron grip of panic seized his heart as he understood how dire the situation truly was.

Shannon tried to turn to see him, but her foot slipped from the concrete and gravity reclaimed her at last. She flailed, knowing it was in vain.

Cody spurted forward with a godlike speed and grabbed her arm, the one she had sliced open, so that she was left hanging over the edge. Shannon screamed in pain. The slick blood coating her arm made it impossible to pull her up, and she was sure to slip out of his hands at any moment. Desperately, Cody pushed himself off the roof and went hurtling down with her toward the unforgiving concrete. As they fell, he gripped Shannon's waist with one arm and flexed his monstrous claws from the other hand to grab hold of a window ledge and stop their fall. Swinging inward while holding her tightly, Cody kicked through a window and catapulted both of them into a bedroom.

Breathing heavily, Cody lay on the floor in front of a bed. Shannon had fallen on top of him, hyperventilating, bleeding profusely and growing steadily weaker as her blood soaked through Cody's shirt.

The door swung open as the greasy-haired man and the two girls peered their heads in to see what had caused the commotion.

"Call an ambulance!" Cody called out.

The man shook his head, "Man, I'm not calling no ambulance. If the cops come up in here and see all thi—"

"Call the ambulance right fucking now before I tear you limb from limb!" Cody screamed. The three suddenly sobered up and scrambled out of the room.

In desperation, Cody tore off his shirt and wrapped the injured arm as tightly as he could. Then he ripped the bottom of his jeans off and created a tourniquet on her upper arm to stop the blood flow. "Why did you do this, Shannon?" he asked through short sharp breaths, fighting tears.

"Because I couldn't live with the pain anymore, Caspian," she said lovingly while putting her hand on his cheek.

The sensation of her touch shook him to his very core. He grabbed her hand and kept it pressed to his face. "Do you finally remember me?"

"In my dreams and in my visions," she whispered, trying to shake away the fuzziness in her head. "I have seen you with green eyes. I saw your love and your dedication. Although I don't know if that love is for me or another."

"Shannon, you must stay with me. You must. You are so close to finally awakening!" The tears finally fell from his closed eyes.

"Don't cry, Caspian," Shannon said, lovingly. "I know you will find me again."

"I'm going to save you, Shannon! You just need to hold on until the ambulance arrives. It should be here any minute," he said, panicked.

"Shh, shh, shh," she soothed. "I'm already dead."

Cody's eyes opened wide in shock as he examined her face and felt her energy waver.

"It seems the drugs have killed me faster than my cutting has," she said, as she looked at her bleeding arm and then back into the gorgeous face of her long-lost lover. "Can we never be together? Is this truly our fate?"

Those words sang in his heart like a lullaby, one he'd never forget. "I promise you that I will never stop, not until this curse has been lifted and we are free to live by each other's side."

"And on that day, I will save you from your curse," she whispered, before darkness consumed her.

"No. NOOO!" Cody screamed in pain as he heard her heart slow. "I can help you!" Hastily, he bit down on his arm until the blood flowed freely into her slightly open mouth. His blood had always been a miraculous life saver and healer of wounds. It had saved many from the brink of death. Why couldn't it save her?

The blood dripped down her throat as the wound healed. At first, her heart quickened and her organs started to move again. Hope filled Cody's chest. Maybe this time would be different. Then everything went horribly wrong: blood gushed from her arm and her organs spasmed angrily. She screamed and began to seize. Realizing his grave mistake too late, Cody held her close to him. Then everything went quiet. Overwhelmed by his grief, Cody numbly watched her entire body burst into millions of tiny purple wisps, leaving him to hold only air. As his arms dropped limply to his side, he watched the millions of tiny purple wisps float out the window and up into the night sky.

"Groovy," he heard the greasy-haired man say. Apparently he thought this was all some cool trip.

Cody wiped the tears from his face. "Did you call the ambulance?" he asked, his voice a monotone.

"Nah, man. She'll be fine. Just let her sleep it off on the bed," he responded.

A dark shadow came over Cody's face as he stood and walked toward the uncomprehending addict, who had no idea death was at his doorstep. Dragging his feet, Cody shoved the druggie aside and went into the living room, where a blue telephone sat on an end table. Numbly he dialed 9-1-1 and held the receiver up to his ear.

"9-1-1 dispatch, what's your emergency?" asked an upbeat female voice.

Lost deep in despair, Cody said the words that would be broadcast to every news station and remembered as the beginning of one of the most horrific events on U.S. soil. "I am going to kill everyone in this building if someone doesn't stop me." Then, without saying another word, he dropped the telephone as the dispatch woman on the other end asked for his location.

The deep red eyes of a monster glared at the others who were too high to help Shannon. Now that Cody had lost everything yet again, he gave in to the dark side … the monster inside of him.

Before the three could even register what was going on, the monster was on top of them, ripping the organs from their bodies—the entrails from Linda, the genitalia from the greasy-haired man and most of his liver, which he forced down his throat. He left the apartment of dying and dismembered people and moved on to the next. Without a human conscience to reason with, the monster was merciless in the way it slaughtered three hundred and sixty-two people in that building.

The SWAT team finally made it there when the monster had reached the second floor. Even with assault rifles and bulletproof gear, those brave men didn't last a minute. As they ran up the stairs, the building's lights went out and death rained down on them before they could bring out flashlights. Shots were fired in the dark without a target to hit. In that stairwell, thirty-six men were slaughtered.

Through the front doors of the Capital Towers Apartments, a lone man in a SWAT uniform ran out, holding his arms above his head. A hundred cops outside, backed up by two helicopters, twenty police cars and three SWAT vans, were focused on this single man in a SWAT helmet that covered his face.

"Remove your helmet and identify yourself!" the shout came from a megaphone.

"I'd like to see you try to contain me." Under the helmet, the monster smiled as his eyes glowed red. Refusing to remove it, he stamped his right foot hard enough into the concrete to create a crack. The ground rumbled, and beneath them all, underground gas lines broke and ignited instantly, shooting purple fire into outlets all over the building and hastening its destruction. The ground beneath the first responders' feet rumbled and cracked as pressure from below expanded into an explosion that blew a crater in the pavement, instantly swallowing everyone in the area as purple fire erupted high into the air. The helicopters fled as the fire quickly incinerated everyone on the ground and expanded to a one-mile radius, in what would come to be called a purple tornado of fire. For ten miles around the epicenter of the fiery tornado there were explosions as gas lines burst and purple fire blew out of fissures in the ground. By the thousands, people screamed and ran to escape what appeared at first to be a natural disaster.

Then, as quickly as it began, it all vanished, leaving behind the massive skeletons of buildings that had been hollowed out by the fire. The only thing left standing in that one-mile radius from the hot site were the blackened steel frames of what used to be buildings. Those closest to the center had been melted into a red puddle of bubbling metal.

Journalists swooped in on helicopters to cover the greatest story of their careers. The haunting footage from that night would mystify and terrify American citizens for decades to come. It was never determined what had started the great underground fire. However, there was one piece of footage saved by a helicopter news reporter who had been able to fly out of the hot site before the fire consumed everything. It showed a building with blood-splattered windows from floors two to fifteen. At the bottom of the building stood a man disguised as a SWAT soldier. Something red glowed from beneath the helmet, moments before the man stomped his foot and fire consumed the town. That man could never be identified, and it was believed that he died in that great fire.

12

THE HIDDEN KILLER

LONDONDERRY, NEW HAMPSHIRE

APRIL 4, 2015

A pair of deep green eyes shifted from side to side suspiciously. The brow furrowed in deep contemplation, followed by a cunning smile. "Aha!" Connor held up a triumphant finger and moved his knight across the chessboard. "Checkmate!"

Morgan held her head in her hand. She was over this game. "Congratulations, you defeated me in six minutes… again." Delicately, she brushed a tight curl from her face to join the rest of her brown hair that was elegantly pulled back in a bun. The sapphire clip in her hair matched her elegant evening gown.

Connor stood up, dressed to the nines in his own well-pressed tuxedo and slicked-back hair. Worry scrunched up his brow, "This shall be one of the most dangerous missions I have ever embarked on— a night that will test my strength and push me to new limits. There might even be a death by the end of the night." With dramatic flair, he gazed out the window, where the sunset was already kissing the treetops.

"Let us play another game of chess to pass the time," Morgan bubbly suggested to distract him from his murderous intent.

"I have beaten you eighteen out of twenty times already, Morgan. I tire of this childish game of strategy," he replied somberly.

"Well, it kept your mind busy enough to prevent you from griping for the past two hours ..." Morgan mumbled to herself and then looked at Connor, who stared out of the window as if it was the last sunset he would ever see. "Oh, come on! Stop being such a drama queen! It's only prom!"

"Prom," he growled menacingly. "A place where boys try to feel their way into girl's dresses. That runt is going to shove his tongue down her throat. I just know it!"

At this point, she'd had about enough of his drama. "Connor, stop this. You are being silly and unrealistic. I'm sure she has kissed many boys already that you don't know about."

Connor gasped, "Don't utter your lies to me, witch, or I'll cut out your tongue!"

Morgan gave him a disgruntled look. "Don't be a tease. You'll turn me on." She gave him a slightly flirtatious smile. "It is just a kiss at the end of the night with Sammy's boyfriend that she's been dating for one month. It is harmless, Connor. Besides, I'm sure you were having sex with women at the age of seventeen."

Lifting his chin regally, Connor answered, "Times were different back then ... and I was fourteen."

"Ha! See!" Morgan pointed at him.

Connor ignored her jest.

Turning to a more serious tone, Morgan walked over and put her arm around him. "Listen, Connor, I know this is going to be tougher on you. It is only natural that you will get possessive of her. Just don't ruin this night for her. Senior prom means everything to a 17-year-old girl."

Sighing deeply, Connor turned around and hugged Morgan. "This past year has been difficult for me," he said, pulling away. "Sammy is growing up. She is spending more time with friends than at home. She is busy at school, in sports and even with these horny boys. I know how teenage boys think. Those lecherous thoughts will get them castrated if they don't watch their hands."

"Connor, it is perfectly natural for Sammy to spend more time with her friends than her guardian. It's part of growing up. It's also natural for her to date boys her own age. You didn't think she would fall in love with you as a teenager, did you?" Morgan asked in a soothing tone.

"Of course not! Our dynamics are far too odd in this life to ever become lovers. I would be happy to be her guardian and protector for the rest of her life. I just loathe seeing these boys eyeing her in the halls at school." Connor scowled.

Morgan rolled her eyes. "And you know you can't interrogate all these boys in your office at school whenever you wish. It is unprofessional and can get you fired from your school counselor position for harassment."

"That doesn't matter. She will be graduating with her high school diploma and her associate's degree this May. Then it is off to university, where she will become a renowned scientist, achieving three PhDs before she reaches the age of twenty-one," Connor said.

"Where she will meet college boys who are even hornier and more forward than high school boys," Morgan added.

"Ugh, how many men must I castrate to ensure her safety?" Connor asked dramatically.

Morgan slapped him across the face. "Stop blowing things out of proportion! Now, this nice young man is going to take Samantha to prom. You will be there to monitor ALL the students and you will NOT interfere. Do you understand?"

Connor nodded his head as if he were a puppy that hat been reprimanded for peeing on the carpet.

"Is he still sulking?" Dorian suavely leaned against the door frame. He wore a white designer suit with a black button-up shirt and a silver tie. His blonde hair was styled similar to Clark Kent's in *Smallville*. Although he would never admit it, Dorian liked dressing up to make all the high school girls swoon over him.

"Obviously," Morgan replied, with a sarcastic hand on her hip.

"Don't worry, old friend!" Dorian said, with a light slap on the back, "If you want to make her truly happy, then you should focus on giving her the best prom night ever!"

A smile crept across Connor's face. "You're right. Thank you, Dorian."

Morgan made a sassy sound of disapproval. "What the hell. I try to talk you down for hours and all it takes is for Dorian to come swooping in ... in that white suit?"

Chuckling, Connor reached over and wrapped his arms around both of them. "Thank you both for helping me keep a level head. I'm so grateful I have kept you with me all these years."

"Aw, you're welcome," Morgan responded, wrapping her arm around his waist.

The doorbell rang.

"The boy," Connor growled as he raced toward the door, speedily undid all the alarms and locks and swung the door open. He might as well have been salivating and growling at the boy, with the way the boy shrank away.

Standing in the door nervously was a tall 18-year-old boy with sandy spiked hair and blue eyes. He wore a traditional black suit with a bright green boutonniere and a green striped tie. In his hands, he held a corsage made of yellow roses. "Um, hello Mr. Roberts ... is um ..."

"Why are you stuttering, boy? A man should hold his chin high and introduce himself properly," Connor lectured.

For a moment, the boy was scared out of his mind. Then, realizing he was being tested, he puffed out his chest and said, "Good evening, Mr. Roberts. My name is Westin. I'm here to take Samantha to prom." Connor glared at him.

Westin lost his resolve and shrank a bit under the pressure of Connor's intense green glare. "If that is all right with you, Mr. Roberts."

"Of course, it's all right," Dorian said, popping into the conversation while patting Connor on the back. "Come on in, Westin, and take a seat. Samantha will be out shortly. Girls take such a long time on their appearance, wouldn't you agree?" Dorian ribbed the boy while ushering him unwillingly into the house. Friendly but with considerable force,

Dorian forced poor Westin to take a seat on one of the black leather couches in the front room.

Connor slithered in, looking venomously at Sammy's prom date. Keeping his eyes fixed on the boy, Connor took a seat directly opposite him. Imitating a villain from a movie, he pressed his fingertips together in front of his chin as though plotting an evil plan. "How long have you been dating Samantha?"

"Um, one month and two days," Westin replied nervously as he watched Dorian stand behind the couch and put his hand down on Connor's shoulder. "Did I, um, do something wrong?"

"Not at all, lad," Dorian replied pleasantly, "Mr. Roberts it ensuring that Sammy remains safe tonight, and I'm here to ensure that you are safe from him."

The boy's blue eyes widened in horror as he gulped deeply.

"What are your intentions for Samantha tonight?" Connor interrogated.

"I, um," Westin pulled at his necktie, "I am going to take her out to eat and then take her to the dance. I just want her to have a good time tonight, sir."

Connor settled deeper into his evil pose. "And if you were given the opportunity to have your way with Samantha?"

"I would do nothing, sir. I promise to keep her safe and will not do anything against her will," Westin replied. His foot and knees started to tremble anxiously.

"Good," Connor said as an evil smile curled upward, "because I'll be watching you, boy. If your hand goes a hair too low to her butt or slips to her breasts, then I will remove one of your balls while you sleep. Do you understand?"

Terrified by the monstrous man in front of him, Westin nodded his head rapidly.

"Not to fret though, son, because Connor will come no closer than thirty feet away at all times tonight, unless you dishonor or harm Samantha in any way," Dorian beamed. The stark contrast between good cop and bad cop was enough to drive any person to hysteria.

Connor broke his intimidating concentration on the boy and turned around to look at Dorian. "Whose side are you on, anyway?"

Dorian and Connor laughed jovially while the boy trembled in his suit.

"Are you giving him a hard time, Connor?" Sammy called out from the top of the stairs.

All of the men got up and raced around the corner to finally see her in a prom dress. Sammy stood at the top of the stairs like a glorious angel on a mountain. Her strapless pastel green dress framed her beautifully with a sweetheart neckline and clung to her perfect form as it rolled over the hips and flowed down to her ankles in a curtain of silk. Starting at her left shoulder, a translucent yellow pastel fabric draped over the shoulder and then melted into the green fabric above the left breast, where it continued to spiral over her right hip, down the back of her leg, finally ending back at her left foot. Upon her feet were golden Roman-style sandals with golden ties that tightly wrapped up her calves to her knees. Part of her hair was pulled up to form a braided crown with flowers woven in. The rest of her auburn hair cascaded down to her mid-back in loose curls. Her makeup was perfectly done to reflect her natural beauty, with mere accents of yellow and green around the creases of her eyes.

They all looked up at Sammy in awe, including Connor, who was blown away by her beauty. It wasn't until this moment that he had actually realized how much she had grown into a woman. When Sammy blushed, Connor realized he'd been staring and averted his gaze to Westin, who was clearly entranced by her beauty as well.

"Westin and I were talking about sports, weren't we?" Connor said, slapping the boy on the back.

Breaking out of his trance, Westin looked dumbly at Connor before getting the hint. "Oh yeah, gotta love those Steelers!"

Connor gave Westin a hidden glare. "So you're a Steelers fan."

"Um, I ..." the boy stuttered.

Laughing lightly, Connor put his arm around the boy. "I jest, I jest. You kids have a wonderful time."

"Oh, Connor," Sammy giggled as she delicately came down the stairs towards Westin. "You look really handsome," she told him, before glancing over at Connor and blushing.

"And you look exquisitely beautiful, Sammy," Westin responded. "Here," he added, opening the clear clam shell that held her corsage. Delicately, he placed it on her wrist.

Sammy admired the flowers for a moment before giving Westin a hug. "It's beautiful, Westin, thank you!"

After they were done hugging, Westin cleared his throat and held out his hand. "My lady."

Feeling like a princess, Sammy took his hand.

"Let's not keep the limo waiting. We have a fun night ahead of us," Westin said and he escorted her out the door.

Before leaving, Sammy glanced back at the trio of guardians, waved her hand like a fan to her face and silently mouthed, "Oh my God!"

Connor chuckled as Dorian waved energetically, "Have fun, you two! We'll see you later!"

The three then calmly watched as Westin politely opened the limo door and escorted Sammy inside before stepping in himself. Once the door was closed, the limo slowly pulled out of the long driveway.

"It sure brings back memories, doesn't it, Connor?" Morgan said with a wistful sigh.

"What?" Connor asked, snapping back to reality.

Morgan gave him a motherly scowl and chided, "Behave tonight, ok?"

"Yeah, yeah," Connor waved her off as he picked up his keys and walked towards the garage.

"Oooh, what are we driving today?" Dorian asked excitedly as he followed Connor. Morgan silently trailed behind both of them.

"Today is a Lamborghini day, my friends," Connor replied as he flicked on the lights to the garage. Over the past three years, the garage had magically grown, thanks to Morgan, to a three-level basement filled with vehicles for every occasion. On the ground level were three motorcycles: a Kawasaki Z1000, a Ducati Multistrada 1200 S Sport and an EBR 1190RS. Included on this level were a Ford F350, a Jeep Wrangler and a Subaru

WRX STI. On the second level, a Corvette Z06, a Pontiac Firebird Trans Am WS6, a Mercedes-Benz SLS AMG and a Lexus LF-A. On the third level, where they ended up, was an array of the fastest cars, including a McLaren MP4-12C, a GTA Spano, an Aston Martin One-77 and a Lamborghini Aventador LP700-4.

"I have to say, the best thing about this decade are the cars," Connor said with a smile.

Dorian giggled with glee as he yelled out, "Shotgun!"

Morgan stamped her foot, "No fair! You called shotgun last time we drove the Corvette!"

Ignoring their squabble, Connor hopped into the driver's seat and adjusted his mirrors. Morgan pouted in the back seat, with her arms crossed. "Come now, Morgan, you can have shotgun on the way back."

Morgan gave a slight smile.

"All right, let's go to prom, guys," Connor said, while putting on sunglasses. With a screech of the tires, he took the car up the ramp to the ground level. The second the garage door was open, Connor put the purring Lamborghini into gear and punched the gas. The car lurched forward at 80 mph out of the starting gate. Connor rolled the windows down to blast AC/DC as he raced through the winding streets of the small neighborhood.

Two hours later, Connor found himself propped up against a wall nearest the punch bowl and dessert table of the high school auditorium. Giant glittery stars and streamers hung high from the ceiling. Near the entrance was a photo booth where some stragglers were now getting their prom pictures taken. Most of the seniors were gathered in the middle of the auditorium facing a large DJ booth that streamed out colorful flashing lights. The whole area vibrated, the bass line of the music doubled by the jumping of a hundred pairs of feet. Among the other teachers, Connor calmly stood and watched Samantha, surrounded by her group of friends.

Westin remained at her side the entire night. He behaved as gentlemanly as he knew how, which was quite disgraceful by Connor's standards. Still

Connor was happy the boy was able to make Samantha happy for tonight.

Connor spotted Dorian whispering into the DJ's ear. Normally Connor could extend his hearing to know what was being said, but with this noise it was damn near impossible.

"Isn't this fun?" Morgan came running over to get a drink. She was breathing heavily from all the dancing, "Will you join me in the next dance?"

"I do not dance," Connor responded.

"Of course you do," Morgan said, catching her breath, "I've seen you dance with *her* many times."

"I only dance for *her*," Connor calmly replied.

Dorian cut in right at that moment. "Morgan, may I have this next dance?" he asked properly, with a low bow, while extending his hand.

"Why of course," she said, with a curtsy.

Eagerly, Dorian took her hand and led her onto the dance floor just as the song ended. They readied themselves for the next one, and an excited smile grew on Morgan's face as she heard the first few beats of "Sing Sing Sing." Instantly, they both jumped into a swing dance from the 1950's.

The crowd of high school seniors gathered around for what they believed was a show put on for them by the school. All wowed in wonder as Dorian flipped Morgan around. Even Connor was impressed by their moves and tapped his toes to the beat.

From the side, Connor felt a fast-approaching force he hadn't encountered in quite some time. The next thing he knew, Peter was by his side, breathing heavily and standing out like a sore thumb among the finely dressed prom-goers. The pockets of his dark brown cargo pants were bulging with gadgets and weapons. His dark green shirt had two large holes in the back and needed a good wash. Two rusty brown messenger bags were slung over each shoulder. His rugged face and messy, sandy hair added to his disheveled look. Nonetheless, it was good to see Peter back from his last mission.

Peter suddenly realized what was going on and sat, mouth agape, watching Morgan. "Is that my Morgan?"

394

"Yes, it is," Connor said with a smile. "Why don't you go clean yourself up and you can have the next dance with your wife."

Peter scowled, "Has Dorian been keeping his mitts off my wife?"

"If you are so concerned, then maybe you shouldn't run off so often," Connor jested.

Not appreciating the joke, Peter made a quick comeback. "I would love to spend more time with her if my slave driver didn't send me on so many missions halfway across the world while he kept my wife next to his side."

"I'm sorry, Peter. Why don't you take the night off to enjoy Morgan's company? She does look spectacular tonight," Connor suggested.

As the song ended, the whole auditorium applauded. Dorian and Morgan bowed and made their exit from the dance floor. Seeing Peter, Morgan's face lit up and she ran into his arms. They held each other and kissed passionately as the next song started, a slow dance that gathered couples under a cascade of blue lights.

It pulled at Connor's heart, watching Sammy dancing so closely with a boy. He had seen her with many men in the past, but this time was different. This time he had created a permanent bond with her that could only be developed over years of love and communication. This time his love for her had deepened in a way he'd never imagined. This time she brought out his human side. This time he would give anything to see her smile.

Connor was brought out of his conflicting thoughts by Peter, speaking in Latin: "Master, I have some important and sensitive information to tell you."

"Oh, well, it must be important if you are using a dead language," Connor responded in Latin.

"As I said, it is quite sensitive information."

Connor looked over at Dorian and Morgan, whose demeanor had become more serious. This must have something to do with the recent errand. After a moment's thought, Connor responded in English, "We will discuss this later."

"But Master!" Peter continued in Latin, "This requires your immediate attention. It's about Kaeda."

"Kaeda?" Connor asked, shocked.

An audible gasp alerted Connor through the pounding beat of the music. Immediately his attention snapped over to Sammy. What he saw, frozen in time, stopped his heart.

Sammy clutched weakly to Westin's suit jacket, her head tilted back and her eyes rolling to the back of her head. Westin was trying his best to hold onto her, but losing his grip.

Before Sammy could hit the floor, Connor ran to catch her. "Sammy! Sammy!" Connor yelled. She gave no response and fell unconscious.

Morgan and the teachers started clearing the area. Dorian grabbed hold of Westin and dragged the boy away as he cried out for Sammy. Though Westin cried out tearful apologies for an incident that wasn't his fault, Dorian still ushered him away from Connor.

Urgently, Connor lowered Sammy flat to the ground and immediately checked her vital signs. Her breaths were slow but steady, her heart rate irregular but strong. Quite contrary to Connor, who was breathing rapidly and had a heart rate that was through the roof. If he had been human, he would surely have been on his way to a heart attack. Tears burst from his green eyes as he continued to check her while the ambulance was on its way. Although chaos erupted around him, Connor could hear only her raspy breathing and see her sleeping face, drifting off to a world of dreams.

* * *

CONCORD, NEW HAMPSHIRE

APRIL 5, 2015

Sammy weakly opened her eyes to a blinding white light. In the distance she could hear the beeping of medical equipment. Her fingers felt stiff, as if they hadn't moved in a while, but when she tried to move her arm, she found it restrained. Oxygen flowed through a breathing tube inserted in her nose. She started to panic and heard the beeping increase in response. Blinking again, she tried to better see the world. Fluorescent lights strained her eyes, but they soon adjusted. She was in a hospital room, strapped to a bed.

Connor sat in the corner of the room, holding his head in his hands. When he noticed Sammy stirring, he raced to her side and spoke soothingly. "Hello, Sammy. How are you feeling?"

"Like shit," she croaked.

Morgan raced into the room upon hearing Sammy's voice. In her hand she held a cup of water. "Sammy! We were so scared! Don't ever do that to us again!" Morgan cried, smearing her makeup.

Sammy tried to reach for the water cup but was stopped by the restraints. Connor realized this and cut the soft restraints off her wrist, explaining, "You kept unconsciously pulling your tubes out, so they had to create a gentle way to stop you."

Morgan handed the water over to Sammy, who drank greedily. Once the cup was empty, Sammy held it out to Morgan. "More please."

"Yes, of course!" Morgan wiped the tears from her face and raced out of the room.

A second later, a nurse walked into the room. "Ah, good to see you finally awake! How are you feeling, sweetie?"

"Like shit," Sammy repeated with a slightly clearer throat. "What happened? What about Westin? He is probably furious at me."

"I'll let your dad fill you in on that," the nurse responded. "Do you know what date it is?" Multitasking, the nurse documented Sammy's vitals and her answers.

"April. … Crap," Sammy responded, holding her head. Morgan came running in and handed the water cup over to Sammy.

"What year is it?" the nurse asked.

"2015?" Sammy responded after drinking another full cup of water.

"Can you tell me your birthday?" the nurse asked.

"Why am I in the hospital?" Sammy demanded, her voice hoarse.

"We are trying to figure that out, Sammy," Connor said, trying to be comforting. "You see, at prom … you fell."

"I fell?" Sammy asked in disbelief.

"You've been unconscious for ten hours," the nurse cut in. "We ran all the tests. The doctor will be in to speak with you about the results and treatment."

"I fell?" Sammy asked nervously, "At prom? That is so embarrassing! Did everyone see?"

Connor and Morgan exchanged eye contact before Connor answered, "Yes, you fainted on the dance floor, near the end of a slow song. Westin helped to ease your fall and I caught you before you hit the ground."

"And everyone saw me?" Sammy amped herself up.

"Yes, they did, but that is why you have so many gifts," Morgan added, pointing to the corner of the room, which was piled with gifts, flowers, cards and teddy bears.

"You are important to a lot of people," Connor added, "and Westin has been calling your cell phone every hour to find out if you are okay. I dare say the boy hasn't had a lick of sleep all night."

"Aww, can I call him back?" Sammy asked eagerly.

"Good morning, Samantha," said the doctor who entered with a cheerful disposition. "My name is Dr. Stanisby. It is a pleasure to meet you, even under these circumstances."

"Good morning," Sammy greeted, while weakly shaking the doctor's hand.

"What's the diagnosis?" Connor asked eagerly.

The smile fell from the doctor's face as he pulled out a clipboard from under his arm. As he leafed through the papers, he told them the grave news. "After running multiple blood tests, we were able to isolate the cause of your fainting spell, which relates to your recent complaints of nausea, fatigue and anemia." —The doctor lowered the clipboard— "I'm so sorry, but you have acute myelogenous leukemia. It's a very serious disease. Luckily, we have an array of treatments to offer. But it is important to start chemotherapy as soon as possible."

The doctor continued, but his voice faded into the background as Connor's heart sank to the bottom of his stomach. Connor honed in on the minute details of her face, wanting to record every detail of her smile and the light of her innocent green eyes. "Is it curable?"

The doctor paused. The look on his face told the story. Success rates for this type of leukemia at the stage she was at weren't great, but he didn't have the heart to tell them at this moment. "We can treat it, but it will require an aggressive regimen."

Connor looked at her perfect, beautiful, tear-streaked face one more time before closing his eyes and walking out of the room. He couldn't hear any more. It was too much to bear. As Connor walked out of the room and down the hallway, he thought back to all the times that she had died, and the times he had managed to make it less terrible for her. This time, there was nothing he could do at all. The enemy wasn't a human or beast he could kill. He couldn't rescue her from a height, or a blade, or even drowning. The killer was in her body. He couldn't save her. This thought struck him hard. Weakness broke him down and tore Connor down to the floor. He wept with his face pressed against a sterile white hospital wall.

* * *

LONDONDERRY, NEW HAMPSHIRE

APRIL 14, 2015

"What do you mean, you can't do anything?" Connor screamed at Morgan from across the kitchen counter. In the middle of chopping vegetables for the beef stew, Connor pointed the tip of the blade accusingly at Morgan. "I know you have plenty of spells to heal the body and prevent ailments. Don't give me this crap!"

Morgan's face was tear-stained. "Caspian, you know full well that magic doesn't do shit for her! You can't prolong her life any longer than I can."

Angrily, he swiped all the vegetables into the pot of boiling broth with the knife. "Prove it to me, then. Prove that it can't be done."

Morgan slammed her fist down on the counter, breaking the marble counter top and cracking the cupboards underneath. "You are not listening to me! It is a waste of magic and could hurt her more than help her. You of all people know that for every spell you cast, there is a cost. What would you pay for a spell that would only do damage to her?"

"I would give up everything to make her live!" Connor yelled as he flung the knife at her head, "Unlike you!"

Morgan dodged the flying blade and looked vehemently at Connor.

"You are going to fix that counter top, and then you are going to march upstairs and rid Sammy of her cancer!" Connor yelled.

Glaring at him, Morgan slowly and seriously explained, "I cannot get rid of her cancer through magic. You will have to do it through medicine."

Defeat washed over Connor as he slid down to the floor and wept on his knees. Snapping her fingers, Morgan was able to restore the counter top. Then she made a circling motion with her pinkie finger as the knife came out of the wall and slowly floated towards the kitchen sink, while the hole magically repaired itself. Then she sat down next to Connor and put her arm around him. "I'm so sorry. I can't imagine how you must feel. Remember when Samantha got her soccer injury? My magic couldn't heal it no matter how hard I tried. In the end, she had to heal naturally with the aid of western medicine. This time won't be any different. Best-case scenario, nothing happens. Worst-case scenario, it speeds up the disease and kills her faster. We can't rely on my magic."

"I have never felt so hopeless in my entire life," Connor sobbed as he attempted to wipe the tears from his eyes.

"I've never seen you cry this much," Morgan said.

A darkness shadowed his eyes. "That's because I am more human today than I have ever been … and I hate it. I've been so tempted to give in to my dark, monstrous side. To do so would give me the sweet release I so desperately crave. It would also make me numb to this … emotion, and that's what I need, desperately."

"You know you can't do that, Caspian." Morgan forced him to look into her calm hazel eyes. "Sammy needs you right now as you are. Cutting yourself off from your emotions would only alienate her. I know you don't want to do that."

"Then what can I do?" Connor raked his hands through his hair.

"What about giving her your blood? It has healing properties," Morgan suggested.

Connor groaned, "Every time I tried to give *her* my blood, it only expedited *her* death and caused *her* greater pain than if I hadn't."

"Right," Morgan said, determined. "Then the only option is to send her to the best medical facilities in the nation. She is the owner of Valda Enterprise. I'm sure she can get the best treatments available through the company's infinite connections."

"What if those don't work?" Connor asked, feeding his own downward spiral.

"Don't think that way," Morgan responded optimistically. "With the best medicine money can buy, Sammy will get better and live a long life. You just have to support her and love her through this arduous journey."

Connor's face brightened. "Thank you. I'm glad I kept you around."

Connor and Morgan were alerted by a peculiar buzzing sound. In the blink of an eye they were racing upstairs to Samantha's room. Startled, they halted in the doorway of the bathroom. Long locks of Sammy's hair lay lifeless on the ground, the glowing auburn color was illuminated by the bright light in the white-tiled bathroom. Only half of Sammy's head was shaved at this point, and it looked quite awful. With a couple isolated tears running down her face, Sammy turned to face Connor. Morgan gasped at the beautiful, intricate orange markings that made up the birthmark on her skull. A magnificent phoenix stretched its wings along the back of Sammy's head, wrapping around to form a crown. The long tail feathers swooped down playfully to land between the crests of her shoulder blades. Connor smiled when he realized that Morgan had never seen *her* birthmark before. In fact, Sammy had never seen the full markings that wrapped around her skull either. In another life *she* had called them the markings of destiny.

"Wh … wh … why are you?' Morgan stuttered.

Sammy held the buzzing electric razor in her hand and said boldly, "I have control over my own life! I have control over when my hair will fall out! I have control over whether I live or die … and I choose to live."

"I'm so proud of you!" Connor said, with dampened green eyes. "How about I help you even it out?"

Smiling from ear to ear, Sammy handed him the razor and turned to face the mirror.

* * *

NEW YORK CITY, NEW YORK

MAY 7, 2015

"I win again!" Sammy squealed as she slid all the poker chips into her lap. Connor and Dorian sat on opposite sides of her hospital bed, holding two cards in their hands. Despite the grimness of the hospital room and its various machines hooked up to Sammy, the trio appeared bright. Even Sammy's sunken face looked cheerful despite her condition. It was her optimism that had kept them all going through this ordeal in the past month.

"Are you cheating, Sammy? I think you are cheating," Dorian joked.

Sammy stuck out her tongue as she stacked her poker chips, just to mock him.

"Mr. Roberts," the doctor announced, sticking his head in the room. "Can I have a word with you?"

"Of course, doc!" Connor said brightly. As he stood up, he kissed the top of her bald head and softly rubbed the back of it, where the magnificent orange birthmark of a phoenix wrapped around her skull.

402

Connor calmly walked outside the room with the doctor and stopped in front of the small window.

"Let's stack the deck so Connor loses horribly," Dorian whispered maniacally.

"Shh." Sammy held up a finger to her lips. Dorian did as he was asked, giving Sammy a chance to hear some of what the doctor was saying. It was hard to make out until Connor threw his hands up in the air and started screaming.

"I can't believe you! You are a man of medicine who follows the Hippocratic Oath. How dare you tell me there is nothing you can do! Do you realize how much goddamn money we have poured into these chemo treatments?"

The doctor responded softly enough so Sammy couldn't hear.

"Other hospitals? Other hospitals? You are a fucking cancer center! Shouldn't you have all the best treatments for cancer?" Connor screamed.

All of a sudden, a slew of hospital guards were standing around Connor and the doctor. Once Connor realized the gravity of the situation, he started to calm down. He looked through the small window at Sammy, who gave him a small smile of encouragement. The doctor continued to talk about other options, which Connor was only half paying attention to. His desire to slaughter all the men in that hallway was greatly outweighed by his need to get Sammy feeling better. In order to not have her blacklisted from other hospitals, Connor had no choice but to play nice.

"Fine, I guess we will try the Mayo Clinic, then," Connor responded, obviously defeated.

* * *

ROCHESTER, MINNESOTA

JUNE 18, 2015

Sammy's lungs were dry and tired from coughing. Every cough made her anxious that blood would come spilling out onto her pillow. She took a gulp of water in hopes that it would calm her throat, which had been sore ever since she started vomiting up bile on a daily basis. Although she knew better than to hope, it was all she had left to hold herself together. At this point, she was the only one who appeared to still hold onto hope.

Connor was worsening as weeks went by without improvement. On the surface he remained calm, but Sammy could see his smile growing more and more fake with each chemo treatment. His angry outbursts happened a couple times a day. Mostly, he just vented to Dorian and Morgan, but sometimes it was directed at a nurse or doctor. In fact, Dorian and Morgan had both suffered burnout from trying to reel in Connor's anger over the past few weeks. Now they took turns monitoring him so the other could go out and decompress. Sammy wondered when they would stop coming at all. At what point would they give up on him?

Though these outbursts never occurred in her hospital room, it was impossible to screen out the desperation in his voice from down the hall. Sammy wondered what would become of him when she died. Would he die as well? Would he be consumed by his own grief and give up completely? These thoughts swam through her mind as she pretended to sleep, fighting the urge to vomit when the bile climbed up her throat. This was a fate she would never wish upon anybody, not even her worst enemy.

The door opened silently and shut just as softly. With her eyes closed in feigned sleep, Sammy guessed whether it was a nurse, Dorian or Morgan who had come to check up on them. She heard Connor stand up from his chair in the corner. The same chair he occupied every day and every night. Once again, he was back to sleepless nights. Yet the lack of sleep didn't appear to hinder him at all, similar to when his eyes were purple.

"Wie geht's?" a male voice asked softly in German. Sammy didn't recognize the voice, and part of her wanted to peek and see who it was, but the other part of her knew that it would be easier to eavesdrop if she continued to feign sleeping.

Sammy's ears perked up and listened intently to the German. It had been months since she had practiced German. Any practice she could get was always a plus.

"Peter, I didn't expect you to stop by," Connor whispered in German. "She isn't improving, but at least she's alive." Connor gave Peter a weak smile.

Peter looked over at her with his ancient blue eyes that didn't match his youthful appearance or his muscular build. Although his sandy hair was still messily sticking out at all angles, he had at least cleaned up to come to the hospital. He wore designer jeans from Italy with bedazzled pockets and black suede shoes. Instead of wearing a shirt, he wore a jacket that could easily be removed for when he needed to take flight. The jacket was lovingly designed after his favorite comic-book character, Deadpool. A jacket he only zipped up halfway in his haste to sneak into the hospital through the roof. He took off both of his tattered messenger bags and lowered them softly to the ground before giving Connor a tight hug.

"I was asking about you, the stubborn dinosaur who refuses to die," Peter joked quietly in German.

"There are many times I wished for death," Connor said, depressed. "If only fate wasn't so cruel."

"Stop your pity party! No one else was invited," Peter joked as he picked up her new set of get-well cards and read through them.

"Why are you here, Peter? I didn't call on you," Connor grumbled with slight disdain.

Peter held up a humorous card. "This one is pretty good. Maybe I should go into writing get-well cards."

Connor impatiently stared at Peter.

Taking the hint, Peter awkwardly cleared his throat and answered Connor's question. "It was convenient for me to come. I have really been needing to talk to you for quite some time, and the other followers are all but worn out from dealing with you."

"You will have to wait. I don't want to hear of your errands until after she is better," Connor replied, as he looked longingly over at Sammy, who appeared to be sleeping soundly.

Peter continued in German, "Master, I understand that you are going through a lot right now. I have tried to give you space and time, but things are moving quickly and I must relay this information to you."

Connor's long silence gave Peter the permission he needed.

Peter leaned in and whispered, "Master, your activities with these hospitals have gained you much attention. You are being watched very closely. It won't take long for them to put all the pieces together and discover who you really are."

"Then *they* will learn *they* can't do anything to me except anger me further. If *they* are smart, then *they* will stay away from me. You can relay that message to Langley, can't you?" Connor asked with a sinister glare.

Peter bit down on his lower lip, hesitant to say more. "It is getting to a point where I no longer have the influence I used to. You know how greedy these politicians are, especially now with all the heat in the Middle East. The U.S. government will use whatever leverage they can spare."

"Is that all you wanted to tell me?" Connor asked, clearly minimizing the importance of this warning.

"No," Peter continued in Latin, "Kaeda's priestess had a vision of you. It isn't safe for me to release all the details to you here, but just know that time is running out. This may be your chance to … you know … fulfill the prophecy."

"I can't abandon Sammy for either of those concerns… not now," Connor returned to German.

Peter also returned to German, "Regardless, you have been requested to speak in person in Japan, which will get you out of the US cross hairs."

"Well both will have to wait. I can't leave her side now." Connor stood up and checked on her vital signs, glowing on the screen. Then he whispered in Latin, "The doctors say she doesn't have long left. Maybe a month. I will come in person after she departs."

Concerned, Peter knelt down on one knee and took Connor's hands in his own, as though he was about to propose. "Master, know that when she passes, I won't leave your side, no matter the hellfire."

No longer could he hold back the tears. Connor clung tightly to Peter and cried into his shoulder. "I don't know what to do anymore, Peter," he cried in English.

Peter rubbed his master's back like a mother would soothe a child. "There is another option, Master. They are currently doing experimental research on people with her cancer in Utah. It could be her last chance to beat this disease."

"I don't know if I can stand to hear those words from the doctor again: 'There's nothing more we can do for her.' Western medicine is pathetic," Connor sniffled and wiped his nose.

Peter pulled away and put a reassuring hand on Connor's shoulder. "Have faith, Master."

Sammy rolled over in bed to face away from them and silently cried into her pillow.

* * *

SALT LAKE CITY, UTAH

JULY 4, 2015

Hundreds of fireworks lit up the Wasatch Front in celebration of Independence Day. From high up on the east bench of the valley, Connor, Morgan, Dorian and Sammy watched the breathtaking festivities light up the night sky.

Sammy leaned forward in her wheelchair as she watched from the massive hospital windows. The brilliant phoenix birthmark on the back of her skull radiated with the same vigor and strength that Sammy had been using to fight this leukemia. "Isn't it magnificent!" she said, admiring

407

the fireworks.

"It truly is," Connor responded, somberly. Her health had taken a turn for the worst. Sammy's flesh had withered to the point of being a living skeleton, too weak and frail to walk on her own. Dark purple circles around her eyes and the sunken cheeks added to the appearance of impending death. The doctors said she didn't have long, but she fought on. She hoped for a healthier tomorrow, even when all others had lost hope. Even in her diminished state, Connor saw her as the most beautiful person in the world … because she was to him.

As in any other precious moment, Connor wished this one would never end. He wanted this one in particular to be endless because then there would never be a death to follow. If he could reverse time, maybe he could erase all this pain and misery.

"Connor," Sammy said, turning around to face him. Her brilliant green eyes reflected the fireworks. "I don't feel well. Can you take me to bed?"

"But you'll miss the rest of the fireworks," Dorian reminded sweetly.

"It's all right, we will come back and see the fireworks on another day," Connor said, picking her up from her wheelchair and cradling her in his arms. Sammy was so skinny that only children's clothes fit her at this point.

The love Connor felt for the girl he raised was reflected in the way he kissed her smooth, bald forehead. The sorrow he felt for the cancer patient in his arms was visible in his watery green eyes and furrowed brow.

Sammy peeked up at Connor with wet green eyes and a warm smile. "I love you, Caspian," she whispered up to him.

Fear clutched his chest. The only time *she* had ever used his real name was right before she died. "I love you more than you know," he said to hide the fear.

A single tear rolled across her shallow cheek as she closed her eyes. Then her body started to tremble and seize, to the point that Connor had trouble holding onto her. Panic choked Connor up, making him unable to talk. Since she was about to fall out of his arms, Connor purposely fell backwards to the ground and then rolled over to gently sprawl her out on the ground. Dorian ran and pressed the emergency red button overhead, which called for a code blue. Morgan ran to Connor's side and helped keep Sammy on her side so she didn't choke on her own vomit.

"Stay with me, Sammy! Don't die on me now!" Connor screamed as tears streamed down his face.

Within seconds of pressing the button, a team of nurses, physicians and interns came rushing in with a crash cart. One of them pulled Connor off of Sammy so the rest could get to her. Seeing how the nurse struggled, Morgan assisted in pulling Connor away to give the life support personnel enough room. He cried out for Sammy, a cry that was drowned out by the rushed orders called out by the medical professionals who were fighting to save her life. Soon, he could no longer see Sammy, as she was surrounded by white coats and scrubs.

Several hours later, Connor sat in Sammy's hospital room with his head leaning against Morgan's shoulder. His green eyes were vacant and fatigued. Pulling up jokes and images from her phone, Morgan tried her best to lighten Connor's spirits as they waited to hear from the doctor. Dorian worked on another drawing for Sammy, since had grown quite fond of his drawings and would tape them up to hide the plain white hospital walls.

Before the door was fully open, Connor was on his feet and wringing his hands expectantly. The doctor walked in, grimly noticing Connor's high anxiety. The way the doctor held her breath only made his anxiety rise further.

"We were able to stabilize Samantha," she said. "She is recovering and will be transported to this room in a couple hours."

"Oh, thank God," Morgan sighed. Dorian also sighed with relief.

Connor however, noticed the concern in the doctor's face. "What is it, doctor?"

She looked away for a moment, then looked down. "Why don't you take a seat, Mr. Roberts."

Simultaneously, Connor's heart sank and fired up. "I don't want to sit down. Whatever you can tell me, you can tell me standing up!"

"Since you have a history of verbal aggression. I would appreciate it if you could please sit down," the doctor said authoritatively, still not giving him eye contact.

Morgan pulled on Connor's shirt, forcing him into the chair. Reluctantly, he sat on the edge of his seat.

The doctor took a long, deep breath before delivering the bad news. "Samantha's condition has worsened. We must stop experimental treatments. She is far too weak for them anymore. All that we can do now is make her as comfortable as possible."

Connor remained silent. His eyes widened in shock.

Taking this moment of silence, the doctor lifted up her clipboard and continued, "I see that Samantha doesn't have any advanced directives filled out. Now might be a good time to make sure everything is in order for ..."

"NO!" Connor yelled as he stood up. "Absolutely not! I'm not filling those out because Sammy isn't going to die. She is going to live a long fucking life. Do you hear me? Just because you have given up doesn't mean that she has!"

"Connor!" Dorian ran forward and grabbed his arm. "Maybe you need to take a break." Morgan also stood up, ready to restrain Connor if the situation called for it.

Pulling his arm away from Dorian, Connor pointed a sharp finger at the doctor. "She is not going to die, do you hear me?"

On cue, the door opened behind the doctor, revealing ten men in scrubs and security uniforms.

"Oh, you think you can scare me with your show of support? Bring it!" Connor screamed.

This time both Morgan and Dorian wrapped Connor's arms behind him. Even with their combined strength, it took all their effort to restrain him.

"Connor, stop this! Think of Sammy!" Morgan admonished, knowing that Connor would happily tear apart every soul in his way until he returned to Sammy— a fact the hospital staff didn't know.

Luckily, Connor did simmer down.

Finding her voice again, the doctor informed him, "We understand that

410

everyone grieves in different ways. Which is why we have decided to not let you see Sammy until you have spoken with our on-site psychiatrist."

"What?" Connor growled, "You would keep me from her?"

"Yes," the doctor nodded, but still took a couple of steps away for safety. "Judging by the impulsive and aggressive behavior you have displayed, not only at our hospital but others as well, we feel you could be harmful to Sammy. Before you can see her again, we advise that you speak with our trained psychiatrist, who specializes in helping grieving parents. Only after she has signed off will you be able to see Samantha again. My team here will guide you to her office."

"How dare you accuse me of putting her in danger," Connor said with pain in his voice, "I would never harm a hair on her head."

The doctor held tightly onto her clipboard as if it gave her protection. "Even so, your aggressive behavior might cause her unnecessary stress that could push her over the edge. If you truly care for Samantha, then you will process your emotions so you don't stress her out and kill her faster."

Having been soundly defeated, Connor sank to the floor in a pitiful lump of his own sorrow. Slumping, he stared at the white tiles on the floor. "Can the rest of her family still stay by her side?"

"Yes, her aunt and uncle can stay with her, so long as you visit the psychiatrist," the doctor confirmed.

"All right, I'll go talk with the psychiatrist," Connor agreed, falling into despair. He looked back up at his two most loyal followers. "Please give her as much comfort and love as you can. I will be by her side as soon as possible."

"She is in good hands," Morgan comforted.

"We will see you soon," Dorian said, smiling ruefully.

Connor took note of the men surrounding the doctor. "All right, take me to the psychiatrist."

"Right this way," one of the men wearing scrubs instructed.

Connor stood up and followed them as if he were a prisoner on death row. Passersby in the hall quickly ducked into side rooms and hallways to let the crowd of men surrounding Connor walk through. Connor had never been so humiliated in his life. Sammy was at death's door and he was being forced apart from her by the institution he was paying to keep her alive. How insufferable people had become, guarded by their belief that rules and regulations will save their lives. How he hated them all and wished all of humankind a fiery death.

After passing through many twisting halls and taking two elevators down, they finally reached an isolated door at the end of the hallway. Without raising a question, Connor walked through the doorway as if he were a cow ushered into a slaughterhouse.

From inside the room, the therapist greeted him. "Good morning, Mr. Roberts. My name is Dr. Powers. It is nice to meet you, even under these dire circumstances. Please take a seat."

Then the door closed.

13

UNRAVELING AT THE SEAMS

SALT LAKE CITY, UTAH

JULY 19, 2015

Sammy awoke to the warm touch of Connor's hand caressing the side of her face. But when she opened her eyes, she was shocked to see his eyes had changed to pitch black. Startled by the change, Sammy gasped and pulled away from him. "What happened to you?"

Ashamed, Connor closed them and turned away. Morgan sat in the background. She, too, was ashamed of the change in his eye color.

"I'm sorry," he apologized as he put some sunglasses on.

The machines started beeping madly in response to Sammy's heart rate dramatically increasing. "Why are your eyes black? Did you kill someone? Is that why you were gone for two weeks? Two weeks, Connor! What the hell were you doing for two weeks?"

"Sh, sh, shhh," Connor soothed as he embraced her tightly in a hug. Sammy clutched onto him and cried into the new black t-shirt he'd picked up from Walmart on the way back to the hospital. The nurses rushed into the room to assess the situation and were surprised when they found that she wasn't in medical distress. Connor waved them away, and they left reluctantly, with suspicious looks.

"I'm so sorry, Sammy," Connor apologized from the heart, "I didn't mean to leave you for that long."

"Where were you?" she sobbed, "I've been so scared without you!"

Connor grimaced, refusing to tell anyone the truth about his disappearance, especially in her current fragile condition. "That doesn't matter right now. What matters is that I am here with you and I promise that I will not leave your side until you are well again."

Sammy cried harder. "We both know I am going to die. There's no use denying it any longer!"

Connor held her tightly and rocked her. No words could soften or justify the fact. At this point, there was no way to stop the inevitable. The first words to come to Connor's mind were, "It could be worse."

"How? How could this be any worse!" Sammy shouted, through her mess of tears.

Once again, Connor choked up. If it weren't for his recent dive back down the rabbit hole into his dark side, he would be crying alongside her. He was grateful for the numbness that came with his monstrous black eyes. "At least ... At least you are surrounded by people who love you. I once knew a girl who didn't even have that."

"Was she trapped in a hospital as well?" Sammy sniffled.

Connor smiled as he pushed the sunglasses onto the bridge of his nose. "Yes she was, but times were different then, and she was locked in a hospital much different than the therapeutic ones you have visited recently."

"I'm scared to die in a hospital," Sammy said with a quivering, blue-spotted lip, "I want to go home."

Sighing deeply, Connor thought for a moment before turning to Morgan, "Morgan, can you please inform the doctor that I'm ready to fill out Samantha's advanced directives and sign the discharge paperwork?"

Morgan smiled softly and stood up. "Of course!"

"And can you please call Veronica to set up a private flight and medical transport to JFK Airport?" he added, holding out his cell phone.

"Anything for Samantha," Morgan said sweetly.

As she walked out of the room, Sammy asked, "What was the name of the girl?"

Connor looked back at her curiously.

Sammy shrugged, "The girl you were going to tell me a story about ..."

He felt uneasy about telling her this story right now, as it was even darker than some of the other ones, and Sammy needed positivity right now. "I'm afraid that is not a happy story, Sammy. It ends quite tragically."

"Well, then, hopefully it is more tragic than my own condition. That way I feel better about my disease, knowing that it truly could be worse." Sammy snuggled under her covers and held her stuffed golden retriever close to her chest. "Tell me a tale of a girl in a hospital."

An old spark returned to Connor's black eyes. "Let me tell you a tale of an asylum!"

* * *

MORRISTOWN, NEW JERSEY

OCTOBER 3, 1911

A young man stood at the entrance to a mammoth building with an iconic domed roof that reached for the sky. To see the top of the 675,000-square-foot building, through the five stories of convoluted hallways and staircases that had been added to the large structure over time, the young man had to tip his bowler hat up with the handle of his black umbrella. His purple eyes scanned the vast grounds surrounding the building. A gentle autumn breeze blew his ankle-length black trench coat around his legs. Although the building that stood dauntingly in front of him bore the name New Jersey State Lunatic Asylum, the young man fearlessly gripped his briefcase and advanced toward the door.

Raising his umbrella, the young man knocked on the massive doors and waited patiently. It wasn't long until they were opened by a nurse wearing a tall white hat. "Ah, you must be Dr. Schroeder. We've been expecting you!"

"Good evening, ma'am. I am expected by Dr. Cotton for a full orientation of the asylum," Dr. Schroeder said, tipping his hat politely before removing it to enter the premises.

With his hat gone, the nurse was able to see his stunningly handsome facial features and his styled black hair, which was combed back with grease. It was his eyes, however, that truly astonished her. "My, Dr. Schroeder! What spectacular eyes you have!"

"Ah, *danke schön*. Please, call me Cyrus. Only my patients call me Dr. Schroeder," he said, correcting the formality while surveying the foyer of the asylum, which was much grander than he presumed.

The nurse blushed. "Well then, Cyrus, would you follow me?" Using a key hung around her neck, the nurse opened the door that led to two mirrored staircases, which led to a long, quiet hallway with large, open windows. "Welcome to New Jersey State Lunatic Asylum. Here we house God's poor children who were unfortunate enough to be inflicted by insanity. Our patients range from hysteric housewives to the criminally insane. Our treatments range from mild medications to surgeries. You will, of course, be given a key to each of the wards, however certain areas of the asylum will be off-limits to you, for your own protection."

"Such as?" he asked, admiring the extravagant decor and lavish furnishings.

Before she opened the next door, she gave the young doctor a serious look. "Such as the criminally insane who will bite your ear off for looking at their chocolate cake." She opened the door with her key and then headed up the staircase.

"Ah! You feed them cake!" he responded, optimistically.

"No. We don't," she clarified.

The young doctor was confused. "But you just ..."

The nurse turned abruptly at the top of the stairs, where there was another locked door. "To the sane person, if it looks like shit and smells like shit, then it is probably shit. To the insane, however, they still want to taste it to make sure it isn't chocolate cake."

"Oh." He was incredibly disturbed by this image.

"Here you are, Doctor," she said, opening the door to a large study.

"Thank you," he said with a small bow as he passed through the doorway. The study was indeed quite expansive and more luxurious than the rest of the asylum. A fire crackled behind an artistically carved mahogany mantel. Rows of book-filled shelves lined the walls around four high-backed upholstered chairs that sat in the middle of the room. In one of those chairs sat an elderly man holding a scotch on the rocks.

"Come in, my good man. Take a seat," the elderly gentlemen said. "I am Dr. Cotton, but you may call me Henry."

"Thank you, sir." Cyrus took off his coat and hung it on a coat rack near the door. Then he straightened his black suit jacket and sat in the chair adjacent to Henry.

"Would you like a brandy? Perhaps a scotch?" Dr. Cotton offered.

"That is quite decent of you, sir, but I must decline for today," Cyrus replied.

"Very well, then," the old doctor said as he took another sip of his scotch. "So you hail from Germany."

"Yes, I studied there," Cyrus responded.

"Yes, yes. You came highly recommended by a Dr. Freud. Very good. We could use a psychologist here at our asylum. Maybe you can make a difference with our stubborn cases." Dr. Cotton laughed heartily. "We will see what you make of them."

"Yes, Dr. Freud believed that most women's problems stemmed from their sex. In some cases, they are cured through therapies that treat their sexuality first and foremost. Can I read over the patients' files tonight by chance?" Cyrus asked.

"My, what an eager young fellow you are. The files are in my other office near the north wing. One of the nurses can show you the way. But that shall all wait until tomorrow. For tonight, drink with me and tell me of your studies and why your eyes are so peculiarly purple," Dr. Cotton said jovially.

"Of course, Henry," Cyrus replied, a glimmer flashing across his dangerous purple eyes.

The next morning, Cyrus was sitting in his new, albeit bare, office. Upon his desk were three boxes of patient files. It had taken him five hours to go through the 178 files before he finally found exactly what he was looking for:

Patient # 20140820

    Patient Name: Summer Winters

    Age: 16

    D.O.B.: August 8th, 1855

    Height: 5'4"

    Weight: 110 lbs

    Hair Color: Auburn

    Eye Color: Green

    Admit Date: 23rd January 1911

Reason for Admission:

    Patient has a history of verbal aggression and acting out. This is assumed to be because of loss of mother at birth and loss of father at age 5. Patient stubbornly defiant at home and in the community. Patient admitted for breaking a whiskey bottle and threatening to kill her aunt and uncle (guardians) with one of the shards.

Diagnosis: Hysteria

Cyrus rubbed his eyes in frustration as he read down the long list of tortures she had been subjected to. Unfortunately, this was what humans believed would heal the mind. Cyrus personally knew better. Underneath the last entry, he added:

10.4.1911 - Reassessment by Dr. Schroeder

Disappointed by the medical field, he turned the page and looked at the picture taken of her upon admission. The black-and-white picture showed a young girl of 16, her long hair pulled back by her bonnet. The ruffled dress she wore was dirty. Even one of her black boots appeared to have a loose sole. What stood out the most were her piercing eyes, which appeared to see him right through the picture. There was so much pain and anger in those eyes. Cyrus only hoped that he could somehow ease her pain and heal her heart. Judging by her recent history, it would take a while to gain her trust.

An hour later, a heavy knock sounded at his door.

"Bring her in." Cyrus straightened his tie and sat up in his chair.

The door swung open, revealing a small, wiry teenage girl with sharp green eyes and auburn hair tied up in a bonnet. She wore a simple white dress that resembled a pillowcase more than an actual dress, but it was what the patients wore here, apparently. Cyrus had already met three patients wearing the same white pillowcase and rough white pants. She appeared nervous about entering and didn't move for a moment.

Impatiently, the orderly pushed her through the door. Luckily, the patient caught herself right before she was about to plant her face on the floor. Concerned for her well being, Cyrus ran over and helped her up, noticing significant scrapes on her knees, elbows, hands and cheeks.

"Don't get too close to her," the orderly said, with disgust. "She bites." It was clear he was speaking from experience.

"Well, perhaps she wouldn't feel the need to bite if you showed her some goddamn courtesy." Cyrus' voice was calm and soothing, but a hint of malice in his voice was clearly noted by the orderly, who sniffed the tobacco deeper into his nostril and then closed the door behind him.

Blushing uncontrollably, she looked up at her new doctor, surprised by his care and consideration. Her cruel past had taught her the untrustworthiness of men and their desires. In a form of self-protection, she pulled her hands away from him and tucked some loose strands of hair into her bonnet. "Good afternoon, Doctor."

"Good afternoon," he replied with a warm smile, taking no offense. "Would you please sit down?" He motioned toward a sofa.

Wordlessly, she took a seat on the edge of the long sofa and fidgeted nervously.

"My name is Dr. Schroeder. I will be your psychiatrist during your stay here," he said, taking a seat in a large, high-backed chair adjacent to the sofa.

Nervously avoiding eye contact, she stared silently at the floor.

"What is your name?" he prompted.

"Patient # 20140820," she said, nervously wiggling her legs and staring at the floor.

"You are not a number," he said kindly. "What is your name?"

Shocked by his acknowledgment of her as a person, her eyes grew watery. "My name is Summer Winters."

"What a beautiful name, Summer," he responded, with an encouraging smile.

Summer glanced up at his swirling purple eyes and quickly looked away again. "Why do you have purple eyes, Doctor Schroeder?"

"I've had these eyes for a long time, Summer. Do they frighten you?" he asked, with genuine concern.

"No," she sat a little farther back on the sofa.

This gave Cyrus some encouragement that she was relaxing. "Good. Now if you haven't already guessed, I am not a normal doctor. I have had a different type of training, which will give you a different kind of treatment." Cyrus pulled out a clipboard and some writing utensils.

Summer tensed. "What sort of treatment?"

Reading her apprehension, he explained further, "I'm here to listen to you and you are going to talk. Then I will make some recommendations on how you should approach difficult situations in the future. Does that sound all right?"

"Doesn't sound like any treatment I've heard about, but at least it's better than the straitjacket." Summer sat back some more; baby steps towards progress.

"For today, I want you tell me your account of what happened to get you into this asylum." Cyrus drew ink into his fountain pen and looked up, the pen poised to write down notes.

"You want to hear my side?" Summer appeared quite shocked.

"Yes, if that would be all right," he responded, smiling.

Summer straightened out her dress nervously. "I was brought in for breaking a lamp and threatening my Aunt Betty with a shard of ceramic."

The case clearly said bottle, but he didn't correct Summer. "Tell me what started this. Why did you break a lamp and threaten your aunt?" Cyrus looked intently at her, waiting for a reply.

After several silent moments she finally found the bravery to respond. "They don't care about me. My aunt and uncle. All they care about is my father's money. My father died when I was quite young, leaving behind a fortune. My aunt and uncle took on the responsibility of raising me so they could have all the money."

"Money?" Cyrus asked quizzically.

"Yes, my aunt and uncle took the money immediately with a promise that it would go to my upbringing. I guess they weren't wrong, because they paid to get me in this hellhole," she said.

Cyrus was disturbed by this level of greed, but didn't allow it to show as anything more than professional concern. "Tell me more about the incident that got you here."

Summer sighed and lay down. "Well, my aunt and uncle wanted me to be the perfect little girl they always dreamed of. You see, they only have boys … but I didn't want to be a perfect little girl. I would rather read books than learn to sew and knit. But *reading gives women dangerous ideas,*" she mocked, "or so I've been told … Anyway, they didn't like my resistance and threatened to bring me here. So, I resisted."

Silence filled the air as Cyrus pressed his fingers against his lips, deep in thought. Finally, he looked directly into her bright green eyes, to which she responded by immediately looking down to the ground. "What are you hiding from me, Summer?"

421

"What do you mean?" She asked, refusing to meet his gaze.

Cyrus took this as a clear indication that she was hiding something. "I'm sorry, Summer, but it doesn't add up. I understand that you are upset about your aunt and uncle stealing your father's money, leaving you an orphan to their care. I also understand that you are not happy about being here. What I don't understand is why a quiet girl who simply wants to read books suddenly attacks her guardians because they wanted her to knit. That is quite a reaction to such a simple request. Is it not?"

Summer wrung her hands, tucked her feet in towards her body, and refused eye contact.

Regardless of her discomfort, Cyrus pressed on. "In order for me to stop these other treatments you have been undergoing, you need to open up to me. What are you hiding from me, Summer?"

Summer sat anxiously in silence as she mulled his words. It was a silence that Cyrus alone was comfortable in. It grew with her rising anxiety and increased fidgeting until she could no longer take it. "They were going to hurt him!" she finally blurted out.

"Hurt who?" Cyrus inquired calmly.

Tears rolled down her face, "Billy … I loved Billy, and they threatened to hang him."

Cyrus sat on the edge of his seat. "Why would they threaten such a thing?"

"Because he's black!" she said, breaking into sobs. "My aunt and uncle are from Mississippi. They don't believe the Negros to be real humans, just sub-humans who tend their plantations in the South. My father never cared. He let us be. Thought kids would be kids. My aunt and uncle could not accept it. They refused. They told me … they … they …"

"It's okay, Summer, you're in a safe place," Cyrus encouraged.

Summer sniffled and wiped her tears with the back of her hand. "They said it was unnatural. That they were going to tar, feather and hang him for his crime of thinking he might violate a white person. I couldn't stand for that! I warned my aunt that if she laid a finger on Billy then I would cut that finger off. My uncle smacked me across the room. When I woke up, I was being dragged into this godforsaken asylum ... Billy is probably already dead by now."

Compelled to make her feel better, Cyrus handed her his handkerchief. After being mistreated for the past couple of years, this simple gesture of kindness shocked her and left her wary. Still, she took it and wiped her eyes with the handkerchief before giving it back to Cyrus.

"That was really brave of you. In fact, I don't think you are insane at all. I believe you are simply a woman who has fought very hard for what she believes in. And that, my dear, makes you strong," Cyrus said, warmth spreading his smile.

"You obviously haven't heard about the other things I've done here," she rolled her eyes, sniffling back the mucous.

Cyrus peered at his clipboard. "Yes, please tell me what happened to put you in a straitjacket on February fifth."

Summer instantly grew distant. "It was bullshit! That orderly decided he wanted to grab my privates while I was helping clean the floors. So, I smacked him across the face. Then him and the other orderlies strapped me up, saying I deserved it for attacking an orderly."

"I'm sorry to hear that," Cyrus genuinely responded as he wrote down in her file: *Indecently assaulted by orderly. Self defense.* "Can you tell me about your week of seclusion that started on February 18th?"

"'Twas the same orderly who started it. That grotesque man. He groped my breast this time and so I screamed at him to never touch me again. The other orderlies surrounded me. They took the other patients out of the sitting room. I was all alone ..." Summer drifted off, horrified by the memory of it.

"Summer, is your virginity still intact? Did they steal it from you?" Cyrus asked, taking care to hide his burning rage beneath his professional demeanor.

"Not on that day," she responded with a spark in her eyes. "On that day I fought back. I clawed and scratched and bit my way out. That was when the needle pricked me. I could still feel it for the first three days I was locked away in that smelly concrete room."

"I know this is hard for you to recollect, but I must be aware of all aspects of your treatment, including the names of these orderlies." Cyrus held his pen ready.

"John. James. George. Edward. Frank." Summer listed them as Cyrus quickly wrote down their names on her record, next to her seclusion date.

"Now please recollect what happened to put you in restraints on March 10th," Cyrus requested, as he continued to write down the names.

Summer gritted her teeth. "I was being good and sewing a dress." Summer paused and stared off into the distance, "Edward called for me to come and speak with the doctor. I went with him, not knowing what would happen next ... they pulled me into the seclusion room ... James ... Edward ... Frank ... and John ... I fought back, but was too weak from my last week of ice therapy. They left me in that seclusion room when they were finished with me ... To be honest, I was comforted by the locked door. I wanted to be alone."

Cyrus put his hand in front of his face to feign rubbing his temples. In truth, he was trying to hide the swirling red anger that was consuming his eyes. "This is really disturbing to hear about. I'm so sorry this happened to you." To keep her from seeing his eyes change, he stood up and quickly turned around to look out the window behind his desk. While he was regaining control of his inner demon, he asked her, "What happened on the day you attacked Dr. Steiner while under hypnosis?"

"I don't remember," Summer said, not at all curious about Cyrus's lack of eye contact.

"What do you remember?" he asked, still feeling the red swirling in his eyes as his heart burned with hatred.

"Fire ... purple fire ..." she responded slowly.

The fire diminished in his own eyes as his curiosity was piqued. "Purple fire? Why purple fire? Have you ever seen purple fire?"

"No," she responded, trying her best to remember. "I sometimes dream about purple fire. It burns twice as fast but doesn't damage my skin. Curious, isn't it?" For a brief moment, she peered into his purple eyes, then quickly glanced away. "Maybe that is why your eyes are so familiar.

They remind me of my purple fire."

This comment warmed Cyrus's heart, but he couldn't reveal this. Not right now. "Do you remember attacking the orderly the next day?"

"No, I don't remember that day, either. I didn't snap out of my delusion of purple fire for three days, according to Dr. Steiner," she recounted.

"And what about April 25th?" Cyrus placed his hands behind his back and paced around the office.

"John got too close to me, so I clawed his face before he got any bright ideas," Summer stated, with her arms crossed.

"This time you attacked the orderly first. That can hardly be justified, Summer," Cyrus reprimanded.

"Can you blame me?" She showed no regret.

Moving on and running out of time, Cyrus asked, "What happened when you attacked a male patient on September 27th?"

"I didn't attack him! He lied!" Summer shouted defensively. Obviously, this wound was much fresher than the last few.

"Tell me more," Cyrus prompted, as he continued to pace around the room with his hands held behind his back.

Summer continued, "Oscar was talking about horrible things he did before he came to the asylum. I couldn't stand hearing him recount his stories of lynching and beating those people. His cruel words reminded me of what happened to Billy. I screamed at him to shut it, but he wouldn't. We were both screaming at each other when the orderlies stormed into the room. That was when Oscar pointed blame at me and said I attacked him. I didn't lay a finger on him, but the orderlies didn't care. They still dragged me away, pricked me with another needle and subjected me to another week of seclusion."

"Was it the same orderlies?" Cyrus confirmed.

"No. Just John, but he leads the rest." She folded her arms.

Cyrus didn't know how much more of this he could listen to before he lost all control and ripped the hearts from these men. In fact, it would bring him more joy to rip their testes off and force-feed it back to them as they bled out— thoughts that he could never share, lest he also be imprisoned in this asylum. Making a note of the time, Cyrus said, "Well, I believe our time for today is up. Thank you for confiding in me and telling me more about your circumstances. I will look into these incidents and make sure you aren't bothered by these particular orderlies again. Until then, I want you to refrain from attacking anyone. If something is dire or you feel as if you are in danger, then please call for me. Do you understand?"

"Yes, Dr. Schroeder," Summer agreed as she stood up.

"Now, return to your duties. I believe you are tending the livestock?" Cyrus gave her a playful little smile.

Summer smiled back. "That is correct, Dr. Schroeder."

"I'm sure you thoroughly enjoy that," he said with a cunning smile. "I will see you again next week."

"Next week?" She looked concerned.

"Yes, I have sixty other patients, so I don't have as much time to spend with each patient as I would prefer. Rest assured, if you are deeply in need, then please inform the staff to fetch me at once." Cyrus finally caught her gaze.

This time she didn't look away. "I understand. Thank you, Dr. Schroeder."

She walked over to the door and knocked on it. As she was turned around, Cyrus noted the bizarre orange birthmarks on the back of her neck. A clear indicator that he had found *her* again. This evidence filled his heart with elation, knowing he was now in control of her safety. The orderly on the other side opened the door and stood to the side to let her through, glaring at her the entire time. After she had passed by him, he politely informed Cyrus, "Your next patient is ready for you."

Cyrus sighed. The next 59 patients would be difficult to get through. The only patient he cared about was Summer. Still, he had to put on the correct presence if he wanted to save Summer from this institution. "Bring her in."

At the end of the next day, Cyrus was rubbing his temples after listening to the rambling of 24 other women. Some were indeed clinically insane, perhaps with faulty genetics that had predisposed them to be institutionalized here. Although he was happy to have gone through forty of his patients, there were still twenty to go. Not to mention all the paperwork and doctor's notes he would be spending all night preparing. It was no wonder that most other doctors at this asylum only visited their patients once a month, sometimes twice if the behavior called for it.

At a bare minimum, he had made sure the five offending men had been moved to another ward. That should make it easier for Summer. At times, Cyrus found it impossible to focus on what his patients were saying. He was far too wrapped up in his own plot to rid the world of those five men as soon as possible.

Before he could dive into the mountain of paperwork, an urgent knock sounded at the door. "Come in," he called out.

The door opened and a frantic nurse walked in, trying to appear calm and professional despite her duress. "Dr. Schroeder, it's Patient # 20140820."

"What's wrong?" He stood up and ran over to her.

"She is making irrational demands," the nurse said, as she led him down the hallway, Cyrus close on her heels.

"Has she been aggressive?" he asked with a lump in his throat.

"No, Doctor. Not yet, but give it time and she will escalate to that," the nurse said as she rounded the corner and opened the door.

Sitting in a wooden chair directly in front of the medicinal window was Summer Winters. She wore a stubborn expression, with tightly folded arms and a furrowed brow. By the looks thrown at her by the white-coat orderlies and nurses, she had been there for a while. Much to their astonishment, Cyrus ran up and knelt in front of her, so that her head was higher than his. Even Summer was astonished at how close he was willing to get to her.

"Be careful, Doctor! You never know when she'll attack!" one of the orderlies shouted.

Ignoring the man's ignorance, Cyrus locked onto her breathtaking green eyes and asked, "What's wrong, Summer? Why are you causing such a scene?"

At first, Summer was in too much shock to respond. Then she recollected herself and responded. "I requested to take my medications earlier. With my current medication regimen, I wake up utterly exhausted. It is near impossible to wake at the crack of dawn to care for the livestock when I am barely awake. I simply want to take the same medications at an earlier time so I can wake up more refreshed to start my morning chores."

"She is up to something! No patient asks to take their medications earlier. I know she is plotting something devious!" one of the nurses shouted in an accusatory way.

"I am not!" Summer yelled back.

Cyrus gently pressed a finger against her jaw to turn her attention back to him, "Summer, look at me. Look at me. I need you to talk with me right now and forget about the rest of them. They are only here because you scared them."

"I scared *them?*" Summer spat.

One of the orderlies started to say something, and Cyrus held up his hand to cease the stupid comment he was about to make. Speaking calmly to Summer, he explained, "Yes, Summer. You frighten some of these nurses with your recent attacks. Whether they were in self-defense or not, they are still scared of you. So, this can end one of two ways. Are you listening to me?"

Summer nodded.

"Good." Cyrus also nodded and kept eye contact with her. "I don't want any harm to come to you. You have been through enough hardship, and my job is to make you better. Since things have escalated to this point, you are unfortunately left with two options. Your first option is to quietly walk back to C Ward, where you will obey the rules and go to bed. No one will touch you with this first option. Your second option is to continue yelling at the nursing staff here in hopes that they will listen to you. I'm going to give you your first piece of advice: when you raise the volume of your voice, everyone else lowers the volume of their hearing. The quieter you speak, the more intently people listen ..."

"Like what you are doing now ..." Summer added.

"Exactly what I am doing now," Cyrus nodded. "Now, in this second option, these fine men and women will be obligated to ensure your safety and their own by tackling you to the ground, pricking you with that needle you hate, and locking you away for another week. And I will not be able to see you until you have served your time in seclusion. Now, which option do you choose?"

Summer tried to make her excuse, "What about my medic—"

"Your medication no longer matters at this point," Cyrus interrupted. "They no longer care about when you take your medications. That is not the issue. The issue is what you decide to do right now. Option one or two?"

Summer scanned the room nervously, noting the posturing and readiness of the staff to pin her to the ground. Then she looked back at Cyrus, who calmly waited for her answer.

"I'll calmly walk to my room, follow all rules and go to bed," she finally decided.

A couple of disgruntled noises came from the orderlies surrounding them. It was quite obvious that they'd been ramping up for another fight. Cyrus ignored this behavior as a positive model for Summer.

"I'm so glad you chose option one," he said with a warm smile. Then he took hold of her hands and gave them a compassionate squeeze. "Nurse?"

"Yes, Doctor?" The nurse who originally summoned him stepped forward.

"Please get her medications ready. She can take them right now," Cyrus ordered.

The nurse was clearly appalled. "But Doctor, that will only—"

"That will only make it easier on the patient!" Cyrus completed her sentence in an authoritative tone. "We are not a prison, we are here to heal our patients. As her psychiatrist, I see no medical reason why she can't take her medication two hours early if it will help her feel more refreshed in the morning. Now, go prepare her medications, and as for the rest of you," he shouted, looking around, "You can all return to your duties. I shall take Summer to her bed, accompanied by the nurse here."

The surrounding orderlies grumbled but slowly found their way to their original assigned spots.

"Thank you," Summer said, with a tear running down her face and resting on her appreciative smile.

"Of course, that's why I'm here," Cyrus responded, with a smile. "I still need you to do your best to remain calm in the future. As I mentioned, you can ask for me instead of making a big scene. You might find that you will have better outcomes."

"That sounds lovely," she said with a smile.

The nurse had returned with a small cup of seven pills and a clear glass of water. "Here you are," the nurse said grudgingly.

Summer took the pills compliantly and finished the whole glass of water. Then, as protocol demanded, she opened her mouth to check that she had swallowed them all. When the nurse was satisfied that no medications were being held in her cheeks, she put the cups on a counter.

"Now, what do you say we calmly walk to your bedroom before your medications kick in and you become sleepy?" Cyrus suggested.

"I would like that," Summer nodded, as she stood up and let go of Cyrus's hands. With the nurse on her left and Cyrus on her right, they quietly went to Ward C. Once escorted there, the nurse in charge of the women's bedchamber in Ward C took over and escorted Summer into the bathroom to get ready for bed.

The moment Summer was out of sight, the medication nurse snapped at Cyrus, "How did you do that? Do you realize the danger you put yourself in? You know nothing of these patients. I have been working with these patients for ..."

Already tired of her nagging, Cyrus put a finger on her lips to instantly silence her. "I am the new psychiatrist. I have been trained in the most effective ways of soothing a patient's mind. I know what I'm doing, and I did not put myself in danger. The rest of the staff unequivocally put themselves in danger by escalating the situation. This whole mess could have been avoided if *you* had come and asked me if she could take her medications early instead of calling every strong man into the room to intimidate and frighten her. A cornered animal will lash out if provoked.

Maybe you will understand that next time something like this happens." After adequately reprimanding the nurse, Cyrus walked away, leaving her in shock. "Don't worry, nurse, I will be sure to be thorough in my report of the incident tonight."

The next day, Cyrus opened the door to his office a moment before the knock. Summer was surprised by his prompt timing but relieved to see him again. "Good morning, Dr. Schroeder," she curtsied in her white dirty pillow-case shaped dress.

"Come on in," Cyrus invited her. "Where is the orderly? Aren't you supposed to be accompanied?" he asked as he closed the door behind them.

"This morning they all kind of avoided me. I am uncertain about their reasoning, but I'm sure you are behind it all," she said with a wink.

Cyrus was disappointed. He had hoped that his tip to Dr. Cotton would have remained anonymous so the orderlies didn't retaliate against her. Still, if the worst thing they did was ignore her, then he was all right with that.

Summer plopped down on the sofa and reclined. Clearly she felt much more comfortable around Cyrus than the other day. "I thought you said you wouldn't see me for another week."

"Yes, well, I was able to finish with the other patients a lot faster than expected. Plus, I find your recovery quite promising compared to the rest." Pulling up his clipboard full of notes, Cyrus prepared for another session.

While he got comfortable, Summer added, "Thank you again for helping me out yesterday. It is quite possible that you are the only one who truly cares for the patients here."

"I find it rewarding to help my fellow man be the best they can be," he lied.

She smiled. "What are we talking about today?"

"How did you feel this morning? Any better with an earlier medication regimen?" Cyrus asked while writing notes down in her file.

"Yes, I felt happier and more refreshed upon waking up," she said with a big stretch. "Right now, the chicks are hatching from their eggs. A sign from God of new beginnings."

"That is excellent to hear, Summer. I'm glad we could get your medications all sorted out. Have you noticed any change in your appetite, or harmful thoughts?" he inquired.

"My appetite improved this morning, along with my mood," she responded brightly.

"That is great to hear." Cyrus continued to jot notes.

While he was busy writing, Summer pointed out, "Your office is a bit bare."

Peering around, Cyrus agreed, "Yes. Yes, it is. What do you think could be added to this room to make it not quite so bare?"

"Hmm…" she thought, with a finger pressed against her lips, "How about a plant? Or a picture?"

"Maybe you could draw me a picture," he suggested.

A red blush appeared on her young cheeks. "I suppose I can do that."

"Good to hear," he responded with a warm smile. "Now, tell me about your mother."

Summer withdrew slightly. "My mother died in childbirth because of me."

"I'm sorry to hear that." Those were the words that came out of his lips, but Cyrus lacked the remorse. It was as if he was expecting that response from her.

Summer found this doctor more intriguing by the second.

"How about we talk about your father, then. How would you describe your relationship with him?" Cyrus began writing again.

A sadness fell across Summer's face as fond memories of her father came to her. She recounted the way he treated her, she being his only child. Among other things, she was taught to fish, shoot, and read far beyond the childish books other girls were allowed. These fond memories were what gave her strength when she felt weak. When she got to the memory of his death, tears streamed down her face. It started out as a simple cold that grew worse and worse until the sickness claimed her father's life. Around that same time, she met Billy and fell in love with him. Everything took a turn for the worse when her aunt and uncle claimed custody and forced her to behave "like a lady." When she resisted, she got the cane to her backside. It was only a matter of time before she inevitably was sent here ... forgotten.

"I ... I ... I don't even know if Billy is still alive or not. Knowing, either way, would bring me some comfort and peace of mind," she said, sobbing into her knees.

"Hmm." Cyrus stood and walked over to his desk to grab paper and a pencil. "Would you say that your recovery would hasten if Billy's memory was put to rest?"

Summer sniffled and nodded.

Cyrus handed her the paper and pencil. "Take a minute to write him a goodbye letter. Don't write a journal entry of your time here at the asylum. Just a simple note describing your feelings for him and a quick goodbye."

Confused, Summer took the paper and pencil. "Why would I write a letter that could never be returned to him?"

"It is a simple method to help you let go," Cyrus explained.

"Okay," she responded, suspiciously. Still, she took the time to write out a heartfelt goodbye to her dearest Billy Reed. Once she was done, she handed the paper to Cyrus.

Taking the paper, he read it over quickly, folded it nicely, and tucked it into his pocket. "Excellent work, Summer. Do you feel a bit better?"

She thought about this for a minute and then responded, "Yes. Yes, I do actually. How odd."

"That is what I aim for," Cyrus said with a smile. "Now return to your duties. I shall see you again in two days."

"All right, Dr. Schroeder, even though at first you told me a week and now it's two days. Soon you'll be with me every waking minute," she jested.

He chuckled, secretly wishing to get to that exact point. "Just remember to stay out of trouble, Summer. You are on the road to recovery, not back to the seclusion room."

"I understand. Thank you, doctor," she said, grasping the door handle. Then her demeanor changed. She froze and spun around. "Dr. Schroeder

… can I ask you one last thing?"

"Of course!" he responded brightly.

Summer bit down on her lip, too timid to say what was weighing on her mind.

"What is it, Summer?"

Finally, she stared into his purple eyes. "Are you a witch or a demon of some sort?"

Cyrus chuckled lightheartedly, "No. I am nothing of the sort. Why do you ask?"

Summer glanced down, abashed that she had said anything. "It's nothing," she responded as she went to open the door again.

"No, really. I'm interested. Why do you think I'm a witch or a demon?" Cyrus probed further.

Summer shyly turned. "It's your eyes. There is something magical about them that I can't quite put my finger on. The way they sparkle and twirl … your eyes confuse me, doctor. They remind me of old memories … a nostalgic feeling, like I have seen them many times before. Yet my logic corrects my mind that I have indeed never seen them before Monday. I had just wondered if you had hexed me, in a way I couldn't explain. Do you think I have truly gone mad?"

Cyrus took a deep breath while he gathered his thoughts. "I don't think you are mad, Summer. Right now is a confusing time for you. These are interesting thoughts you have, though. Please take the time to reflect on them. I look forward to hearing what reflections you discovered. You are now excused."

Without saying another word, Summer promptly left the room.

As Cyrus closed the door behind her, there was a sinking feeling in his stomach. The letter in his pocket also seemed to weigh him down. After coming all this way to find her, he no longer knew what he was doing. His goal, the only goal, was to steal her away to safety and reignite those old memories— the same goal it had always been. However, now he felt lost … and worse than that, he felt trapped.

To make things more difficult, he couldn't just steal her away. First, there was no concrete evidence that she felt drawn to him enough to trust him. Trust would be key to winning her over and sneaking her away from this place. That was where the second complication came in. He now had a paper trail as a doctor, one that led back to Europe for him, and her. The only way to get her out would be through his referral as a physician. And there was the third point: he needed to prove she had recovered. When he releases her from the asylum, she'd be returned to her aunt and uncle, who would continue to mistreat her. It was all terribly complicated.

The letter weighed on him with an intensity that could have burnt a hole through his pocket. Irritated by this nagging thought, Cyrus pulled the letter from his pocket and stared at her handwriting until the words blurred on the page.

Suddenly an idea struck him. An idea so simple he wondered why he hadn't thought of it immediately. This letter was the key to everything!

Later that night, he stood on the rooftop of the asylum, a cigarette burning in his hand though never touching his lips. The smoke drifted up to the sky in view of the guards down below, who thought nothing of seeing the young doctor smoking on the roof and moved on down the yard to double-check all the windows and doors.

Cyrus gazed up at the dark, moonless sky and drank in the tranquility it gave him. In the shadows of the stars swept a dark figure in the night, too large for the average bird and too silent for an airplane. Cyrus smiled and flicked the cigarette to rid it of ashes.

The powerful sound of flapping wings was quickly followed by a snarky remark. "So, the day has finally come! Whoever knew you would finally see how mad you really are and check yourself into an asylum?"

The half-burnt cigarette was gently placed on the edge of the wall. "I'm pleased that you came so quickly, Peter. I have a mission for you."

Peter walked over to Cyrus's side and picked up the cigarette. Putting it to his lips, Peter inhaled deeply, savoring the long drag of the tobacco. "Yeah, well, the only time you ever call me is to go on a mission ... I thought you didn't smoke."

"I don't," Cyrus said with a smile. "Tobacco doesn't do anything for me, but I know you enjoy a good drag." On cue, Cyrus pulled the remaining packet of cigarettes from his pocket and placed it on the wall.

"Ha ha!" Peter laughed triumphantly as he pocketed the packet, "Are you trying to bribe me?"

"Think of this more as a thank-you gift for the errand you are about to run for me," Cyrus responded with a devilish smile.

"So, who am I killing this time?" Peter asked, as he took another long, satisfying drag of the cigarette.

"No one." Cyrus pulled out the letter in the envelope and handed it to Peter. "This will be a simple mission for you. Take this letter to a black man named Billy Reed. He is to write back that he is also saying goodbye to her. Then give him the motivation to move far away."

"*Her? Her?* Fuck! What is it about *her*? I swear *she* makes you crazy. Maybe you should check yourself in here, doctor. I think you've gone cuckoo again," Peter mocked as he opened the letter and read it.

"You of all people know that I am bound to *her*," Cyrus said somberly, as if he understood the severity of his imprisonment.

Peter carefully folded up the letter and stowed it away in his messenger bag. "Doesn't mean you can't fuck out your frustrations in the meantime. I mean seriously, when was the last time you were with a woman?"

"Is that what you do? Maybe some day when you finally find a soul mate you will understand," Cyrus joked.

"Are you loony? I'm far too much of a man for any mere woman to handle. Women can only handle my magnificence once. I'm afraid twice might be too powerful for them and kill them," Peter laughed, spitting out the butt of the cigarette and pulling out another fresh one. "Do you happen to have a light?"

"You really are an asshole ... an asshole that deserves a woman who can shackle him and make him her slave," Cyrus spat with disgust. Lazily, Cyrus snapped his fingers, making a purple flame appear from the top of his thumb. Peter used the flame to light the tip of the cigarette and then inhaled the smoke.

"Try to keep your humor to a minimum and keep those wings tucked away while you are in town. I don't need you causing another commotion like you did with that Joseph fellow in New York," Cyrus lectured.

Peter snickered as if he were five. "You have to admit that it was pretty hilarious! I'm practically a god now in Utah! And all it took was some gold paint ... But I couldn't have pulled it off without my main man!" Peter kissed his fingers and then reached them up into the sky, "Wouldn't have been able to convince poor Joe without my thorough knowledge of the scriptures."

"Peter! Focus!" Cyrus snapped his fingers. "Find this Billy Reed. He's a black man who lives in New Jersey. Shouldn't be hard to find at all. Give him this letter. Make him write a letter back saying farewell to Summer and that he is traveling out west. Then bring that letter back here! I need him to give Summer peace so she can move on."

"Then can I kill him?" Peter asked pleadingly.

"Go!" Cyrus commanded in German.

"Ja! Herr Doktor," Peter saluted, jumped up into the air and then bulleted through the sky. Cyrus watched him fly away until he was only a speck.

The next morning, Summer was delicately collecting eggs from the chicken coop when she heard a light knock on the door. Careful not to break any of the eggs bound up in her apron, Summer turned around to find Dr. Schroeder peeking his head in.

"Good morning, Dr. Schroeder. It's a bit odd to see you here," she greeted with a slight curtsy.

Cyrus smiled wide, "I have come to bring you something. Although it does appear your hands are full."

"Give me a moment," she said as she sneaked past him and over to the basin. An orderly watched her from afar as she carefully placed the eggs in the basin to be cleaned.

Cyrus patiently waited a couple of feet away while she finished up her task. The orderly glared at him, which Cyrus responded with a friendly wave. This only caused the orderly to turn his nose up.

"What was it you wanted to see me so urgently about that it couldn't wait until our session tomorrow?" Summer asked as she wiped off her hands.

In his hands was a brown paper package. Explaining it suddenly became much more difficult than he thought. "Dr. Cotton, our chief medical officer, agreed that some patients should be allowed to wear proper clothes as a regard for good behavior. Well, I took it upon myself to personally retrieve your belongings for you to wear."

"Really?" Summer blushed. "I get to wear real clothes?"

Cyrus handed the package to her. "I felt it would help your recovery."

Excited as a five-year-old opening a present, Summer tore the paper off to reveal a beautiful Victorian dress with intricate layering and needlework that would put the president's wife to shame. It obviously wasn't the dress she had come in with. Cyrus made an extra trip to buy her this exquisite and expensive dress early this morning— a token to express his dedication to her health. Summer knew this wasn't her dress, but that didn't mean that the rest of the hospital had to know. "Doctor ... I ..."

Before she could finish, he interrupted, "I know this is yours. I made sure of it."

A tear glistened in Summer's eyes. "Thank you, Dr. Schroeder. This means more to me than you could ever imagine."

"I'm glad it was able to put a smile on your face. That was what I aimed for. Once your duties here are done, you have my permission to go put the dress on and wear it from now on. Perhaps later I can write to your aunt and uncle to send more if your good behavior continues." Cyrus nodded with a slight tip of his bowler hat. "Good day, m'lady."

Early Friday morning, Cyrus rushed back to the asylum, making sure to slip in unseen. After such a grueling long day of listening to these women's tragic tales, he really needed a small release out in the woods. Still, the quick release he received from a run in the woods did little to help him decompress from the stressful day. And now he was running late for an urgent training that Dr. Cotton requested.

The snap of rubber gloves echoed down the hallway, followed by the squeaking of door hinges. Gowned in white coat and rubber gloves, Cyrus joined Dr. Cotton, Dr. Morrison and four nurses surrounding a young woman strapped to a procedural table.

"Nice of you to join us Cyrus," Dr. Cotton greeted sarcastically.

"I apologize. I had a small errand to run," Cyrus fixed the medical mask to his face.

"Well, as I said before, Fridays are the days we do the surgeries. Since our demand has increased for these procedures, we will need your help in administering them," Dr. Cotton explained.

"I swear I'm all better!" the woman on the table shouted. Her white uniform had been stained with urine and dirt, so that it matched her soiled skin and brown frizzled hair. Her appearance did little to help her appeal to sanity, nor did her wide eyes, which rapidly switched focus from person to person. "Please doctor. There's no need for this," she begged, then suddenly snapped her head to the side and shouted under her breath, "Shut up, you fool, or they'll hear you." Then she resumed to look back at each of the doctors.

The doctors ignored her. She was no longer a patient. She was no longer a person. At this point, she was nothing more than a disease to be experimented on.

Dr. Cotton turned to Dr. Morrison and instructed, "Will you please read the diagnosis for your patient; #07563254?"

"Certainly," Dr. Morrison nodded his head and peered down his glasses at the clipboard with her file, "Patient #07563254, female, was admitted to New Jersey Asylum for grandiose thoughts. During her stay, her delusions increased with reported instances of hearing and responding to voices in her head. #07563254 has experienced moments of aggression toward male orderlies, but otherwise is harmless to others. #07563254 repeatedly peels the skin away from her fingertips because of the voices she hears. #07563254 denies this even after repeated observations. After other treatments have failed, I have submitted the orders for surgical removal of the uterus in hopes that it will calm her hysteria and silence the voices. #07563254 will be monitored in a controlled environment post-surgery and left in isolation to better heal from the treatment. Are there any questions?"

The patient was wide-eyed and terrified, which reminded Cyrus of a frightened dog about to be punished for sneaking into the pantry at night. Cyrus' heart throbbed with pity for the poor woman who was so tortured by her own lunacy. "What is her name?" he asked.

Both doctors appeared taken off guard for a moment. Even the nurses looked at each other in astonishment. Apprehensively, Dr. Morrison flipped through the pages in her chart, "Uh, #07563254 name is Polly Anne Roth."

Looking past all the doctors and over to the frightened woman strapped to the cold metal table, Cyrus told her sympathetically, "Don't worry, Polly. Everything will be all right."

This little human touch miraculously made her face muscles smooth out and her eyes close to a more relaxed position. "Thank you."

Irritated by the new doctor, the rest of the treatment team turned their backs to him and prepped her for surgery. The nurse's rough and forceful hands spiked Polly's anxiety. The ether mask was dropped roughly over her mouth and nose without an explanation of how inhaling the smelly liquid would make her go to sleep. The straps to her limbs were tightened without any consideration for the pain the pressure might cause her. No one looked her in the eyes or soothed her wild fearful ramblings. Once again, she was no longer human; just an experiment.

"Let us begin!" Dr. Morrison commanded, pulling the gloves up to his forearms. Everyone in the room stepped forward. Everyone that is, except for Cyrus, who remained two feet away from the metal table. He was the only one who noticed Polly's darting eyes that the ether sedation had not yet taken effect.

Dr. Morrison began the first incision into her abdomen. Polly's whole body shook violently, pulling against all the restraints. The ether didn't take effect for a whole two minutes. To Polly, it must have felt like an eternity. Urine soaked into her uniform and trickled off the side of the table. There was a brief pause to confirm she was still breathing before Dr. Morrison continued to dig his scalpel deeper.

Cyrus couldn't take it any longer. He yelled out, "For God's sake, removing her ability to reproduce will not make her affliction leave her …"

It was true that Cyrus had killed hundreds of thousands of people in the past. Men, women, children, it never mattered to him. He killed ruthlessly and unforgivingly. It was even true that he tortured people for days on end, to the point at which it became a form of art for him. He artfully kept his victims alive for weeks while he slowly seared and tore the flesh from their bodies. Still, this form of torture sickened him. For he had never lied to his victims, telling them that the torture devices he used was a way to heal them in the end. Such a deception was unworthy of any sympathy. This sickening lump in his stomach seeded into hatred— a hatred that might end in the destruction of this entire asylum.

Annoyed by Cyrus' resistant attitude, Dr. Morrison instructed, "Shut your trap or you might cause my knife to slip. Even Freud agreed that hysteria was caused by the wandering womb."

Dr. Morrison continued the procedure, with Cyrus silently stewing in the corner. After removing the uterus, Dr. Morrison stitched her back up and checked his watch, "At 10:13, on October 6th, 1911, patient #07563254 has successfully undergone surgery. Nurse, please check her blood pressure and then take her into isolation to limit disruptive sounds that could impair the healing process she will experience over the next week. #07563254 will be reassessed for diagnosis in one week."

Making sure to double-check their elbow-length rubber gloves, the nurses advanced on the unconscious patient. They took a moment to document her respirations and heart rate before unstrapping her from the table and rolling her body over into a wheelchair. Cyrus watched as the nurse wheeled the unconscious, limp body out of the room.

"Congratulations! You witnessed your first surgery here at the asylum. We will have you watch two more and then you will lead the last three," Dr. Cotton said brightly.

"How many of these will I do each week?" Cyrus asked through gritted teeth.

"Well, this week we only have seven surgeries, but you should expect five to fifteen each week, depending on the doctors' orders," Dr. Morrison said.

"*Only* seven?" Cyrus grimaced, thinking of how horrific this treatment was and how casually these doctors talked about it. "What is the success rate for such surgeries?"

Dr. Cotton appeared quite pleased. "Due to our strict protocol, our success rate is really high! Fifty percent of all patients recover from their past ailments."

Cyrus was disgusted by the filth around him. "What is the death rate with this procedure?"

"With our advanced methods, we haven't had a death in over seven months!" Dr. Cotton stated proudly.

I'm going to kill you when this is all over, Cyrus thought as he responded, "The new techniques used for treating the insane have done very interesting things for western medicine."

"Wonderful to hear! Let's power through these next few treatments," Dr. Cotton boasted optimistically.

I am seriously going to kill the lot of you, Cyrus promised himself.

After several emotionally draining hours, Cyrus was ready to escape back to his study to complete the paperwork on his patients. This task was far too taxing for his meager humanity.

The only way he could follow through with these procedures each week was to give up the little bit of humanity he had protectively built up over the last two years.

"Thank you so much for an educational day. I shall now be off," Cyrus said, with his fake smile plastered to his face.

"Oh, we are not done yet, my boy!" Dr. Cotton spouted cheerfully. "We have one more surgery to do today. A removal of the liver and uterus to reduce our patient's aggression and lust."

Cyrus could feel his blood run cold.

Dr. Cotton laughed. "Oh I know you want to start your weekend— hit the town and meet the ladies."

All of them laughed, except Cyrus, who was close to losing his composure.

"Who is the patient?" Cyrus asked calmly.

"Let's go," Dr. Morrison said with a wave. The group of nurses and doctors walked over two doors to the operating room.

When Cyrus rounded the corner into the room, he was shocked to see who occupied the chair. His eyes grew wide and his anger began to boil. "That is my patient! I didn't give consent for this!"

"No, I did," Dr. Cotton said sternly. "You are a new doctor who is not authorized to prescribe this kind of treatment. Besides all surgeries must be signed off by me to prevent abuse of the treatment."

Just like in the other room, the nurses gathered around and began to strap down the patient's limbs to the chair and leaned it back slightly. Another nurse carried out a silver tray which held several instruments with some gauze. The two doctors examined the patient closely for a moment, blocking out Cyrus' view.

Finally, Dr. Cotton ordered, "Dr. Schroeder, will you read off the diagnosis?"

Sitting on the counter was the file that Cyrus was repelled by. He knew that reading that file off would indefinitely be finalizing signature on her surgery.

"Cyrus!" Dr. Cotton prompted.

Cyrus flinched in response, trying so desperately to not tear every person in this room limb from limb. Obediently, he picked up the file and opened it up to the front page. Before he started reading, Cyrus looked over at the desperate blue eyes of his patient and pitied her. "AnnaBelle Brown. Patient #33485625. Admitted to New Jersey State Asylum on October 7th, 1910 for aggression towards husband and the whore he was with. Concerned for his new fiancee's safety and his own safety, AnnaBelle's husband admitted her here. During AnnaBelle's stay at the hospital, she has shown aggression towards male staff, whom she reported to be sexually forward with their suggestions."

Cyrus paused, recognizing a common trend among the female patients in this asylum, "Sir, I do not believe AnnaBelle should receive this treatment. She is just another woman acting in self defense ..."

"I'm going to give you some advice, my boy. Follow my orders at all times! Do that and you will survive your time here. Disobey orders and you might find yourself on the other side of the bars," Dr. Cotton threatened.

"But she is not a fit candidate for this procedure sir," Cyrus continued to defend her.

The chief of medicine's face went bright red. He shoved a stubby little finger in Cyrus's face, "That patient was under my care for an entire year, with no improvement! This is the only option for recovery for someone like her, plus it has already been paid for by her husband. A price that I daresay was not cheap. Do you understand me?"

"Perfectly," Cyrus responded, with dangerous eyes and a voice dripping with venom.

"Then I want to hear no more of your objections! We have protocols to follow here. Precedence to maintain!" Dr. Cotton went back over to the patient and picked up the scalpel.

Cyrus couldn't bring himself to watch and abruptly left with the file in his hand. In a clash between numbness and rage, Cyrus took no detours on his way to locking himself away in his office. Closing the door brought the most relief he'd had all day. The seclusion of his office gave him little peace, however. Cyrus collapsed in his chair and stared at the closed file of Patient #33485625 ... The patient formerly known as AnnaBelle Brown.

The numbness had taken over him for so long that he didn't snap out of it until a loud commotion caught his attention. Forgetting all about the file in his hand, Cyrus bolted out of the door, fearing the commotion had something to do with Summer. He followed the frantic screams and the barking of orders until he came upon a large group of orderlies and nurses who were huffing and puffing outside the seclusion room.

"What's going on here?" Cyrus demanded to know.

John, the untrustworthy orderly, stepped forward. "We got this under control, Doc. Go back and drink your gin in peace."

The prisoner in the seclusion room frantically banged on the door, crying hysterically, "Let me out of here! Please! Someone help me!"

The voice sounded a lot like Summer's, which infuriated Cyrus further. Grabbing John's white collar, Cyrus proceeded to scream in his face, "Who is in that seclusion room? Tell me this instant!"

The screaming and crying continued from inside.

"It's Patient #20140820," one of the nurses spoke up.

Cyrus rounded on the nurse and towered over her threateningly. "What happened?" he growled.

The screaming started to taper off, but the crying continued inside.

The nurse gulped but stood her ground, "Patient #2014 ..."

"Summer! Her name is Summer Winters! Use their goddamn names, for Chrisake!" Cyrus screamed.

Summer continued to weakly rap her fist on the door, crying for it to be opened, hoping her pleas weren't falling on deaf ears.

The nurse took a deep breath and glared menacingly at Cyrus. "She woke up screaming. Another patient tried to console her and was knocked back. *Summer* was thrown into the seclusion room because she was a danger to others."

By now, Summer was sobbing on the floor of the dirty seclusion room, giving up all hope.

"Open the door," Cyrus commanded in a low growl.

"But Doc, she must pay her time," another orderly responded.

"I said, open the fucking door!" Cyrus screamed. "She had a nightmare! You don't punish someone because they were frightened by a nightmare. Would you do that to your children?" he asked accusingly, glaring at each of the female nurses. "No, you wouldn't. You would soothe them back to sleep and rest their mind that no monsters lurked in their closets. Now open the fucking door before I fire you incompetent lot!"

Reluctantly, one of the nurses unlocked the door and swung it open. When Cyrus saw Summer curled in a ball, weeping on the floor, he couldn't help himself and ran into the room to comfort her. "Summer. Summer." He lightly laid a hand on her shoulder.

Instinctively she flinched away. But then she opened her eyes to see

Cyrus crouched next to her with a loving concern in his purple swirling eyes. Desperate for some comfort and protection, Summer wrapped her arms around his neck and cried into his shoulder. The gawking orderlies and nurses gasped at the abnormal behavior. This was not protocol.

Cyrus held her lovingly in his arms. "It's okay, Summer. You're safe." Summer continued to sob, so Cyrus made the decision. "Let's get you to bed."

Cyrus wrapped his arm around her and picked her up. While he cradled her in his arms, she clung to his neck tightly and buried her head in his shoulder so she didn't have to see the angry faces of the orderlies around them. Cyrus, too, ignored the angry looks he received from doing the unprecedented and showing a patient more compassion than the rest of the staff were capable of.

As he carried her to her room, he soothingly asked her, "What nightmare shook you so?"

Summer clutched tighter onto his white coat. "I dreamed of fire ... purple fire. It swallowed and consumed everything in sight. I dreamed of death ... so much death around me. It was so frightening!"

"That does sound like a terrible dream," Cyrus verified.

"It was ... so terrifying!" She shuddered and then loosened her grip on his shoulder to look him in the eyes. "The fire was the same color as your eyes. The hypnotic way it destroyed everything in sight ... it reminds me of the intensity in your eyes."

"Did the purple fire burn you?" Cyrus asked, intrigued.

"No," she responded. "The fire licked my skin but never burned me. It was as if the fire was protecting me."

"Then maybe, just maybe, your mind believes that I am protecting you from the dangers around you," Cyrus suggested. Finally, they had made it to her ward room, where the rest of the patients were awake and waiting for Summer to return. A few rejoiced when they saw her again, almost as if they were a family of some sort. It was comforting to see the support the patients gave one another despite all this hardship. Gently, Cyrus set Summer down in her bed. At the head of the bed hung the beautiful green

446

dress he bought her.

"Thank you, Dr. Schroeder," she said as she wiped the tears from her face.

Cyrus sat down on the bed for a moment, fully aware that other patients were watching him. "Summer, I honestly believe you are getting better. I plan on discharging you from this asylum in the next couple of weeks. To do that, I need your help. You have to stay under the radar the best you can. Doing so will help you be released sooner. Do you understand?"

Summer nodded. "Yes, thank you so much! You bring me hope ... hope that I never believed could be possible."

Cyrus tucked her hair behind her ear. "Sleep well, Summer. I will see you again on Monday."

"Okay, Dr. Schroeder." She smiled.

"Good girl." He smiled and stood up.

As he walked out, another patient asked, "When will I get to leave, Dr. Schroeder?"

"You can leave when you stop pulling your hair out and scratching your skin," Cyrus responded with a wink. The girls in the ward all giggled and whispered their flirtatious opinions of the new doctor as he left the room.

It wasn't long until Cyrus found himself on top of the roof, staring at the stars. How peaceful and calm they always appeared. No matter the hell that was unleashed upon Earth, the stars always remained the same. At times, Cyrus wished he too could be up there in the stars.

The sound of beating wings disrupted his thoughts. Expecting the company, Cyrus addressed his winged friend without turning around. "I could use some good news right about now."

"Woooh, that rough of a day, huh?" Peter said with a long, drawn-out whistle. Magically, the gigantic wings folded up behind Peter's back until they disappeared into the curling purple marks that glowed.

"Every year, I believe humanity is at its worst. Then the next year rolls around and I find out that humanity can indeed dip to new lows. It is a species that is doomed to fail. Why not eliminate them right now?" Cyrus' eyes glowed red with hatred and malice as the darkness in his heart festered.

Peter shrugged and leaned against the wall next to Cyrus. "Because you don't want to destroy the world that your perfect little soul mate calls home. Plus, you still have a human side buried deep ... very deep ... the deepest penetration that any man can withstand ..."

"You really need a woman." Cyrus shook his head.

"Ugh! I really do!" Peter whined. "It's been three months since my last fuck. At this rate it's going to fall off."

"I wasn't talking about another one-night stand, Peter." Cyrus gave him a critical look, "Besides, we are getting off-topic. Did you finish your mission as requested?"

"Eh," Peter wobbled his head side to side.

"Peter," Cyrus growled.

The face of the comedian peeled off and Peter showed a rare serious side. "I have something important to share with you, Cyrus. I found Billy Reed and gave him the letter, which he was tearful about. After much persuasion, I got him to write this letter." Peter held up the letter and handed it to Cyrus.

Concerned, Cyrus read the letter, which appeared to be poorly written, with shaky handwriting and incredibly poor grammar. It read:

Deer Sumar,

It mak me sad to heer yu sai goodby. I will alwais luv yu. I will wate for yu in caleefornya were we can be free.

Yur Billy

Cyrus read it over a few times before finally asking, "Why should I be concerned with this? This is exactly what I wanted. Minus the California message."

Peter sighed, "The note is not what would interest you. It's Billy Reed ... He's not who she says he is."

"Then who is he?" Cyrus asked, very much intrigued.

"Billy Reed is not just a black man. He is also an Indian of the Algonquin tribe," Peter said.

"Why would I care about that?" Cyrus remarked.

"Because Billy Reed is not human. He's a Mishipeshu." Peter maintained a cold stare. This beast obviously made him feel uneasy.

"Oh! How interesting!" Cyrus said with a spark in his eyes. "Mishipeshu are extremely rare."

"And extremely dangerous," Peter added. "I'm surprised he didn't rip your girl apart already."

"Yes, well she does choose the odd ones for some reason." A warm smile spread across Cyrus's face, thinking about her. "I want to meet him."

"Right now?" Peter complained.

"Yes," Cyrus replied bluntly.

"That means I have to carry your old heavy ass around," Peter continued to complain.

A stern parental look washed over Cyrus' face. "I will ground you if you refuse."

Peter rolled his eyes. "Fine. Hop on." Great black wings burst from Peter's back and spread out to display their immense power. Along the edges of the sharp, black, leathery wings was a faint purple glow that pulsed rhythmically. From his messenger bag Peter withdrew a long, silver rope with a few buckles running along it. As if he had done this a thousand times, he looped the rope several times over until it sat snugly around his body. Cyrus stepped up and put his back to Peter's back and began fixing the rope around his own body. Soon they were strapped together, back to back.

Without warning, Peter beat his strong wings enough to push them high into the sky. Once the air grew thin and the condensation from the clouds moistened their skin, Peter shot through the sky like a bullet.

On Monday evening, Cyrus quietly walked into the chapel with his hands behind his back. The chapel was simple enough, with a bare wooden cross at the end of the aisle and two rows of beaten-up wooden pews. The altar was simple but was bare of any bible, which was kept at the priest's side at all times. The brilliant stained-glass windows depicted Christ, the Virgin Mary, saints and angels in a wide array of colors.

A dark figure sat at the front of the pews, writing on some loose paper. So engaged was she in writing, she didn't notice him sit down next to her.

"They tell me you have stayed in the chapel since Sunday morning," Cyrus finally said.

Summer startled and gasped, "Dr. Schroeder!"

"I didn't mean to scare you, Summer. I sometimes forget how quiet I can be." Cyrus gave her a warm smile.

Summer couldn't return the smile. She couldn't even look him in the eyes. This only lengthened the pause as Cyrus waited for some sort of response. After five minutes of silence, Cyrus reiterated, "Why have you been in here since Sunday morning, Summer?"

"I need to pray and reflect in the presence of God," Summer said simply as she read the bible that she had stuck her loose papers into.

"Or is it because this is the one place where you can be left alone? While they can control your schedule in every other manner, they can't force you out of the chapel." Cyrus watched Summer stare down at her green dress. It was obvious that he was right. She just couldn't admit it. "I'm assuming that is why you refused to see me this morning."

"I'm doing as you said. I'm keeping a low profile and being good," Summer responded, refusing to make eye contact.

"That's all right. We can have your therapy session in the chapel," Cyrus leaned into a more relaxed position. "You can start by telling me what happened over the weekend while I was gone."

"I was good. I didn't cause trouble. I was compliant," Summer said so robotically that he was instantly concerned.

Alerted by her forced answers, Cyrus took note of her stiff and uncomfortable posture. There was also a bruised hand print on her upper right arm. "Summer, I know something happened. Please tell me. You can tell me anything."

Her body posture remained tense and she refused to give him eye contact. "I just want to get out of this place."

Cyrus could tell that she felt incredibly uncomfortable talking about this and thought maybe a more private setting would be easier on her. "How about we go to my office, Summer. I can escort you there and escort you right back here …"

"No!" Summer exclaimed loudly and then grew sheepish again, "I don't want to go to your office. I want to get out of this place." No longer able to contain herself anymore, Summer covered her face with her hands.

Though she tried to hide them, Cyrus could see the tears dripping off the palms of her hands. "Summer, I am doing everything I can to discharge you as soon as possible, but I need you to be patient. It might be for another two weeks before I have enough proof to discharge you."

"Leave me alone right now," Summer sobbed.

"Summer." Cyrus felt hurt by her sudden change.

"Just go," she whispered through tears.

"All right, Summer. I'll see you tomorrow. Remember, if you need anything, you can always call for me," Cyrus reminded her. On his way out of the chapel he had a sneaking suspicion that something happened in his office. Truthfully, he hadn't spent the day there at all. He was far too busy going to the morning meetings, where each of the doctors criticized his methods. Then he had to check on each of the patients who received treatment the prior Friday to make sure there was no long-term damage done over the weekend. Quite simply, it had been too hectic a day for him to reflect in the sanctity of his office.

However, he couldn't rid himself of his nagging curiosity about Summer's reluctance to enter the office. He made a beeline there, pausing before he entered. Normally when he locked the door, he turned the knob just enough to the left to create the need for a slight jiggle before unlocking it. This adjustment was gone, suggesting that someone had opened his door at one point. He opened the door, stepped in and breathed deeply.

Instantly his purple eyes swirled red as he caught the familiar scent of blood. His eyes sharpened to be acutely aware of all the details. Papers and

451

files were scattered on his desk. Drawers were slightly open, indicating someone had been fishing around for something. A pencil in the corner, spotted with blood, used as a failed defense weapon. Dried drops of smeared blood were scattered on the wooden floorboards. There was enough evidence for Cyrus to prove that these orderlies had harassed Summer in some way … in his office, of all places!

Cyrus was furious at the orderlies, at men, at humanity, at the world, and even at himself. He released a terrifying roar that ended in a low, rumbling growl. "I'm going to kill them!" In his frustration he punched the wall, causing bricks and pieces of mortar to fly across his office. The deep, angry rumble of his voice resonated with fury.

When the moon had risen and the stars twinkled in the sky, Cyrus went to the rooftop. A cloud of cigarette smoke drifted up to the stars, occasionally joined by perfect rings of smoke. Behind that purple ring of smoke was a fantastic display of black wings that were each as wide as Peter was tall. Currently, the wings were being used to create a small draft so the smoke traveled up to the sky in what appeared to be a spiral.

"Will you put those away before someone sees you?" Cyrus barked.

"Ooooh, someone is in a bad mood," Peter teased sarcastically. "Will the girl not spread her legs for you?"

Cyrus became a blur as he ran over to Peter, grabbed one of the wings and slammed him down to the ground, hard enough to create a small imprint of his head in the concrete. "Don't you ever fucking talk about her like that again!" Cyrus growled.

"I'm sorry, Master. I am so sorry. I crossed the line," Peter whimpered and held his hands up in surrender.

Cyrus continued to hold Peter down by the base of his wing. Some darkness deep inside of Cyrus wanted to fight with Peter, no matter the casualties it would cause. When the wings disappeared into the purple mark on Peter's back, Cyrus was able to snap out of it. Although Peter could take the beating and would eventually recover from the wound, it would still debilitate him, keeping him from assisting Cyrus with the task at hand.

"I'm sorry." Cyrus looked up at the moon, wishing it would wash away his uncontrollable rage.

"What happened, Master? I haven't seen you this enraged in quite a long time." Peter sounded quite concerned.

"I have very strong reasons to believe that *she* was attacked last weekend while we were out," Cyrus grimaced. It deeply hurt him to say it. "Because I was not here to protect her, she ..." he couldn't even think what might have happened.

Sympathetic to his master's guilt, Peter stood up and put a reassuring hand on his shoulder. "What is your plan, and what can I do to help?"

"I thought I could get her out of here the right way in a couple of weeks, but now I understand that she doesn't have that time. I need you to find Veronica. She should be up in Vancouver at this moment. Tell her to get the safe house ready and two of her body guards in place around the safe house. I need everything ready no later than Wednesday."

"I love to see that spark in your eyes. It reminds me of the good old days," Peter said with a smile as he lit another cigarette. "Times were simpler back then."

"No, humanity has always been a plague on this Earth. It's just that now they have discovered new ways to torture each other with chemicals and guns. The whole lot of them should be extinguished," Cyrus vented.

"Awww, but that means no more beautiful ladies!" Peter joked.

Before Cyrus could give him a hard time, a siren went off. The grounds below suddenly were abuzz with commotion. Guards and orderlies started roaming the grounds with flashlights. All the lights in the asylum turned on, as each of the rooms were being checked.

"What's going on here?" Peter asked curiously.

"Probably an insane patient attempting to leave. It rarely ever happens, according to Dr. Cotton," Cyrus explained as he curiously peered around from the rooftop. After a moment, the thought came to Cyrus that the escaping patient might be Summer—a thought that tightened his throat, making it hard to swallow.

Peter alerted Cyrus by pointing to a dark gap to the east. "Found 'em!"

Down below, a woman with short black hair that stuck out at all angles bolted across the lawn. She had waited patiently for this moment, when the guards had separated and left a pocket of space for her to sneak through. Amused by the escape, Cyrus watched her and mildly hoped that she could make it to the forest line. Once there, the rest would be easier, if they didn't release the hounds on her. The woman grew smaller as she ran towards the edge of the asylum property. Unfortunately for her, the moment she reached the fence, there was a loud bang that echoed in the night sky. Struck by the bullet, she fell to the ground and began twitching. Three guards closed in on her, one of them checking her pulse. Cyrus continued to watch as one of them flung her over his shoulder like a trophy and carried her back to the asylum.

"Wow, I can't believe they killed her," Peter said, mildly amused.

"They didn't kill her. With the range and distinct sound of the shot, it was obviously a tranquilizer gun. Come on, Peter, I thought you knew your weapons," Cyrus teased.

"I thought I did, but apparently I need to study up." Peter laughed.

Cyrus started to relax when he suddenly realized they weren't done hunting. The guards and orderlies were still frantically searching. That meant only one thing: there were more escapees.

Suddenly the door to the roof on the building to the west burst open and two dark figures bolted from it. Closely following behind them was a pile of guards that spilled from the door similar to water breaking through a dam. Cyrus turned to Peter. "Peter, I need you to vanish right now! Go! Find Veronica! Make haste!" Understanding Cyrus's sense of urgency, Peter unfolded his wings and shot up into the sky at such velocity that it cracked the concrete roof.

Cyrus turned back and watched the two figures run along the rooftop. Even though he couldn't see their faces, he was positive one of them was Summer. The two figures reached the ledge of the first building and, without faltering, jumped off it to the second rooftop. The first made it with room to spare. The other, however, only made it to the ledge. She desperately called out for help. The first figure ran back and pulled her friend up onto the roof.

The guards took advantage of this opportunity to shoot the second figure in the back. More darts flew in their direction, quickly making the first figure change her plans. She abandoned her twitching friend on the ground and continued to run along the rooftop. By the time she made it to the ledge of the second rooftop, she stopped dead in her tracks.

Cyrus looked into Summer's eyes across a twenty-foot gap. "Summer, don't jump. You won't make it."

The 16-year-old girl showed grit as she backed up to give herself a running start. "Watch me!"

"Summer, don't!" Cyrus yelled upon deaf ears.

The guards were closing in, their whistles blowing. This only gave Summer more motivation as she ground her back foot. In a runner's stance, Summer pushed off, running as hard and fast as she could. Her last foot curled around the ledge of the roof right before she jumped.

It was more obvious to Cyrus than it was to her … she wasn't going to make it. Risking everything to save her life, Cyrus, too, jumped off the ledge from the opposite building. Both were suspended through free fall. Summer was motivated to make it out of the asylum, dead or alive. Cyrus was motivated to keep her alive.

In a maneuver too fast to perceive with the human eye, Cyrus reached her in midair. He grabbed hold of her wrist and pulled her into him. As they fell towards the building, Cyrus wrapped himself around her and ensured his back was facing the building they were about to crash into. Bracing for impact, he tucked her head into the crook of his shoulder and held tightly onto her waist. Reflexively, she pulled her legs into her chest.

The glass mosaic of the chapel window shattered into thousands of shards when the two bodies came flying through it. Thanks to Cyrus's superhuman speed and agility, they flew through the window at a speed fast enough to blast through the large wooden cross on the altar, sending wood splinters flying, and then into the wooden pews, toppling them row by row like dominoes. Dust lingered in the air in the aftermath. Doctor and patient lay wrapped in each other's arms with a nest of destruction surrounding them.

Summer coughed a few times. She would be sore, but otherwise uninjured from the fall. Gingerly she removed Cyrus's hand, which had been protecting her head, and sat up.

"Doctor, thank you for ..." Summer stopped when she turned around to see the condition he was in. The backs of his arms and legs were shredded, bits of flesh removed. A large piece of a pew had broken off and stabbed him through the other shoulder. Blood spilled from the back of his skull where it was cracked open.

"Dr. Schroeder! Dr. Schroeder!" Summer panicked as she shook his body. "Don't be dead. You can't be dead. You just saved me! Why the hell would you save me and then just DIE!" she screamed.

Guards and orderlies burst in through the hole in the wall. The shock of seeing the destruction made them hesitate only a moment before they returned to the task at hand. Summer stared up at them as if she were a deer in headlights, right before they shot her in the shoulder with a tranquilizer gun.

"No!" she screamed, as she clutched tightly onto Cyrus's body. Soon the drugs kicked in. Despite the erratic twitches the tranquilizer gave her, she never let go of Cyrus.

Cyrus slowly opened his eyes to a bright light blaring down on him and shadows hovering around him. His head throbbed and his body felt stiff. In fact, it was difficult to move anything at all. Cyrus blinked a couple of times to clear his vision.

"He's awake," a nurse said, with a slight hint of fear in her voice.

Cyrus's head lolled to the side as he saw a familiar blurred figure approaching him.

"Good morning, Cyrus Schroeder, if that is indeed your real name," Dr. Cotton said brightly, but there was a slight quiver to his voice.

"What? Whe— Where am I?" Cyrus asked, desperately trying to wake up his lagging body, still recovering from flying through the chapel window.

Dr. Cotton slowly approached the table, inspecting Cyrus's body. "Well, to be honest, we were going to put you in the morgue, but all of a sudden you showed signs of life: a beating heart, deep breathing, murmurs in your sleep. What I normally would figure to be impossible, given your dire condition. Curiosity got the better of me, you see. So, I decided to bring you to the operating room instead, to monitor you on my own. Needless to say, you have proved a remarkable specimen. I don't know what you are, but your healing ability is profoundly inspiring."

"Where is Summer?" Cyrus asked groggily while lifting his head to search for her— a motion which caused his head to throb worse. Hopefully that would be gone in several more minutes.

"Yes, about that ... I am taking her off your patient list. In fact, you don't have a patient list anymore. Your potential as a specimen is much greater than that of a doctor." Dr. Cotton rested his hands on Cyrus's forearm.

Testing his reflexes, Cyrus tried to reach up and grab the doctor's throat. The most that came of it was some violent struggling against a five-point restraint system that had him tied down to the metal operating table.

"Woah! No need to be aggressive!" Dr. Cotton said, while backing away a couple of steps.

"Where is Summer Winters?" Cyrus growled.

Dr. Cotton stalled and resumed pacing around Cyrus. Every step the doctor took was another second that Cyrus had to regenerate his strength. "Summer Winters and her conspirators are too dangerous for this hospital. It was tragic to lose Polly ... she proved a very capable specimen as well. The others will be medicated and remain here until their dying days."

"You better not touch a hair on Summer's head, or I will rip out your throat myself!" Cyrus growled.

"That manipulative little vixen did certainly put a wicked curse on you, didn't she?" Dr. Cotton laughed and then proceeded to exit the room.

"Where is she!" Cyrus yelled.

Before completely leaving the room, Dr. Cotton made this last comment, "We are not accustomed to doing major surgeries at midnight, but we are more than happy to make exceptions for special individuals."

"No! NOOOOO!" Cyrus screamed. Even though he wasn't completely healed, he didn't care. He ripped right through the leather restraints. Two orderlies and three nurses rushed to push him down on the table. Releasing the monster within, Cyrus ripped through all five of them and jumped over their mangled bodies to get to the door. Time was of the essence as he raced through the winding corridors of the asylum. Some people were lucky enough to jump away, while others were trampled to death in Cyrus's rage and determination to get to Summer in time. Steel doors and cement walls wouldn't stop him in his pursuit to save Summer.

Finally, he reached the surgery room and kicked the door off the hinges with enough force to make the entire door fly back and hit the opposite wall. "STOP!" Cyrus roared as he barreled over to the operating chair, shoving a screaming nurse away so violently that she hit the wall and was knocked unconscious. The other doctor and nurse stepped far enough back to be out of the line of fire.

Tenderly, Cyrus held Summer's shoulder and gently shook her, hoping it wasn't too late. "Summer. Summer, it's me. You're safe, Summer. Do you hear me?"

The only response he got was a glazed-over look from her perfect green eyes—the look of a medicated mind. The proof lay in her swollen belly and the bowl of organs sitting on the operating table. The idea of removing essential organs to ail hysteria was an abomination. The only result this surgery would do is to keep her weak and feeble until her dying day, which appeared much closer now.

At this point, Cyrus had lost everything. All his willpower was gone and he melted to the floor, keeping a hand on Summer's forearm. "Summer … Summer … Summer …" he cried consistently, wishing she would snap out of it by some miracle.

If only that could be how this story played out. However, fate was never so kind as to reverse a permanent procedure such as this. Cyrus lost all his resolve and all his strength.

He was numb to everything … even the three needles stuck in his neck.

* * *

Connor rested his hands on his lap and looked into the distance.

Sammy leaned in, "That is a truly horrible story. Did they really used to remove a woman's …" Sammy gulped down the discomfort.

The rhythmic beeping of the nearby vitals machine droned into a numbness that Connor found comforting amidst the depressing reality around him. It was true, conditions used to be worse in mental hospitals. Patients were treated worse than animals … like test subjects. The memories of Summer's strong will defeated by such inhumane medical treatment was akin to a hot needle in his brain, searing away the numbness and reopening the painful wound. Despite the torture that brought him to see Summer succumb to such cruelty, it was a paper cut compared to watching Sammy slowly die from cancer.

"Connor?" Sammy brought his attention back to reality. Even Morgan appeared distraught from the retelling of that story.

Sammy deserved something from that story. A recognition that the world had gotten much better since then. Hope that things were going to get better, because at least she hadn't lost any organs to surgery. Even a history lesson. Anything!

Connor couldn't find the moral in the story. Couldn't find the reasoning for telling her such a tragic tale. All he did was ramble on about some horrific story about how a handful of patients were treated in the early 1900s.

That was when Dorian swooped in to save the day. "There is no comparison to how far medicine has come. What used to be stone walls and unsanitary conditions has transformed into hospital systems that function in synchronized flowing processes. All the staff you have interacted with at all these various hospitals have been passionate about saving your life. In Connor's story, there was only one lowly doctor who believed in patient recovery through non-invasive methods. That same passion now lives in every nurse, physician and supporting staff member. They all believe in providing you with the highest quality of life possible."

Sammy bowed her head and focused on her frail hands. The skin so white and paper-thin that she could see all the veins struggling to circulate blood.

"Which is why Connor had to leave," Morgan lied. She didn't know what happened to Connor during his absence. No one did, and no one was graced with the knowledge of what Connor did during those days, other than give in to his own form of addiction.

This got Sammy's attention. Along with everyone else in the room.

Improvising the best of her abilities, Morgan continued, "Connor was away finding the best possible living situation for you so you might have the best quality of life. There is a place far up in the mountains of Pennsylvania that looks like a fairy tale castle— similar to the stories you grew up on. It seems right that your final days are spent being doted upon as the princess we all know you are."

"But," Sammy glanced at Connor's black eyes, "That doesn't explain..."

"Can you really blame Connor for wanting to find some way to escape from all the stress for a little while? It's been tough on all of us," Dorian said, giving him the benefit of the doubt in front of Sammy despite the aggressive conversation they'd had before entering her hospital room.

Connor appreciated the others' efforts to cover for him when he knew he didn't deserve it. "Thank you all," Connor said. He bowed his head and gave Sammy the best strained smile he could offer despite his shame. "What do you say we discharge you from this place and take you to your magical castle, your majesty?"

"I'd like that," Sammy said, with her own strained smile.

Connor nodded and motioned for the bedside nurse. The rest of the time was a blur. The staff buzzing about him similar to busy bees while he could hardly muster the energy to move a finger. As everyone around him maintained a hopeful composure, he dipped back into the horrific memory that now plagued him like a chorus line that annoyingly replayed in his mind. Connor closed his eyes, and revisited the ending to Summer's tragic tale.

* * *

Some twenty-six hours later, the tranquilizers were wearing off enough that Cyrus started to hear voices in the distance. The dark had been comforting for the past day, so much so that Cyrus wanted to forget the voices and return to sleep. His conscious mind perked up when he heard John, the orderly.

"Of course I'm sure I want to do this! He's completely sedated, see?" John said, as he delivered a hard smack across Cyrus's cheek with enough force to break a normal jawbone. For Cyrus, it merely shifted his jaw out of place for a second before it readjusted into place. Cyrus faintly felt himself being pushed in a wheelchair. The squeaking wheels confirmed as much.

"All right, but let's at least keep a couple more shots ready, just in case he awakens. Did you see what he did to all those people yesterday? That was terrifying!" Frank said.

"Yeah, he is a monster," George agreed. There was a distinct sound of a heavy metal door being unlocked and opened.

"Wheel him over here," John instructed. "I want him to get a front-row view of this shit!"

"Are you sure about this?" Frank asked for confirmation, terrified of the consequences.

"Definitely. This monster deserves every bit of torture after everything he has done. What better torture than this?" John laughed.

I deserve it. I deserve whatever these weaklings can give to me, Cyrus thought to himself. *I couldn't protect her. I failed in the worst sort of way, and now I deserve the most severe pain imaginable.*

"Sit her right here," John barked.

There was a pause.

"Goddammit George! She's practically an old woman at this point. Restrain her to the chair!" John screamed.

A fire burned deep in Cyrus's stomach. All of his senses rapidly returned and his body quickly fought off the sedation. With his acute hearing, he could hear John's shoes tap on the cement as he approached. With his acute sense of smell, he could smell John's horrible body odor and rank breath. With acute sensory abilities, he could feel the weak metal melting under his fingertips. With his acute sight, he could see John's shocked face, even with his eyes half open.

"Whoa! John, we need to give him another shot!" Frank panicked.

"No, boys, it's okay. This monster is far too drugged to move a muscle. Besides, I want him to see this." John got really close to Cyrus's face, which still presented as drugged. "Revenge sure is sweet, isn't it, Doctor? But not as sweet as your patient's mouth will be."

Adrenaline flooded Cyrus's body, awakening all his muscles. In the blink of an eye, Cyrus was biting down on John's neck. Blood squirted everywhere as John screamed under the vice grip of Cyrus's jaw. George came running over with another shot, ready to plummet into the monster's neck. When George was in range, Cyrus extended his right arm. The handle of the wheelchair broke off, but still remained dangling from Cyrus' wrist. Using this broken piece of metal, Cyrus ripped the armrest across George's face. Chunks of flesh and bone flew from George's head and splattered Frank's face. Deformed and now unrecognizable, George fell to the floor, bleeding profusely. Frank stood frozen in horror as he watched this all happen.

Cyrus ripped the screaming John from his teeth, tearing off large chunks of flesh and creating a steady flow of blood from John's neck. As John fell to the ground, Cyrus grabbed him by the groin and ripped his penis completely off.

Before John could die, with eyes wide from shock, Cyrus leaned over him. Blood dripped from Cyrus' mouth and chin. Long sharp teeth protruded out of his mouth. Red fire danced in his eyes, which burned with hunger. "You're right, John. A monster deserves every bit of torture. Revenge is sweet." Hatred continued to burn deep in Cyrus's eyes as he shoved the ripped off penis into John's gaping mouth before he died.

Finally, Cyrus turned his attention to Frank, who had cowered in the corner. His pants reeked of piss and his eyes were wide with fright. Yet Cyrus felt no mercy for him. Cyrus lifted his bare foot and stepped through

Frank's groin, crushing his pelvis to mush. Frank only screamed for a moment before Cyrus wrapped his clawed fingers around his victim's neck and pulled until the head wrenched free from the rest of the body. Blood and spinal fluid dripped down from the head as the eyes twitched in shock. After all the nerves stopped firing in the body and decapitated head, Cyrus dropped the head, which rolled across the room towards George's body.

The most monstrous features vanished from Cyrus's body as he jogged over to Summer. Through all the horrific death, Summer remained oblivious, staring at the ceiling vacantly, her eyes glassy. More than anything, Cyrus wanted to hold her in his arms. What held him back was the blood that stained his hands. One look at Summer's vacant expression made the decision for him. Affectionately, Cyrus pulled her into his lap and held her tightly against his chest.

"Summer, I am so sorry. I am so, so sorry." Tears streamed down his face.

Though Summer was far too weak to comprehend what was going on around her, she felt the deep sadness of the person who tenderly held her. Tears rolled down her face while she struggled to lift her heavy eyelids and whispered, "Kill me."

Cyrus was so shocked by this that he turned her chin around to look him in the eye. This simple task took many attempts before he was finally able to get her to look at him directly. "Summer, I can't do that."

A bit of her real self returned to those drooping green eyes when she commanded, "Caspian. Kill. Me." Then her eyes closed and she was lost once more.

At this moment Cyrus understood that there was indeed a fate worse than death ... and he allowed her to suffer that fate. The only true mercy for her would be death. It almost felt beyond his control as he placed one hand over her mouth and plugged her nose. He didn't want to do it but he had no other choice. It was the hardest kill he had ever done. Taking a life had always been much easier than saving one. But this moment would scar Cyrus for the rest of his life. She barely struggled as the life was choked from her body. Cyrus knew it was all over when her body burst into millions of tiny purple wisps that floated out the window into the night sky.

At first Cyrus watched them peacefully drift away, until he could no longer stand to look at the evidence of what he had done. Cyrus closed his eyes to shut out the tears. When he opened them, they were blazing red, with a monstrous hatred that consumed his despairing human side.

It only took one hour for the monster to sweep through the building and ruthlessly murder every patient, nurse, orderly and doctor caught in his tantrum. Over four thousand souls drifted to the night sky through the hungry purple flames that consumed the entire asylum and all the land on it. The further he walked from his massacre, the lower the flames dropped. The blood from the thousands he killed remained stained on his bare skin.

A shadow appeared from the trees, running at a superhuman pace. Cyrus's red eyes looked up at the shadow, prepared to kill the next thing in his path.

"Caspian!" Veronica called out, "Caspian!" Not afraid of the monstrous beast in front of her, Veronica ran straight up to him and embraced him tightly in a hug. The moment she embraced him, all of the flames magically vanished from the hospital, leaving behind a metal and concrete skeleton of the asylum. The fire in his eyes diminished to pitch black. Simultaneously, he went limp in her arms and fell unconscious.

Veronica helped his naked body lie down on the cold earth and cradled his head in her lap. "Oh, poor Caspian," Veronica whispered as she gently brushed a lock of hair from his face.

The sound of whooshing wings was quickly followed by, "Is he going to be all right?"

Veronica's eyes glistened with bloody tears as she looked up at Peter. "I don't know if he will." Then she saw the destruction he caused. "I can't remember a time when he went on this massive a rampage."

14

MEMORIES

POCONO MOUNTAINS, PENNSYLVANIA

JULY 20, 2015

Sammy lay curled up in Connor's lap, fast asleep. Given her condition, the frequent naps were expected. This didn't make it any easier for Connor, who stared out the window of the moving limousine. He tried his best to focus on the trees that quickly passed by and the occasional rivers that flowed underneath the many bridges they crossed. Every time his eyes would lose focus on the familiar landscape, he would catch a glimpse of his eyes reflected in the window and be utterly disgusted with himself. Although one eye had returned to his deep green, the other remained a swirling purple. He hated to see his wildly strange eyes because they only reminded him of the divided feelings that tormented him: the human emotions that brought him to tears, and the uncontrollable rage of the monster that threatened to burst out and destroy everything in sight. He wanted to feel both ... but wished he could only feel one. His only solace from being violently pulled in two directions was Samantha.

Gently, Connor rubbed the top of her head, where the brilliant marking of a phoenix spread its wings across her skull. Connor kissed her bald head affectionately.

Sammy stirred. "Are we there yet Connor?"

"Yes, actually," Connor replied with a plastic smile. "We should be coming around the bend now if you want to sit up and see it."

It took a little effort, but Sammy eventually was able to sit up and peek out the window. The trees parted to reveal a grand mansion. The red bricks and black roof stood out against the green forest surrounding the house. Ivy climbed up the walls in several places, and some of the windows were open, revealing beautiful curtains drifting out with the breeze.

Sammy pressed her face to the window to see thousands of unique flowers artistically planted along the side of the long driveway and even more that surrounded the front of the mansion. As they slowly drove up the driveway, Sammy was sure she saw a shirtless man with large muscles and blonde hair carrying a shovel over his shoulder. The man turned to look at her, but when Sammy blinked, he was gone.

The limousine pulled up in a large circle that led to the front steps. Right in front of the mansion stood a magnificent fountain featuring an angel blowing a trumpet as stone lions guarded the four corners for any danger. On the other side of the fountain was what appeared to be an old-fashioned horse and buggy patiently waiting for the rider.

When the limousine came to a complete stop, Sammy looked away for a moment to see Morgan fetch her wheelchair from the trunk. Then, when she looked back at the horse and buggy, it was gone. Sammy blinked a couple of times, confused by these ghost-like mirages.

"Are you all right, Sammy?" Connor noticed her rubbing her eyes a few times.

Sammy shook it off. "Just side effects of the medications."

Acting as chauffeur, Morgan opened the door and prepared the wheelchair.

"Well, after you get a quick tour, then I can put you to bed," Connor said, as he got out of the car and pulled the readied wheelchair closer. Then he reached in the car and gingerly picked Sammy up. "Here we go. One. Two.

Three." And she was in the chair. Even though it was summer, Connor still tucked a blanket around her lap in case she got cold.

"You were right, Morgan! The mansion does look like something out of a fairy tale," Sammy said wistfully.

Connor chuckled. "Something like that, yes." He rolled her toward the entrance of the mansion.

"Connor, why are we coming here instead of going home to New Hampshire?" Sammy asked curiously.

There was a brief pause as Connor braced himself to admit the horrible truth again. "Because you don't have much longer left of this life, Sammy. I want to make you feel like a true princess, pampered with luxury in your final days. It is the least I could do for failing to save you from this disease."

"Connor, this wasn't your fault," Sammy chided.

Mighty black doors opened wide, revealing an ancient royal crest on the inside. Coming out of the mansion, her arms spread wide, was a Japanese woman dressed in modern athletic apparel, but her long black hair was tied up in a traditional Japanese topknot. By the way she was perspiring, it was evident that she had been exercising right before they arrived.

"Welcome to the Legna Estate! It is so good to finally meet you, Samantha. My name is Sakura Legna," she said, offering a warm smile and a firm handshake.

Sammy returned the handshake with her own shaky one. "Haven't we met before? I'm positive I've met you."

Shock peaked Sakura's eyebrows for a moment. She eyed up Connor, who was also intrigued. Sakura brushed it off. "I don't believe we have met, but trust me, I understand the confusion. All Asians look the same to white people." She laughed, but no one joined her in the racist joke.

Connor finally broke the silence. "Did Dorian arrive already?"

"Ah yes," Sakura replied with a sharp head nod. "He arrived a couple hours ago, so we decided to have a little fun."

"Who won?" Connor asked with a devious smile.

"I beat him at sword every time," Sakura proudly said, with her hands on her hips.

Connor chuckled. "Obviously. Shall we take our tour?"

"Yeah!" Sammy's spirits rose.

"Excellent! Let me show you around, Sammy," Sakura said with an enthusiastic clap.

Connor pushed the wheelchair, with Morgan quietly trailing behind, and Sakura led the way. "Welcome to Legna Estate. This house was established in 1872 when a young nobleman from Switzerland decided to migrate over to America with his beloved wife. He built this house for her. Over here to the left we have the main study," Sakura pointed.

Sammy craned her head to look in as they passed by. The door was slightly ajar to the antique-filled professional office. For a moment, she saw a man wearing an outdated sheriff's uniform sitting across from the mahogany desk. Right when he was about to turn around to look at Sammy, she was wheeled out of sight of the room.

"Connor, have we been here before?" she asked.

Connor continued to push the wheelchair to the back of the manor, where Sakura was leading them. "I haven't been here in a very long time, so I don't see why you would have been here before. Why do you ask?"

"No reason," Sammy said, dismissing the idea. It was probably all in her head.

Sakura opened the next set of doors and held them open for her guests to enter. "Here is the kitchen, which I am quite proud of," she said with a wink. "I recently remodeled it with granite counter tops and brand-new appliances."

Leaning around the wheelchair to look at Sammy, Connor added, "Sakura makes incredible sushi and yakisoba. If you are good, maybe she can make some for you as well."

"Mmm, that sounds delicious going down and coming back up!" Sammy jokingly rubbed her sunken tummy.

Connor chuckled at her morbid joke. Sakura was not amused.

On the counter was a display of a beautiful gold-rimmed china tea set. From the spout of the floral teapot came steam that smelled wonderful. Sammy pointed towards the teapot. "Can I have some tea, too?"

For a moment, Sakura appeared confused. "Sure, I can make you a pot of tea once the tour is over."

"But," Sammy looked back over at the teapot and was shocked to see that it had vanished. "Okay, I can wait." A blush of embarrassment spread on her cheeks.

"Uh, *hai*," Sakura said in an attempt to move past this awkwardness, "let me show you the garden!"

"Did you remodel that as well?" Connor remarked while pushing the wheelchair towards the back door.

"Of course! I gave a Zen appeal, similar to the gardens from my home country," Sakura said sounding upbeat.

The sun was blinding for a moment, and then Sammy's eyes were able to readjust. The first thing she saw was a crowd of women huddled together under a large canopy. A brilliant rose garden surrounded their little tea party. Each of the women wore clothing similar to that of the early 1900s. Their giggles drowned out the whispered gossip that was shared over shoulders and behind fans.

From a side door came a young woman who appeared alarmingly similar to Sakura. Only she wore a modest black kimono and carried a large silver platter full of desserts. The reflection of the sun from the silver platter caught Sammy in the eyes, forcing her to blink. After her gaze readjusted, the whole group of gossiping women had disappeared. Sammy tried to wrap her brain around what was going on, while Sakura and Connor distracted each other with conversation.

"Who did you hire to tend the garden?" Connor asked.

"Oh, my son does that," Sakura replied, as she looked over her half-acre Japanese garden. "I have done my best to keep everything in the family. It is just easier that way. Fewer questions are asked."

"Are there still horses?" Connor asked.

"Just two for now," Sakura replied. "We always keep a couple on hand just in case we get …"—she looked over at Sammy, who was rubbing her eyes—"special guests. My grandson tends to them."

"Oooh,"—Morgan bounced out the door with a skip in her step— "I love horses!" Sakura shook her head as she watched Morgan bound away to the stables.

Connor looked down at Sammy with some concern, "Are you feeling all right?"

"I, uh." Sammy didn't know what to say. She would sound completely insane if she told them both that ghosts wandered the halls. Worse than that, Sammy feared she was growing delusional and seeing things that simply were not there at all. "I'm just tired, I suppose," she finally responded.

"We can finish the tour some other time when you have the energy for it," Connor replied, worry etched into his face. "You have had a long day of travel."

"Let me show you where you'll be staying, then," Sakura replied proudly. "I left the remainder of the house alone. Thought it best to keep the bedroom the same."

Connor didn't reply but simply pushed Sammy back into the manor. He did, however, strike up more conversation with Sakura about elements of the house that had changed. Somehow, he didn't appear pleased with these changes.

On their way to Sammy's bedroom, they passed a music room with high, vaulted ceilings and large windows with translucent curtains. There, Sammy saw something even more alarming and bizarre: Connor, standing next to the piano. His black hair was slicked back tight against his skull. He wore a tuxedo pressed to perfection. His purple eyes glowed softly as he held a violin under his chin. A woman that Sammy couldn't quite make out was sitting at the piano. She wore a gorgeous green dress that flowed around her. Her long, auburn hair was tied up in a bun with little curls artistically falling down at certain twists in the bun. They were obviously playing a duet together, but Sammy couldn't hear the music. She could only observe them playing to each other. The woman playing the piano started to turn around, as if she heard Sammy approaching down the hall. Unfortunately, Sammy was pushed past the doorway before she could see the woman's face. It was all so confusing and starting to make her head pound.

All three stopped in front of two large doors that were much taller than any other. The door handle was made of crystal and an ivy floral design was etched into the frame. "Sammy, this is where you will stay," Sakura said with a warm smile.

The doors opened wide and Connor pushed the wheelchair into the room. It was one of the biggest and most elegant bedrooms Sammy had ever seen. A four-poster bed sat regally with a white, airy silk canopy. White, lacy pillows covered the top of the bed and two large lamps sat on each side of it. In the corner of the room were two antique wardrobes with roses etched into the doors. A vanity sat against the opposite wall with a large mirror and antique containers waiting to be used. The door to the bathroom was left slightly ajar to reveal a jetted bathtub that was four times the size of the one Sammy had at home.

"What do you think?" Connor asked.

Without warning, hundreds of visions flashed through Sammy's head, simultaneously, overburdening her brain until it felt as if her skull would split in half. "Why … why is this happening? … My head!" Sammy cried, holding her head.

Immediately Sakura began checking Sammy's pulse while Connor kneeled down in front of her.

Sammy's heart surged with emotion. First, the deepest agony she had ever felt. Followed by an anger that burned hotter than the fires of hell and a vengefulness to act upon it. A cold despair washed over the anger like an icy sea extinguishing hot lava. Fear mixed with love in a confusing knot that couldn't be untangled. "Why … WHY!" Sammy screamed, as she violently pushed the chair away with more force than Connor thought she was capable of.

Now on her hands and knees, Sammy held tightly onto her head for fear that it would burst open. Unable to control the forces on her, Sammy screamed as loud and long as she could.

The piercing scream shattered mirrors and crystal. Sakura fell to her knees and covered her bleeding ears. Even Connor struggled to cope with

471

it his body shaking and struggling to move under the disorienting high pitch of Sammy's cry. Sakura fell to the ground, unconscious, as blood trickled out of her ears. Trying to silence Sammy, Connor wrapped his arms around her frail body, brought his lips close to her covered ear and tried to soothe her, saying, "It's okay, Sammy. I'm here. I'm right here. It's going to be okay."

As suddenly as it started, the screaming stopped. Exhausted, Sammy slumped over on her knees. Connor caught her and held her upright. Blood trickled from his ears, but this mattered nothing. He gave Sammy a moment to catch her breath and to allow his eardrums to heal. Then he asked her, "Sammy, what happened? What did you see?"

Sammy weakly lifted her head up to look into Connor's glistening green eyes. "I've been here before, Connor. I was here in the 1920's. My name was Sylvia Legna, the owner of this manor. What a traumatic life I lived …" tears streamed down her face.

Connor's breath was taken away. It had finally happened! She remembered! Never before had anything such as this ever happened at such a grand level! She remembered! It was a miracle! Euphoria filled Connor's soul at the impossible finally becoming possible. Perhaps this time she would be able to remember it all. Perhaps this time, she could save him from the cruel, immortal curse that had tortured his existence. Thousands of years had come to this one moment. Finally, hope had returned.

Tenderly, he lifted her chin up until he could see her watery green eyes. "Sammy … tell me! Tell me *your* tale of the Legna Estate."

A serious expression washed over Sammy's face. "Let me tell you a tale … of revenge."

About the Author

Brooke Stayrook is professionally trained in mental health research with a Masters degree in Healthcare Administration. While her day job focuses on improving process problems using Lean Six Sigma, Brooke's passion for travel has driven her wanderlust heart across the globe. learning about other countries' history and culture.

You can connect with me on:

🌐 https://brookestayrook.wixsite.com/home
🔗 https://www.instagram.com/brookestayrook

CPSIA information can be obtained
at www.ICGtesting.com
Printed in the USA
LVHW100916240722
724274LV00003B/110